BOUND BY FOREVER

A TRUE IMMORTALITY NOVEL

S. YOUNG

BOUND BY FOREVER

A True Immortality Novel

By S. Young

Edited by Jennifer Sommersby Young

Cover Design By Hang Le

Cover Image by Regina Wamba

OTHER TITLES BY S. YOUNG

War of Hearts (A True Immortality Novel)

Kiss of Vengeance (A True Immortality Novel)

Kiss of Eternity (A True Immortality Short Story)

Other Adult Contemporary Novels by Samantha Young

Play On

As Dust Dances

Black Tangled Heart

Hold On: A Play On Novella

Into the Deep

Out of the Shallows

Hero

Villain: A Hero Novella

One Day: A Valentine Novella

Fight or Flight

Outmatched (co-write with Kristen Callihan)

On Dublin Street Series:

On Dublin Street

Down London Road

Before Jamaica Lane

Fall From India Place

Echoes of Scotland Street

Moonlight on Nightingale Way

Until Fountain Bridge (a novella)

Castle Hill (a novella)

Valentine (a novella)

One King's Way (a novella)

Hart's Boardwalk Series:

The One Real Thing

Every Little Thing

Things We Never Said

The Truest Thing

Young Adult contemporary titles by Samantha Young

The Impossible Vastness of Us

The Fragile Ordinary

Young Adult Urban Fantasy titles by Samantha Young

The Tale of Lunarmorte Trilogy:

Moon Spell

River Cast

Blood Solstice

Warriors of Ankh Trilogy:

Blood Will Tell

Blood Past

Shades of Blood

Fire Spirits Series:

Smokeless Fire

Scorched Skies

Borrowed Ember

Darkness, Kindled

Not so much now. A burn flared to life in her chest sometimes. It had taken her awhile to realize it was anger. Aggravation.

She'd changed.

Not for the better.

With a sigh, she threw off her maudlin thoughts and paid for entrance into the club. The bored-looking woman behind the desk gestured to her hand, and she held it out. The woman proceeded to press a wet stamp to the back of it.

The club name glared at her in bold, blue ink.

Drifting off toward the double doors manned by two more bouncers, she held up the hand with the ink and they allowed her entrance. One of the men winked at her. She gave him a coy smile and sauntered through the opening.

Although she didn't feel it the way a human would, the thick change in the air informed her that the deafening club was roasting hot.

And no wonder.

It was packed with bodies all jumping to the pounding bass of electronic music. As tall as she was, she still had to stretch onto tiptoes to see above the crowd. At the end of the colossal space was a stage and on it, a deejay.

With her heightened senses, for a moment all she could hear was a thunderous din. All she could smell was fresh sweat and the choking, mingling scents of beer, cologne, and perfume.

She stopped and took a deep breath. After a moment or two, the noise was manageable.

But her heart still thudded out of time with the drumming bass.

It must have been hella hot in the space because her hair was starting to stick to the back of her neck. All she wanted to do was take the hair tie that circled her wrist and capture the pale-blond locks up into a messy bun. But over the years, she'd found that her hair was a feminine weapon. And the vamps would like it.

Leaving it to sway against her bare back, almost touching her arse, she pushed with determination into the clogged club. Eventually she would sense them.

The burn she'd been feeling lately flared now and then as hands took advantage of her in the crowd. Pats on her bottom, caresses across her bare waist. When a girl groped at her breast, the burn inside her spit out embers and she grabbed the girl's wrist. Careful of her strength, she gave it just enough of a twist to cause the girl to cry out in pain. Releasing her, she continued pushing through the crowded club.

Then she felt it.

All the fine hairs on her body rose as if static electricity charged the air.

There was another supernatural in the vicinity.

She veered between triumph and anxiety.

Hoping neither showed on her face, she turned her head to follow the feeling and her eyes locked with a vampire's.

Beams of light flickered across the vamp's face, causing his eyes to flash mercury silver.

With a coquettish tilt of her head, she gave him a deliberately bashful but inviting smile and then continued to push through the crowd toward the edge of the room where there was space to breathe.

To her gratification, the nape of her neck tingled. Awareness tightened her muscles.

He was following her.

Once she'd stepped out of the wave of human bodies that pulsed toward the stage, she turned to lean against a wall. It wasn't hard to pretend she needed a moment to compose herself.

How anyone thought this was good *craic*, she'd never understand. It was minus craic, as they said back home.

She'd take a cozy fireplace, an armchair, and a bloody good book over this shit any day of the week.

You were born an eighty-year-old woman, you know that?

Pain clawed at her throat and she grit her teeth, forcing *his* voice from her head.

Then the vampire was there.

He was the same height as she was with a wiry, ropy physique that belied his strength. None of the humans would know just how strong he was. His dark hair was slicked back off his forehead and looked oily under the lights.

She supposed, though, he had a pretty face with his cut cheekbones and pouty, full lips.

She brushed her fingers across the imaginary sweat on her forehead and gave him a shrug. "It's a bit warm in here!"

He smirked as he approached and then as he inhaled, he tensed. His eyes flashed silver and he stared at her, completely arrested.

Pretending to be oblivious to the reason why, she tucked a strand of hair behind her ear and asked shyly, "Something wrong?"

He shook his head. "No. You are just very beautiful."

The vamp had an accent. Not Lithuanian. She wasn't sure where he was from. Her vision didn't tell her that much. He was perhaps Scandinavian or Nordic. She wasn't schooled enough in accents to be certain either way.

Does it matter? She felt that familiar burn of irritation, this time at herself.

"You're very kind!" She had to keep pretending that she thought she needed to yell for him to hear her. In truth, they'd both be able to hear each other if they whispered, even in this racket.

What kind of music was this? Could a person even categorize it as music? What happened to melody and lyrics and storytelling?

Christ, I really am an eighty-year-old woman.

The vampire touched her waist, reminding her to focus. She tried not to stiffen at his touch. He smelled faintly of blood beneath his sandalwood cologne. She forced herself not to recoil when his head dipped toward her ear. "Would you like to go somewhere? A place we can talk?"

Her pulse skittered and she knew he probably heard it. Hopefully he mistook it for sexual awareness. She nodded, and he pulled back to smile triumphantly. There was nothing in his eyes but malice and hunger.

She wondered how his victims couldn't see that.

And where was his partner in crime?

Allowing herself to be led around the edges of the crowd toward a door at the back of the club, she pretended not to notice that when he pushed down on the handle, he snapped the lock.

She further pretended not to notice the way her whole body tightened with renewed awareness, the hairs springing up on her arms.

The female vamp was near now too.

Bracing herself, she gripped the vamp's hand tightly as he led her down the dank hallway. Everything in this building was built from thick concrete. It was no wonder the noise from the deejay was just a dull thud outside.

Even here in the hallway it was significantly muffled. So much so she heard the door at the top of the hallway slam. Even a human would have heard it, so she knew it was okay to glance over her shoulder.

The female vampire sashayed toward them in a long, seductive, electric-blue dress that clung to her slender curves. Rich red lipstick painted her lips. She walked in six-inch stilettos like they were sneakers. God, this vamp was such a bloody cliché.

"My wife." The male vamp's mouth was at her ear. "You don't mind if she joins us, do you?"

She scanned the hallway for cameras and spotted one above the door entrance on the opposite corner. Ignoring the vamp whose hands were clamped tight on her hips, she turned in his arms and saw the other camera at the opposite end of the narrow corridor. It was pointed at the exit door.

"What are you doing?" His fingers bit into her skin.

"Looking at the cameras," the female vamp observed as she approached. "Looks like she's nervous of us. I wonder why?" Then she inhaled deeply, her eyes silvered. "Oh, she smells so wonderful."

"I know." His voice rumbled in her ear. "I caught her scent as soon as she entered the club."

It was hard to ignore them, but she needed to concentrate. Lifting a hand, she flicked her fingers and sent out magic toward the first camera.

She twisted in his hold and did the same to the other.

"What the fuck?" He shoved her into the wall with enough force to cause her head to crack against the concrete.

She winced at the slight ache and glared at the two vamps.

They might not have seen her magic, but they sensed its energy.

"She's a witch!" The female vampire smacked her lover's biceps. "You fool."

A witch.

That's what most supernaturals thought.

Oh, how she wished it were true.

Life would be so much easier if she were a mere witch.

"I saw. I saw what you were going to do to that girl here tonight." She was quiet, her words just above a whisper, but she knew they could hear her. "I saw what you've done to all the girls before."

Violation, blood, gore, terror.

They were psychopaths. Or sociopaths. She always got those two mixed up. Either way, they were particularly nasty feckers.

"You can't do that anymore."

"And I suppose you're going to be the one to stop us?" The female vampire laughed.

Such arrogance.

And there was something about the dynamic between the two, something she'd missed in the visions.

The female was the one in charge. Which usually meant she was the oldest and therefore the strongest.

Keeping her right hand behind her back where the vamps couldn't see, magic tingled at her fingertips as she conjured one of the wooden stakes she'd left on her bed back at the hotel.

Without a word, she moved.

She was a blur.

Unstoppable.

It all happened in two seconds.

Her wooden stake plunged with precise accuracy into the female vamp's chest, up underneath the rib cage to pierce the heart.

The vampire's silver eyes widened in outrage before her entire being burst into ash.

She was so shocked by her first vampire kill, she could only stare at the cloud of supernatural dust that caught in the harsh light of the aluminum bars on the ceiling.

Rookie mistake, that, losing focus.

An animalistic roar filled the corridor seconds before the male vampire slammed her to the floor. Burning pain flared up her neck, disorienting her for a moment until he lifted his head and she stared, aghast.

His long incisors, his lips, his mouth were covered in ... her.

Wet gushed from her neck even as she felt the tingle of her skin repairing itself.

The bastard had torn out her throat.

His eyes widened as he watched her heal in a way no ordinary supernatural could.

And there was that burn in her chest again.

Except worse.

It was growing in a blaze and suddenly, it wasn't the vampire she saw in front of her. It was *him*.

It was *them*.

And *they* deserved to die for what they did to *him*.

The rage consumed her.

It was like a black veil over her eyes.

When it eventually lifted, there was another pile of dust in the corridor.

What had happened ...

Tears filled her eyes as she looked at her blood-covered hands. The rust of it was thick in her fingernails, like she'd clawed someone apart. Her hair swung into her vision and she saw it was wet.

Nausea roiled in her gut and she stumbled back against the corridor wall.

She slammed her eyes closed and thought of her hotel.

The dull noise of the club faded, replaced by the hum of late-night traffic. When she opened her eyes, she found herself in the middle of her hotel room. Weariness hit. The building was in Old

Town, and *traveling* always shattered her. She used to call it teleporting until ... a friend offered her a different name for it.

Afraid but needing to know, she moved slowly toward the bathroom, careful not to touch anything with her bloodied hands.

She stared at her reflection in the mirror above the sink.

Blood splattered her face, the globs of wet dark red in her hair turning those strands a muddy brown. Her clothes were stained with it.

Clearly, she'd inflicted some serious damage on the vamp before she dusted him.

She'd obviously torn him apart.

She couldn't remember.

How could she not remember this level of violence?

She lunged for the toilet just in time.

Shuddering, shaking, she hovered over the bowl for a while before she could gather the courage to stand and look at herself again.

What she'd seen those vamps do in her vision was traumatizing. They'd inflicted terror and pain beyond imagination.

But what had she done in return?

Tears slipped down her cheeks.

Who was she?

With a swipe of her hand, the tingle of magic, the blood was gone. Her clothes gone, replaced with clean ones. It was like it had never happened.

But as she peered into the mirror with the same aquamarine eyes as *his*, she still saw the blood in her hair, even though it was gone.

Who was she?

She didn't know anymore.

All she knew was that she wasn't the woman she used to be.

Raising her hand, she gave her wrist a flick and magic transformed her hair color.

She was now a brunette.

You couldn't see blood spatter on dark hair, could you?

A chill shuddered through her at the wicked thought.

1

February
Moscow, Russia

It had been many years, but he still remembered winter in Japan during his mortal life. The icy burn of a brittle wind on his cheeks, the heavy wet of snowfall soaking his clothes, and the tingling sensation from the relief of fire from the hearth they called an *irori*.

Now Kiyo didn't feel the cold as he had when he was human.

Then again, he'd never experienced a Moscow winter.

For the first time in a long time, he felt the chill. Not as the humans did, but still ... the icy dampness tried to invade him as he stalked through the well-lit darkness of the Kitay-gorod district.

To blend with the humans he wore a winter coat and scarf, forgoing a hat and gloves. His feet were sure and steady on the paved ground of Manezhnaya Square. Although the square was mostly clear of snow, small patches of ice and muddy rocks of frozen, dirty water lingered here and there.

As he neared the hotel his quarry resided within, Kiyo slowed.

His timing couldn't have been more perfect.

The tall brunette stepped outside the entrance of the Four Seasons and forged out into the subzero temperatures without a glance left or right.

He narrowed his eyes on her short dress, her legs bare and uncovered except for her calves, protected by a pair of knee-high wedged boots. She turned left, walking with a steady grace, uncaring of the weather. Her conspicuous behavior knew no bounds, apparently. Humans shook their heads at her supposed stupidity as she walked through Moscow without a coat.

They didn't realize that as fae, although she felt the freezing temperature, it didn't affect her.

Following, Kiyo tried to keep enough distance between them that she wouldn't sense him. He'd been told that her kind had a radar for fellow supernaturals.

Impatience niggled beneath his skin. He wanted this part of the job over with.

At first, he thought she was heading north, but then she took another left, leading them east. He had a sneaking suspicion regarding her destination. As difficult as it had been these past few weeks to keep up with her, reports placed Niamh Farren at nightclubs throughout eastern Europe.

Either the fae-borne woman liked to party after playing Superwoman, or she was still playing Superwoman at these bars. As cliché as it was, vampires loved a dark nightclub.

Kiyo knew Niamh was rescuing people from bus crashes and burning buildings, but if she was also playing dark hunter, she was in more trouble than he'd thought. And according to his employer, Fionn Mór, Niamh was already buried under a pile of enemies. The last thing they needed was the Consortium coming after her on top of the Blackwood Coven and The Garm.

Twenty minutes later, he watched from a distance as the brunette disappeared into a club not far from the Kitay-gorod Metro station. Kiyo waited a minute and then followed her in after two huge doormen gave him a once-over. He hated clubs. He much preferred the ruckus of an underground fight.

He immediately felt enclosed by the dark, concrete walls of the venue. Kiyo paid the entrance fee and took the stairs upward to an open landing. Music pounded and pulsed behind a set of double doors guarded by two men as large as the doormen outside. To the right was a cloakroom where clubbers removed their layers of winter clothes to reveal uniforms of mostly jeans and T-shirts.

Relieved to be rid of it, Kiyo removed his coat and scarf and took the ticket he'd need to recover them, already knowing he'd have no time to.

He pulled out his cell and typed a quick message to Val to let him know which club he was in.

Stepping inside the main venue, Kiyo scowled as he tried to focus out the noise of the rock band playing on stage at the north end of the room. It wasn't a huge space, and it was crammed full of mostly young people. He looked up into the darkness; lights flashed overhead, revealing a U-shaped gallery crowded with more humans.

From the ages of the average patron, the kind of music the band was playing, and the low-cost entry to the club despite its location in the most tourist-driven area of the city, Kiyo would guess this was a local student spot.

Ignoring the jostling of the surrounding bodies, Kiyo grew very still as he attempted to filter out the band and zero in on his prey.

His cell vibrated in his pocket.

Val had replied. He'd hired Val, a local criminal with a reputation for keeping his mouth shut, to drop the car where he'd need it. There was a parking lot behind the club, used for its employees and those of the businesses in the surrounding buildings. Val had left the keys on top of the driver's side tire.

With his exit strategy confirmed, he slid his cell back into the ass pocket of his jeans and pushed into the crowds. With his nose and ears on high alert, he scoured the throbbing space for the fae.

A whiff of familiar caramel caught his attention and his head snapped to the right.

There.

She stood in among the crowd as the humans jumped around her, fists pumping in the air, voices rising with the music as they sang along with the band.

Her base scent was the same as Fionn's and his mate Rose. Rose's and Fionn's individual scents had joined, proclaiming their identity as true mates. The notion of true mates was ridiculous to Kiyo, but he couldn't deny that such a thing existed—two souls fated to be tied to one another for all eternity.

It sounded like hell.

Niamh's base scent held the same heady caramel sweetness as the fae couple, but it was overlaid with something spicy. Almost like cinnamon, but not quite.

It was such a distinct scent that it would make it easy to keep track of her from now on when she was in the vicinity.

Niamh had no apparent interest in the band.

Instead, she stared intently at something in the middle of the crowd.

Kiyo followed her gaze, searching ... searching ... and then he spotted what had her attention.

There was a man harassing a young woman in amongst the revelers, and no one seemed to be paying attention except Niamh. The girl kept trying to push his wandering hands off her body, but he was having none of it. He laughed like it was a joke.

Looking back at Niamh, Kiyo caught the hardness in her expression as a beam of light lit her face.

Fionn had explained that Niamh was psychic. That she'd spent most of her life following her visions. Is that what was happening here? Had Niamh seen something that brought her to this nightclub, to this girl and this man?

Moving toward the couple, Kiyo lifted his head and sniffed the air. They were definitely both human.

But if Niamh was here to stop something from happening, then it was his opportunity to divert her attention. A werewolf stalking a human would be of much more interest to her, no matter her visions.

She'd probably even think *he* was the reason her visions had led her there.

Kiyo reached the struggling couple and took a small amount of pleasure in shoving the man off the girl with just enough strength to put him on his ass. The place was so packed, the prick took down a couple of people in his path. But Kiyo couldn't be sorry.

Especially when the girl looked up at him with hero worship and interest in her dark eyes.

Well, this is going to be easy.

Her cheeks flushed prettily as Kiyo stared down at her. She was perfect for snaring Niamh in his trap.

The girl leaned onto her tiptoes and he bent his head toward her. Her lips brushed his ear as she said, "*Spasibo*."

He nodded and lifted his head. "You're welcome."

She frowned.

He searched his memory for the little Russian he knew. "*Pozhaluysta*."

Beaming, she grinned flirtatiously. Kiyo took hold of her hand and gave it a gentle squeeze. He mimed taking an invisible drink with his free hand and raised a questioning eyebrow.

The girl lowered her lashes and nodded coyly.

Kiyo led her through the surging bodies. But not toward the bar at the back of the room. As he moved, he looked for a glowing exit sign. Discerning the green one that read выход was it, he stalked toward it. He felt the girl wrap her other hand around his wrist and give a tug. Glancing over his shoulder at her, he found her frowning warily.

As he offered her a reassuring look, he tried not to appear triumphant as the smell of caramel and spice grew closer. His skin tingled with awareness, the hair rising on the nape of his neck.

Niamh was following them.

Gripping the girl's hand tighter, he pulled her to the exit door, ignoring the barely there sting of her nails on his skin as she resisted. He yanked open the door and hauled her past him, thrusting her into the darkly lit hallway. Steep concrete stairs led down to a fire door.

The exit door slammed shut behind him and the girl backed away, her eyes round with fear.

Kiyo let the growl of the wolf rumble in his voice as he ordered, "Run."

She might not have understood English, but she understood his command. She ran. Without hesitation.

She took the stairs three at a time and blasted out through the fire door without looking back.

A shiver cascaded down Kiyo's spine, shocking him as his claws unleashed, as if his body had a mind of its own. Something satisfying and needful tugged at his gut. It was like the call of a full moon. As her scent tickled him, Kiyo realized the sensation was Niamh drawing near.

Darting into the darkest corner of the hall, he retracted his claws and held his breath as the exit door opened again.

Niamh stepped into the hall, her scent enveloping him.

The hair on his arms rose.

His heart raced.

What the hell?

"Hello?" She turned toward the staircase.

Kiyo knew Niamh was fast. Faster than even him.

It was a risk to take her like this.

But he really saw no other choice.

Niamh tensed, turning her head so she was in profile. Her lips parted in surprise and he knew she'd sensed him.

Too late.

Faster than most werewolves, Kiyo was a speedy blur as he crossed the short distance between them, grabbed her head between his large hands, and snapped her neck.

The fae crumpled, and he quickly swept her warm body into his arms. Her head lolled horribly, but he refused to feel guilty. Guilt was a foreign emotion. Anyway, a fae didn't stay down long from a broken neck. Or so Fionn and Rose had told him.

As he pushed out into the freezing Moscow night, he searched the parking lot for witnesses and was relieved to find none. They were alone. He rounded the vehicle and swiped the keys off the tire, pressing them to open the car. Remembering how important this woman was to Fionn, Kiyo found himself easing her onto the back seat of the car with a gentleness that did not come naturally.

And was pointless, really, considering he'd just broken her neck.

Before coming for her, he'd torn open the leather of the car bench and lined the inside with pure iron, and then taped the leather back up. If Niamh awoke before he returned to the apartment, the iron would weaken her without hurting her.

Pure iron, Fionn had confessed, was the only weapon on earth that could harm a fae. They did not have pure iron on Faerie, which was why the fae were truly immortal in their own world.

Sometimes he had to remind himself this shit was no longer a fairy tale supernaturals scoffed at or the religion that some of them clung to, to explain their existence.

It was real.

Still, Kiyo reckoned it would never feel truly real unless he, one day, saw Faerie. And if that happened, the world was screwed.

Moving with urgency, Kiyo got in the car and tried not to speed out of the parking lot. The heat from the traffic within the city center melted the snow and ice, but Kiyo drove west at an inconspicuous speed. At this hour the traffic wasn't bad, but it still took thirty-five minutes for them to reach the apartment in the Solntsevo District.

Niamh had been awake for most of that.

She healed with remarkable speed.

Kiyo knew she was awake because only five minutes into the drive, an almost imperceptible whimper had escaped her lips. Glancing in the rearview mirror angled toward her, he found her lying limp, eyes closed.

But her neck no longer lolled at a hideous angle, and her chest rose and fell ever so slightly. His gaze darted down her sweetly curved body to the long legs that he'd had to bend at the knees to make them fit on the bench.

Staring back at the road, Kiyo felt every muscle in his body lock with tension. He had no idea if the pure iron sewn into the seat would work.

Eventually, he relaxed. The fact that she hadn't attacked him the entire ride or *traveled* out of the car using fae magic was evidence that his strategy was a success.

Parking the car in a dark neighborhood of dangerous reputation, one chosen specifically so if anyone saw him hauling a woman into his apartment, they might be less likely to do anything about it, Kiyo waited a moment. He had excellent vision and even in the car's dim light, he could make out Niamh's every feature. She still pretended to be unconscious.

That strange shiver cascaded down his spine again, and his pulse jumped. He frowned. It was unlike him to be anything but calm in a situation.

Reaching into the glove box, Kiyo removed the handcuffs he'd had specially made. They were pure iron but covered in thick leather so they wouldn't burn her. He'd seen the burn scars on Rose's wrists from whoever had held her captive. To press pure iron to Niamh's skin would be tantamount to torture.

And while he wasn't in the habit of torturing innocents, Kiyo also wasn't keen on testing the unbreakable contract with Fionn. If he hurt or abandoned Niamh, Fionn would be able to summon Kiyo to him using magic. Though Kiyo was unkillable, he was pretty certain Fionn would be able to imprison him for all eternity or until he found a way to end Kiyo's life. Kiyo didn't mind the ending his life part, but he knew with absolute certainty there was no way to kill him.

Unlike every other being on Earth, Kiyo *was* a true immortal.

Eternity was a terrifying prospect Kiyo avoided the thought of by working as a mercenary and battling in underground fights.

Eternity in prison ... he didn't dare contemplate the hell it would be.

So, he'd do as Fionn asked, even if Niamh Farren turned out to be the biggest pain in the ass. He was being generously compensated to do so.

Kiyo exited and rounded the car to the passenger side where Niamh's head rested. He didn't want to take the chance of opening the other side and her using what strength she had to kick him to Timbuktu. Moving at wolf speed, he fastened the handcuffs around her wrists. She couldn't hide her flinch.

Frowning, Kiyo double-checked the iron wasn't burning through the leather.

It wasn't.

Her reaction had to be the weakening effects of the iron.

"I know you're awake."

Her eyes flew open and it was like the breath was knocked from his body.

Her irises were liquid gold.

The gold suddenly melted, and she stared up at him with the most extraordinary aquamarine eyes. Striations of gold remained in them.

He was surprised by the fear he saw in her gaze. He hadn't imagined a powerful fae capable of fear.

But she didn't know his intention, and she wasn't completely invincible.

Plus, he'd gotten the drop on her. Of course she was afraid.

"I'm not going to hurt you," he promised. "I'll explain everything once we're inside. But first ... apologies for doing this to you again."

Her lips parted in question, but Kiyo broke her neck before she could speak.

Sliding her carefully out of the car, he gathered her into his arms, annoyed that her dress was now showing an indecent amount of skin, skin he'd touched and was adamantly ignoring the silken softness of.

Using his supernatural speed, he hurried across the lot, into the building, and up the five flights to the apartment he'd acquired for his purposes. Once inside, he laid Niamh on the graying mattress and pulled her dress back down around her thighs.

Retreating, he stared at her sprawled across the mattress on the floor of the dingy apartment. Her long, brown hair cascaded around her face in wavy tendrils. It wasn't her natural hair color. The first surveillance photos Fionn's research guy, Bran, had provided showed Niamh with light blond hair.

Tension drained out of Kiyo's body as he settled into the grubby armchair that made up the small collection of furniture in the two-room apartment. Kiyo had kept the three table lamps lit for his return, preferring the warm light of those to the glaring overhead bulbs.

The beige paint was peeling off the walls, marred with food stains and fingerprints and even graffiti. But you couldn't see that now. Nailed on top, without an inch of space between, were thin sheets of pure iron.

He'd made Niamh a cage.

Kiyo wasn't sure how Fionn would react to his methods, but what else did he expect? Niamh Farren could teleport herself out of any room, and Kiyo needed to disable that skill long enough to explain who he was and why he'd come.

And if he felt she wasn't amenable to the idea of him guarding and stopping her from using her powers without circumspection, then he'd have to consider keeping her here indefinitely.

Thinking of the vile bathroom he'd scrubbed clean with bleach only hours ago, Kiyo really hoped Niamh would get over his aggressive methods and trust he was who he said he was.

Months of living in this shithole as a prison warden instead of a bodyguard didn't exactly appeal to him.

But Fionn Mór was not someone you crossed. Kiyo had known Fionn since the late '60s. Kiyo had left New York several years before because it was no longer safe for him to remain there. Although he'd kept to himself and moved from borough to borough, he'd begun to encounter one too many older people who remembered him from their youth.

Since then, Kiyo had lived the life of a nomad, a mercenary for hire. He'd been a silent assassin, hostage negotiator, soldier, bounty hunter, kidnapper, bodyguard, and thief, to name but a few occupations in the unseen wars of the supernatural world. Even in the human world. There were humans who were aware of the supernaturals, some to fear and avoid, others who paid a great deal of money for the advantages of supernatural power.

The supernatural world questioned Kiyo's longevity, considering he was a werewolf, and there had been those who'd tried to kill him as an abomination, and failed. There were those who'd tried to use him and failed at that too.

Among all the supernaturals who had guessed at his immortality, only one man had garnered a modicum of Kiyo's trust. Fionn. Kiyo had thought him a powerful warlock. They'd met fighting each other in the underground matches, and Kiyo was satisfied to have found someone who could finally challenge him. Fionn never pried into his personal life and vice versa. As the decades passed with Fionn never aging, Kiyo had surmised the Irishman had been cursed with immortality as he himself had.

Until last year when he arrived at an underground fight with his mate, Rose. Fionn hadn't known she was his mate then, but Kiyo had understood Fionn was fighting his attraction to the woman. He'd come to the fight to take out his pent-up frustration on Kiyo, and in a moment before the fight, Fionn's eyes had flashed gold.

He'd demanded Kiyo forget he'd seen it, and Kiyo had obliged.

But the origin stories had filled his mind. Stories of the fae and the gate, how it had been opened over two thousand years ago, and the fae's interference with the humans on Faerie had brought about the creation of vampires and werewolves. The fae had been true immortals, beautiful, beguiling ... and with eyes that flashed gold when their passions were high.

Fionn Mór was fae.

Of course, now Kiyo knew the whole story. Fionn had once been human. An ancient warrior king in what is now Ireland. He'd fought the fae as a human king and in punishment for killing a fae prince, the Faerie Queen, Aine, had enslaved Fionn. In return, his wife and children were spared. But Fionn lived on Faerie for several years as the queen's consort. Before she'd decided to close the gate between worlds and send the supernaturals and humans back to Earth, she'd turned Fionn into fae to keep him with her.

However, he escaped. Upon his return to Ireland, his wife, now remarried to the new king, wanted to kill him for what he'd become. But in respect for the king he'd once been, Druids cast a sleeping curse over him and buried him in the earth instead. Personally, Kiyo thought that was worse than death.

In the early 1700s, the Blackwood Coven found Fionn. They were a powerful North American coven obsessed with reopening the gate to Faerie. It took them two years, but they eventually broke the Druid spell and woke Fionn. They thought he'd be the one to help them open the gate. The ancient Irishman had plans to do that but only to take revenge on Aine. He waited, as a few others of his time had, for the fruition of a spell that Aine had cast before she closed the gate. She'd prophesied the birth of seven fae children born to humans who would have the ability to open the gate between worlds.

Rose Kelly had been one of those fae.

Fionn found Rose and wanted to use her to open the gate. In a twist of fate, Rose turned out to be Fionn's true mate. Now he was determined to protect her and to protect the gate from reopening. He knew what the fae could do to the human world. Aine knew. That's why she'd closed the gate in the first place. But the twisted fae bitch couldn't help herself from toying with the supernaturals and the humans by casting that goddamn spell.

There were only three fae-borne left.

The now-dead leader of The Garm, a supernatural group made of vamps and wolves, who were religiously against the opening of the gate, had killed three of the fae before his death. He'd died at the hands of the fourth who had been turned into a werewolf by her werewolf mate and was now no longer a person of interest to those who wanted to open the gate.

At the head of that group was the Blackwood Coven. They'd been focused on Rose for a while, but she was extraordinarily powerful, as was her mate. So, for now, they seemed to have abandoned her as prey. They were focused on one of the two fae left. The second was an unknown. Not even Fionn knew who the last fae-borne was.

But the first was lying on the old mattress in front of Kiyo.

Niamh Farren.

Fae-borne.

Hunted by many.

Protected by few.

One of those protectors had apparently been her human brother, Ronan. And Ronan had been killed by an Irish coven hunting Rose Kelly.

Since then, Niamh had lost all sense of self-protection. She used her powers in front of humans, bringing attention to herself from the supernatural world.

From the enemies who hunted her.

Kiyo was now one of her protectors. Fionn was paying him a lot of money to be.

Protecting Niamh from her enemies was one thing.

Protecting her from herself was a far greater challenge.

2

The smell of bleach tickled her nostrils.

It was quickly overwhelmed by the more pleasant scent of earth and ... something else. Like aged ambergris and smoke.

Fear flooded her.

She knew that scent.

The werewolf.

Her vision had led her to a girl in a music venue in Moscow. It was a vision of the girl being raped and then murdered. When she'd spotted the girl, and a human was harassing her, she thought he was the one she had to deal with. Until the werewolf arrived on the scene.

Niamh kept her eyes closed tight, feeling something soft beneath her body.

"I'm not going to hurt you. I'll explain everything once we're inside. But first ... apologies for doing this to you again."

He was American.

At the venue she'd watched him approach the girl and could only make out a tall, well-built man with dark hair tied back into a top knot.

Her skin had tingled in awareness, the hair rising on her arms, and she'd realized he was supernatural. Watching him lead the girl through the crowd, she'd gotten the impression of broad shoulders, large, dark eyes, and a brooding expression.

It was only when she'd stepped through the exit door and sensed him behind her that she'd caught his base scent. Earthy, heady, like the soil after a rainstorm.

Werewolf.

The bastard had broken her neck. She'd healed quickly, waking up to discover she was not only in the back of the werewolf's car and that she was the one he was after, not the girl, but that he'd done something to weaken her. Her limbs felt heavy and lethargic and as much as she tried to *travel* back to her hotel room, her magic wouldn't work.

Then he'd had the audacity to tell her he wasn't going to hurt her right before he broke her fecking goddamn neck. Again!

Niamh tried to twitch a hand, tried to focus on *traveling* from where she was, but it was even worse than it had been in the car. Her body felt so heavy and weak. She'd never experienced anything like it.

Realizing she couldn't put off the inevitable forever, Niamh opened her eyes and found herself staring up at a cracked ceiling. There was a single light fixture in the middle but it wasn't on. Yet warm light filled the room from various points. Lowering her gaze, she saw a doorway that led into a grubby-looking bathroom. Next to the doorway was, possibly, the world's smallest kitchenette. Along from—

Her breath caught in her throat when she registered the walls.

Nailed to almost every inch were sheets of a silvery-gray metal.

Pure iron.

Feeling his eyes on her, Niamh's flew to the right.

The werewolf sat, legs sprawled, arms relaxed on a worn armchair that might have been red once but was now a muddy brown.

He stared expressionlessly at her.

If it weren't for his worryingly blank countenance and the fact that he'd kidnapped her, Niamh would think he was quite possibly the most beautiful man she'd ever seen. And that was saying something.

With his gorgeous fawn skin, large black eyes, broad nose, high cheekbones, thick black hair, and full-lipped mouth, it was hard to look away.

"Who are you?" she asked.

"My name is Kiyonari. You may call me Kiyo," he replied casually, as if they'd met under normal circumstances.

With a name like Kiyonari, Niamh would guess he was Japanese. Japanese American if his accent was anything to go by.

"I reckon you already know who I am." Her gaze flew to her hands. They were locked together with leather handcuffs but they weighed a ton.

Beneath the leather, those handcuffs were made of pure iron.

The wolf wanted to incapacitate her but apparently didn't want to do any permanent damage. That should have been more of a relief than it was.

She'd had no vision of this man. It made no sense. Anytime she was in danger or someone she loved was, she'd always gotten a vision before it happened. Why not this time?

Who was he really?

With a smirk that belied her fear, Niamh pushed herself up into a sitting position with great effort. She had to rest against the wall behind the old mattress she lay on. Thankfully, it was the only patch of wall not covered in iron.

"You're Niamh Farren."

"So ..." To her shock, she felt sweat bead on her forehead. The iron *really* did weaken her kind. It was her first experience with it. "Iron handcuffs, iron walls ... Are you working for The Garm or the Blackwoods?"

"Neither." He leaned forward, resting his arms on his knees. Niamh found herself held captive by his dark eyes. "I work for Fionn Mór."

An image of the huge six-foot-six, suit-wearing Irish warrior king filled her mind.

But if he worked for Fionn, why had this bastard kidnapped her? "I don't understand."

"I know what you are. I know the whole story. I'm an old acquaintance of Fionn's. When you started lighting up all over the map, playing Superwoman, he and Rose tracked me down. Fionn is paying me to act as your bodyguard and, more importantly, convince you to stop bringing attention to yourself." His expression was mildly disapproving. "You do realize the Blackwoods think you killed their heir and his two sisters?"

Indignation stung. "What? I didn't."

"No. Fionn and Rose did. The Blackwoods kidnapped Rose against their father's orders. Death was the consequence. But the Blackwoods were under the impression Layton and his sisters were tracking you. And since they died in Ireland, they've put two and two together and come up with you."

"Fionn sent you because he feels bad for setting them on me?"

"I don't know. All I know is he's paying me a lot of money to protect you until the heat is off."

Although it took effort, Niamh grinned.

Kiyo's eyes narrowed on her mouth and he glowered.

Ignoring his apparently perpetual bad mood, Niamh said, "Fionn does realize that the heat is never off? Not even for him and Rose."

"Yeah, but they're good at hiding. You seem to have made it your mission in life to bring our world to the attention of humans. You're not only pissing off the Blackwoods and The Garm but you're going to piss off the councils and the Consortium. Never mind every supernatural on the planet who enjoys anonymity from the humans, or the human governments who don't want their human citizens to know what they know."

Ignoring that—because Niamh couldn't really argue when he was right—she contemplated him a moment. "Fionn hired you to protect me ... so you decided to break my neck, kidnap me, break my neck again, and handcuff me in a room lined with pure iron. Yeah, that sounds like someone whose word I can trust."

"If I'd approached you, you'd have *traveled* before I could explain myself."

"You don't know that."

"You're telling me you wouldn't have suspected I was The Garm?"

"To be honest, I'm still not convinced you aren't. It's probably that neck breakage and iron cage thing I mentioned earlier."

"I'm not The Garm. For a start, I work for no one but myself."

"You just said you work for Fionn."

"He hired me. There's a difference."

"Is there? Okay, then. Why you? What makes you so special? Not to be a bitch, but when there isn't a plethora of pure iron in the vicinity, I can pretty much kick the arse of any supernatural who comes at me."

"Yeah, I've seen that." He pulled out his smartphone and began scrolling. "Bran has been keeping me posted on your exploits these past few months."

"Whose Bran?"

"Fionn's friend. A vampire. The information guy."

Niamh's head lolled to the side. Her eyelids were beginning to feel heavy. "What makes you so special?"

"I'm stronger than the average wolf. Smarter too."

And more handsome.

Seriously, he was so bloody gorgeous, it was almost like staring at the sun. You couldn't look at him without him blinding you with his attractiveness. But Niamh was never one to fall victim to a pretty face.

"Well, obviously, I'm going to need confirmation from Fionn and Rose that you are who you say you are."

"That I can do."

"And then they're going to have to *un*-hire you."

"I doubt they'll do that."

"Call them."

Without a word, Kiyo hit a button on his mobile and then another, and a loud ringing filled the room. Loudspeaker. Niamh forced her eyes to remain open, trying to stay alert.

"I'm about to talk a very attractive blond and her equally, sexy-as-fuck boyfriend into coming back to my apartment, so this better be good," a man with a thick Dublin accent answered.

"Bran, I have Farren, but she refuses to believe me until she speaks to Fionn."

"You don't have Fionn's number?" she asked.

He cut her a dark look as Bran chuckled, having overheard.

"Let me patch you through. Say hello to my fellow countrywoman for me."

Niamh smirked because it was obvious Kiyo had no intention of doing anything so congenial. A click sounded and there was silence, followed by a ringing.

The phone rang several times before finally someone picked up.

"What is it, Bran?"

"It's Kiyo. Bran patched me through."

"Have you found Niamh?"

Niamh's eyes narrowed. Fionn had been stalking her for years, intending to use her to open the gate. Then her visions changed suddenly, and she realized Rose, one of her fae siblings (of a sort), could change the path Fionn was on. They were true mates. Niamh couldn't tell Rose that for fear of changing her destiny, but she'd tracked Rose down to try to convince her that it was important she give her time and trust to Fionn to save the entire world—and Niamh herself.

Still, Niamh had only heard Fionn speak once, and it was during a time she'd rather forget.

"I have her," Kiyo confirmed. "But she refuses to believe I'm here because you sent me."

"Is she there? Can she hear me?"

"Yes," Niamh spoke up. "I'm handcuffed with leather-covered pure iron, in a room filled with iron, while your dog sits guard."

Kiyo bared his teeth at her.

"What's this?" Fionn's voice lowered, a dangerous edge to his tone. "That's not what we discussed, Kiyo."

"There wasn't a better way to keep her in one place while I got her to trust me."

"I doubt this is inspiring trust," he drawled.

"Amen to that," Niamh agreed. "Also, I can't remember talking to this Fionn character," she lied, "so how the bloody hell am I supposed to know if you're really him?"

Fionn grunted. There was a rustling sound and then, "Hello, Niamh?"

She stiffened.

The new melodic voice with its American accent was familiar.

Rose.

"It's me, Rose. I'm sorry if Kiyo has hurt you. That wasn't in the plan and I'm going to kick his furry ass when I see him next."

The said furry arsehole remained impassive against the insult, but she noted a muscle ticking in his jaw that gave away his annoyance. Niamh snorted with humor.

She'd know Rose's voice anywhere, which meant he was telling the truth. He was her new bodyguard.

"There's no permanent damage," she assured Rose with a sleepy breeziness. "He broke my neck a few times, but he hasn't let the iron touch my skin, so I guess that's something."

"Kiyo, you're a dead man," Rose said, sounding impressively scary. Well, at least Niamh thought so.

Kiyo looked unperturbed.

"So ... may I ask why you felt the need to have me kidnapped by a werewolf who proclaims himself my bodyguard?"

"You weren't supposed to be kidnapped," Rose insisted. "We sent Kiyo to watch over you. Niamh, the Blackwoods think you killed their son and daughters. I'm so sorry. It's kind of my fault."

"Not really." Niamh meant it too. "Those wicked bastards had it coming, Rose. And I don't need your help."

"You do. Niamh, you're not being safe. You can't keep using your magic out in the open like this."

"What else am I to do? I stopped receiving visions about us, about the fae-borne and the gate ... so I have nothing else to do but follow the visions I *do* receive. That's what I'm doing. They must mean something. They feel different from my other visions. Angrier, insistent. Important."

"Those visions are going to get you killed. Please. Just ... stay with Kiyo for a while. He'll take you somewhere safe."

"And if I say no?"

Rose sighed heavily. "I'm sorry but that's not an option. I can't leave you unprotected. We're connected, Niamh. We owe each other. I owe you. But more than that, I can't let you be the one to open the gate. So please, don't fight Kiyo. Just lie low for a while."

Exhaustion was pulling Niamh under. It was a struggle to reply. "It won't just be for a while. We both know this is our lives forever. On the run. Hiding. This werewolf you've hired, he can't protect me indefinitely."

"He'll protect you until he's sure you're in the right frame of mind to protect yourself. He'll protect you until we've found a way to deal with the Blackwood Coven permanently."

"That's your plan?"

"It wasn't ... but Fionn and I have decided they need to be dealt with. But in a way that's orchestrated so it doesn't look like the fae-borne had anything to do with it. That could take awhile. So Kiyo will stay with you. Please, Niamh, tell me you'll allow this without a fight."

That burn of irritation swarmed Niamh's chest. "I will if your dog will take off these damn handcuffs and get me out of this bloody awful apartment."

"You heard her," Rose practically snarled. "Kiyo, do it."

"Are you sure?" Kiyo narrowed his eyes on Niamh. "I'm not convinced she's seeing things your way."

"Niamh Farren is the sweetest soul I've ever met, Kiyo, and you are so lucky I am not in that room to eviscerate you for hurting her."

Rose's words eased the burn somewhat in Niamh's chest. Guilt replaced the irritation.

Kiyo glared at his phone. "I think I might have the wrong Niamh Farren, then."

Ugh, very nice. She gave him a dark look.

"Just do it."

"Fine."

"And let us know when you're on the move. We don't need to know where ... we just need to know she's okay."

"*Fine*." He hung up.

Kiyo stood slowly and Niamh drank in his powerful body. Beneath his T-shirt and jeans were very broad shoulders, a narrow waist, and long legs.

"You don't like her very much, do you?" she asked.

He walked toward the mattress. "I thought you'd have mixed feelings about her, considering it was her coven who killed—"

"That wasn't Rose's fault."

Thankfully, Kiyo said no more. Instead he lowered to his haunches and reached out to take hold of the leather cuffs. A small key appeared in his hand as if from nowhere and he unlocked them.

"Throw them away, please," she begged, feeling tears of relief sting her eyes.

He frowned but did as she asked, sending them soaring to the other side of the room.

The deep lethargy began to fade from her body, although the iron walls meant it wouldn't alleviate itself completely.

"So, what's the decision. Really?" Kiyo asked.

They stared at one another a second, and Niamh had the alarming feeling she could drown in his big dark eyes. They should have been soulless and dull considering he had all the warmth of an icebox. But they weren't. His eyes glittered with intelligence and determination.

Her gaze dropped to his lips. He had the most prominent cupid's bow she'd ever seen on a man. His mouth was beautiful and tempting as hell.

Pity, really, they'd met under these circumstances.

It took every inch of strength Niamh possessed, gathering it like a cyclone in the center of her being.

Kiyo's eyes widened as he sensed her energy building.

But he was too late.

Niamh sent her magic out like two hands gripping his head and she snapped his neck without even touching him.

"Fair play and all that," she muttered wearily as she crawled along the mattress past his now-unconscious body.

It took Niamh much longer than she'd ever have thought to crawl to the apartment door. Her body was soaked with sweat by the time she reached it, all the while worried the wolf would awaken and stop her.

But finally, her hand grasped the lock and the doorknob and it swung open. She fell out of the doorway and scrambled to shut it behind her.

Though still tired and weak, the heaviness left her limbs and she managed to push herself up to standing. She had to move at the speed of a human, but Niamh hurried as fast as she could out of there and used what energy she had left to start the engine of a car out in the lot.

She breathed a very real sigh of relief as the car pulled away from the apartment building.

Because Niamh didn't care what Rose and Fionn wanted. They didn't have the visions like she did. And if she didn't follow her visions, then what was the point in this long, bloody awful eternal life? If the visions led to her eventual death, then at least she would have died for something and not been killed in a pointless act that had led to nothing.

3

An aching burn of pain woke Kiyo. His eyes flew open and he stared up at the cracked ceiling, frowning at the hurt in his neck and spine as he tried to orient himself.

Niamh.

The memory of her hit with the same force of a sucker punch. Fury filled him as he flew to his feet and swayed. His body wasn't quite done healing itself.

The fae woman had broken his neck without even touching him.

He growled as he marched toward the door of the apartment, following the faint traces of her scent out into the hallway. Kiyo knew he shouldn't have listened to Rose. Behind Niamh's blasé but iron-weakened attitude had been a hard glint of determination in her eyes.

Either she didn't give a damn she was putting the gate in danger or she was so blinded by her own mission, she couldn't see what she was jeopardizing.

Thankfully, her scent still lingered, which meant it hadn't been long since she'd escaped. She'd underestimated how quickly Kiyo would heal. Not as fast as a fae, maybe, but faster than the other wolves.

Her scent led out to the parking lot and beyond, so Kiyo jumped in the stolen car he'd parked out there and rolled down the window. Niamh's caramel essence tickled his nose and he drove in the direction she'd taken off in.

The whole time he drove, he tried to contain his anger. Playing nice wasn't second nature to Kiyo, but his fury at her would definitely push her further away.

He'd never regretted taking on a job more.

She hadn't escaped from the apartment for more than five minutes when the two cars appeared behind her.

Niamh's pulse jumped. It wasn't the wolf following her. Wolves didn't heal that fast. But her knowledge of her pursuers' identity came from more than that.

Fae could sense when they or others were in danger. The hair on Niamh's body rose, her pulse rate increased, and a feeling akin to dread swam over her. That hadn't happened with Kiyo and now she knew why. Rose and Fionn *had* sent him to protect her.

So the three cars behind her ... nothing to do with Kiyo.

It was either The Garm or the Blackwoods.

The bloody wolf had led them right to her. She scoffed in irritation at his interference.

And because of his interference, she was too weak to *travel*!

Niamh had been heading back into the city to collect her things from the hotel, but even if it was the early hours of the morning and there were only a few cars on the road, she couldn't lead them into a fight where innocents might get hurt.

She was currently on the motorway and as she passed the buildings on her left, she caught glimpses of thick, dark forestation in the distance. One of Moscow's national parks, maybe? She knew there were areas of natural beauty scattered throughout Moscow that could make folks forget they were even in a city.

Niamh could head into the park and lose them in there. Her

strength might even come back in a place like that and she'd be able to *travel.*

Mind made up, and seeing no way off the motorway but to cross it, she swerved the car onto the opposite side of the quiet road and shot across and off it. She hit the grass as she took a road on the left, past a Burger King, down a tree-lined street toward the wooded area she'd seen in the distance. Plowed snow sat piled along the edges of the sidewalks in graying, icy borders.

Glancing in the rearview mirror, she saw the two cars were still following her.

Clingy buggers, aren't they? she thought in aggravation as she approached a glowing-red traffic light perched beneath a railway bridge.

Niamh took a breath and flew under the tight bridge, thankfully not meeting any oncoming traffic. As soon as she came out of it, her headlights lit up a path leading into the park.

Skidding to a stop, the car hit ice and swung haphazardly into the tall curbside. She barely even felt it. She was too busy jumping out of the car. Niamh dashed toward the opening in the snow-dusted trees. She could see the pathway under a thick layer of snow. Tires squealed behind her as her pursuers witnessed her escape. Sweat beaded under her arms as she pushed through the lethargy that still clung to her body.

Come on! She gritted her teeth in frustration as she ran up the snowy path, fast but nowhere near the speed she was capable of. The snow didn't bloody help matters.

That fecking fecker of a werewolf!

He was going to get her killed!

The path seemed to just keep going, the trees thick on either side, and Niamh could hear the crunching of very fast feet through hard snow in the distance. Panic bloomed in her chest as she hit an intersection in the path.

She turned left, feeling her speed pick up in increments. Fast, but not fast enough.

Breaking off the path, Niamh disappeared into the snowy trees, hoping to lose her pursuers in the darkness. She had superior night vision, but so did most supernaturals.

The birch trees towered above like skinny giants holding out their snow-peppered arms protectively, urging her to hurry. She tried to detect the scent of her pursuers but she didn't have a nose like a wolf and all she could smell was the freshness of snow, the earthiness of the soil beneath, and the sweet, sharp, clean scent of the birch. There was also the faint mustiness of animal. Not werewolf, but from whatever animal lived in the park.

Niamh picked up speed, calmed by the enveloping darkness of the trees and the fact that the crunching footsteps had grown fainter in the distance. She kept pushing, pushing until she burst out of the trees into an open field thick with snow. Gathering her speed again, she flew across the openness—wet encapsulated her ankles as her feet disappeared in and out of the snow—and into the tree line ahead.

Not long later, as Niamh caught the glimmer of another opening in the distance, a familiar sick sensation built in her gut.

No.

No, not now.

Tears of defeat pricked her eyes as she rushed out, skidding through the snow of another small clearing.

In the distance, she could hear the thrashing through the forest. The thrashing of her pursuers growing closer.

And there was nothing she could do as the first image blasted into her head, throwing her to her knees. She didn't even feel the icy wetness soak through her clothes.

The pain was too blinding, an electric, white-hot heat that blazed around her head as she saw green.

Grass.

And on the grass, four stone circles. Like a small druid circle. Like standing stones.

Then a face appeared through that image. A woman. A face she'd seen before but not since her death.

And then Elijah.

And Rose.

And herself.

The image was obliterated as another slammed into her skull. A pendant. A jade pendant shaped like a water droplet. It flickered and there was a city. A mountain towering over it. A garden. A water garden. A Japanese garden. The images kept coming, one after the other, each like a mallet to her head.

SELF-DIRECTED frustration and irritation held Kiyo immobile for a few seconds.

He'd followed Niamh's scent down the highway, across traffic and down a road that led him under the railway bridge to a park.

And scattered across the road by the entrance to the park were three vehicles. One smelled of Niamh.

The other two of vamps and wolves.

The Garm.

They'd found her.

For a moment, Kiyo wondered why the hell she had led them to a park instead of *traveling*, and that's when he realized that she probably couldn't.

Kiyo's trick with the iron had depleted her strength.

And if she died today, Fionn would make the rest of his eternity a living hell.

Biting back a curse, Kiyo took off into the park.

He was faster as a wolf, especially in snow.

So as he ran, a blur through the wintry darkness, following Niamh's scent and the fresh footprints, he called on the change.

Not many wolves could run and change at the same time, but as Kiyo liked to remind himself, he wasn't like normal werewolves.

Usually, he had time to enjoy the transformation. Changing was like a satisfying pleasure pain. Like a deep stretch of a knotted muscle. Bones cracked and muscles contorted and it all sounded horrific but ... it wasn't. Kiyo, however, didn't have time to feel any of those things.

He slowed, kicking off his boots, just before he began to run on all fours. Eventually he skidded through the snow, halting in the density of the woods to let the transformation take over. He pushed it. He didn't savor it. And in a flash, he was staring through the eyes of his wolf with his wider peripheral vision.

He contained the growl he wanted to unleash but didn't for fear of losing the element of surprise. Kiyo instead left behind his tattered clothes and ran.

He soared through the woods with such speed, even if it had been daylight, all anyone would have seen was a blur so fleeting, they would be sure they imagined him. The wind whipped through his fur; the snow barely had time to soak his paws he was so light across it. He felt the violence building within him at the thought of The Garm harming Niamh Farren.

She was his charge.

She was his job.

His to protect.

And Kiyo did not like to fail.

Hearing voices ahead, his ears twitched as a male voice asked in a thick Russian accent, "What do we do with her?"

"Kill her," another grunted in exasperation.

"But she's ... she's seizing or something," a female said. "Maybe she's already dying."

Seizing?

The word caused Kiyo more than a flicker of unease.

Rose said Niamh's visions physically incapacitated her. She said she resembled someone in the midst of a seizure.

Niamh couldn't even protect herself.

"Take that piece of iron and kill her!" the exasperated male ordered. Kiyo could see the man through the opening ahead. Tall. Burly. Another wolf.

Kiyo leapt out of the trees at his back, jaw open, and clamped his teeth into the man's neck. The force of his hit took them both to the ground. He tore out the wolf's throat, hearing the surprise from his companions as he rolled off to face the others.

His eyes darted to Niamh. She was collapsed in the snow, eyes wide and staring unseeingly at the night sky as her body convulsed.

Rage blasted through him as he turned his attention to the two vampires and two werewolves who bared their incisors and canines at him. Only cowards with no honor would take down Niamh while she was in no state to fight back.

He would enjoy this hunt.

The female wolf came at him first. Kiyo lunged to meet her. She was so distracted by his open jaws, she missed his claws. As she triumphantly punched him with impressive force in the muzzle, Kiyo pushed the change, his front forelegs shifting back to his human arms as he slashed her across the belly with his wolf claws.

As her howl of agony lit the air, momentarily disconcerting her companions, Kiyo made the full shift. Uncaring of his nakedness, he spun back to the female as she dropped to her knees, retracted his claws, and punched through the solid cage of muscle and bone in her back.

The force of the hit shuddered up his arms as his hand clamped around the hot, wet muscle of her heart.

He yanked it out and she sagged lifelessly to the ground.

A roar of fury filled his ears as the remaining wolf and the two vampires sped toward him. Claws out again, Kiyo ran at them, leapt into the air in a spin to give his body enough momentum and force so that when he brought his arm around, his clawed hand out, he cut through the wolf's neck like his hand was a blade. His teeth rattled with the impact, but the wolf's head rolled from his body with satisfying results.

The sight caused the two vampires to stare in disbelief.

He doubted they'd seen many werewolves decapitate someone with their bare hand.

Realization that Kiyo wasn't at all what he seemed flooded their expressions, and the male and female vampire shared a concerned look.

Self-preservation was a typical characteristic of a vampire and they shot off into the woods. Kiyo couldn't let them get away and back to The Garm.

The less The Garm knew about Niamh, the better.

He raced after them, catching up to the male first. He tackled the vamp to the ground but felt hands wrap around his neck and throw him backward.

Kiyo hit the ground hard but the snow cushioned the impact. He glared up at the female vamp who had surprised him by coming back for her companion. That was something he could respect.

He lunged, canines out, misleading her as he had her werewolf counterpart. She was a blur of movement, lashing out to grab him around the throat and hold off his teeth from her neck.

But Kiyo wasn't aiming for her neck.

He punched through her chest, up under her rib cage, gripped her heart, and squeezed it until it popped.

She burst into a thick cloud of dust, speckling his face and body.

He grunted in annoyance, stepping back from the ash cloud as a blur moved behind him.

Pain screamed at his scalp as the male vamp gripped hold of Kiyo's top knot and yanked, pulling Kiyo down toward the ground onto his back. At the last moment, Kiyo thrust his lower body upward and he flipped backward, the movement relaxing the vamp's hold on him.

He landed with a deadly silence behind the confused vampire and was about to treat him to the same end as his female companion when the vamp suddenly turned, incisors out, and clamped his strong jaw down over Kiyo's neck.

His long teeth sliced through Kiyo's throat and the toxins in the vamp's saliva tickled at his senses, trying to confuse him into believing he was receiving pleasure, not pain.

Goddamn dirty trick, that.

Kiyo gripped the vampire's head, trying to part him from his throat, but he had the strength of a boa constrictor now that he'd sunk his teeth into him. His arms were a vise around Kiyo's upper body, and Kiyo knew the vamp had every intention of draining him dry.

It wouldn't kill him, of course, but it would weaken him.

And mightily piss him off.

Kiyo dug his claws into the vampire's sides but other than a grunt of pain, it didn't shift the bloodsucker. As calm as ever, despite his growing anger, Kiyo searched for the most expedient way to kill him.

That's when he caught sight of the perfectly angled, sharp-ended branch sticking out of the skinny white birch tree in the distance.

Pushing his hand between the tight compression of their two bodies, Kiyo dug his claws into the vamp's chest around his heart. It was enough to make the vamp loosen his hold.

With a roar of power, Kiyo broke the vampire's cage, feeling part of his throat come away with the pressure of his removal. Warm blood spurted down his neck as he watched the vampire soar through the air and hit the tree with accuracy.

The vamp stared down at the branch sticking through his chest with a look of abject disbelief.

And then he exploded into a burst of ash dust.

Hot pain throbbed at Kiyo's throat and he muffled his curse as he dropped to a knee.

Despite the icy wetness surrounding him, sweat soaked his naked skin. Blood ran in rivulets down his chest as his wound slowly knitted together. The blood loss made him slightly woozy, but the thought of Niamh, vulnerable in the clearing, had him pushing to his feet.

When he stumbled out of the woods, he found Niamh staring in confusion at the dead werewolves surrounding her.

Her eyes flew to his, widening at either his nakedness, his injury, or both.

"Vision over?" he croaked out, clamping a hand over his still-bleeding, gaping wound.

Niamh nodded, blinking rapidly. Then she observed, "You're butt naked. In the snow."

"Yeah."

"You have a gory tear in your throat."

"Yeah."

Her eyes dropped to the werewolves. "You saved me."

"Yeah."

"I wouldn't have needed your help if I hadn't been weakened by the iron." When her eyes flew back to his, there was irritation in them.

"Maybe, maybe not."

"You're a man of few words, huh?" At his answering silence, Niamh sighed and pushed to her feet. She swayed, and he noted her skin was paler than usual. At his frown, she waved him off. "The visions take it out of me. We better get going." Her eyes dropped to his throat. "How long do you take to heal?"

"Faster than the average wolf."

"That's your favorite saying." Her eyes flickered down his body, and he saw a satisfying tinge of red crest her cheeks as she averted her gaze. "Where are your clothes?"

"Had to shift fast. They got ruined."

With a nod, she marched over to the largest wolf, the one Kiyo had taken by surprise first, and began to remove his jacket.

Seeing what she was about to do—and not too happy about wearing a dead man's clothes but knowing there was nothing else for it—Kiyo helped her undress the corpse.

"I think this might be the lowest moment of my life thus far," she said, but there was a hint of humor in her voice.

Kiyo raised an eyebrow.

She huffed. "What? You want me to feel sorry for the supernatural arsehole who had every intention of killing me?"

"Rose said you were the sweetest soul she'd ever met," he replied. *A sweet soul wouldn't find humor in stealing from a dead man.*

A pucker appeared between her brows. "Rose knew me ... before."

Realizing she wasn't about to elaborate, Kiyo merely grunted and changed into the dead wolf's clothes. Despite the slimness of Kiyo's waist, he had a very broad chest and shoulders, so the material of the wolf's shirt strained against his muscles. The jacket didn't even fit. The jeans would do, however.

Niamh had averted her gaze as he changed but now she stared at his chest. Her eyes flew to his, that pretty blush still staining her cheeks. "Well, you are an impressively proportioned individual, aren't you?"

He hadn't known a fae could blush. He found he enjoyed the notion. A smirk tickled Kiyo's lips, but he didn't respond. Instead he marched back into the woods. "We need to move."

Her light, crunching footsteps sounded behind him as she hurried to follow. "What about shoes?"

Finally feeling the cold seep into his feet, he shrugged. "My boots are in here. We'll find them. Then go. The sooner we get the hell out of Moscow, the better."

"I guess I'm stuck with you, then."

"I guess so."

"About the getting out of Moscow part ..."

If she was about to argue about that, Kiyo would lose his patience. He didn't have much of it to begin with.

"I know where we need to go next. That's what my vision was about."

In all the fighting, he'd almost forgotten about the vision. He glanced at her. She was so tall, they were nearly on eye level. "Oh?"

"Tokyo. We need to go to Tokyo."

Shock hit him first.

Then anger.

Because surely this fae woman was totally and utterly yanking his fucking chain.

4

Although Niamh was grateful the werewolf had come to her rescue, ultimately that wasn't why she'd decided to stick with him.

Part of her vision had been about him. His name had tickled her mind as images of Tokyo came at her. The mountain was Mount Fuji so the garden must be in Tokyo ... and it all had to do with Kiyo.

Unable to return to either her hotel or Kiyo's apartment, Niamh had used her steadily building strength to conjure a backpack Kiyo had described that was in the dingy flat. It had his passport and a change of clothes inside it.

Niamh conjured the emergency bag she kept ready to go in her hotel.

"So this vision ... it's about me, right?" he asked as he reluctantly drove toward the airport. "That's why you want to go to Tokyo and all of a sudden, you want me to come with you."

She sighed, knowing it was too obvious to hide the truth. "Yeah. There's something there about you, and it's important. I don't know what. My visions don't work like that. They come in waves ... almost like chapters in a story. Each chapter provides a little more information and usually it happens the closer I get to my destination or quarry."

"Tell me what you saw."

Niamh remained stubbornly silent. She didn't know why this new flood of information in her vision included Kiyo, but she knew she didn't trust him enough to confide in him. About any of it.

"Are you kidding?" His voice was worryingly calm and low.

Glancing at him, their eyes met as he took his off the road to glower at her. She wondered what his smile was like.

"Seriously? You want me to haul my ass back to a city I haven't been to—" He cut off abruptly.

Interesting. "You haven't been to ...?"

"You tell me nothing, I tell you nothing."

"Can you really blame me?" Her tone was conciliatory. Niamh wasn't the type to be at loggerheads with someone. It wasn't in her nature. And it seemed she was stuck with the werewolf for a while. "Think about it from my perspective. You kidnapped me using the only weapon on earth I'm vulnerable to. For a start, not many folks know what I am or what can hurt me, so you're immediately in my 'be wary of' category.

"Plus, when I came out of my vision, there were dead bodies everywhere, hearts ripped out, and one of them was decapitated. When you appeared in all your naked glory, you had no sword in hand—actual sword, I mean." Her cheeks bloomed hot and she cursed the nonsense blushing this man incited in her. She'd rarely ever blushed in her life before. Damn him. "So, one can only conclude that you ripped a man's head off with your bare hands."

The werewolf didn't respond. Instead he gestured to a gas station. "We can change here."

Niamh rolled her eyes at his evasiveness. "Fionn wouldn't hire just anyone to watch out for me. He'd hire the strongest supernatural he knew that he could trust."

Kiyo flicked her a considering look as he glided the car into a parking spot.

"He trusts you, but that doesn't mean I do. I only started to trust *him* a few months ago, for goodness' sake." She sighed. "It's going to take a lot more than a bloody fight in the snow to assure us of one another's intentions. I can't tell you about the vision. Not yet. If ever. But I promise you that we absolutely should go to Tokyo. I feel it in my gut. And my instincts about these visions have never let me down. I'm the reason Rose and Fionn are together. Did they tell you that?"

"They're together because they've become Fate's bitch. True mates."

Niamh raised an eyebrow. "You have a low opinion of the bond?"

"I have a low opinion of anything that tries to control me."

"That's a funny way to look at love."

Apparently done with the conversation, Kiyo moved to get out of the car.

Niamh grabbed his arm to stop him, and he cut her a bored, questioning look.

Feeling a strange tingling sensation running up her arms from her fingertips, she released her grip. "I just need you to know I'm not messing you about, taking you somewhere you don't want to go for the hell of it. I'm sorry if I've upset you."

His beautiful upper lip curled into that irritating sneer of his. "I don't get upset."

She grinned, mostly just to annoy him. "Well, you do a wonderful impersonation of it, then."

The wolf's eyes narrowed ever so slightly on her smile. "Please tell me you're not one of those 'I can make sunshine and roses out of piles of shit and pools of blood' kind of people?"

Niamh chuckled and pushed open the passenger-side door but she didn't answer him.

Her lack of response to his curtness seemed to perturb him. He grabbed their bags out of the back and handed over hers. His eyes scoured her face, as if he couldn't quite figure her out.

They separated inside the twenty-four-hour gas station to their respective restrooms. Despite lingering weariness, Niamh's mind turned over and over at the recent developments. Kiyo's anger at returning to Tokyo only validated the vision. And he *was* angry. He was good at hiding how much, but Niamh sensed it. It pulsed beneath his skin. There was something important there, though not just to the werewolf but to her, and possibly others. It was maybe even about the bigger picture. The rest of the vision certainly had been.

For weeks she'd wanted her visions to have a coherent direction and mission. Like the visions before when she was trying to save the other fae-borne.

Well, wish granted. The visions had returned to the fae-borne.

And now Niamh bloody wished they hadn't.

Despite her turmoil, or perhaps because of it, as Niamh changed into dry clothes, she imagined Kiyo changing in the men's restroom. Heat bloomed on her cheeks, and other places on her body tingled in delight at the thought. When he'd come rushing out of those trees naked and wounded from defending her, she wasn't going to lie—a very deep thrill moved through her.

The werewolf might be a brooding pain in the ass who'd tried to coerce her into accepting his guardianship, but all that beautiful fawn skin wrapped around taut muscle made him very fun to look at. Granted, she was somewhat wary that he was powerful enough to remove someone's head from their body with his bare hands.

Also he moved faster than other wolves. He'd caught her completely off guard back at the club. And only someone fast and powerful could have taken down five members of The Garm by himself.

The airport was only forty minutes west in the light, early-morning traffic. They were both tense, on guard for The Garm in case they'd sent more than one unit after her. Once they abandoned the car in a parking lot, they strode determinedly toward departures.

"Why are you doing this?" Niamh asked as they reached the entrance.

"Doing what?"

"Acting as my bodyguard. I mean, a fairly terrible one who breaks my neck and all, but ... yeah, for lack of a better word, my bodyguard."

"Terrible?" he asked in his bored tone. "I saved your life. I wouldn't call that being bad at my job. And that's why: It's a job I'm being paid to do. Extremely well paid."

"There's more to it than that. Someone who is secretly seething underneath at the thought of going to Tokyo wouldn't go, not even for money."

With a sigh of irritation, he gripped her arm and pulled her toward the airline desks. "It's called an unbreakable contract. Basically, a spell. If I fail to protect you, the spell brings me to Fionn. He's promised retribution."

Niamh's brow puckered. "Why on earth would you sign up for that?"

"Because I was bored." He gave her a hard smirk. "Believe me, I'm regretting it."

"Why?" she said. "Nothing about the last twenty-four hours has been boring, has it?"

Then she saw it ... a definite twitch of his lips and a slight glitter of amusement in his eyes.

Something swelled in her chest at the sight, and she found herself grinning like a moron. "Thought not."

"Shut up," he said gruffly. "And let's book this flight."

Having the ability to make humans see what she wanted was one of Niamh's less honorable tricks, but it had come in very handy over the years. She changed the name on Kiyo's passport, which was currently Ryan Green.

"Very imaginative," she muttered dryly.

He really could cut the most delightfully dirty looks.

And she presented a piece of paper that the desk staff would see as a passport.

They had no bags to check, so it was a fairly quick business. Kiyo attempted to pay for the tickets but Niamh didn't want to give anyone a chance to track them. She paid in cash.

Their first flight was to Istanbul, and they had over six hours to wait until takeoff. The thought left Niamh feeling antsy for more than one reason. Six hours was too long to be in one place after being attacked by The Garm. Worse, she hated hanging around airports. Airports seemed to exist on some plane of existence where time slowed to a painful, sloth-like crawl. Her boredom always increased tenfold.

When they moved through security, she had to use mental manipulation again to stop security from questioning her about the pile of cash in her bag. She had over $30,000 in different currencies.

"Did you steal that cash?" Kiyo asked as they strolled out of security.

Guilt pricked at her. "What of it?"

"There is no honor in stealing."

"I know," she said so quietly, it was almost a whisper.

Kiyo frowned at whatever he heard in her voice. "Then why?"

"I've been on the run for over half my life." She shrugged. "I did what I could to survive."

"Luxury hotels, empty penthouse apartments, and piles of cash is merely surviving?"

Realizing he knew more about her than she'd thought—and hearing the judgment in his tone—Niamh clamped her lips tightly shut. He wouldn't understand, so there was no point engaging in conversation about it.

"Unless, of course, it was your brother who convinced you living it large made up for being on the run."

His words hit so close to the truth, Niamh felt them like claws in her chest. She turned to snap at him, to tell him to mind his own business, when a roll of familiar nausea turned over in her gut.

She felt the blood drain from her face.

No.

Not now.

Not so soon after the last.

"Kiyo," she said, frantic.

He stopped, expression alert. "What?"

"Vision." She got the word out just before the first image slammed into her head. Vaguely she was aware of her body moving and then a strong band of power wrapped around her. It steadied her as images of a young, pretty, dark-haired girl pounded painfully through her brain, one after the other. A man. Older. Connected to her. Owner. Husband. Sexual violence. Beatings. Abuse. Servitude. Exhaustion. Pain. Despair. Loathing. Rage. Despair. Rage.

Despair.

Rage

Despair.

RAGE.

Shuddering as the last image faded from her mind, Niamh realized the usual juddering convulsions were restrained. Cognizance returned, and Niamh lifted her head to lock gazes with Kiyo.

He'd guided her to a corner of the airport, his body covering hers, his arms bound tight around her.

"If anyone saw, they only witnessed two people embracing," he whispered, his hot breath tickling her face.

The hairs on Niamh's arms and nape rose as a shiver skated down her spine.

He smelled wonderful. Earthy. Smoky.

And his arms felt safe.

They felt good.

It had been months since anyone had been there to hold her through her visions.

As tears burned her throat and stung her eyes, Niamh dropped her gaze so he wouldn't see. She pushed gently at his chest.

He slowly released her.

"Thanks," she muttered, turning away from him.

Her bag had fallen to the floor. She quickly grabbed it and hurried in the direction of the ladies' restroom.

"I don't suppose you'll tell me what the vision was about?"

"Same one," she lied. "Must be important."

They reached the restroom and Niamh raised an eyebrow at him. "You know you can't come in here, right? Why don't you go buy us some breakfast?" She gestured to the food court. "I'll meet you over there."

Niamh wasn't sure if anyone had ever bestowed such a suspicious look on her before. Everyone else saw a sweet girl with a sweet demeanor who couldn't possibly lie ... not Kiyo. It was like the bastard could see right through her.

With a roll of her eyes, Niamh pushed into the restroom and let the door slam behind her.

There were several other women inside.

She pretended to use the facilities as quickly as possible and then followed one of the other ladies out.

Thankfully, Kiyo was gone, which meant he was at the food court.

Good.

Niamh took off in the direction for terminal transport. By the time Kiyo realized she was gone, it would be too late. And she'd find him again. Something told her that whenever the wolf was in the vicinity, Niamh would be able to find him, even blindfolded.

Ignoring the ghost of his embrace that still clung to her, Niamh got on the elevator that took her down to the terminal's bus stop. A bus was already there waiting. Perfect timing.

Her patience strained as the bus sat there for five minutes and then finally, the doors closed. It moved, skirting the runway and waiting planes as it drove toward the next terminal.

No one would notice if she raced from this point on because people were always in a hurry at the airport. Niamh dove off the bus in the direction of the girl from her vision. This vision had explained more than the last. Unlike the last, but much like the latest others, this vision was tinged with insistence and aggression. She'd never had visions like these up until a few months ago ... like they were trying to make her *feel* something, not just relay information.

The girl and the man she'd seen were human. She'd been sold into marriage by her own family. And this man was abusive in every way he could be. The girl's spirit was strong but she was breaking, and she was hours away from murdering her captive. Niamh didn't exist to play God, but she'd seen what this man had done. He was evil to his core.

The violence he'd enacted ... Niamh had seen a lot in her visions over the years, and he sat among the worst of the monsters she'd experienced.

Niamh couldn't let this girl go through so much only to end up in prison for killing her torturer, her abuser, her enslaver. And if it was worthy of a vision, it was worthy of her dealing with the problem.

"And where is it you think you're going?" Kiyo suddenly stepped in front of her.

Niamh skidded to a halt seconds before crashing into him.

She gaped in confusion. "How did you ... what? How?"

He had a to-go cup of coffee in his hand. He took a casual sip as he stared at her. "You think I'm that stupid?"

"Well ..."

"You have a vision and then you urgently need to use the restroom and get rid of me at the same time."

That burn of irritation she hadn't felt in hours swarmed her chest. "Look, I'm not running away from you. I just have something I need to do."

Kiyo chugged back his coffee and then threw it, with perfect aim, at a recycle can twenty meters away. Without taking his eyes off her.

"Show off."

His expression darkened. "I can't let you go play savior. Not hours after The Garm tried to kill you. Are you insane?"

"I can't ignore my visions." She moved to brush past him.

"Niamh." He grabbed her arm, and she whipped around to rail at him, the images from her vision causing that burn in her chest to flame. She felt it flooding out of her; her eyes widened as she watched Kiyo's grow round with shock.

His body shuddered as his grip on her arm became bruising.

"Kiyo." Concern eased the burn as his eyes fluttered and his body convulsed ever so slightly.

He gasped, releasing her arm.

His dark eyes, filled with disbelief, flew to hers. "What the hell was that?"

"I don't know." She shook her head in truth. "What ... I ..."

"I saw things." He grabbed both of her biceps and gave her a shake. "What did you do to me?"

"I didn't do anything." Niamh yanked at his unyielding hold. "I promise, I didn't do anything."

His grip eased, his eyes desperately searching hers. "I saw a girl and a man. But it was more than just images. It was ... their life together." Anger darkened his expression. "She was sold to him. He abuses her. They're here. And she's going to kill him."

Niamh's legs almost buckled. "Not possible."

"What was that, Niamh?"

"My vision. You saw my vision."

How ...

She shook her head. That had never happened. Not with anyone, not even with *him*.

"Not possible," she repeated. "What are you?"

He released her like she'd burned him. "*I* didn't do this. I've never experienced anything like that. That was you."

"No!" She flinched at the loud denial and glanced around to see they were drawing attention to themselves. "We have to move."

Kiyo studied her intensely for a few seconds. "You've never shared a vision with anyone before?"

"Never."

He released a shaky exhale. He was completely thrown by this, and Niamh could tell he wasn't used to anything disconcerting him.

"We have to go, Kiyo. Now."

"Yeah, we do. Back to our terminal."

Her eyes narrowed, the burn of irritation returning. "I can't leave her to him."

"You're not. He's about to get what he deserves."

"But she isn't. All that pain." Her eyes brightened with tears of compassion. "I know you felt her pain. If she does this, she spends the rest of her life in prison. Or worse, they cart her back home and they execute her for it. You can't tell me, after what you saw, that you think she deserves it."

As hard as Niamh tried to hold them back, tears of sorrow, for what the girl had endured, escaped. Kiyo seemed fascinated, watching the tears roll down her cheeks.

"What do you plan to do?"

"Find him. End him. And help her start a new life somewhere else."

"So you're judge, jury, and executioner?"

Niamh shrugged wearily. "It's my burden to bear. I have a long life ahead of me ... maybe. I want to know I made a difference. And I don't care if it makes me dishonorable or a different kind of monster. If I can rid the planet of his kind of evil, I'll take Fate's judgment when She comes for me with my head held high."

Something happened then. Something Niamh didn't understand glittered with a sharpness in Kiyo's dark eyes. Fustratingly, Niamh didn't understand what that look meant.

"Fine. We can wait until he goes into the restroom. There are no cameras there. I'll follow him in and deal with him. But we'll have the problem of the body. It can't be found while we're still here."

Niamh was momentarily taken aback by his willingness to help. It took her a second to reply, "Don't worry about that. I can turn a body to ash."

He quirked an eyebrow. "And you didn't think to do that back at the park?"

Oh shit, yeah.

Her lips twitched. "Must have slipped my mind."

He huffed. "You can't find any of this amusing."

"It's hysterical laughter," she promised. "I've had quite a shock."

"*You've* had a shock," he muttered under his breath as they searched for the abuser.

It was weird watching as Kiyo spotted their perpetrator first. He'd seen him too. There had to be a reason she'd been able to transfer her vision to the werewolf. For twenty-one of her twenty-six years on this planet, Niamh had never once physically shared a vision with another person.

Her emotions seemed to have fueled the transfer, but she'd been plenty emotional after her visions over the years, and it hadn't happened before. Why was Kiyo receptive to them?

None of it made sense.

They had to wait for over an hour, watching the evil fecker sitting next to his young wife. Niamh spotted him pinching her thigh a few times as he snapped something at her.

Although Kiyo's expression never changed as they waited, she noticed he tensed ever so slightly every time the man pinched the girl, which meant he'd noticed it too.

And he didn't like it.

Something warm flooded Niamh's chest.

"You're staring at me," Kiyo said, attention still on their prey.

"You're nice to look at it," she answered honestly but evasively.

He gave her a wry look. "You're trying to figure out how I saw your vision. If you think I might know, you're wrong. I'm as baffled as you." His gaze cut back to the couple. "He's moving."

Niamh's attention returned to the man as they watched him head toward the restroom.

"What if he's not alone?" she asked Kiyo before he moved to follow.

"I'm an alpha," he replied. "I give off energy that I can turn up. Makes humans flee my vicinity."

"Sounds very helpful for a being who so clearly prefers his own company."

"Funny," he muttered before casually strolling toward the restroom.

As soon as he disappeared inside, Niamh followed.

Just as she reached the door, two men hurried out, looking confused and disturbed.

Alpha energy indeed.

She waited a minute, made sure no one was watching, and then darted inside.

In the farthest corner, she found Kiyo standing over the corpse of the girl's abuser. Kiyo glanced over his shoulder at her, his expression grim. He seemed to take no pleasure in death. That was reassuring. "Your turn."

As she approached the man, all the terror and hurt and torment the girl had felt wrapped itself around Niamh until she could barely breathe ... and she could technically survive without oxygen, which said much of the size of the girl's pain and fury.

Kneeling, she placed a reluctant hand on the man's knee and felt her magic pulse from her palm. Slowly it crawled through his whole being and they watched as his face cracked.

Then he just crumbled.

To ash.

"I've never seen anything like that."

Niamh stood. "We fae have many tricks up our sleeves."

His gaze sharpened on hers. "We will never do this again."

She narrowed her eyes at his bossy tone. "I'll do what I have to do."

"No." He shook his head. "I understand now that you feel everything these victims feel, and I appreciate that you want to help them. But this"—he gestured to the ash—"it's bad enough interfering in supernatural lives when it's not your job, because we have rules for a reason, Niamh, and it's all about our survival and avoiding war with the humans. To interfere in *their* world is so far beyond dangerous ... It's not your right."

His words penetrated, making her feel guilty and indignant at the same time. "But my visions ..."

"I don't know why they're coming to you, but every time you do something like this, you leave a signature. And that signature is how the Blackwoods or others like them are going to find you. Is this girl's life—the lives of the other people you've interfered with—worth the lives of every single person on this planet?"

Deep down she'd always known she was playing a dangerous game with the world, but Kiyo had hauled her harshly into the light of reality.

He was right. She knew he was right.

She couldn't keep doing this.

She couldn't be responsible for opening that gate because once upon a time, she'd seen what could happen if the wall between worlds fell.

Yet, it was so hard not to answer the call of the visions.

"I just wanted … I want to be useful."

He exhaled slowly. "The vision, the Tokyo one, is that truly helpful or is it another one of these?" He gestured to the ash.

"It's important. I promise. It's about the fae-borne."

"And you won't tell me more than that?"

More guilt pricked at her but even after the last hour, she still wasn't ready to trust him. She shook her head.

His expression closed down. "Fine. Let's get back to our terminal."

"But the girl. I want to help her. Change her passport. Give her money."

"And how do you propose doing that without using magic that makes her aware of our world?"

Niamh scowled because he was infuriatingly right.

"You've helped her enough. She's on her own. Now get your ass back to the terminal."

His demanding tone licked down her spine like fire, causing her to snap to attention. "Or what? You'll make me?"

"Niamh, I just killed a human in a public restroom and watched you turn him to ash. This, after receiving visions I had no business receiving from a pain-in-the-ass Irish woman I'm bound to protect by a spell that pretty much screws with my freedom until Fionn's happy you're safe. My patience is wearing very thin."

She sniffed haughtily as she moved past him. "It can't be wearing thin if it doesn't exist in the first place."

His growl rumbled at her back and while it should have frightened her, it didn't.

It had a much more disturbing effect on her body.

One that made her flush hot from head to toe.

5

"You can relax now, you know," Niamh said quietly.

The plane had just leveled out and Kiyo wanted to believe he could relax, but his body refused to. Waiting at the airport had been tense. He'd been constantly on alert for any sign of The Garm or another enemy. Moreover, he still couldn't figure out how the hell Niamh's vision had transferred to him. He wondered if it could happen again. The stubborn fae wouldn't tell him about her Tokyo vision, and since she'd admitted it was partly about him, Kiyo felt he had a right to know.

Especially if it was taking him back to a city where he had enemies.

"Can I?" he muttered, glancing around at the busy plane. The passengers were reading, watching the TVs on the back of the seat headrests, or sleeping. When was the last time he slept?

Having his neck broken and being unconscious for a few minutes didn't count.

"I have a spider sense," Niamh leaned in to whisper. Her spicy-sweet scent tickled his senses, and his gut tightened.

Kiyo glowered at her, noting the delicate golden freckles scattered across the bridge of her nose and cheeks. "I don't care about your spider sense?"

She quirked an eyebrow. "You're in an awful mood."

"Niamh ..." There was a growl of warning in her name.

"Okay, fine." She considered him, questions in her big, golden-aquamarine eyes. "Do you not like flying?"

"Breaking the contract might be worth it," he muttered.

She rolled her eyes. "My spider sense is pertinent, so I'm telling you about it whether you want to know or not. I can sense when danger is lurking. I knew I was being followed by The Garm before I saw the cars. And if there was anyone on this plane that meant to cause me harm, I'd feel that too. So ... you can relax, bodyguard. Why don't you try to catch some z's?"

Tempting, but he still didn't trust the woman he'd been hired to protect. And since she had the ability to pop herself out of the plane to somewhere else, he was staying awake and alert.

"I'm fine."

Niamh leaned into him again and his fingers curled into tight fists. "Do you want to talk about why you don't want to go to Tokyo?"

"Do you want to tell me about the vision?" he countered.

She flicked him a dry look and thankfully relaxed back into her seat.

"You could share it with me, couldn't you? Like at the airport with the girl."

Niamh frowned. "I don't know how I did that."

"Want to try again?" He reluctantly held his hand out, palm facing up.

Her gaze dropped to his hand. Her long, spiky lashes drew his attention as she considered his offer. Then, to his surprise, she reached out and placed her hand in his, wrapping her cool fingers around his. Kiyo's skin sparked and tingled where she touched, like he'd caressed a live wire. It had to be because she was fae and made of potent energy.

"Well?" he said gruffly.

Niamh gave him a sad smile. "Oh, I don't know how to give you the vision. I just wanted to hold your hand. I haven't held someone's hand in a long time."

Her words disarmed him.

If anyone else had dared to hold his hand, he'd have shoved them off with impatience and irritation. When he took a woman to bed, it was all about sex. Any affection shown was for sexual gratification. It never involved cuddling or hand-holding.

Yet the thought of rejecting Niamh so brutally ... well, he didn't like the thought of doing that to her.

Kiyo didn't understand his reaction.

He hadn't experienced soft feelings toward anyone in a very long time.

Disturbed by his response, he lifted their clasped hands and placed them in her lap before easing out of her hold. "I'm not good at providing comfort," he said as gently as he was able. "I'm not that guy."

She stared at him, assessing, her eyes moving to his now-free hand, her brows puckering. Wondering at the confusion on her face, he followed her gaze to his hand and realized he was flexing it.

Because it still tingled, like she'd given him an electric shock.

He abruptly dropped his hand out of sight. "Go to sleep," he commanded.

The goddamn woman needed to give him a break for just a while.

"It's okay to need human contact, Kiyo," she whispered. "A little comfort. It doesn't mean anything."

Patience thinning, he sneered at her. "Neither of us are human. And I wasn't the one who needed to be comforted. If you need that, find someone who's interested when we land in Tokyo."

Hurt flickered across her stunning face before she could hide it.

Another sensation he hadn't felt in a long time caused an ache to flare across his chest.

Guilt.

Goddamm it.

He'd never regretted taking on a job so much in his entire existence.

"What happened to make you so cold?" Niamh asked, but he could tell by the hard edge to her words that she wasn't really asking him. She was merely observing facts.

Kiyo turned to look at her, and his agitation built tenfold. For someone as fast and powerful as she was, a woman who could break his neck without even touching him, she was irritatingly soft. She cared too damn much, and it would get her killed ... or worse, put the entire world in jeopardy.

"You're soft," he said, his voice barely above a whisper.

Her head whipped around toward him. "What?"

"You're soft. You care about strangers and it makes you weak. That's not to be admired, Niamh, when that weakness could cause a war. So stop being weak. You could learn a thing or two from me, and it might just keep us all safe." The words were harsh, and he knew as soon as he said them that she didn't deserve them. But she made him off-kilter and he didn't like it.

That's when she reminded him that he didn't know her at all. A cool hardness crawled across her features, and she suddenly looked strange and ethereal and every inch the fae woman she was. Her words, however, were very human and very irate. "I have nothing to learn from you other than how to be a complete and total arsehole. Go to sleep, Kiyo. Give the world a rest from your delightful presence."

The guilt he'd felt over his words was nudged to the side by amusement.

She had a fire in her. Spirit.

And he couldn't help but admire it.

That was the problem. He couldn't help but admire—

The hair on Kiyo's neck rose, stalling his thoughts. He felt strangely disconcerted.

Something wasn't right.

Growing still, tense, he tried to feel out his surroundings.

"Kiyo, what's wro—"

He held up a hand to cut off Niamh.

And then it hit him.

Tapping the screen on the headrest in front of him, Kiyo searched for confirmation.

He brought up the map.

His muscles locked tight. Niamh leaned in to look at his screen and he heard her slight exhalation.

"We're going the wrong way."

He nodded, quickly tapping off the screen. "We're not heading south. We're heading west." Kiyo studied her shocked expression. "You can't sense anything?"

They both tried to look circumspectly around the plane. Something about what he saw wasn't right.

"Kiyo ..." Niamh's voice was hushed with fear. "Everyone is ... sleeping."

Every single passenger had their eyes closed.

He turned to Niamh as she lifted a hand into the air and flexed her fingers. Her cheeks paled as her horrified gaze flew to his. "They're dead."

"Get up," Kiyo bit out. "We need to get off this plane."

They both unlatched their seat belts and Kiyo slid out first, holding a hand to help Niamh onto the aisle. He was still holding her when every hair on his body rose. A figure appeared out of a shimmer in the air at the head of the aisle; he walked toward them. Behind the man, the air shimmered again and someone else appeared.

"Cloaking spell," Niamh said as the three warlocks and two witches lined up on the aisle ahead of them.

"How?" Kiyo growled. Niamh was supposed to be able to sense magic and supernaturals.

"They can cloak themselves, even from me." Tears brightened her eyes. Eyes that were filled with rage as she stared down the coven members. "But at great sacrifice."

Kiyo knew about magic. He knew that unlike Niamh who was made of energy, connected to it, and could use her powers with no need of an exchange, witches and warlocks couldn't. To cast spells, to use magic of any kind, they required fuel for the energy. A tree in the woods in exchange for an offensive spell in battle. An animal in exchange for wounding an enemy.

A human being in exchange for a spell of invisibility against the most powerful species on earth.

White witches and warlocks had great limitations upon them because they refused to hurt others for their power.

Some covens, like the Blackwoods, however, were large enough that their combined natural energy allowed them to do much that individual witches and warlocks couldn't. That's why most magic users wanted to belong to a coven. It made them more powerful.

And then, of course, there was the fact that when covens became as powerful as the Blackwoods, they got away with using dark magic while pretending the very thought abhorred them.

"They killed everyone on the plane to cloak themselves from me," Niamh said in furious horror, grief darkening her eyes.

"Not technically necessary." The warlock leading the charge gestured to the dead passengers. "But we did need about half of them. You're very hard to trick, you see."

"Why kill all of them?" Kiyo stared blankly at this warlock who had no honor. It was something Kiyo had mastered over the years. Keeping what little emotion leaked through locked down tight. He'd seen much in his life ... but even as soulless as he felt most days, Kiyo knew in that moment that he still had one. Because he felt the deaths of all those passengers pressing in on his chest.

He couldn't look at them.

At the humans who had gotten on a flight like they'd probably done many times, and their energy, their lives had been snatched mindlessly so five fucking magic users could hide from one fae woman.

Dirty, dishonorable pieces of shit.

"I don't like loose ends," the warlock said. His pale gaze was fixed on Niamh. "You're lucky we need you so badly or I would kill you for what you did to Layton and his sisters. But Layton's father doesn't want that. You're too important."

"She didn't kill them." Kiyo spoke for her.

The warlock flicked an irritated look at him. "And I would believe the word of a mercenary? What business have you here, you filthy, mangy half-creature?"

Absolutely the wrong thing to say to him when he was already feeling more than he wanted to.

Kiyo was a blur, closing the short distance between them.

His fist smashed through the warlock's chest; he gripped the son of a bitch's heart and yanked it out. The warlock's eyes closed and he flopped to the floor like his battery had been removed.

Which it kind of had.

Kiyo had just dropped the heart on the warlock's body when he felt invisible fingers tightening around his throat. The sensation was unpleasant, startling him to his knees. It wouldn't kill him, however, and he pushed to standing to face the witches who were using their combined power to choke him.

Suddenly, he smelled Niamh brush past him. He barely saw her. She was so fast, just a whirl of color and movement. The first time he'd seen someone move that fast was a few months ago when Rose and Fionn tracked him down in Bucharest. They'd been attacked by coven members then too.

One by one, like dominoes, the coven members dropped to the aisle floor.

Niamh stood in amongst the carnage, her chest heaving with emotion, tears streaking her face as she stared down at the bodies. Kiyo didn't know if they were unconscious or dead.

She lifted her tortured gaze to his, and Kiyo had the strongest urge to go to her.

To comfort her.

It made no sense.

Then the plane lurched, stealing him from the disturbing thought. "What the hell?" he bit out, getting to his feet only to stumble against a seat as the plane lurched again.

"The coven!" Niamh flew at him. "They must have been controlling the plane." She wrapped her arms around him, shocking him. "Hold on tight! Don't let go!"

Kiyo did as she demanded without thought and abruptly everything went black.

And then cold.

Wet and cold and darkness surrounded him, pressure pushing down on his chest.

It took him a moment to realize where he was.

In water.

Drowning in the dark depths of the sea.

6

Breaking through the surface, Niamh gasped for breath. Even though she'd never die from lack of oxygen, her "human" mind liked to trick her into thinking she would. She blamed it on having been raised among them. "Kiyo!" she yelled as she scanned her surroundings. In the distance, she could see the coast.

Traveling had limitations. As much as she would have loved to have taken them to land, they'd been flying over the Baltic Sea, which was at least a thousand miles long. Considering she could only travel around six miles or so, it was a bloody miracle she'd gotten them this close to land.

Well, gotten herself this close to land.

Panic clawed at her. "Kiyo!"

Nothing.

"Oh my God, I've killed him." Her teeth chattered. Not from the cold, since she barely felt it, but from emotion. From grief.

First all those people on the plane ... "KIYO!"

"I'm here!"

Relief flooded her as she turned. Kiyo was swimming the front crawl at a rapid pace toward her. Niamh swam to meet him. A human would have struggled in the choppy water but they reached each other in good time. Fighting the urge to throw her arms around him in relief, knowing he wouldn't welcome it, Niamh gave him a tremulous smile. "Sorry. That gift has its limits."

Kiyo's narrowed eyes flew above her head, and it was then she became aware of the terrible, mechanical whining sound. She turned in the water, kicking to keep afloat, and stared in horror as she watched the plane come down in the distance.

"It's gonna hit the water and we'll probably feel it," Kiyo said, his voice urgent.

"Waves, you mean?"

"Yeah."

That wouldn't be a problem for her but werewolves weren't immortal. They could drown. At least, if Kiyo was worried, she assumed he could.

The wolf was a giant mystery.

"Okay. I might have another bout of *traveling* in me." She pointed to the coast. "I can get us there."

"Do it."

Niamh moved into him, her body hyperaware this time of being pressed tightly to his. His hands had just settled on her hips when she gathered her energy around him.

The blackness of *traveling* was quick.

They fell onto the beach, this time not separating.

Kiyo's grunt reverberated through Niamh's body since he'd taken the brunt of the fall and she was straddling him. Their eyes locked, and a thrilling shiver cascaded through Niamh that had nothing to do with the soaked clothes stuck to her skin.

He was still holding on to her hips and she felt his fingers flex, squeezing her.

Heat pooled in her belly.

His dark gaze dropped to her mouth.

The sound of something making terrific impact in the water broke the electric moment, and Niamh was brought crashing back to reality. She pushed her exhausted body from his and stood to turn and face the sea.

Waves rippled, coming toward them. They grew smaller and smaller as they headed for the coast.

"All those people." The grief hit her anew.

"Why do they keep doing this?" Kiyo asked, irritation lacing his words. "They've sent so many coven members after you fae-borne, and you've all triumphed over every one of them. Why won't they stop? Is it idiocy or arrogance?"

"Fanaticism," she answered. "They're so obsessed with the idea of unlimited power, they'll sacrifice themselves to get it." Niamh looked over at him. His hair had come out of its top knot and fell in wet, thick strands around his face, the ends hitting his chin. He had grains of sand in his hair; his back was covered in it.

His beauty hurt her a little. She wished it were enough to distract from what had just happened, but not even Kiyo could do that. "They killed all those innocent people. I killed them," she confessed.

"It wasn't your fault," he replied gruffly. "You're not responsible for someone else's actions."

"No, I mean, I killed the coven members."

She could feel his eyes burning into her.

"So? You were defending us."

"I could have just knocked them out."

"They'd have died in the crash, anyway. Drowned."

"I've killed people."

At his silence, she remembered his words on the plane.

"You're soft. You care about strangers and it makes you weak. That's not to be admired, Niamh, when that weakness could cause a war. So stop being so weak. You could learn a thing or two from me, and it might just keep us all safe."

Niamh didn't want to be cold like him, but she also didn't want to be vulnerable in front of him. Sucking back her tears, her grief, she turned and made her way wearily up the beach.

Kiyo followed. "You okay? You're moving slow ... for you."

"*Traveling* exhausts me. I'll be fine in a bit."

Silence fell between them.

She broke it. "What now?"

He studied the cliff tops ahead of them. There was a pathway cut into rock that would lead them off the beach onto grassy fields. "My guess is that we're on one of the Swedish islands."

As they walked up the beach, Niamh studied the werewolf. There was something about him she was missing. It wasn't as though she had a ton of experience when it came to werewolves. She'd run away from a few, either because they were members of The Garm or they sensed she was different and got overly curious about her.

But Kiyo seemed much stronger than most. Definitely faster. Werewolves were fast, but they were generally slower than other supes. Of course, some alphas were exceptions to the rule. Just over a year ago, when she started having visions of one of the other fae-borne, a woman called Thea, she'd seen Thea's true mate. Niamh never met him in real life but she knew from her visions that he was one of the strongest and fastest werewolves ever. His name was Conall. He was the alpha of the last werewolf pack in Scotland, and he had a gift for tracking. Once he had someone's scent, he could track them anywhere in the world. He'd been hired to track down Thea by the man who had tortured and experimented upon her.

Niamh flinched inwardly every time she thought of Thea. Not one of the fae-borne had escaped tragedy, but Thea had been brutally tortured at the hands of a madman.

Her mission back then had been to protect Thea from him, but her visions had revealed that Conall was actually Thea's true mate and that their joining would save Thea, and them all, in the long run. She'd tried to convince Thea to trust Conall without giving away why. She'd done the same for Rose and Fionn. It worked for both couples. Thea, however, was stabbed in the heart with an iron knife, and Conall bit her to change her into a wolf to save her life. Because they were mated, it worked, and now Thea was safe from this madness, this war for the gate to Faerie.

For a while, Niamh had been concerned for Thea because she seemed intent on finding her. Thea's determination was born out of a sense loyalty Niamh reciprocated. But she'd stopped having visions of Thea coming for her, so she reckoned someone had finally convinced the newly turned wolf to stay put in Scotland. To stay safe there.

Thank goodness.

Memories of her new vision, the one with the standing stones, came at her, causing her heart to pound.

Niamh couldn't believe what she'd seen was true.

"People will have witnessed the plane come down. The authorities will be all over this beach soon."

Niamh looked at Kiyo. He'd said this to her over his shoulder as he led the way up the rock face. He didn't offer her help but she assumed that was because she didn't need it. She had the balance of a tightrope walker. Better, even.

"We'll need transport," she replied.

"I would call Bran to see if he has any contacts here, but everything we had was on that plane, including my cell."

Including all her cash. "We'll need to steal a car."

She could tell by the tension in his shoulders he didn't like that idea. The wolf was a contradiction. He was quite willing to kill if necessary and had probably been hired to do just that many times. But he thought stealing beneath him.

When you lived your life on the run, sometimes you had to sacrifice what little honor you had. Grimacing at the reminder of all the immoral crap she'd pulled over the years, Niamh followed the werewolf up onto solid ground and gaped.

Stretching before them was a frost-covered plain and beyond that, trees. Lots and lots of trees.

"Where the hell are we?"

Kiyo scowled and scanned their surroundings. His eyes narrowed on something in the distance to their right. He pointed. "That's a road." His finger followed the flash of bright concrete in amongst the frost-dulled green. "And it goes right into those woods." He turned to her. "We follow that road but keep to the trees."

"And you think this is definitely Sweden?"

He nodded. "When I checked the map on the flight, we were heading toward the south of the Baltic Sea."

"But doesn't that mean we could be in any one of the countries with coasts along the southern end of the Baltic Sea?"

"No. We *traveled* west."

Niamh frowned. "How do you know that?"

His expression was shuttered as he strode toward the road in the distance. "I have an excellent sense of direction."

"Is that a wolf thing?"

He shrugged. "Not that I'm aware of."

That now-familiar burn of irritation flared in Niamh's chest. She knew Kiyo could be like Conall, an extraordinarily powerful alpha with his own quirky gift. But her gut instinct told her there was something more here. How did he and Fionn know one another? And why was Fionn so sure that Kiyo was the one supernatural on earth powerful enough to protect a fae? Niamh was stronger, faster, and almost unkillable. Yes, she could be overpowered by too many people at once and was absolutely screwed if they used iron on her, just as Kiyo had proved. Strength in numbers helped.

But that didn't explain why Fionn chose this guy of all supes to send as her bodyguard.

And it was bugging the crap out of her that she'd received a wishy-washy vision about him that told her nothing except that Tokyo was important.

She thought of that moment on the plane, when he'd wanted her to share her recent vision and Niamh had held his hand. She'd allowed herself to be vulnerable because, for a moment, she'd felt an inexplicable connection with him.

Kiyo had rejected her. Niamh reckoned he'd tried to be as nice as someone like him could be, but he'd still rejected her need for comfort. And in the end, he hadn't been very nice about it at all.

"Who are you really, Kiyo?"

He stopped mid stride and turned to look back at her. His expression had been blank until his gaze dropped down her body and his eyes narrowed.

Frowning, Niamh glanced down. Her white T-shirt was plastered to her skin, leaving very little to the imagination. And now that she was aware of it, her skinny jeans were soaked through and rasping like sandpaper against her legs.

Kiyo was in much the same condition. His T-shirt delineated the powerful muscle she'd seen in the woods back in Moscow. She remembered his nakedness and the scar on his belly. At one point someone had come at him with silver.

She noted a slight tremor move through him. A shiver.

The wolf was cold.

It occurred to Niamh that it was February on a Swedish island, and they'd just been in a sea that was probably subzero. The ground beneath was crisp with frost and sparkled in the sunlight. Werewolves ran hot, but they still felt the chill.

She walked toward him, and his whole body locked with tension. Niamh reached out a hand to touch him and his snapped up in reflex. He grabbed her wrist, holding her away from him. "What the hell are you doing?"

A needle of hurt stung near her heart.

He still didn't trust her.

Was it because he didn't trust anyone ... or because she was fae?

"I was going to use my magic to dry your clothes." Niamh tugged on his hold but his grip tightened. "Let me go."

His dark eyes searched hers, the suspicion fading to bemusement. Slowly Kiyo uncurled his hand from her wrist. "Fine."

Feeling less charitable toward him than she had been a minute ago, Niamh hesitated.

The wolf cocked his head, contemplating her. "Did I hurt you?"

For a moment, she panicked he could see right through her. Then she realized he meant her wrist. Niamh gave him a somewhat mocking smile. "It takes a lot to hurt me." Reaching out, she placed a tentative hand on his shoulder and poured her energy into drying the clothes on his body and also into his skin to warm him up.

"Why do I think that's not true?" Kiyo's question was almost a whisper.

Her eyes lifted to his as her energy moved through him. "What?"

"You said it takes a lot to hurt you. I doubt that somehow."

Seeing his clothes were now dry, she wrenched her hand away. "Because I'm soft, you mean? Soft and weak." Refusing to meet his gaze, Niamh strode past him, her clothes drying as she used the same magic on herself. "I meant physically. It takes a lot to hurt me physically."

The werewolf moved to catch up with her. "I meant what I said on the plane. You'll survive longer if you start thinking about your own survival over others. Emotion is weakness."

A pang of sympathy cut through her. "Oh, Kiyo, what happened to you to make you think such a thing?"

His expression darkened at the sight of her pity. "Don't condescend. I'm old enough to be—"

Suspicion lit through Niamh at his abrupt silence. What had he been about to give away? "I don't care if you're older than me." She skirted the now-intriguing subject of his age. "It doesn't mean you know better. And if you think emotion makes a person weak, then you're greatly mistaken. Emotion makes you strong."

"It causes you to think irrationally, to make mistakes."

"Maybe," she agreed. "But it's also what fires you. What is the point in any of this without emotion?" She gestured around them, indicating their very existence. "Whether it's passion, lust, love, anger, vengeance, compassion, ambition, determination ... emotion gives us reason to live. If you don't have that, what's the point?"

"Okay, I'll concede to that. But there is such a thing as too much emotion. *You* care too much. You grieve for strangers and put yourself in danger for them without knowing if they'd ever do the same for you. And, news flash, ninety-nine percent of them wouldn't."

She heard the angry edge in his voice and it soothed her. Kiyo might like to think he was emotionless, but he was an opinionated son of a bitch and he was genuinely irritated by her putting her life in danger for others. Because it made his job harder or because he cared what happened to her? Niamh would like to think it was the latter, but it was probably the former. After all, they'd known each other all of forty-eight hours.

"It's who I am." She cut him an apologetic smile. "I care about people."

"Even when they don't deserve it?"

She considered this just as they reached the man-made road. It had two lanes and led right into the woods ahead. They walked along the side of it toward the trees. "Most people deserve to be cared about. The man back at the airport in Moscow ... he didn't. He was evil, in my book. Missing a conscience. It's not his fault he was born that way, but it was his fault he gave into the darkness. So, no, people like him don't deserve it."

"What about a drug dealer or a rapist?"

His condescension rankled. "Stop trying to make this more complicated than it is."

"It is complicated," he snapped. "There are levels of good and bad in all of us. Are you going to go through life weighing and judging, so you can decide if you care enough to help a person? That's exhausting and ridiculous."

"So I just write everyone off like you do?" she snapped back.

Kiyo shrugged. "I'm happier for it, aren't I?"

"You're the unhappiest person I've ever met in my life." She brushed past and marched ahead, using her supernatural speed to get away from him.

Unfortunately, he was fast too. "I'm not unhappy. I'm not anything. That's my point."

Jesus Christ, this wolf was delusional. "Oh, please. Beneath that stoic facade, there's an army of emotions just waiting to burst out and wage war on the world."

"You don't know anything about me." His voice was like ice.

"I imagine very few people do. That's what happens when you don't let anyone in."

"Who says I don't? Because I don't want to let you in? Has it occurred to you I just don't like you or trust you very much?"

Her heart, she realized, was racing. "Well, the feeling is mutual. And *I* like nearly everybody."

"And trust nearly everybody too. Something that *will* get you killed."

"I don't trust nearly everybody, you bloody arse!" She halted and pushed at his chest.

He didn't even move. Just quirked an annoyingly patronizing eyebrow at her.

"I have been on the run since I was twelve years old. I am one of only five beings left in this world with powers beyond anyone's wildest imagination. I'm capable of things you couldn't conceive of." She stepped into him, forcing him to hold her gaze. "And out of all my incredible gifts, my soft emotions, as you call them, my kindness, my compassion, my love, are my greatest. Because without them, I am the darkest, most dangerous being you'll ever meet.

"Be grateful I am who I am, Kiyo. For everyone's sake."

The werewolf studied her with his intense expression and then shocked the hell out of her by tipping his head in a slight nod of acknowledgment.

She hesitated before she resumed walking again. Because what Kiyo didn't realize was that she'd said it out loud not just to snap him out of his superior attitude but as a reminder to herself.

There were days she crossed the line and let herself be pulled into the shadows.

She had to fight harder to stop that from happening.

They were silent as they strode side by side, but tension hummed between them. Tension that continued to make Niamh's pulse race.

As they hit the woodlands, the wolf gestured and they stepped inside the forest. The trees, though not snow dusted, were covered in frost, and the bracken snapped and cracked with an extra icy crunch beneath their feet.

Niamh desperately wanted to prod Kiyo about himself. Who he was? Why was he different from other wolves? Because he was. Definitely. However, she didn't want to get into another argument. The werewolf had the ability to prick her pride and irritate her more than most.

"What do we do next?" she asked instead.

She noted the way his eyes darted all around as they walked. He was constantly on guard, watching his surroundings. "You still think we need to be in Tokyo?"

"Yeah." Niamh was eager to learn more about her companion.

"I think we should check in with Bran and Fionn. They might be able to help us map a safe route there."

"I'm surprised you'd rely on someone else for help." She winced as soon as she said it. She had this annoying habit of needling him. "Sorry."

He shook his head. "You're not wrong. But I trust only one person in the world, and it's Fionn, and he trusts Bran."

"Why Fionn?"

He cut her a look. "Because someone like Fionn doesn't entrust the dire secrets of his very existence—and more importantly, those of his true mate's—to someone unless he trusts him. He trusted me. Regardless of the unbreakable contract. He trusts me with Rose. I've always respected him, and by trusting me with Rose's secrets, I'm honor bound to return his trust."

Niamh smiled at the uncharacteristically sweet words. Kiyo might not think he was being sweet, but he was. He and Fionn had a bromance. "I thought you scorned the true-mate bond?"

"I do. That doesn't mean it isn't powerful. Rose is what matters the most to Fionn. Any fool can see that."

A twinge of something flared within her.

She realized it was envy.

"You can trust me," she offered.

He surprised her with a small smile. Okay, it was more of a smirk, but still ... it was hot. "Do you trust me?"

"You're the reason I experienced pure iron for the first time, so I should really say no ..."

Kiyo gave a huff of disbelief. "But you're beginning to anyway?"

Niamh shrugged. She'd probably regret being vulnerable again, but she was who she was. "I *want* to trust you. There's something about you ... I don't know."

A frown puckered between his brows. "You can trust I don't want to break the contract with Fionn."

Silence fell anew between them and this time, Niamh let it. She'd never been the type to crush on a bad boy, and she didn't want to start now. But she couldn't deny she felt an electric awareness of the wolf or that he didn't fascinate her. Niamh wished he didn't. But he was a mass of intriguing contradictions, and she'd always loved a good puzzle.

Feeling her cheeks heat at the thought of Kiyo discovering her crush on him, Niamh clamped her lips closed and decided it best not to speak for a while.

Not long later, they strode out of the woodlands and saw a small cluster of houses in the distance. They were mostly surrounded by frost-speckled fields.

But coming toward them from the direction of the houses, they spotted an SUV.

Kiyo took hold of her arm to halt her, his expression granite hard.

"It's okay," she reassured him.

"We're strangers out in the middle of nowhere, not exactly dressed for winter, and a plane just fell out of the sky," he reminded her.

"Trust me."

He still scowled, but he released his grip on her and they waited as the SUV slowed beside them. A man jumped out of the vehicle. He was probably in his late thirties, early forties, and he wore a suede jacket over a thick cable-knit sweater. His brown trousers were tucked into working boots.

"*Var kom du ifrån*?"

"Do you know any Swedish?" Kiyo muttered under his breath.

"Do I look like I'm a master of languages?" Niamh stepped toward the stranger. "Sorry, sir, we don't understand."

The man raised his eyebrows as he came to a stop before them. He gave Kiyo a wary look. "You're English?"

"Irish."

"You're not survivors of that plane crash. It's impossible."

"Plane crash? What plane crash?"

"You didn't see anything?" His English was perfect. "We just received a call that a plane went down in the sea."

"I'm sorry, we don't know anything about that," Niamh lied. She moved closer to the man and put her hand on his arm as their gazes locked. He immediately relaxed and began to drown in her eyes. "Where are we?"

"Ottenby. On the island of Öland."

"How far to the mainland?"

"It's just over an hour's drive to Kalmar."

"We have an emergency to get to. It's imperative we get there as quickly as possible. You'll give us your vehicle, won't you?"

He nodded slowly.

"And when anyone asks what happened to it, you'll tell them you sold it to a young couple in need but you can't remember what they looked like ... and that's what *you'll* believe."

"I sold it," he agreed.

"Where do you live?"

He turned and pointed back up the road he'd come.

"Not far, then. We'll drop you off as close as we can. Keys?"

The man pulled them from his coat pocket and held them out.

Niamh nodded to Kiyo who took them from the man's hand. A wave of uneasiness moved through her, but she ignored it. All three of them got into the SUV, and Kiyo turned it around so they were headed back toward the houses.

He stopped at a crossroad near the houses on the right and large buildings on their left.

"You can get out now," Niamh said. "And thank you."

The man got out of the SUV with that dazed expression on his face, and Kiyo pulled away, speeding out of the small town as he tapped the screen in the middle of the dashboard.

"I'll do that," Niamh offered, moving to brush his hand away.

He snapped it away before she could touch him.

She sighed heavily as she touched the screen, searching for the

GPS. The map appeared, and she entered the name of the mainland town the man had mentioned. Kalmar.

The GPS lady spoke in Swedish. Niamh shot Kiyo a wry smile, but he was staring blankly ahead at the road. Water appeared on their left as they drove north up the west coast of the island. According to the maps, it was called the Kalmar Strait. "You don't like it, do you?"

"Like what?"

"The mind-warp gift."

"Is it a gift?"

She considered his question. "No," she eventually said. "I suppose you're right. It's not."

"You're messing with people's free will."

"I know. But what else would you have me do?"

His hands flexed around the steering wheel. "In this circumstance, we're doing what we have to do to survive. But it seems to me that you use it whenever the hell you feel like it. To stay in fancy hotels. To fly where you need to fly." He flicked her a look. "To rob banks."

Guilt suffused her as she looked quickly away. "Old habits die hard, I suppose."

"I guess I should be grateful you can't use it on other supernaturals." He flicked her a look. "Fionn said you couldn't. You can't, right?"

"I can't," she confirmed. "It doesn't work against you."

He nodded and then ... "It was your brother, wasn't it? He convinced you to use your *gifts* to live well while you were on the run."

The mention of ... him ...

Niamh glared at Kiyo. "I'm a grown-up. I take responsibility for my actions."

"Yeah? It's just a strange contradiction. You care so much about people ... it doesn't make sense that you'd enjoy stealing from them or playing games with their minds."

"Well, you'd know all about contradictions. You're one big giant one."

"I'm right, aren't I?" He ignored her weak comeback. "Ronan convinced you to use your gifts."

"You owe me, Nee. There's no harm in it."

Niamh flinched at the memory of his voice. "Don't ever say his name again."

A chill fell over the car and Kiyo's mask of indifference slipped. His eyebrows rose in surprise at the icy cold in her tone, the freeze emanating from her very being.

Their eyes met and she dared him to push her on this.

Kiyo looked away first, watching the road ahead. "When we get to Kalmar, we need to find a phone so we can contact Bran."

The chill in the vehicle dissipated. "Perhaps they can find us a safe flight out of this place. As beautiful as it is."

"I've never been to Sweden," the wolf muttered. "Traveled a lot but never Sweden."

"Well, you can cross it off your bucket list. 'Plummet into the Baltic Sea and swim to Sweden.' Check!"

To her delight, Kiyo's lips twitched. Just a little.

7

After Niamh programmed the GPS to find the nearest hotel, it took them just over an hour to reach it on the mainland of Sweden. Crossing the Ölandsbron Bridge from Öland to the mainland had been the only moment where the tension between Niamh and Kiyo was forgotten.

The sun had disappeared behind heavy, dark clouds, and the water on either side of them was like glass. Gray-blue sheets of stillness. There were hardly any other vehicles on the bridge, and for a moment it felt like they were on some lonely, safe corner of the planet. It was incredibly peaceful.

Kiyo enjoyed it for what it was. A moment of tranquility in amongst the chaos and danger.

He suspected Niamh appreciated it as well. Or maybe she just appreciated not having to interact with him for a while. Other than the bridge, the drive felt longer than an hour.

"... out of all of my incredible gifts, my soft emotions, as you call them, my kindness, my compassion, my love, are my greatest. Because without them, I am the darkest, most dangerous being you'll ever meet. Be grateful I am who I am, Kiyo. For everyone's sake."

Her words echoed in his mind—more than that, his reaction to them.

He respected her, and it took a lot to gain his admiration.

More alarmingly, he *wanted* her.

Lust, Kiyo could deal with. He had a strong sexual appetite and no particular preference. His body reacted to all kinds of women, in all their varied glory. Sex was the one thing in this harsh existence that Kiyo could be thankful for. However, he never let his sexuality control him.

That was easy when you were just attracted to a body, a face.

The moment he'd seen Niamh, he reacted to her. She was beautiful. He was aware of her, as a male would be.

But it would never control him.

Being attracted to who she was as a person, to her mind, her heart ... that was more concerning.

Kiyo had a job to do, and he couldn't let softer emotions that hadn't touched him in decades creep in. He had to keep her at bay, and if that meant pretending to have the moral high ground because of her talent for mind trickery, then so be it. She didn't need to know he'd done the kind of wicked shit that made her look like Snow White in comparison.

This strange feeling toward her also meant he wasn't going to push about her brother, even though her reaction was ... damn, he didn't even know what that was. He thought she was going to turn the entire SUV into an icicle. As much as he wanted to push, distance between them was best.

They'd crossed the bridge and were now on a highway flanked by trees when a lake appeared to their right. Kiyo glanced at the GPS. "We're getting closer."

Following the road around the lake, they turned right. They seemed to have hit the outskirts of town. It wasn't much to look at it, especially on a gray day. Or at least that's what he thought at first.

But then they turned left toward their hotel and the concrete road changed to wobbly cobbles and the buildings became older, quainter. Each was painted in a different soft pastel. Cafés offered outside seating. An empty market square was probably filled with stalls and flowers during the summer. Bicycle racks upon bicycle racks suggested cycling was a popular form of transport here.

The road narrowed the farther they drove, the SUV handling the cobbles with ease.

"It's pretty," Niamh murmured.

Following the GPS, Kiyo took a left turn down another tight, cobbled road and followed it nearly to the end where the hotel was located.

The hotel wasn't as pretty as its neighbors with its roughcast exterior but it had a Dutch roof that gave the building some interest. Noting the lack of available parking, Kiyo's irritation spiked. He didn't tire easily, but after what they'd been through and having not slept for days, he just wanted a moment to stop somewhere without aggravation. "Where the hell am I supposed to park?"

"Just park in front of the hotel. They might have valet."

Niamh's patient tone irritated him even more. She *would* be calm with her fae ability to recover from anything, including damn exhaustion. "At this shithole?"

"It's a four-star hotel, Kiyo," she scolded gently. "What did you expect? A towering modern structure in the heart of an historical town? Don't be precious." She hopped out of the car while he gaped after her.

Precious?

No one had ever dared to call him *precious*.

With a growl of annoyance, he followed her out of the car and into the hotel. Inside it was Scandinavian in style with simple, modern, comfortable midcentury furnishings. But in Kiyo's mind, the European star system didn't reflect what it did on other continents. In the States or Japan, this would be three-star, not four.

Not that he goddamn cared.

He was getting pissy about things that didn't goddamn matter.

What he needed was a bed. Food first. Then bed.

Niamh was already using her mind-trick shit on the front-desk clerk by the time he appeared at her side. The woman handed over the keys to two rooms.

"One room," Kiyo demanded.

Niamh turned and raised an eyebrow at him. He stared at her, noting that the golden freckles on her cheeks and across the bridge of her nose stood out in sharp relief against the paleness of her skin. Perhaps he'd been wrong. Perhaps fae did tire after all. "One room?"

"I'm not letting you out of my sight."

"And I'm not sharing a bed with you."

"Many women would be happy to."

She grimaced. "Well, you cocky bastard, I'm not one of them."

Something like a lie lingered in the air between them.

Kiyo felt an answering tug in his gut.

Shit.

"Fine. Two rooms." His hand clamped around hers as she took the key cards.

Her golden-blue eyes widened.

"But if you run from me, it will piss me off."

She sighed, pulling her hand away only to hold out one of the key cards. "Can I ask, is there anything that *doesn't* piss you off?"

"Sex," he answered instantly. He shouldn't have said it, but she seemed so unflappable all the time while he most certainly felt ... flapped.

To his pleasure, he watched a pretty pink blush stain her cheeks. "Oh." Her gaze dropped as she turned away from him and the dazed receptionist. "Well, I can't help you there."

Kiyo's eyes lowered to her perfect sweetheart ass showcased superbly in tight skinny jeans and the long legs attached. He allowed himself a torturous second of imagining those long legs wrapped around him. With Niamh's power and grace, he bet she was epic in bed. "Lies," he muttered.

"What?" She cast him a narrow-eyed look over her shoulder.

He cleared his face of all expression as he fell into stride beside her. "I didn't say anything."

They took the stairs instead of the elevator, and he remembered the SUV.

Niamh shrugged at his reminder. "Just leave it. Someone will come and ask us to move it if they need us to."

"Right. Then first things first, we need to call Bran."

"And how do you propose we do that?"

"With the phone in my room. I know his number."

"You memorized it?"

"Of course." He cut her a mocking look. "Never rely on technology to remember anything of the utmost importance."

She threw him an amused smile. "Wise words."

As it turned out, their rooms were opposite one another. "Come into mine," he said as he swiped the key card, "while I talk to Bran."

The room was much like the lobby. Sparse, simple, and clean. Kiyo's gaze drifted longingly to the bed. He couldn't remember the last time he'd been this tired. Gesturing to the chair at the small desk by the window, he watched Niamh settle into it before he grabbed the phone on the bedside table. Hitting the country code for Ireland first, he tapped in Bran's cell number.

It rang and rang before going to voicemail.

"It's me," he said, trying to hide the bite of impatience. "Call me back. We hit some trouble." He replaced the receiver and said to Niamh, "He probably didn't answer because he didn't recognize the number."

Less than a minute later, the phone rang. Kiyo snatched it up. "Yeah?"

"It's Bran."

Pressing the speaker button so Niamh could listen in, he explained to Bran what had happened on the plane and the events after.

"I told you the Blackwoods would be watching airports and train stations."

"All of them? In the entire world?"

"Who knows at this point? Suffice it to say, we need to get you where you're going under radar."

"Do you always point out the obvious?"

"Someone's in a bit of a mood."

Niamh snorted.

"Bran, don't make me come to Ireland."

The vampire chuckled down the line. "Okay, okay. First off, this trip to Tokyo, if it involves the fae-borne, then maybe Fionn should know about it."

Kiyo looked over at Niamh who was shaking her head frantically. He wished like hell she'd just tell him what this vision was about. "Niamh doesn't seem to think that's a good idea."

"Fine. Then here's what we'll do. I'll get you money, new passports, and I imagine you need clothes?"

"I can get us clothes." Niamh shrugged.

"You mean, steal them?" Kiyo said flatly.

She flushed guiltily and looked away.

"Yeah, we need clothes, Bran."

Bran tutted. "I detect a hint of judgment in your voice there, Kiyo. Didn't your mother ever tell you not to throw stones at glass houses? Or something like that. Don't listen to this Judgy Mcjudgerson here, Niamh. He's committed more crimes than you'll find soaked into the walls of Alcatraz."

Niamh raised an eyebrow at Kiyo, and a snarl of annoyance escaped his throat.

Bran heard and chuckled harder. "Did you just lose your moral high ground, wolf?"

"When this is over, you're my new personal punching bag," Kiyo promised.

The vamp seemed completely unconcerned. "Before we both get to enjoy that delightful moment together, I'm going to get you the hell out of Sweden. A package will arrive at your hotel within the hour with everything you need, including a cell. I'll call you on it with your travel schedule." Bran hung up abruptly.

"He's funny." Niamh stood. "And efficient."

"The only reason I put up with him. The latter, not the former."

"What did he mean?" She crossed her arms over her chest, studying him. "About your crimes and the moral high ground?"

"Not anything you haven't already guessed about me."

She nodded. "You're a mercenary so I knew you'd probably done a lot of questionable stuff over the years. It does make me wonder what right you have to judge me about my gift for tricking the human mind?"

Needing to keep the barrier between them, he shrugged. "In all the things I've done, I've never messed with someone like that."

It was a lie.

But it worked.

Her expression closed down. Flicking him a wounded look, she headed toward the door. "I'll be in my room."

"No, you won't."

"Excuse me?"

"You haven't eaten. Neither have I. We'll go downstairs to the dining room. We'll eat while we wait for the package to arrive."

"I don't feel like eating."

"I'm not giving you a choice."

Suddenly, she was a blur across the room and Kiyo was pinned to the wall by the force of her forearm against his throat. She pushed her stunning face close to his and bared her perfect, straight teeth, her eyes flashing gold.

Heat flushed through his body, surprising the shit out of him.

"I'm not yours to push around, Kiyo. And don't you forget it." She released him, stepping away.

Kiyo didn't let his expression betray him, even though it took a lot of control not to react physically to her. He wanted to take her down on the bed and show her how much she'd enjoy submitting to him. And he wasn't that kind of wolf. He thought himself above those baser instincts.

What the hell was happening to him?

He impressed himself by the steady blandness of his tone. "That was kind of an overreaction, wasn't it?"

She gaped at him. "No, I don't think it was. You're being a bully."

"I'm not the one who pinned you to the wall."

"Are you always this irritating when you're hungry and tired?"

He growled. "Are you always this irritating, period?"

"I imagine a male like you *would* find a woman who had her own mind irritating."

"You don't know anything about me." Brushing past her, ignoring her scent because it was driving him mad, he yanked open the hotel room door and gestured for her to go ahead. "We eat first."

Niamh narrowed her eyes as she walked to the door. "Is this bossiness or concern for my well-being? Because you should know that it takes more than a day before I start to feel the effects of hunger. Like, around a week, actually."

Kiyo knew she hadn't meant to, but she'd just given away something of her past to him.

Niamh had known hunger.

He closed the hotel room door and quickened his stride to catch up with her. "You and your brother went hungry at some point."

It wasn't a question.

She flicked him a surprised look, then her brows puckered as if she'd just realized what she'd conveyed. "Not me and my brother. Just me. Thank goodness."

"What happened?"

She didn't answer.

A sting grew hot in his chest. Kiyo ignored it and they strode in silence, following the signs for the dining room. It turned out to be buffet-style service, the food less than appealing. Yet it *was* food, so it would do. There were only a few other hotel guests in the room.

They separated while they filled their plates and then Kiyo spotted Niamh at a table for two in the corner, far away from anyone else.

He sat down, noting for someone who wasn't hungry, she'd piled her plate almost as high as he had. Kiyo raised an eyebrow.

She flashed him a quick, sheepish grin. "I got hungry when I saw the food."

Amusement eased his earlier irritation and his lips twitched around a forkful of deli meat.

"I went into hiding for a while," Niamh said abruptly. At his obvious confusion, she continued, "You asked what happened. With the going-hungry thing."

He was silent but nodded for her to go on.

Niamh shrugged. "I disappeared off the map a few months ago. I disappeared even from myself. Does that make sense?"

Yeah, that made total sense to him. Kiyo nodded again.

"I don't even remember how I got to the room or when or ..." Her lovely eyes were dark and hollow with an emotion he recognized.

Grief.

This was about her brother.

"I don't know how long I was there exactly. I estimate about ten days or so." Her rueful smile was limp, joyless. "I felt the hunger pains, but it was the cramps from dehydration that pulled me out of the black hole. I knew I wouldn't die ... but I also didn't know it would hurt so much." She gave him a considering look. "It didn't last. By the time I pushed myself to my feet to get out of that room, the pain started to dissipate. And I felt strangely stronger but hard. Brittle. Like I was made of stone." Her eyes rounded with shock, like she hadn't meant to give that much away. She dropped her gaze to her plate. "Anyway, I stepped out of the room into an apartment I didn't recognize, into a city I didn't know. Turned out I was in Hamburg. I don't even remember getting there from Munich ..."

Kiyo studied her as she got lost in her memories. What she said, about the hunger and dehydration pains eventually disappearing, her body growing stronger for it, reminded him of what she'd said about her kindness being her greatest gift. Maybe it was generally her *human* emotions they had to be thankful for. It sounded like her human habits were what kept her from becoming fully fae.

Her gaze lifted to meet his again and the hair on the back of his neck rose with awareness.

"You've known hunger, too, haven't you?"

How the hell did she know that?

He looked down at his plate and stabbed his fork through half a boiled egg. "I've known many things," he answered evasively.

Kiyo felt Niamh's annoyance, and perhaps hurt, without even looking at her.

She didn't ask him any more questions.

In fact, she didn't talk for the rest of the meal.

And considering Kiyo liked the quiet, it unnerved him that he missed the sound of her gentle voice with its lilting Irish accent.

The silence stretched between them as they finished their meal and then as they walked back to their rooms. As they strolled into the lobby, the girl behind the desk flagged them down.

"This arrived for you." She gestured to a large duffle bag.

"Bran," Kiyo muttered, taking up the bag.

Niamh thanked the girl and they strode upstairs. They seemed to have come to an unspoken agreement that using the elevator was a bad idea for two people who didn't want to find themselves cornered.

Gesturing for Niamh to follow him into his room, he threw the bag on the bed and unzipped it. Inside were two new passports, more cash than Kiyo knew what to do with, a couple of pairs of jeans and shirts, clean underwear and bras for Niamh as well as jeans and tees and underwear for him.

"These will fit perfectly," she said, holding the jeans against her body. Her eyes flickered to the bras and twinkled with amusement. "How did he know?"

Kiyo ripped his attention from the new bras to the dark jeans and black tees Bran had put in the bag for him. He grunted in acknowledgment, realizing they'd fit him perfectly too. There were even black hair ties, and he knew they were for him. He was no longer surprised by Bran's unnerving accuracy and efficiency.

And, as if on cue, a cell rang inside the bag.

Kiyo dug through it and noted the flash of silver at the bottom.

A katana.

He almost smiled.

Instead he pulled out the old-fashioned cell phone. He answered it, hitting the speaker button. "Yeah?"

"Good, you got everything, then? I did good, didn't I? I even remembered your hair ties so you're not walking around with your hair hanging in that gorgeous face. I know how much you don't like feeling too sexy," Bran said.

A burst of laughter brought Kiyo's gaze to Niamh who was grinning widely, her shoulders shaking with amusement. The compelling vision of her laughing amused him, stifling his irritation with Bran. He bared his teeth in a half grin, half snarl, and she blinked rapidly, as if surprised. Her gaze lowered to his mouth and stayed there long enough for him to feel as if she'd caressed his lips with her fingers.

"Hello, anyone there?" Bran's voice yanked Kiyo back to himself.

"Yeah, we're here. We got everything. What's next?"

"There will be a private plane waiting for you at Kalmar Airport tomorrow morning at six a.m. sharp. The pilot is called Stephen and he will meet you at the entrance. It's a small airport so he won't miss you."

"How far away is the airport from here?"

"Ten minutes. You left an SUV outside the hotel, right?"

Kiyo frowned. How did he know these things? "Yeah ..."

"I've gotten rid of it. You'll find a Honda Civic parked just down the street. Keys are in the duffle bag." Bran rattled off the car's registration number.

"Wow," Niamh said. "You're brilliant, Bran. You think of everything."

"Why, thank you," he answered with more than a hint of flirtation. "I just want to make sure you're safe and comfortable. Are the clothes good? I stuck to jeans but I know you like your dresses, so ..."

Kiyo raised an eyebrow. How did he know Niamh liked dresses?

"Oh, it's fine. Jeans are easier to run in," she observed ruefully.

"You two have never met, right?" Kiyo asked.

"No," Bran answered. "But keeping an eye on Niamh for Fionn makes me feel like we have. Maybe one day I'll get to meet your stunning loveliness in person, Niamh." There was a definite purr of invitation in his voice.

And a red flush crested Niamh's cheeks, meaning she'd caught it too.

He stemmed a growl. "You sound like a stalker, Bran."

"I like to think of myself as more of an extremely hot guardian angel of the night."

Seeing Niamh suppress a charmed smile, Kiyo felt his impatience grow. "What happens after Kalmar Airport?"

"Right, that. So, Stephen can take you to Düsseldorf where we'll have Fionn's private jet waiting for you. The jet will take you to Tokyo."

"Fine. We'll call if we need anything else." Kiyo hung up.

Niamh gaped at him. "You hung up before we could thank him."

"He's paid very well by Fionn to do his job. That's thanks enough."

She shook her head. "Oh, you are such—" She faltered, letting out a small, anguished moan.

Her hand flew to her temple, the color draining from her face.

Kiyo was immediately at her side, gripping her biceps. "What's wrong?"

"Vision," she whimpered. "Another one—" Her head flew back too sharply on her neck, her eyes rolling as her lids fluttered at a rapid pace.

Feeling her body convulse, Kiyo pulled her into him and lowered them both to the carpet so he could hold her while she shuddered.

He watched her features strain with the pain of the visions. An ache flared across his chest, and his arms banded more tightly around her. The strength of her physical reaction to the visions was such that Kiyo wondered how Ronan ever comforted her through them. Surely a human couldn't contain her while she was like this?

He cupped her nape to stop her head from jerking so much and caressed her neck with his thumb, hoping the comforting gesture might reach through the visions.

Part of him hoped the vision would transfer to him, too, so he'd finally know what was going on inside her head. But nothing happened.

Other than the strange realization that it disturbed him to see her like this.

His grip on her tightened and he bent his head to her ear. "It's okay," he murmured, "I'm here, I've got you."

Finally, her convulsions eased and relief moved through him as he felt her hands rest on his chest as she came back to herself.

Her eyelashes fluttered and as her eyes opened, the gold bled back to aquamarine. Only golden flecks remained.

She felt warm and solid and real in his arms, and her sweet, spicy scent made him want to bury his face in her throat and breathe her in deep.

Hot awareness sprung between them.

This was becoming a problem.

In fact, at some point, Kiyo needed to leave her safe in her hotel room and go get laid to deal with the damn problem.

"Well?" he demanded gruffly.

At his sharp tone, Niamh's hands dropped from his chest and she pushed away, forcing his hand from her neck.

He let her go and stood up.

He wanted to hold out a hand to help her to her feet, but he knew he shouldn't.

Niamh slowly stood on shaky legs, looking exhausted.

"Well?" he repeated impatiently.

She looked at him steadily. "What are you, Kiyo?"

He blinked at the abrupt question. "What?"

"I know you're not an ordinary werewolf. Tell me what you are and why Fionn sent *you*, of all people?"

Wondering if she'd seen something about him again, he took a step toward her. "What did you see in your vision?"

Niamh lifted her chin, a stubborn glint in her eyes. "First, tell me what you are."

"There's nothing to tell." It was his rote answer. The one he gave anyone who got suspicious about him. "I'm a werewolf. An alpha. Stronger and faster than most ... now tell me what you saw."

Niamh stared blankly at him for longer than made him comfortable and then she sighed. "It was the same. Fate is impatient for us to get to Tokyo. I know the vision is about you … I just don't know why. And it looks like I'm not going to get the answers from you." She picked up the clothes from Bran. "Can I count on you to wake me in the morning?"

He swallowed hard against the frustration choking him. "Yeah. I'll wake you at five."

She gave him a nod without meeting his eyes and slipped out of the room.

Kiyo sank with exhaustion onto the bed, staring at the door.

It didn't sit well with him, hurting Niamh's feelings, but the sooner she realized he was just here to do a job, the better.

For them both.

8

Niamh had made her decision. In that moment, when Kiyo once again refused to divulge anything personal about himself, anything that would prove that he trusted her at least a little, she'd made up her mind to leave him behind.

It had been shockingly easy to slip out of the hotel undetected. Kiyo was exhausted from the last few days of constant activity and stress. She'd heard his soft snoring behind the door of his hotel room and known he was out for the count. Which was good because she didn't really want to break his neck again to get away from him.

The latest vision hadn't been about the fae or Tokyo.

She'd lied.

To her disbelief, the vision had been about an O'Connor witch.

The O'Connors were the Dublin coven Rose was born into, but after her parents died, the coven decided Rose's existence was too dangerous. To stop the chance of her ever opening the gate, they planned to kill her. However, her aunt and uncle stole her away to the States and changed their identities so they couldn't be found. When Rose was finally awakened to what she really was, the O'Connors learned of her whereabouts and went after her.

Unfortunately, Niamh and Ronan were there when she did.

Niamh's pulse raced as her mind took her back to the memories she'd tried so hard to bury.

The coven had killed her brother.

Stolen Ronan's life force to power themselves against her and Rose. It was a pointless, mindless death because his life energy was not enough. While she'd tried desperately to save him, Rose and Fionn had decimated the coven.

All but one.

At the beginning of the fight, Niamh had fought a witch and used her magic to throw her out the window of the apartment they were in.

According to this latest vision, that witch, Meghan O'Connor, was alive and hiding out in Paris.

The only thing that had kept Niamh from losing her mind when Ronan died was the knowledge that the coven had paid for what they'd done.

But they hadn't.

One of their attackers still lived.

And vengeance like nothing Niamh had ever felt or ever believed herself capable of pumped black in her blood.

There had been a tiny part of her that had hoped Kiyo would trust her and in turn, she could trust him with the truth, that maybe he'd come with her while she dealt with the O'Connor witch.

Yet he was closed up tighter than a clamshell. Any illusions of feeling she felt between them were just that—the imaginings of a silly woman with a crush.

No, Niamh would deal with this alone. As she would deal with everything. The vision of the four stones, the four fae ... the one who was supposed to be dead but wasn't. Niamh would deal with it all because it was *her* job. Kiyo was just a well-paid guard. Nothing more. She couldn't entrust him with the important knowledge she had.

Using the shadows to cloak herself as she moved through the tight, narrow, dark streets of Kalmar town, Niamh was a blur. Her first stop was an ATM. She pressed a hand to the machine and forced it to open its mouth and spew out cash. She slipped the money into her bag and then used her fae speed to arrive at the bus terminal. It took her about thirty seconds, what was otherwise a four-minute walk for a human.

While Kiyo had fallen asleep quickly, Niamh had gone downstairs to chat with the desk clerk about the bus routes out of Kalmar. She'd checked for Niamh and there was a night bus to Zadar, Croatia. One of its first major stops was near Copenhagen Airport. Niamh could get a flight from Copenhagen to Paris.

Using mind trickery to make the clerk forget they'd had the conversation, Niamh had returned to her room to shower and change into the fresh clothes Bran had provided. She conjured a bag from the nearest store and put her new clothes into it.

The bus terminal was quiet at midnight. There were only a few passengers, like her, waiting for the bus to Zadar. Every second she had to stand, ticket clutched in hand, waiting for the bus, was torturous. Any minute now, she expected Kiyo to appear and foil her plans.

Are you really going to hunt this woman and kill her?

Why was Kiyo now the voice of her conscience?

It was no business of his.

And Meghan O'Connor deserved it.

Ronan's face, frozen in death, flashed before her eyes and her heart raced harder with determination.

By the time Niamh made it to Copenhagen Airport, it was just past four in the morning. She'd been a nervy, jangled mess on the bus, expecting someone—Kiyo or an enemy—to pop out of nowhere and stop her. But she'd made it. The next part of the waiting game was her flight to Paris. It didn't leave until six-thirty in the morning.

Kiyo would wake soon, and although she knew it would be impossible for him to reach her in time, she still couldn't wait to be more than four hours away from him.

No one could stop her.

Her mind was made up.

If she'd been provided with a vision of Meghan, it meant something. She was supposed to give Ronan justice. Maybe then, she'd find some peace at last.

~

THE SOUND of a sharp beeping seeped through Kiyo's consciousness and his lids fluttered reluctantly open.

It was the alarm on the hotel's bedside table.

Groaning, he reached out and hit the top of it to shut the damn thing up. The time glared at him in neon red.

It was five in the morning.

They were supposed to meet this Stephen guy at Kalmar Airport in an hour.

Pushing up from the bed, Kiyo buried his head in his hands. He'd fallen asleep at seven thirty, which meant he'd slept for almost nine hours. No wonder he felt like crap. Kiyo was used to six hours a night. Anything longer made him feel drugged.

Damn it.

Rolling out of the bed, he decided to give Niamh a few minutes longer by taking a shower first. He hurried through his ablutions and tied his wet hair into a top knot.

Feeling more awake and refreshed, he set out to cross the hall and wake up his pain-in-the-ass charge. Anticipation thrummed beneath his skin.

To his dismay, he realized he was almost looking forward to the day ahead.

Nothing ever went to plan around Niamh. She definitely wasn't boring.

Perhaps if he'd been more himself, he would've realized he hadn't picked up on her scent when he stepped out into the hall. But he was so lost in his thoughts, it wasn't until she didn't answer his repeated knocks that he realized something was wrong.

Uneasiness settled over him. He grasped the doorknob and

twisted until it broke, the electronic lock rendered useless. The door swung open and Kiyo marched inside Niamh's room.

He took in the unmade bed and the fact that her scent barely lingered.

There was a stronger hint of it coming from the bathroom. He strode toward it, thrusting the door back against the wall. His nose lifted into the air and he followed her scent to a comb lying by the sink. It was one of the hotel's free amenities. The cardboard packaging laid beside it.

Kiyo clutched the comb with Niamh's tangled hair caught in its teeth. He almost broke it he gripped it so hard. She'd used the shower. The complimentary shampoo bottle was half-empty. There were soap suds on the bottom of it. A wet towel on the floor.

Hurrying back into the bathroom, his anger built as he swept the space for any trace of her. Nothing.

The new clothes Bran had provided were gone.

She'd left on her own.

Damn her!

Racing back into his room, he quickly gathered his shit into the duffle bag, throwing the comb in, too, and got out of there. To his annoyance, the woman on reception last night had been replaced by a guy. He questioned him anyway.

No, he hadn't spoken to a young woman with long brown hair this morning.

Eyes searching the lobby, his gaze wandered high near the ceiling, and satisfaction slammed through him when he spotted the security camera. The guy at the front desk watched him suspiciously, so Kiyo pretended to make his way back to his room. Instead, as soon as he was out of sight, he searched for the hotel office. The security tapes were likely in there.

Finding the office, he also found a security camera trained on the door.

That was fine. He'd just need to steal the tape for that too.

Making sure no one was watching (which there wasn't because it wasn't even six o'clock yet), Kiyo tried the office door. Locked.

He took care of it and slipped inside, shutting the door quietly behind him. Dumping the duffle bag, he searched the room and found three small TVs and old-fashioned VCRs for the security tapes inside a walnut cabinet. Using the remote, he rewound the tape on the first TV, which was for the camera trained on the reception desk. To his dismay, he had to rewind the damn thing back to just before midnight. There she was.

Niamh. Leaving the reception area.

She hadn't spoken to the desk clerk.

He frowned.

Winding it back further, he found her again.

At around eight thirty last night, Niamh appeared at reception and had a ten-minute chat with the female clerk.

He noted the dazed way the woman looked at her.

No doubt, she'd used her powers to make the receptionist forget their conversation.

His fury was a burn in his throat.

Abandoning the tape, he found the one for the office and ripped it out of the VCR. Hiding it in his duffle bag, he got out unseen and returned to reception. He didn't even look at the guy behind the desk. He just kept walking until he was outside beneath the breaking dawn.

Compounding his anger was the fact that his fingers shook as he removed his cell to call Bran. He hated that he had to make this call.

Never in his life had he failed on a job.

Bran answered with, "It's my nighttime, arsehole, so this better be good."

Kiyo bared his teeth, wishing the vamp was there in front of him so he could take his bad mood out on him. He needed a fight. But no one challenged him like Fionn, so what was the point?

"I lost her."

There was silence. Then, "You what?"

"I woke up this morning and she was gone. I checked the hotel tapes. She had a nice chat with the front-desk clerk last night and then around midnight, the tapes show her strutting her ass out of the hotel."

"Did you question the clerk?"

"No point. I could tell Niamh had used that mind-fuck thing she does. And I know from watching her do it, she covers her ass. She'd have told the girl to forget their conversation."

"Did anything happen last night after we spoke?"

The memory of Niamh convulsing in his arms came to him instantly. "She had a vision. She said it was the same one, but ..."

She'd asked him about himself and had seemed more disappointed than usual when he didn't answer. What did it mean?

"She might have been lying," Bran said. "What about her room? Is there anything that might suggest where she went?"

"No."

"Are you sure?"

"Bran, this is what I do for a living. I have no leads other than Tokyo."

The vampire was silent for so long, Kiyo thought he might have fallen asleep. He was about to growl his impatience down the line when Bran said, "Do you have anything of hers?"

"What do you mean?"

"An item belonging to her?"

"Yeah. A comb. Can we use it to find her?"

"Preferably, Fionn could come to the bloody rescue and use a tracing spell to find her. But, unfortunately, he and Rose are pretty far away at the moment. And I don't trust any other magic user to find Niamh. So there's only one solution."

"What is it?"

"There's an alpha in Scotland. He has a rare gift. For tracking."

"Are you talking about Conall MacLennan?" Kiyo asked, surprised.

"You've heard of him?"

"Most wolves have. His is the last werewolf pack in Scotland, and he's taken down any alpha who tried to win it from him." Not to mention that once he had your scent, there was nowhere on earth you could hide from him. The wolf was a legend among their kind. "Why would you trust this guy?" Suddenly it hit him. "Wait—Conall is the werewolf who mated with one of the fae-borne and turned her?"

"Yeah, he's the one. He was hired to hunt Thea. Instead he discovered they were true mates. The man that was after her ... his son stabbed Thea in the heart with an iron knife. She was dying, so Conall bit her. Turns out, because they were mated, he could turn her into a werewolf. It's one of the reasons the Faerie Queen wanted all the supernaturals out of Faerie. When she realized that a werewolf bite could destroy their immortality and turn them to mortal wolves, it didn't make her happy. But it certainly made Thea and Conall happy."

"So you think this wolf would be willing to help because Niamh is some kind of pseudo-sibling to Thea?"

"That, and Niamh was the one who convinced Thea to trust Conall. She had a vision, you see. Knew they were mated."

He remembered Niamh mentioning she'd played matchmaker to not just Rose and Fionn but Thea too. "So I have to go to Scotland and get him to track Niamh using this item of hers?"

"Yup."

"Wouldn't it be faster to just call Fionn and get his ass back here?"

"He's really, really far away."

"How far?" Kiyo snapped.

"Like Oceania far."

Dammit. "What the hell is he doing out there ?"

"Living his fucking life, wolf, all right? He didn't know you were going to be so incompetent you'd lose the luscious Niamh in the first seventy-two hours."

"You better hope you and I never meet, vamp."

"Because I'm calling you a failure or because I think your charge is delicious?" He drawled the word *delicious* like he was imagining sinking his fangs into Niamh's throat.

Kiyo held the phone away from him, afraid he'd crush the thing in an effort to ram his fist down the line and crush Bran's windpipe.

"You still there?"

A growl rumbled from deep in his belly. "You're straining my patience."

"So I can hear. All right, then. Conall lives in a place in the Highlands called Torridon. We're going to get Stephen to fly you to Inverness, which isn't far. I'll have Conall meet you there. I'll call Stephen to let him know the change of plans, but you better get your arse to the airport now."

Kiyo hung up to do just that.

He found the Honda Bran had left for them outside the hotel. As he drove toward the airport, he tried not to dwell on how angry he was. Not just at Niamh.

He was furious with himself.

Because something told him he could have prevented her taking off.

That didn't mean he wasn't still raging at the fae.

"She better have a good excuse," Kiyo muttered.

And more than that ... if anything happened to her ...

If the Blackwoods or The Garm got to her first—

Don't think about it.

He'd reach her first.

The alternative wasn't an option.

9

"It isn't the nicest place we've stayed, but it'll do." Ronan flopped down on the L-shaped sofa, his arms spread across the back of it.

The apartment in the center of Munich was somewhat deceiving. It didn't look like much from the outside, but the inside was ultramodern and chic. Whenever they came to a new city, depending on the circumstances, they usually looked up all the places to rent and found the nicest to take over while it sat empty. They were squatters, basically. Sometimes, though, Ronan was in the mood to be looked after, so they stayed in luxury hotels to enjoy the perks of room service.

"How long will we be here?"

"Long enough to see what's wrong with Rose."

"I miss Rome." He glowered at her.

He didn't miss Rome. He missed the married Italian woman he was shagging every night. But Niamh had been overcome by the need to be in Munich. She wouldn't take no for an answer, no matter Ronan's reticence. She'd told him she'd go alone. But no matter how much he grumbled about it, Ronan wouldn't let her out of his sight.

So they flew to Munich and within five minutes of landing, Niamh got a vision of Rose Kelly.

She would be at the train station tomorrow, and she needed Niamh's help.

"You know how I feel about you spending time with these people. It's one thing to set them on the right path, another to be in their company for more than a few minutes. It's too dangerous."

Her brother wasn't wrong, but Niamh couldn't turn her back on Rose. Unlike most of the others, Niamh had been born with the knowledge of who they were and even had snippets of the fae history buried in her consciousness. Worse, she'd had visions of alternative versions of the future depending on the decisions certain key players made.

The other fae-borne, all but one, had walked around blind, fumbling to find their way in a human-dominated world, confused by their strange abilities. When three fae-borne were hunted and killed by Eirik before Niamh could get to them, two of them didn't even know what they were.

It was Niamh's duty to try to save the others. She'd succeeded with Thea Quinn, now MacLennan. And she'd succeed with Rose, no matter what.

"Are you even listening to me?"

Niamh turned and looked down at her brother. "I need to do this."

His expression darkened. "I need to be in Rome."

"I told you to stay."

"You know that's not an option." Something dark flickered in his countenance. "Everything I do is for you. I gave up my life in Ireland for you. I'm not going to let you wander alone now, am I, after all that?"

This life suited Ronan. She knew it did. He liked not being tied down anywhere. Liked the money and the travel and the unknown. He could protest until he was blue in the face, but she knew her brother didn't care about leaving Ireland. He just liked to remind her that she owed him.

Guilt prickled as she remembered the many times she'd come out of a vision to find Ronan straining to hold her, his face stark with concern.

He did love her, though.

She knew that too.

Just sometimes a traitorous question crossed her mind: Which did he love more? Her or her powers?

"Niamh."

She looked back at him.

His expression had softened. "I just worry about you. Every time we do this, we put ourselves in the path of the Blackwoods and The Garm."

"I know." She felt terrible for thinking badly of her brother. "But we know who our enemies are. We can protect ourselves."

Ronan opened his mouth to respond but instead of his voice, Niamh heard the roar of shattering glass. She flinched, shutting her eyes against it, and when she opened them, they were surrounded by witches and warlocks. Rose was there. She stood between Niamh and Ronan looking fearful and confused.

"What's going on?" Niamh asked. She turned to face the unfamiliar coven as they held hands and surrounded them.

And then the image slammed into her head, taking her to her knees.

Ronan.

Losing energy, soul, heart ... everything he needed to live.

Leaking out of him and into them.

To the coven.

"No!" she screamed, coming out of the vision.

Ronan held her, his expression pale with worry. "Nee?"

"Run," she whispered. "Ronan, run."

But it was too late.

Suddenly, he grew limp, falling onto his back, his eyes staring vacantly at the ceiling.

"Ronan." Niamh scrambled over him. "Ronan!"

Cracks appeared in his skin. Cracks. Cracks. Cracks.

Until his body crumbled inwards and there was nothing left but a pile of ash.

"No!" Niamh's eyes flew open, her pulse rushing in her ears, her chest heaving with frantic breaths. Disoriented, it took her a moment to realize she was on a plane.

"Are you well?"

She glanced at the woman to her right. The stranger's brow puckered with sympathy.

Niamh lifted a trembling hand to her forehead and gave the woman a pained, embarrassed smile. "Nightmare. Fear of flying."

The woman reached out to pat her hand in motherly comfort. "Air travel is the safest mode of travel."

Niamh gave her a tremulous smile and relaxed into her seat. She closed her eyes against the bright lights of the cabin interior. She hadn't dreamed of Ronan in a while. For a long time, she wouldn't even let herself think his name.

The nightmare never depicted the exact reality of his death, but it was a succinct summation of the event.

Meghan O'Connor would pay for it.

A *bing* sounded above Niamh's head.

The seat-belt sign was lit up.

Then the PA crackled. "Ladies and gentlemen, the captain has now switched on the seat-belt sign as we begin our descent. Please make sure any larger items, including laptops, are stowed in the overheard bins. Any smaller items can be stowed beneath the seat in front of you. Please stow away your tray tables and return your seats to the upright position. We hope you've had an enjoyable flight with us this morning and wish you a pleasant stay in Paris. And if you have a connecting flight, we wish you a safe onward journey. From all of us at Helm Airlines, thank you for flying with us and we hope to see you again soon."

Niamh released a slow exhale. She felt twitchy and impatient to get off the plane now that she was so close to Paris. To being in the same city as Meghan.

When the fighting had started, Niamh remembered the witch coming at her. She'd used her magic to blast the girl out of the apartment window. Niamh had assumed that the descent, or rather the impact, had killed her.

But she'd survived.

Ronan hadn't.

That just couldn't be allowed.

Obviously Fate agreed with her by sending her the vision.

The hum of the plane's engines grew louder as they descended toward Paris-Charles de Gaulle Airport. The knots grew tighter and tighter in Niamh's stomach. Vengeance was a nasty business, not something she'd ever thought her heart would hunger for.

But here she was.

Starving.

~

Inverness, Scotland

After leaving New York in 1960, Kiyo traveled. His first stop was Britain. After exploring England and Wales, he'd backpacked north and up through the highlands of Scotland. Even after he'd wandered mainland Europe for the next decade, Scotland stayed with him. Being more mountainous than the rest of the island, it reminded him a little of Japan.

Back in the '60s, he'd climbed Ben Nevis. It was almost three times smaller than Mount Fuji, which Kiyo never had occasion to climb. Yet the mountain of his home was far from his mind standing at the top of Ben Nevis. All that had mattered was that he was alone up there in a way that finally made sense. Standing on a clear day, staring out at the majestic glory that stretched before him, the panoramic vistas conveyed a lonesome beauty that caused an ache in his chest for the first time in decades. The mountain peaks, the rolling valleys, the glistening, placid lochs, the startling greens and earthy browns and the harsh, rugged rock face. It reminded him there was still unspoiled places in the world. Places that made feeling alone no longer a joyless desert; that aloneness could offer its own bounty. Its own peace.

The contentment he found in the Highlands surprised Kiyo. After he left, the hunger for something that always seemed out of reach returned to plague him.

Over the years, Kiyo had traveled back to the Highlands of Scotland searching for that elusive serenity. The roads there, however, were busier now. Tourists descended in their masses at certain times of the year. But he could still find moments of tranquility standing on lonely, empty golden sands or mountain peaks during the tourist off-season.

If it had been for any other reason than chasing a fae woman who'd abandoned him, Kiyo would have been happy to arrive at Inverness Airport. The airport was surrounded by the Cairngorms and the Moray Firth. It was a sunny, wintry day, the water glistening a perfect blue in the distance.

Kiyo stood outside the entrance of the small airport, the duffle bag at his feet. The humans who passed gave him a wide berth while throwing him looks that veered between wariness, awe, and attraction.

He was used to it.

What he wasn't used to was the unnerving impatience and urgency that thrummed in his blood.

An old Land Rover Defender rolled to a stop outside the airport in front of him and the hair on Kiyo's arms rose before its driver even got out of the vehicle.

An alpha.

He pushed off the wall of the building and grabbed his duffle bag as the Alpha and chief of Pack/Clan MacLennan jumped out of the Defender and rounded the hood. His piercing gray gaze set stonily on Kiyo.

Kiyo would have known this was Conall MacLennan without feeling the impressive alpha energy emanating from the wolf. He was a huge male at around six foot six, made of solid muscle. A deep scar was visible down the left side of his face, from the tip of his eyebrow to the corner of his mouth, where someone had clearly slashed him with silver. If humans were wary of Kiyo, he could only imagine how they feared this wolf.

But none of that was the reason Kiyo knew who Conall was.

The Scot was the spitting image of his father.

"Kiyonari." Conall halted before him.

"Kiyo," he corrected.

Conall gave him an abrupt nod. "You've been hired to protect Niamh but she's run from you?"

The question was asked without censor. "She had a vision ... I don't know what it was about, but I think it's the reason she took off without me. Had I suspected for a second—"

Conall held up his hand. "You dinnae need to explain yourself to me. They're tricky creatures, these fae women. Believe me." He grinned, the action transforming his face entirely. "I have firsthand experience of their trickery."

"Your mate?"

"Aye." Conall nodded to the SUV. "Get in."

Kiyo followed him to the Defender, pulling out Niamh's comb from the duffle before he stowed it in the back next to a large backpack he assumed was Conall's. Once settled in the passenger seat, he handed the comb to Conall. The wolf took it, his brows drawn together in thought.

Waiting impatiently, Kiyo watched as the hard concentration left Conall's expression and he flicked Kiyo a weary look of acceptance. "I assumed we'd be leaving Scotland," he gestured to the backpack, "but hoped that we wouldnae."

"But we are?" Kiyo asked, though he'd assumed so as well.

"We are. My mate will be pleased."

Noting the alpha's sarcasm, Kiyo waited silently as Conall pulled out his cell and hit a speed-dial button. With his wolf ears, he heard it with clarity as the call connected and a husky female voice with an American accent answered. "What's happening?"

"Thea, love, I'm heading out."

"Where is she?"

"Not sure exactly. We're heading south. She doesnae feel too far ... so perhaps France."

France? What the hell could Niamh want in France? Kiyo searched his memory for any mention of it.

"I should come."

"You shouldnae come," Conall answered patiently. "We've already discussed this."

"I'm not fae anymore. It's not dangerous."

"It's always dangerous." An edge entered the alpha's tone. "You have scars on your body from silver bullet wounds that prove my point."

Kiyo heard Thea give a huff. "It feels wrong to stay out of it. I owe Rose and Niamh."

"And I'm fulfilling that debt for you."

"Conall—"

"Thea," he bit out, flicking Kiyo an annoyed look. "Please. It's not just you anymore."

There was silence. "I know. I'm sorry. I'll stay. But I want to hear from you every four hours."

The alpha smirked. "I can do that."

"I love you."

"I love you too," the wolf said, completely unabashed to admit so in front of Kiyo.

He sighed inwardly. It seemed he was surrounded by fools in love.

When Conall hung up, he turned to Kiyo, all business. "Let's park the car. We need to get a flight to London."

TRAVELING with Conall MacLennan had been somewhat easy at first. The wolf had asked Kiyo if he'd ever visited Scotland. He answered that the Highlands were among his favorite places to visit, which seemed to please the Scot. But Kiyo already knew that pride of their country was a huge part of a Scot's national identity, and nothing endeared you more to them than to compliment the beauty of their homeland.

When Conall noted he must not have visited Torridon before, for he would have sensed him there, Kiyo nodded vaguely. After all, he couldn't tell the alpha that he'd met Conall's father and grandfather back in 1961 when he'd stumbled across Pack MacLennan on his travels. At the time, he'd been running in wolf form through the woods near Torridon when he'd come across a cornered alpha. Another alpha and a beta had the alpha pinned. Without even thinking about why, Kiyo had joined the fight.

That cornered alpha turned out to be Conall's father. Although strong, he was young and inexperienced. The two wolves were from a pack in the Lowlands of Scotland. Kiyo had insinuated himself into a war. When the Alpha of Pack MacLennan discovered Kiyo had saved his son, he welcomed him into his home in Torridon. Always a lone wolf, Kiyo had been intrigued by pack life, but he knew it would never be for him.

Still, he stayed awhile. Long enough to see the end of the Lowland pack. It was a small pack, having lost members and much power over the years. The attack on Conall's father, Caelan, had been a last desperate attempt to gain leverage over Pack MacLennan, to force a submission.

Lennox MacLennan, Conall's grandfather, was having none of it. He'd given the Lowland pack many chances to assimilate, but they didn't want to. They wanted to take over Pack MacLennan. Foolish arrogance as far as Kiyo could see.

He lived with Pack MacLennan for three months before setting off on his own again. By the time Kiyo left, Lennox had wiped out the last of the Lowland pack, and Pack MacLennan was the last werewolf pack in Scotland.

Conall wasn't even a glitter in Caelan's eyes at the time as he hadn't found a mate yet.

There was no way Kiyo could confide his history with the pack without revealing his immortality. Wolves lived longer and aged slowly ... but not *that* slowly.

After his query about Scotland, Conall stopped talking. Much like Kiyo, he wasn't really a conversationalist. It suited Kiyo nicely. Theirs was a comfortable silence.

However, the urgency and irritation that hummed beneath Kiyo's stoic facade must have betrayed him because as soon as they got into the rental car hours later after arriving at Heathrow, Conall asked, "Do you have some feeling for Niamh?"

Conall was driving since he was the one following Niamh's scent.

Kiyo tried not to glower at him for the ridiculous question. “Obligation,” he replied flatly. “I’m being paid to keep an eye on her, and I don’t like to fail.”

“So, the somewhat oppressive sense of desperation coming off you is just out of obligation?”

“Desperation?” Kiyo asked, his voice dangerously quiet.

Conall was not intimidated by his warning tone. “I’m an intuitive alpha,” Conall explained. “I often sense things in other wolves, especially other alphas. I hadnae realized it until my mate pointed it out. She had the audacity to suggest it’s why I always win in a fight.” He grinned, shrugging. “Perhaps she’s right.”

“I’m not desperate,” Kiyo insisted.

“You’re something.”

Glaring out the passenger-side window as they sped along the motorway away from Heathrow Airport, Kiyo considered this. It would be a lie to suggest he wasn’t feeling something. “I’m annoyed,” he admitted. “I should have realized what she was planning.”

“Why?”

“What?”

“Why should you have realized?”

Kiyo looked at the alpha. “It’s my job.”

Conall gave a slight shake of his head. “It’s more than that. You think you missed something.”

Damn it, the wolf *was* intuitive. Kiyo thought on the night before with Niamh, going over every inch of their interaction. And there it was. In among everything. The thing that bothered him most. “After her vision … she asked me … well, something personal. Something she’d been plaguing me with almost from the moment we met. I won’t get into what. But she asked again after her vision, and there was something in her expression when I didn’t give her the answer she wanted.”

“What?”

Kiyo shook his head. “Nothing,” he answered, realizing what this sounded like. “It’s nothing. I’m looking for answers out of nothing.”

"I doubt it." Conall glanced quickly at him before looking back at the road. "I can guess what you saw."

He almost rolled his eyes. "Now you're clairvoyant too?"

The alpha let out a low rumble of a growl, but it was tinged with amusement. "Thea would call me wise, not clairvoyant."

"Are you sure you're not using Thea as an excuse to hide the fact that you have an ego the size of Scotland?"

Conall gave a bark of laughter. "Thea would say so."

The wolf was mate-whipped. Kiyo had come across a pair of true mates decades ago, but he'd forgotten how insufferable they could be until Fionn and Rose crossed his path. And now this alpha. A veritable legend among his species. And he was practically bubbling with contentment and happiness, like an oversized pup, all because of a supernatural mating bond that had shattered his freedom.

Not that Kiyo dared voice that out loud. Even if Kiyo was the stronger of the two of them, he was sure Conall MacLennan could turn lethal in seconds, and he owed Caelan more than to bait or belittle his son.

"You broke her trust," Conall said abruptly. "Niamh. That's what you saw in her expression."

"How could I break her trust when I've never had it?"

"Then that's your problem. Niamh will continue to run from you if she doesnae trust you or think she has your trust in return."

"She doesn't have my trust."

The alpha sighed heavily. "Then you'll never have her. Niamh will always escape you. And the ... failure, you feel"—he said the word *failure* like he wanted to exchange it for another word entirely—"will only grow worse over time."

Silence fell between them. Silence Kiyo was grateful for as his agitation grew. He'd thought that was the end of the discussion. Little was said between them as Conall followed Niamh's scent.

Sure enough, around an hour into their car journey, Conall grunted, "Dover. Her scent is taking us to cross the water for Calais."

"France, then?"

He nodded. "Aye. She doesnae feel far from Calais." He glanced at Kiyo. "Ferry or tunnel?"

Conall referred to the Channel Tunnel that connected Britain to mainland Europe. Kiyo had never used the tunnel before. Apparently, you drove your car onto the Eurotunnel shuttle and it only took around forty minutes to get to France.

"Tunnel. It's faster."

The half-hour journey to Folkestone for the Eurotunnel was quick, and they were only another twenty minutes boarding a shuttle. Inside the brightly lit space, Conall pulled the Land Rover to a stop behind the vehicle in front and cut the engine.

For some reason, now that they'd stopped, the silence felt awkward.

As much as it was against his nature to converse easily, Conall was doing Kiyo a favor, and he didn't want to seem like an ungrateful dickhead. "I appreciate this."

"No problem. We owe Niamh a debt. And Thea worries about her. Especially now that her brother has been killed."

Ronan's death was the reason Niamh was as unpredictable as she was. Kiyo was sure of it. But he didn't know how to deal with it without digging himself deeper into Niamh's life and confidence.

"How do you know Fionn?"

Kiyo glanced at Conall. "We met at an underground fight."

"Aye, I've heard of those. They can be quite brutal."

"No more brutal than an Alpha challenge." He flicked a hand to Conall's face, indicating his scar.

He gave a lift of his chin in acknowledgment of the comment. "Do you have any?"

"Silver scars?"

"Aye."

Kiyo nodded and lifted his shirt to reveal the long scar across his abdomen. "A werewolf hunter. Rogue. Not one of the dark hunters from the Consortium."

"Human?"

"Yeah. Had a prejudice against wolves."

"I hope you taught him a lesson."

"*She*," Kiyo replied with a wry smirk. "I thought she was just an attractive human eager for sex. I smelled her arousal. I had no reason to be suspicious. So she caught me unaware ... and *she* taught *me* a very valuable lesson."

"You don't trust women," Conall responded.

"I don't trust anyone." Well, except Fionn. A little.

"Lone wolves often feel that way."

Kiyo curled his lip at the condescending assumption, but out of respect for Caelan and Lennox, he held his tongue and stared broodingly out of the car at ... nothing. The ferry would have been longer, but at least there was water and sky to look at.

Twenty-five minutes passed.

No words spoken between them.

And then, "My father had a photograph. It was of him and my grandfather with a friend of the pack. A Japanese American lone werewolf. It was taken almost thirty years before I was born. My father was barely eighteen and he wouldn't fall in love with my mother until twenty years after this photograph was taken."

Kiyo held still, willing his pulse not to race and give the alpha, with his exceptional hearing, knowledge of his anxiety. It was a trick Kiyo had learned years ago.

"I remember my father's stories of the Japanese wolf. He admired him. Looked up to him. I think it disappointed him that the wolf never returned to visit the pack. He would take out that photograph and tell me of Kiyonari. A brooding, quiet, noble, honorable, cold son of a bitch, with a quick sense of humor, a deep admiration for the Highlands, and natural loyalty that not even his lone status could diminish."

Now Kiyo struggled to slow his breathing as a strange feeling of emotion and nostalgia filled him.

"I'd recognize you anywhere." Conall's gaze burned into his profile and not to face him would be cowardly.

Their eyes met.

"Fionn Mór wouldnae entrust Niamh to an ordinary wolf. And

the energy emanating from you is … different. I remember my father speaking of that as well." Conall's eyes narrowed. "Wolves live for a long time and age slower than humans, but I know of no wolf who looks exactly as they did sixty years before."

Damn it. Was everyone to know what he was? He glared at Conall. "You know nothing."

"I suspect you're immortal. I have no idea how … but you're no ordinary werewolf."

"And what do you want for your silence?"

Conall raised an imperious eyebrow. "You would dishonor me with such a question? Do you not remember your time with the MacLennans?"

Kiyo exhaled slowly, looking away. "I've lived a long time with very few people guessing what I am. It's irritating that Fionn, Rose, and Bran know. Now you too. I don't like people knowing my business."

"Obviously. I'll tell no one. Not even Thea. As long as you protect Niamh, you have my loyalty. You have it anyway … for saving my father's life."

They shared a tense look, and seeing the sincerity in Conall's gaze, Kiyo offered him a nod.

"Is this what Niamh asked of you? The personal thing she wanted to know and you wouldnae tell her?"

Aggravated by the renewal of that conversation, Kiyo cut him a dark look.

Conall grinned. "It was. Bloody fae woman sensed it."

"Yes. She sensed it."

"Then why not tell her the truth of what you are?"

"Are you kidding?" Kiyo stared at him like he was dim-witted. "The fewer people who know, the better."

"I dinnae know the whole truth. Your story. Niamh doesnae need to know either. Just tell her the part about your immortality. Although I must say, I cannae imagine how that came about." Curiosity glinted in Conall's eyes. "It must be an interesting story."

Interesting.

Not the adjective Kiyo would use.

"Just tell her that. Tell her something. You know what Niamh is. That knowledge is dangerous in the wrong hands. So whether you think Niamh trusts you or not, she has to at least trust that you willnae betray the secret of her identity. All the lass is probably looking for is some sign that by offering her knowledge of *your* identity, her trust in you is not misplaced."

Letting Conall's advice sink in, Kiyo had to admit that the alpha made sense. He'd never thought about it that way.

"And you think she'll stop running from me?"

"I think there's a far greater chance of it, aye."

"Then I'll consider your advice."

Conall smirked. "You do that."

10

Saint Denis, Paris

It had become a habit to stand in front of the mirror and look.

No, not look, Niamh thought. Look suggested vanity.

Search.

She was searching.

Who are you?

She glanced over the muddy-brown hair she'd piled on top of her head, tendrils falling around her face. She fingered a brown lock, remembering the light blond color that hid beneath it. With the touch, a memory flooded her, so sharp and clear it felt like it happened only yesterday ...

NIAMH HUDDLED ON THE BED, her arms wrapped tight around her small knees as she stared hard at the crack beneath the bedroom door. Light spilled through it from the hallway. Everything had been good for a while.

And things had been awful for ages before that, so Niamh had been grateful for the good.

When Mam died, she and Ronan had been sent to live in a group home. She'd hated it. It was hard to keep the strange things that happened to her under wraps when there were lots of other people around. She'd shared a bunk bed with Ronan, but they'd shared a room with four other kids.

Ronan had hated the group home too.

He hated having to watch their backs constantly and cover up Niamh's weird behavior.

But then things got better when Siobhan came into their lives. Siobhan knew what it was like to lose her mam. And her dad. They left her lots of money so she didn't have to work. Instead she decided to foster kids. Her house was four times the size of the old flat they'd lived in with Mam. When they'd first come to live with Siobhan, she was fostering a baby girl named Shannon. But three months later, Shannon got adopted. Niamh was sad. She'd grown attached to the little thing. For a blissful six weeks, however, Niamh and Ronan had Siobhan's undivided attention.

She was the best. And because she didn't work, she could give them more attention than even Mam had.

The strange part was that in all that time, nothing weird happened with Niamh. It was like being in such a safe place made all the weird stuff stop. Ronan was over the moon.

Then Joe arrived to stay with them, too, but he was only thirteen months old, and as busy as he kept Siobhan, she still had time for them.

They'd started attending a really nice school, small classes, and the kids weren't too bad. A few were a bit snobby, but nothing Niamh couldn't handle. Ronan was two years ahead of her, and now that she wasn't using any powers or getting any visions, he wasn't hovering so much. Niamh couldn't decide if she liked it or not.

She hadn't liked sleeping in separate rooms.

Back when Mam was alive, Niamh and Ronan shared a room in their tiny two-bedroom flat. Living at Siobhan's was the first time Niamh had slept alone. It had taken weeks for her to get used to it, but she didn't want to be a baby, and Ronan was fourteen now. She knew he needed his space. And eventually she liked having her own space too. Especially once her period started. She was glad she didn't have her big brother around when that first happened two months ago.

She was kind of surprised it did. Part of her wondered if her body would work the same way as a human's. In that respect it did, which Niamh thought was pretty rubbish, actually. Surely being a magical creature from another world should have come with perks like not having a period?!

Siobhan had been really nice about it, though. Siobhan was nice about everything.

Yeah. It had all been grand. Until now.

Niamh's heart raced as her eyes stayed trained on the crack of light beneath the door.

About a month ago, Siobhan started bringing Miller around. They knew she'd been dating someone because every Friday, either Ronan babysat them or if he was out with his friends, Siobhan got a babysitter so she could attend these dates.

Then, after two months of dating the guy, she decided it was serious enough to introduce him to them.

Niamh had gotten a bad feeling off Miller from the moment they'd met.

He was overly affectionate with Siobhan in front of them, always kissing her, petting her, pressing his lips to her neck or patting her arse, and Niamh thought it was a bit much, considering they didn't know him. Ronan had commented on how much he didn't like it either.

But it wasn't just that. It was the way he looked at Niamh when he didn't think anyone was watching. And he winked at her a lot.

Yet nothing was worse than the last week. He'd started touching Niamh. Nothing terrible at first. Placing a hand on her shoulder when he asked her something. Then on her lower back, when he sidled up to talk to her in the kitchen.

Then brushing his fingers through her hair when they were alone, telling her what beautiful hair she had.

Stroking her knee when he sat down on the couch beside her and Siobhan was in the kitchen feeding little Joe. Telling her what gorgeous legs she had.

Hot looks and compliments that Niamh understood too well. She'd always known things other girls her age didn't know. Born with the sight,

Ronan said. She'd seen things someone her age shouldn't have seen, understood things about human and not-so-human nature that had chipped at her innocence. Or hammered away at it, really.

And she knew that Miller was after what was left of her innocence. She knew because anytime Niamh felt danger, the hair on her neck rose. Her pulse raced. Dread filled her tummy.

Since as long as she could remember, she'd had a sixth sense for danger and understood exactly what all those feelings meant.

And this evening, when Miller came over for dinner, her whole being went into high alert.

Looking into his eyes, she knew. Whatever sickness was inside of him, he couldn't hold it back any longer and he was planning to hurt her.

Niamh didn't know what to do.

She loved Siobhan.

And Ronan was happy. Finally happy.

Niamh didn't want to ruin anything.

Perhaps she could deal with it herself and no one would ever know. She'd give Miller a fright and he wouldn't want to speak of—

A shadow flickered across the crack of light beneath her door. Niamh's pulse throbbed and she could barely hear a thing over the rushing of blood in her ears. Energy crackled around her and she felt it tingling on her fingertips, even her toes.

The doorknob turned.

Chest heaving, arms tightening around her knees, she watched as the door opened inward without a sound and then closed behind the tall figure as he stepped inside. She could see him looking at her in the dark. He wouldn't know how clearly she could see him. Niamh had excellent night vision. He had sweat on his upper lip, and he was breathing too heavily.

He moved quietly toward her.

"I'll scream."

"What for?" he whispered as he lowered himself onto the bed. He reached out and placed a hand on her knee and everything within Niamh revulsed. "I'm not going to hurt you, little one."

Lies.

"I just want to make you feel good."

And then he lunged, covering her mouth with his hand as he attempted to push her small body beneath his.

He grunted as Niamh resisted, stronger than any human twelve-year-old could ever be.

And something dark flickered inside her.

Something foreign to who she was.

Something angry and vengeful.

Because she couldn't imagine she was the only child he'd tried this with. Had he succeeded with others?

The thought turned the rage to a flame and as they grappled, the energy tingling through Niamh's extremities grew hotter and hotter and hotter—

Miller hissed in agony and scrambled off her, staring at his hands in horror.

Niamh did too.

His fingertips glowed like golden fire ... and then they just ...

The golden fire chased black ash, and the ash began to crumble. His finger, palms, wrists, arms all crumbling to dust.

Niamh gaped at his face and watched as it cracked and blackened and caved in on itself.

Until there was nothing left but a pile of ash on the bed and floor.

Skittering away from it, Niamh fell off the other side of the bed. Sickness swarmed from her gut and she threw up on the carpet, heaving until there was nothing left.

Sensing someone's presence, Niamh looked up and saw her brother standing in the light spill from the open door.

His attention swung between her and the ash.

"What happened?" His eyes blazed fiercely.

"Miller," she replied, falling back on her rump. Tears spilled in hot rivers down her cheeks. "He tried to hurt me."

Ronan skirted the vomit and kneeled beside her, pushing her hair off her face. He looked murderous. "What did he do? Where is he?"

"He was going to hurt *me, Ronan."*

"I had a bloody awful feeling about him," he choked out. "It woke me up. I'm sorry, Nee. I should have said something sooner. Did you hurt him *instead?"*

Her lips parted to speak but she couldn't quite say it out loud. Instead she stood and Ronan put his arms around her, holding her. She pointed to the ash on the bed.

She felt her brother stiffen. "Nee?"

She sobbed, trying to muffle the sound so she wouldn't waken Siobhan. "I didn't mean it," she gasped softly. "I don't know how I did it. It just happened."

Her brother released his hold on her, stumbling toward the bed to stare closer at the ash. "Are you saying ... you incinerated him?"

Nausea rolled through her again. "I didn't mean it."

Ronan stared back at her. And for the first time, she saw fear in his eyes.

It made her cry harder.

"Shh, Nee." He patted her shoulder tentatively.

He was afraid of her.

"We have to go." He ducked his head to hers to meet her eyes. The fear hid behind panic. "No one can know. They'll take you away."

"Maybe they should."

Anger clouded his features. "Don't ever say that. This was self-defense, Nee. The bastard was a sick fuck. You hear me?"

She nodded quickly.

"Okay. Pack a bag. Quietly. Pack only what you need."

"But what about Siobhan?"

Sadness flickered across his face. "She can't protect you."

"But how—"

"Just pack a bag and meet me at the front door." He darted out of the room.

Niamh stared at the ash.

They couldn't leave it there. It was evidence.

As easily as the horrible magic had come to her to defend herself against Miller, it didn't come so easily as she tried to open the window with it. Ronan didn't want her using it a lot, so she was out of practice.

And exhausted from what had just happened.

Sending her energy like powerful arms and nimble hands toward the window, she pushed down the handle and watched it open silently.

Then, with a flick of her hand toward the ash, it swirled into the air like a cyclone, the room sparking with the electricity of her magic. With an aggressive thrust of her hand, the ash cyclone swept out of the room, through the window, and out into the night sky.

Trembling with weariness, Niamh used what little energy she had to locate the things she needed without moving from the spot. Then she used her magic to clean up the vomit, tidy her bed, and teleport downstairs.

Ronan was already at the front door and he jumped a mile when she popped out of thin air.

He surprised her by saying, "You probably should practice."

"Why?"

"Because a fourteen-and twelve-year-old won't survive out there without magic."

His words followed Niamh as they disappeared out of the nice house on the nice street in the nice neighborhood. She ached for Siobhan, and her mind railed against the truth.

She'd killed a man.

She didn't deserve nice.

A touch of darkness had bled into her soul.

"Don't feel guilty," Ronan had lectured her a few days later as they sat in the first-class carriage of a train heading for mainland Europe. Niamh had used her ability to trick humans into seeing whatever she wanted them to see to get them on the train without passports. When she accidentally did it to her mam the first time, her mam was so angry, she made Niamh vow never to do it again.

Ronan wanted her to use it all the time now.

"We need to survive. And that's what you did back at Siobhan's. You survived."

"They're looking for us."

It was all over the news back in Cork. They thought Miller had kidnapped them.

"Aye, well, that's why you should do something about your hair." Ronan gestured to her long, light blond hair. She didn't know where it came from. Although she and Ronan shared the same green-blue eyes, he had brown hair. Just like their mam. They didn't remember their dad. He left before

Niamh was born. Mam had said he was a loser, anyway. But she also said he didn't have blond hair. No one in her family had blond hair like Niamh's.

"I don't want to dye it," she said petulantly.

"Dye it, cut it," he insisted. "And stop dressing like a fairy princess."

"But I am a faerie," she teased, trying to break the tension between them.

Ronan scowled. When she was younger and she first started spouting stories about Faerie, her mam and Ronan thought she just had a wild imagination. As she got older and her powers started to present themselves, Ronan at least began to believe Niamh was one of the fae. She explained about the Faerie Queen's spell that had brought about Niamh's existence in the human world along with six other fae children, but Mam insisted it was nonsense.

"I gave birth to you!" she yelled in exasperation on Niamh's tenth birthday. "I remember the bloody pain! I'm your mother, and stop saying otherwise, you ungrateful shit, or they'll put you in the nuthouse!"

It was the nastiest thing her mam had ever said to her. She hurt any time she thought of her mam and how one day she was alive, and the next, she was gone. And they'd never really known each other. While Niamh and Ronan had an unbreakable bond, Niamh and her mam had never forged one. Ronan was close to Mam. Her death hit him the hardest.

It hit Niamh hard for a different reason. She'd always thought that one day, her mam would eventually believe her, and the bond would grow between them.

They never got the chance.

"Don't say that stuff out loud," Ronan reprimanded her. "And from now on, stop dressing in a way that will get attention and dye and cut your bloody hair," he repeated. "We need to move around without being noticed."

But Niamh refused.

In her vanity, she refused.

"You're going to get me killed," her brother said in exasperation.

Niamh blinked rapidly, coming out of her memories.

"You're going to get me killed, Nee."

How many times had Ronan said that?

And she'd just taken it for granted that she'd be able to protect him.

"I couldn't even dye my bloody hair for him," she muttered angrily.

Turning from the mirror, Niamh strolled into the sitting room of the small apartment in the shitty neighborhood.

A small blond was huddled in the corner.

Lights of gold encircled her wrists and ankles, holding her in place.

She'd never used such magic before. Every day, Niamh learned something new about her capabilities.

She'd also used her magic to silence the witch. She couldn't bear her nonsensical pleading: *"It wasn't me. She made me. She made us."* Assuming she referred to the leader of the O'Connor Coven who'd led the charge that day, Niamh didn't want to hear it. An adult was responsible for their own decisions.

When she'd hunted Meghan O'Connor down to a café in Sèvres, she'd waited until the witch left the café and followed her. The entire time, Niamh had felt like she was being watched, as though someone was following *her* following the witch. The sensation made her fear that Kiyo had, by some miracle, found her. But when she glanced behind and all around, there was no one there, and she needed to focus.

So she abandoned the feeling with reckless pursuit. Meghan entered a park and as soon as they were alone, Niamh *traveled* until she was right behind her and hit her carotid with energy until Meghan passed out. She *traveled* to her rental car, the witch in tow, and drove thirty minutes north to the shithole neighborhood she'd chosen to carry out the murderous deed.

When a neighbor came out of her apartment as Niamh easily carried Meghan's limp body upstairs, she'd made an amused, casual remark in muddled French about her girlfriend not being able to day drink. The neighbor just shrugged and pushed past them.

Niamh stared at the terrified O'Connor witch.

She should have just killed her in the park.

Why was she drawing it out like this?

Who are you?

Her conscience sounded like Kiyo again.

Please, please don't hurt me.

She flinched, remembering Meghan's pleas when she'd first gained consciousness hours before.

Do you know who I am?

The witch had shaken her head.

Your coven murdered my brother trying to take down Rose Kelly.

Meghan's eyes widened with recognition. *I remember you. You threw me out the window.*

You survived. Ronan didn't. Your coven murdered him.

I'm sorry. It wasn't me. She made me do it. I'm sorry.

Me too.

Niamh glared at the witch now. *I'm so sorry, Ronan.*

11

As Conall slowed the rental car to a stop, Kiyo scowled at their surroundings. The neighborhood was one big dumpster fire. Between buildings was garbage and piles of discarded junk. Old, stained mattresses were stacked next to an ancient, rusted-out washing machine, flanked by rotten pallets and black garbage bags long decimated by vermin.

The buildings themselves were old and run-down. Some were covered in graffiti. Washing hung out of the windows of apartments on the upper floors while plywood had been nailed across windows on the lower floors.

It was the exact kind of place he'd choose to hide out if he'd, say, kidnapped a fae woman or was planning on hurting someone. What was Niamh doing? His gut knotted.

"This car might not sit here too long," Kiyo observed grimly, trying to hide his anxiety.

"Aye." Conall shot Kiyo an equally grim look. "This is a side of Paris I've never seen before."

"Every city has places like this. No matter how beautiful the rest of it is."

"Even the Highlands has places like this," Conall agreed as he pushed open the driver's-side door. "If the world existed as a wolf pack does, wealth would be distributed equally, and no place on earth would look or feel like this."

If he wasn't so concerned about tracking down Niamh, Kiyo might have smirked at the wolf's idealism. Conall had apparently inherited it from his grandfather who could wax lyrical for hours on the advantages of pack life. And Kiyo had to admit, one of the things he'd admired most about Clan MacLennan and its chief was that everyone within the pack was provided with a pack stipend. No one would ever go without in their pack.

Following Conall out onto the sidewalk, Kiyo caught sight of two men farther down the street, leaning against an apartment building, staring at them. Or at the car.

He stared defiantly back, emitting as much alpha energy as he could and watched in satisfaction as the two men not only averted their gaze but hurried away in the opposite direction.

"You'd make quite the leader if you ever fancied creating your own pack," Conall said.

He turned to find Conall watching him with a glint of admiration. Kiyo cocked an eyebrow.

"Your energy," Conall explained. "I didn't expect it, and it almost took me to my knees."

"But didn't."

The Scot grinned. "Not once I fought it off with my own."

He gave him a distracted nod. "Where is Niamh?"

Conall's smile disappeared. He lifted his chin toward the building behind him. The one with the mattresses and other used shit spilled out on its "lawn." They hurried toward it and found the entrance system broken. The building door swung open easily.

"Up here," Conall said in a low voice.

Kiyo had to admit, he was envious of Conall's tracking ability. It guided them to an apartment door on the third floor. Kiyo knew it was accurate because he could smell Niamh. He smelled that spicy-sweet scent of hers in the tight, graffiti-covered stairwell, and it grew stronger the closer they got to the apartment.

Something like nervousness twisted his gut, which made as much sense as his anxiousness. Kiyo was never nervous or anxious.

What the hell was happening to him?

And what the hell was happening to Niamh?

His urgency and worry overpowered that twist in his gut, and he grabbed the door handle and yanked until it broke. He and Conall moved into the apartment at speed and came to an abrupt halt at what they found in the small space.

Kiyo stared at Niamh, vaguely aware of Conall closing the apartment door behind them.

Niamh was huddled in the corner of the sparsely furnished room, her arms tight around her knees. Her cheeks were pale and tear streaked, her eyes huge in her face and filled with the kind of grief and pain that cut through Kiyo like a katana.

"Kiyo." Conall's voice stopped him just before he moved to go to her.

He glanced back at the alpha. Conall gestured to the wall adjacent.

Kiyo followed his gaze and found a small blond woman. Her back was pressed against the wall, her own face saturated with fear. His eyes narrowed at the sight of the gold rings that encircled the blond's wrists and ankles. He'd never seen anything like it. The rings were made from light. Golden light.

Fae magic.

His eyes flew to Niamh. "Who is she?"

Niamh shook her head in despair.

He took a tentative step toward her. "Did you do that? The magical restraints?"

She nodded slowly.

Kiyo looked back at Conall who stayed where he was, guarding the exit. "Have you seen anything like that?"

"The restraints? No." He shook his head, his attention moving to Niamh. "My mate had no idea what she was, had barely tapped into her potential before the change. It seems Niamh has had more practice."

Niamh looked at Conall but immediately refocused on Kiyo.

He took another step toward her. "Who is the woman?"

Her haunted eyes filled with fresh tears, and Kiyo was done. He hurried across the room and lowered himself in front of her.

"Niamh," he said, his voice soft, coaxing. "Tell me what's going on. Let me help."

"She"—the word croaked and cracked, causing Niamh to swallow hard and try again—"Meghan ... Her coven killed my brother."

This was vengeance.

"I thought they were all dead." Her grief-stricken gaze moved toward the woman behind him. "But that night at the hotel in Kalmar, I had a vision of her. Alive. Here in Paris." She looked back at Kiyo, seeming to plead with him. "All those visions of bad people, all the justice I mete out. How could I ignore this one when it's the most important?"

He lowered a knee to the floor and moved closer, his hand covering hers as it rested on her knee. "Then why is she still alive? And why are you balled up in a corner like this?"

"I'm taking my time," she said in an almost comically petulant tone.

"You're procrastinating."

"I'm going to do it. Ronan deserves justice."

His hand tightened over hers. "This isn't justice, Niamh. This is vengeance. Trust me. I know the difference."

"Whatever word you want to give it, I owe this to my brother."

Kiyo recognized guilt when he saw it. "You're not to blame for Ronan's death."

The surrounding air crackled dangerously.

"Kiyo," Conall warned.

Niamh glared at him. "I never said I was."

Denial.

Great.

"Niamh. Let the witch go, and you and I can get the hell out of this shithole."

Her eyes lowered and she shook her head.

Frustration churned in his gut.

"Kiyo ..." Conall's voice came at him again.

And this time he understood why. The alpha's words of wisdom regarding trust filtered through his mind. With a heavy sigh of discomfort, Kiyo moved to sit beside Niamh, his back pressed against the wall, the side of his body touching hers. He looked at her profile, taking in the pert nose that turned up a little at the end, the wide cheekbones, and the spiky, long lashes wet with tears.

Something tightened in his chest.

Agitation thrummed through him, but he called on the self-control he took much pride in and cleared his throat. He had a job to do and apparently making himself vulnerable was going to be part of that job.

"You don't want to do this, Niamh. I told you before that deciding who lives and dies is too big a judgment to lay on your shoulders. It's not up to you, and it shouldn't be."

She stiffened next to him but he pushed on. "It's not who you are. There's too much darkness in it. The line has been blurred between vengeance and justice in everything you've been doing these last few months. But this"—he gestured to the witch—"this is vengeance, pure and simple."

"It doesn't matter. Nothing matters."

"Your soul matters," he said gruffly.

Her head whipped toward him, her eyes wide with surprise.

"You told me I should be grateful that your greatest gift was your kindness, your compassion. What you really meant was that I should be grateful your humanity was your greatest gift."

Niamh's beautiful eyes glistened once more.

He wanted to reach out and catch the tear that escaped but instead, he clenched his hand into a fist and held back. "You were right about me," he confessed. "I'm more than I seem. I'm ..." He exhaled slowly, disbelieving he was going to say the words out loud when he never had before. "I'm immortal."

She seemed surprised, but he didn't know if it was the nature of the confession or the confession itself.

"I was born in Osaka in the winter of 1872."

Her eyes searched his face, curiosity bright in them.

"I've lived a long time, Niamh, and I personally understand vengeance." He ducked his head toward her, inhaling her scent, and his fist unfurled with a life of its own. He found himself cradling her face with his hand, sweeping his thumb down her cheek in a tender gesture he didn't know he still had in him. "Trust me when I tell you that once you have your vengeance ... there's nothing but emptiness at the end of it. It took everything from me. I don't want that for you."

Fresh tears spilled down her freckled cheeks as she wrapped her hand around his wrist and squeezed gently. "Okay," she whispered.

Relief moved through him. She capitulated so quickly that he knew she was just waiting for someone to talk her down. This wasn't who she was. He stroked her cheek one last time and then moved to stand, pulling her up with him. He studied her as she seemed to gather herself, throwing her shoulders back as she turned to look at the witch.

Conall gave him a nod of respect, which he appreciated considering how goddamn exposed he felt right then.

Then Niamh flicked her wrist and the golden light encircling the witch's wrists and ankles disappeared.

"It wasn't me," Meghan said, her eyes wild. "It wasn't us. She made us do it."

Ignoring the witch's stressed babbling, Kiyo turned to Niamh. "You're doing the right thing."

"I don't think I know what the right thing is anymore, and that scares me. It should scare everyone."

"I'm not afraid," he promised her. "Everyone, no matter how good they are, can be taken to the edge of darkness. Pain has a way of doing that. But you'll never cross that line, Niamh. It's not who you are."

"You're so sure?"

"I know dark when I see it. You're not it."

A groan of agony caused the hair to rise on the back of Kiyo's neck, and he and Niamh jerked toward Conall, who had fallen to one knee, his hand clutching his chest. His eyes flew to Meghan, whose whole being seemed to crackle with electricity.

Something like fear for Conall flooded him, and he crossed the room to protect him just as the silvery gray weapon appeared in the witch's hand.

A dagger.

An iron dagger.

His gaze flew back to Niamh, who seemed momentarily paralyzed with shock at the sudden turn of events.

The dagger flew across the room, crackling with magic as it headed directly toward Niamh's heart.

A roar of outrage escaped him as he sped back toward Niamh, a blur of movement as he threw himself in front of her. Pain blazed through his chest, taking his feet out from under him.

The iron dagger was embedded in his heart.

NIAMH GAPED in horror at the sight of Kiyo falling to the floor with the dagger lodged in his chest. Fury at the witch and at herself for stalling burned within her as she felt her eyes bleed gold.

Meghan paled but reached out a hand toward Conall, the magic sparking the air as she tried to use him as her coven had used Ronan.

As Niamh moved toward Meghan, Conall bellowed at Niamh to see to Kiyo just as Conall transformed into a black wolf. He lunged at the witch. Stunned, Niamh could only stare for a second. She had never seen a wolf transform that fast before. As his wide jaw opened, his sharp teeth glittering in the dull light of the apartment, Niamh fell to her knees to help Kiyo.

She flinched, feeling somewhat sick at the sound of Conall tearing apart their foe, screaming in torment. Niamh ignored it and turned Kiyo gently onto his back.

He hissed, his handsome face contorted with pain. "Just ... yank ... it out."

"Are you sure?"

He nodded.

Trusting him, Niamh conjured thick gloves to cover her hands. She then wrapped them around the dagger's hilt and shuddered as a feeling of utter lethargy crawled through her. Fighting the sensation, she gave the dagger an abrupt, quick jerk.

Kiyo convulsed, falling to his side to vomit up blood.

"Kiyo!" she cried in fright. Perhaps being immortal didn't mean he couldn't be killed like her. Maybe it was just a spell of long life, not invincibility. "The dagger." Her hands shook as she brought it to her wrist. "My blood can heal you."

He turned with a fierce abruptness that surprised her, wrapping his hand around her wrist that held the dagger. His lips and chin were smeared with blood. "Don't," he choked out. "I'm healing, I'm healing. Don't."

Reassured he would be okay, Niamh discarded the dagger and the gloves, using her magic to send them away from her.

"He's all right?" The deep voice brought her head from studying Kiyo whose color was returning by the second.

Niamh stared at the huge werewolf that towered over them and almost blushed. He was naked. Her eyes moved behind him to where his clothes were tattered across the room. Her gaze snagged on a limp female hand.

"Dinnae look." Conall caught her chin and pulled her head up gently to meet his eyes. "I'm afraid the pain she inflicted caused me to lose control over the wolf for a few moments." Remorse flickered across his face.

Niamh gave him a sympathetic look. "It's okay. You did what you had to do to protect us."

He nodded grimly, and Niamh became all too aware again of his nakedness.

Lucky, lucky Thea.

However, sensing Thea wouldn't be happy at the thought of her mate flaunting his rather impressively beautiful body in front of another female, Niamh flourished a hand in his direction and clothed him.

He jerked in surprise to find himself fully outfitted in a T-shirt, jeans, and boots that fit perfectly. He threw Niamh a bemused look.

"Sorry. Should have warned you," Niamh said wryly.

Conall let out a weary, bitter laugh.

Niamh didn't know him well, but she could tell he was extremely upset about Meghan.

"I'm sorry," she said and then looked at Kiyo as he pulled himself up to sit. Guilt irritated her. When she'd left, Kiyo had obviously contacted Bran or Fionn who had put him in touch with Conall. With the alpha's tracking gift, it was no wonder Kiyo had found her so quickly. "I'm sorry for putting you both in this position."

"It's my job," Kiyo reminded her.

She glanced down at the slice in his shirt.

He'd thrown himself in front of her to save her life.

Niamh didn't know what to do with that.

She just knew she needed to start trusting him.

Even if she was just a job.

Conall helped Kiyo to his feet and then held out a hand to her. She took it, letting the alpha pull her up. "Because of you, Thea trusted me. And Rose trusted Fionn. We owe you for that."

"You didn't owe me." She shook her head. "But if you did, the debt is paid. I'm sorry, Conall."

"Dinnae be sorry. My debt to you will never be repaid."

Niamh felt a pang of envy. She wondered what it was like to be loved as Conall loved Thea.

"And better the witch than you or I." His piercing gray eyes turned cold with determination, and Niamh realized he'd compartmentalized what happened. This was an alpha who allowed himself only a moment to grieve before moving on.

And he was right.

He'd done what he had to, to protect them.

Niamh held out a hand to him to shake. As soon as he settled his large hand in hers, energy shot from him and into her. Images slammed into her mind, forcing her head back in a jolt of sharp pain.

"Niamh!" She heard Kiyo yell but the images took over.

Warmth flooded through the pain as emotions, beautiful emotions of adoration and protection and laughter, filled her. Years of happiness and family and safety and inclusion. Thousands of days of love that if bottled could change the world for the better.

Quite abruptly, they stopped. Her eyes flew open and she found Conall holding tight to her hand while Kiyo's front was pressed against her back as he held on to her.

"Are you okay?" he asked gruffly, his breath hot on her ear.

She shivered at the feel and scent of him surrounding her but nodded, her eyes locked on Conall's.

"Congratulations," she offered.

Conall frowned.

She squeezed his hand. "Thea's pregnant."

His expression hardened. "You saw?"

Niamh gave him a soft smile. "I saw. I saw much." Tears of happiness for Thea filled her eyes. "You have a beautiful future to look forward to, Alpha MacLennan. Such a beautiful future as I've never seen before."

Kiyo's hold on her eased as Conall's features slackened with surprise ... and then gratitude.

12

The car, to both Kiyo's and Conall's surprise, was still there when they left the building with Niamh. She'd cleaned up the apartment and discarded Meghan's body as she had the man at the airport in Moscow.

Kiyo didn't know how to react to what had happened. For now, he was focused on getting the hell out of Paris.

They drove to the airport in silence. Niamh huddled in the back of the car and quickly fell asleep as Conall drove northwest.

"You did the right thing," Conall said, his voice low so as not to wake her.

"What?"

"Telling her the truth about your immortality."

Kiyo wasn't sure. He wasn't sure about anything at the moment.

"It's a story I'd be interested in hearing one day."

Kiyo smirked. It wasn't a story he was interested in telling.

Conall seemed to understand his silence and didn't take offense. "So, where to now?"

"I need to call Bran. Let him and Fionn know I have Niamh. They'll probably organize safe passage to wherever we need to go next."

"You're following her visions?"

"Yeah. But they seem to be all over the place. It doesn't make sense. Some are about what they've always been about—the other fae-borne and protecting the gate. It seems that since her brother died, the visions have gotten interrupted by others that have led her on this vigilante path. It doesn't make sense to me."

Conall frowned. "No, it doesnae sound right." He glanced in his rearview at Niamh. Kiyo turned to follow the male's gaze, his chest tightening at the sight of her asleep. Exhausted. It took a lot to bring her down. She was wrecked inside.

The job of protecting her, not from others but from herself, felt impossible.

It frustrated him beyond bearing.

And he didn't understand the intensity of the feeling.

"You can do this," Conall said.

Kiyo frowned.

The alpha flicked him a look before turning back to the road. "You know this is bigger than just protecting one fae woman."

Unfortunately, yes.

"But you can do it, Kiyo. Keep her trust, help her. No matter what you have to sacrifice to do it."

Conall's words brought silence to the car as Kiyo pondered exactly what they might mean ... and dreaded the possibilities.

Thankfully, it wasn't a long drive. After waking Niamh, they dropped off the rental and made their way to departures. Conall bought his ticket to Edinburgh, where he'd get a connecting flight to Inverness.

"You call again if you need me," the alpha said, holding out his hand to Kiyo.

Kiyo shook it and found himself saying, "I admired and respected Caelan and Lennox very much. I was sorry to hear of their passing."

Emotion flickered across Conall's face before he cleared it and gave Kiyo a slight nod of thanks.

Kiyo gripped Conall's hand tighter. "You honor their memory, Alpha MacLennan."

Conall's gray eyes turned piercing and he shook Kiyo's hand with a firm fierceness. "Stay safe, Kiyo."

They turned from one another, Conall's eyes alighting on Niamh as she stepped toward him.

"Thank you again." She held out a hand.

He took it, covering hers with both of his and he smiled. "No. Thank you."

Kiyo assumed he referred to Niamh's vision of the bright future he and his mate had ahead of them.

"Give Thea my love," Niamh offered.

"I will. And you have hers. You have our loyalty, Niamh. You know where to find us if ever you need us."

Watching as Niamh fought tears of gratitude, Kiyo felt frustrated. She had no one now. No family. And she wasn't like him. She wasn't built to survive without someone to love. Days ago, he would have sneered at her for the weakness.

Now he felt powerless in the face of her loneliness.

They watched Conall stride through the airport, drawing stares from almost everyone who passed him. He disappeared up the escalators toward security, and Kiyo turned to Niamh.

"We should call Bran."

"Who were Caelan and Lennox?" she replied instead.

Still uncomfortable with Niamh knowing about his curse, he hesitated before replying. "Conall's father and grandfather. I knew them before Conall was born."

To his gratitude, she left it at that.

"Call Bran." She sighed heavily, crossing her arms over her chest. "Our only lead is Tokyo. So let's go there. As safely as we can."

Kiyo nodded, glad to have a plan and to get her the hell out of Paris. Although she was acting calm and collected, there was a strain around her eyes and the color hadn't returned to her cheeks. The problem was *definitely* Niamh's guilt over her brother's death. With that hanging over her head, she was a ticking time bomb, and Kiyo wasn't sure how to broach the subject or if he even should.

Leaving his concerns behind for the moment, Kiyo contacted

Bran and got him up to speed. Minutes later, Bran had checked the security tapes in the airport and cross-checked all passengers logged on flights in and out of Paris in the next few hours with the names of members of the Blackwood Coven and The Garm. No names came up. They seemed to be safe, so Bran booked them on a flight to Tokyo using the false passport information he'd given them back in Sweden.

Kiyo had wandered off a bit to talk to Bran. When he hung up, he collected his and Niamh's tickets from a self-service machine and turned to find her. Niamh leaned against the wall near the entrance doors, her eyes closed. She appeared suddenly very young and lost.

He knew what it was like to lose the one person who kept you anchored. Home wasn't a house or a building somewhere. Home was a person. Kiyo knew that better than anyone. Ronan had been Niamh's home, and without him ... *Tamashii ga nuketa*. She was a lost soul.

Striding toward her, his eyes fixed on her, his pulse leapt when she opened her eyes to meet his gaze. Ignoring the sensation, he slowed to a stop before her and held up the ticket with a wry smirk. "Bran booked us first-class tickets to Tokyo." It had been awhile since Kiyo had traveled first class anywhere. It wasn't that he couldn't afford it; he'd just already been through what he considered the extravagant, indulgent phase of his life in the '80s. He grew bored with it quickly. It wasn't him.

"That was nice of him." She took the proffered ticket. "Did he say anything else?"

"Just that we seem to be safe." He explained Bran's security checks. "Our flight leaves soon but we have time to eat. Why don't we head to the first-class lounge and get something there?"

Niamh nodded docilely and fell into step beside him. He kept looking at her out of the corner of his eyes, worry niggling at him.

She frowned at her feet. "Why did it take you so long to come to the apartment?"

He frowned in return. "Considering the situation, I think Conall and I got there pretty fast."

"But weren't you following me in Sèvres? When I was following Meghan?"

Kiyo drew to a halt. "No, I wasn't."

Niamh stopped with him.

"You were followed?"

She searched his face, his worry reflected in her eyes. "I can't say for sure. But I'm rarely wrong. I felt like I was being followed. I was so focused on the witch and I didn't feel any danger, so I just ignored it. Then when you and Conall showed, I just assumed it had been you following me."

"You didn't feel any danger?"

"None."

Shit. Kiyo did not like mysterious subplots. He glanced around them, searching the crowds for anything out of the ordinary. "You sense anything now?"

"Not at the moment."

"Okay. We keep moving." His expression hardened. "But you tell me if you feel anything like that again. If you feel anything out of the ordinary, I want to know." His head dipped toward her. "You have to trust me, Niamh."

Her eyelashes fluttered at his closeness. "I know. I'm going to try."

Although more than a little annoyed that she needed to *try* considering he'd thrown himself in front of a damn dagger for her, Kiyo merely grunted and continued toward the small security lounge for first-class travelers.

They moved through it quickly. Kiyo had already abandoned his katana in Conall's Defender back in Inverness so he could board the flight to London. Niamh's backpack held only a small amount of cash and her clothes.

Afterward, as they followed signs for the first-class lounge, Kiyo spotted the bookstore and stopped so fast, Niamh collided into him. He felt the brush of her breasts against his biceps just before she pulled back. "What is it?"

He gestured toward the store. "Give me a minute?"

She nodded and followed him inside.

As he perused the English language fiction bestseller list, he spotted the new Stephen King and grabbed a copy without reading the blurb. He moved toward the checkout counter.

"Wait ... you're buying a book to read on the plane?" Niamh asked incredulously.

Kiyo scowled at her over his shoulder. "And?"

"You read?"

"Yeah. I've also been known to use my opposable thumbs."

She chuckled. His lips twitched at the sound, but he had his back to her so she couldn't see.

"I just never took you for a reader." She sidled up beside him as he stepped to the counter to pay for the book.

"You don't really know me," he muttered.

She slipped a book up onto the counter. It was a copy of *Schindler's Ark* by Thomas Keneally. Kiyo had already read that one. He quirked a brow at her. Niamh shrugged, smiling at him. "I've never read it and I like books about history."

He turned to the checkout assistant, ignoring the hint of curiosity in Niamh's tone when she stressed the word *history*. "That one too."

"Thanks."

He flicked Niamh a wary look. "No problem."

For a few seconds Kiyo thought she wasn't going to push it. But as they walked out of the bookstore with books in hand, Niamh shocked the absolute shit out of him.

So how does a werewolf become an immortal?

At the sound of her voice, clear as day in his head, an invasion and not a thought, he staggered to a stop and gaped at her.

She gave him a sheepish smile. *Yeah, I can talk to you like this.*

Grabbing her by the arm, he led her across the airport in quick, long strides until they neared a set of double doors reserved for airport staff only. Kiyo pushed Niamh into the corner, dropping his bag at their feet, so he could cage her in with his arms braced on the wall at either side of her head.

Her cheeks flushed as he glared at her.

"What the hell?" he bit out, not sure how to feel about this latest development.

"Do you want me to keep talking telepathically or is it freaking you out?" Before he could answer, she put her hands lightly on his chest as if in a calming gesture. He looked down at them, wanting to push her off. He didn't want her feeling how hard his heart was racing right now. Her soft words stopped him. "It's useful. When ... Ronan and I were on the run, being able to talk to him like that was useful."

Kiyo frowned, considering that. "Can you hear me if I did the same?"

She shook her head. "No, it doesn't work like that. But it's still useful." She dropped her hands, as if touching him burned. Niamh shrugged and he caught the uncertainty in her expression before she looked away over his shoulder. "I just ... I thought maybe it was time I trusted you with it. It might come in handy."

There was something brittle about her now. As if she half expected him to judge her for it.

"You just surprised me." He pushed away from her. "I can see how it could be useful."

He watched the hard uncertainty melt from her face. Her expression softened, her lips quirking at the corner and drawing his attention.

He looked at her mouth for a few seconds too long. When their eyes met again, Kiyo's whole body bristled with hot tension.

An aching silence stretched between them, and Kiyo didn't know how to break it. He was afraid if he moved or opened his mouth, he'd lose hold of the self-control he prided himself on.

The decision was taken out of his hands when Niamh's eyes widened with shock. "No," she whispered, tears of frustration filling them. "Not again. Kiyo—vision." She bit it out just in time.

With his fast reflexes, he gripped her head just as it jerked back on her neck. If he hadn't caught her, she would've slammed it into the wall with force. Gut churning, Kiyo encircled her and tried to contain her as she convulsed and shuddered in his arms.

He hated this.

He absolutely hated seeing her like this.

And these visions … there seemed to be a lot of them. Too many.

Hoping no one was paying them any attention, Kiyo muttered soothing words in Niamh's ear until her body finally grew still. He held her a few seconds longer, and she didn't make a move to retreat.

Finally, he eased away from her.

Her cheeks were pale again, her expression wounded and frazzled.

"They're happening too often," Kiyo observed.

She nodded wearily. "I started to get more after Ronan … but these past few weeks. When Ronan was alive, I used to only get a vision every few months, sometimes only once or twice a year."

"What does it mean?"

"I don't know." Concern strained her beautiful face. "I don't know."

"What was the vision this time?"

She stiffened beneath his touch, drawing Kiyo's attention to the fact that he still held her. He released her quickly but blocked her path so she couldn't walk away from him.

"Well?"

Niamh stared him directly in the eyes. "There's a child abuser here. At the airport."

Frustration filled him. "No."

"No?"

"Did we not just have this conversation back at the apartment?"

Looking away from him, Niamh sighed. "We did."

"But?"

"It's hard not to do anything about it."

"But you have to. Niamh, what did I say about the darkness?"

Her eyes flew to his, guilt filling them. "I know. I know you're right. But I can do something about evil people like that … and why do I keep getting the visions if I'm not supposed to do something about it?"

He didn't know how to answer that. Instead he focused on

appealing to her common sense. "Every time you veer off the right path, you put yourself in jeopardy. You put the gate in jeopardy. As hard as it is to walk away from these visions, you need to. For the greater good."

"Do you really believe in the greater good?"

Surprised by the question, Kiyo took a step back. "I have to."

"Have to?"

"If I don't ... then what the hell is the point of anything?"

She nodded, understanding. "I want to ignore these visions but I'm afraid of the guilt if I do."

Yeah. Kiyo bet she was. She was carrying enough of that shit around. "Niamh."

She seemed to shiver at the sound of her name on his lips, and Kiyo's body tightened in reaction.

"You don't understand."

"Make me understand." His tone was harsher than he meant.

"This one's personal."

"You know this child abuser?" His gut twisted at the thought.

"No." She shook her head. "But ... the first person I ever killed was one."

His pulse raced at the implications. "Niamh," he whispered her name, sorrow and anger beginning to fill him.

"No," she reassured, pressing her hands to his chest again. "I got away. I was twelve. He was my foster mother's boyfriend. I ..." She broke off, and then her voice was in his head. *I killed him. Accidentally. Just turned him to ash. Ronan found us and we ran. We've been running ever since. We* had *been running ever since ...* As her voice trailed off, she dropped her hands from his chest again and stepped back, her gaze pleading.

Kiyo thought of that sick bastard touching Niamh as a child, and he could find no sympathy or horror for the guy. Everything he felt was for Niamh. Everything he felt ... was too much.

"I get it," he bit out. "But no, Niamh. This has to stop. Every time you answer a vision ... I think you lose yourself a little more."

Tears glittered in her eyes. "I know you're right."

"Come on," he said, his voice gruff as he grabbed his duffle bag with one hand and took hold of her elbow with the other. "Don't think about it. One foot in front of the other. We'll go to the lounge, we'll eat, and then we'll board that plane."

Kiyo wasn't fooled by her sudden docility. He didn't know if it was weariness, confusion, or agreement that caused her to keep up with him, he just knew he wasn't letting his guard down. Any second now, he expected her to try to slip away from him and go after whoever it was she had seen in her vision.

When she suddenly stumbled to a stop, his grip on her tightened. "Niamh," he warned.

She shook her head, pulling at his grip as her eyes darted around them. Searching. "It's not that," she promised. "I feel it again."

"Feel what?"

Uncertainty filled her gaze. "Someone's following me."

13

The creeping, crawling sensation that tingled all over her at the park back in Sèvres had returned as she and Kiyo made their way toward the lounge. Like before, the feeling wasn't accompanied by a sense of danger, but it was still unsettling. She pulled again on Kiyo's grip, and this time he let go. She turned, searching the faces of the people moving through the airport.

"Do you sense anything else?" Kiyo asked at her back. She could feel the heat of him down the length of her body.

"No. I just ..." She frantically searched but the feeling was dissipating. "I don't understand."

"Niamh, if this is a trick—"

She spun on him in indignation. "It's not."

"What the hell is going on, then?" he snapped.

"I don't know, you impatient furball," she snapped back, ignoring the dangerous narrowing of his eyes. "I just know ... someone is here and they're following me. Or they were ..." She trailed off in confusion as she searched their surroundings again. "The feeling is gone. It came as fast as it arrived." A wave of nausea rattled up from her gut, and her eyes flew in horror to Kiyo. Something was wrong. They never came in twos! "Vision," she choked out.

Images slammed into her brain with one painful instruction after another. Four stones. Four faces. Hers. Elijah. Rose. And Astra. Astra. ASTRA. Mount Fuji. Kiyo. A garden. Kiyo. Astra. Astra. ASTRA.

Shuddering as the images faded, Niamh's eyes flickered open. To her shock, she found herself on the cold floor of the airport, huddled against Kiyo as strangers peered down around her in concern.

What the hell? she asked Kiyo in his mind.

His grim face came into clear focus and he bent to whisper in her ear. "Your vision transferred to me. It took me down too. I couldn't hide us."

Well, that was shit on multiple levels.

Exhausted, Niamh was grateful for Kiyo as he helped her to her feet. The people surrounding her included an airport security guard. Questions about her welfare came in several languages.

Calling on all her energy reserves, Niamh took turns looking every single person in the eyes as she assured them she and her friend had merely tripped and they were fine. It took longer than it normally would for the mind manipulation to take hold.

However, eventually it did, and the group wandered off in a daze.

Kiyo's warm, strong hand came down on her shoulder.

She glanced up at him and flinched at his expression.

"What the hell did I just see?"

The urge to divulge the truth was great, but Niamh needed time to gather her thoughts. She was still reeling from what she'd nearly done to Meghan and her awful demise at the hands of a quite rightly pissed-off werewolf. Her head was muddled. And she needed to process the information from the vision before she could talk about it. "Not now."

His expression darkened; he looked angrier than she'd ever seen him. "There's something about me in that vision."

"Did you understand that part?"

He looked incredulous. "You think I would tell you if I did, knowing you don't trust me enough to explain why we're really going to Tokyo? I saved your life."

Remorse flooded her. "I know that. And I'm grateful. But I'm just a job to you, Kiyo. And this ... this is much bigger than you or me. I just need time to process."

"Then why are we going to Tokyo? Why did I feel myself in the vision somehow? How the hell are the visions transferring to me?"

All valid questions.

Niamh's head swam.

"And who the hell is Astra?" At her silence, he exhaled in exasperation. "Whether we like it or not, we are now a team. I'm getting your visions. There's something there about me. If we're going to get through this, we have to trust each other." He stepped closer. "Never mind I took a blade for you ... I have never told anyone what I am."

She frowned in disbelief. "What about Fionn and Bran?"

"They guessed. But even they don't know my story. I told you what I am." He seemed to swallow hard. "That took a lot more than you think."

A flood of emotions filled her. Emotions she didn't quite understand. Emotions that pushed her to clam up when she might not have if he'd just given her bloody time to think! "Kiyo, I'd like nothing more than to have someone I could confide in again. To have someone fighting by my side. But we both know that this"—she gestured between them—"is temporary. I can't give you everything. In fact, I think it's better for me if I give you very little and you do what you're being paid to do."

"Being paid to do?"

"Jumping in front of iron daggers and such." She lowered her gaze, unable to see his expression. "You saved my life because you're being paid to. Let's not pretend it was for any other reason."

A terrible silence fell between them.

Then he practically growled. "That doesn't explain why I'm getting your visions."

"I don't know why. And I need time to ponder it." She pushed past him abruptly, her heart racing and aching at the same time. Niamh was alone. Pretending she wasn't, that Kiyo was something more than a paid bodyguard, was dangerous.

She was *all alone.*

"What about the frequency of the visions?" Kiyo caught up to her, grabbing her elbow to stop her. "Niamh, that can't be good."

No, it wasn't. "That's not your problem. You guard me as we follow the clues."

"It would be easier to do that"—his grip tightened almost painfully—"if I understood the clues."

Niamh lifted her chin in an air of studied arrogance. "You'll understand what I allow you to understand."

Kiyo released her. He searched her face in suspicion. "What just happened? What did you sense in that vision that I'm not getting?"

He was too perceptive for his own good.

Niamh looked away and continued onward more slowly toward the lounge. All she knew was that the game had changed because the players had changed.

Astra was alive.

How she'd tricked Eirik, Niamh didn't know.

But the fae-borne was alive.

And if she was still alive ... the future was more uncertain than ever.

Niamh was quietly panicked that she'd endured one vision after another. Something wasn't right. She could feel the wrongness of it. And she didn't understand why, which was worrying in its own right.

Never mind that when her emotions were particularly high, she seemed to be unwittingly transferring these visions to Kiyo when he was holding her.

She knew he was frustrated and angry with her about not explaining the vision, but she might have eventually done so if he hadn't pushed. Part of her wondered if she'd hurt his feelings by not trusting him after he'd taken that iron blade for her.

Guilt niggled at Niamh.

But then she couldn't think of Kiyo having feelings that could be hurt. She had to remind herself that Fionn was paying Kiyo to protect her. These warm, fuzzy feelings she had toward him ever since he'd taken a dagger to the heart for her had to be quelled immediately. It was bad enough she had a crush on the wolf. Letting those feelings develop into anything deeper for a man who had inexplicably been alive for nearly one hundred and fifty years and had few bonds of friendship to show for it would be a gigantic mistake.

As a bit of an expert brooder, Kiyo seemed only too happy to let the silence fall between them. They ate quietly in the airport lounge as Niamh stewed over her concerns. The latest vision hadn't shown her anything new from the last one. She still only had Tokyo to go on.

And Kiyo.

Somehow he was a part of this new future. She didn't understand why.

But running away from him again wasn't an option. She shouldn't have in the first place.

The thought of Ronan and Meghan made her nauseated, so she threw it from her mind for now to focus on the present. By the time they boarded the plane, Niamh was mentally exhausted. Gratitude toward Bran filled her as a flight attendant led them to the first-class cabin at the front of the plane. They each had a suite in the middle aisle with a connecting window between them. Niamh was surprised Kiyo didn't press the button to close the window to shut her out.

Once they were settled in, a man stopped by her suite to personally introduce himself as the senior flight attendant and welcome her on board. She tried not to blush or flinch when he called her "Ms. Wainwright," the name from the passport Bran had supplied.

She waited until the flight attendant made his way around the cabin, stunned when one man impatiently waved the attendant off and bit out, "Go. Away." That burn in her chest flared as the flight attendant quickly stood and apologized for bothering him.

Knowing how impatient and brooding Kiyo was right now, Niamh tensed when the attendant finally crouched down at Kiyo's side, referring to him as "Mr. Kaneshiro" as he gave him the same speech he'd given her. While not friendly, Kiyo was polite and gave the man his attention. He even thanked him.

She relaxed and decided she really must stop assuming horrible things about him.

Not long later, another attendant appeared to offer them a choice of champagne, orange juice, water, or a mimosa. Niamh gladly accepted a mimosa, ignoring Kiyo's inquiring gaze.

Of course, he took water.

She wondered if he ever indulged in anything ever. Other than sarcasm and fighting.

Determined not to spend the entire flight overly aware of the werewolf, her attention moved to the man who had been rude to the senior flight attendant. Who the bloody hell did he think he was?

Watching him sip his champagne, Niamh gave a flick of her fingers and stifled her laughter as the glass jerked sharply in his hand, causing the champagne to splash all over his face.

A prickling sensation shivered down her neck as she felt a warm breath at her ear. "I saw that," Kiyo's voice rumbled.

She turned her head slightly to find him leaning into her suite.

He was rude to the flight attendant, she answered in his mind.

His lips twitched with amusement, making her stomach flutter. "I know." He gave her a slight shake of his head and settled back into his suite. "Just be careful."

She nodded, not at all chastened, and frowned as he picked up the Stephen King book.

Niamh would never have guessed Kiyo was much of a bookworm, but clearly it was a form of entertainment he favored over the movies or music supplied on the flight. Niamh preferred a good book, too, but right now, she could barely focus on anything. She decided to watch a movie—a new sci-fi flick—hoping it might distract her.

Since they were on an evening flight, they were served a meal early on. It was surprisingly delicious and when the flight attendant returned not long after she'd eaten to ask if she'd like the turndown service (transforming the suite into a sleeping pod), Niamh worried she'd never be able to return to economy travel ever again.

She did like a little luxury in life and flying international first class was bloody nice so far. Using the bathroom to change into the brand-new pajamas supplied by the airline, Niamh thought of Ronan. He'd liked nice things too. They'd traveled first class a lot, but they'd never taken a long enough flight to travel first class like this. Ronan would have loved it.

Tears burned in her eyes and Niamh forced them back. Ignoring her reflection in the mirror, she left the bathroom and returned to her suite to find it was now a bed. She glanced over at Kiyo who had refused turndown.

"You're not going to sleep?"

He glanced up from his book, his gaze moving down her body now clad in soft jersey pajamas that hung too big on her torso but clung to her hips. "Maybe later." He returned to his book.

Summarily dismissed, Niamh tried to ignore the conflicting emotions rioting inside her. She slipped into the bed just as the cabin lights dimmed. Noting Kiyo hadn't turned on his overhead light, she whispered through the window, "You can turn on your light if you want. I can wear the sleep mask." She'd found a bag in her suite with a sleep mask, a pair of socks, lip balm, a toothbrush and toothpaste, a comb, and a mini deodorant in it.

Kiyo didn't look at her. He just whispered back, "Night vision."

Of course. He was a werewolf.

Sighing at his monosyllabic responses, Niamh pulled up the duvet and closed her eyes. Now and then, the plane would bob against the airstream, and the sensation lulled her to sleep.

Ronan's face gleamed through the dark of her subconsciousness until she was falling and falling toward him.

Her feet landed on the ground.

She was back in Munich.

Back in that apartment.

Back where she couldn't save him.

14

Kiyo was aware of every move Niamh made.

To his frustration, he'd had to go back and reread passages in his book because he kept getting lost. It was her fault. He was pissed at her. Really, truly pissed at her. It was better for him to stay silent so he didn't say shit he couldn't take back.

The problem was that he liked her.

Kiyo could admit that.

Niamh had a good heart. She was funny and determined. And he liked her.

Considering he didn't like many people, it was frustrating that she wouldn't confide in him. And it was even more frustrating that even experiencing her vision, he couldn't work out what it meant for himself. There were a few images of Niamh and Rose with a man and a woman who *felt* similar to them. He couldn't explain that feeling, but his common sense told him these two people were fae-borne. Niamh hadn't been lying. This vision was about the bigger picture, about the gate ... so why the hell was Kiyo mixed in with it?

It didn't surprise him that Niamh found sleep so quickly on the plane. She must have been mentally drained. Kiyo heard her breathing relax, telling him she'd found sleep. This allowed him to concentrate fully on his book, and he found himself distracted by the story.

Not long later, however, in the dark, quiet cabin, Kiyo noticed the muted lighting flicker. He didn't think anything of it. Sometimes that happened on flights.

But it happened again.

And again.

Niamh began to whimper.

He leaned over the window between their suites and saw she was shifting restlessly, her lashes fluttering. Small moans escaped between her parted lips.

Then the seat-belt sign pinged above his head, even though there was no turbulence. The senior flight attendant hurried down the aisle past him and disappeared into the cockpit. Kiyo frowned, his sixth sense telling him something was wrong.

He got up out of his seat and casually strolled down the aisle, pricking his wolf ears to hear beyond the cockpit door.

"... no idea. There's no turbulence, no storm, but the instruments are going haywire."

The hair on his neck stood on end and he looked toward Niamh. Glad most of the other passengers were asleep, Kiyo darted around the aisle and toward his companion. The energy radiating from her swarmed him like he'd just hit a cloud of hot air.

It was her.

She was causing the problem with the plane.

Shit.

Leaning into her suite, he gently shook her. "Niamh. Wake up."

An agonized moan fell from her lips.

She was having a nightmare.

Without thought, Kiyo climbed onto the bed, stretching out beside her so he could pull her into his body. He pressed his lips to her ear. "Niamh, wake up. Come on, wake up. Everything's okay."

She shuddered against him and her eyes flew open.

The leaking energy seemed to whoosh back into her like a vacuum.

Turning her head, her eyes widened in confusion to find him lying beside her. "What happened?"

"You were dreaming," he murmured, his grip on her tightening. "You were causing some electrical issues with the plane."

"Oh hell. Is everyone okay?"

Kiyo nodded and settled more comfortably beside her as she turned to face him. Niamh rested her cheek on the pillow, her hands curled up by her chin. She looked young and so very lost, staring into his face with those big, wounded eyes.

"Do you want to tell me what you were dreaming about?"

"Ronan. I dream about the day he died. It gets all muddled up with other stuff. Things that happened in the past."

"What happened to him?"

She released a shaky exhale. "I haven't spoken about it."

"I think that's the problem."

Kiyo thought she wasn't going to respond, but her hushed voice carried between them. "I made us leave Rome because I just had this feeling we needed to be in Munich. And when we got there, I had a vision of Rose. I knew she needed me. Sure enough, we found her running away from Fionn and being chased by The Garm. We took her back to an unoccupied apartment we'd broken into. Unbeknownst to us, Rose's coven was also chasing her and they found us there. I had a vision ..." She broke off, one of her hands curling into a fist beneath her chin. "I saw him die before he did. But it was too late. I told him to run ... but it was too late."

Kiyo released a pained huff. How damn awful to see that and not be able to prevent it. Her vigilante efforts via the visions made a lot more sense.

"The coven did what Meghan tried to do to Conall. They stole Ronan's life force, his energy, to make them more powerful so they could take Rose down." Rage flared gold in her eyes. "They had to know he wasn't enough. That killing him was pointless. I tried ... I tried to give him my blood, but my wound kept closing because I heal so fast and he was too far gone. He just ..."

Kiyo reached out, wrapped his hand around her tight fist. "It wasn't your fault."

"Wasn't it? My very existence is the reason my brother is dead."

"Your brother loved you. He wouldn't have stayed by your side otherwise."

Tears filled her eyes. "That's the worst part. Just hours before he died, I had a thought that I had been having more and more as time went on. Did my brother love me or what my powers could do for him? That's what I thought. That was my ungrateful pondering. And he was killed because of what I am."

A frown puckered Kiyo's brow as he considered this. "You must have thought that for a reason." He caressed her fist with his thumb. "What made you think that?"

She shrugged wearily. "Ronan was the one who talked me into using the gifts to make our lives easy. Stealing. Manipulating people. We were always on the move, but we lived well. He loved the life. He loved what my gifts could give us. And he was overprotective of me. In a way that felt stifling sometimes. Like ... he was afraid if he lost me, he'd lose the life he loved." Guilt filled her expression. "How could I think that of him when he died because of me?"

"Niamh," Kiyo said and moved his head closer to hers, "people are complicated. Nothing is straightforward. We're not all good and we're not all bad. And let me save you from torturing yourself: Your brother wasn't perfect. His death doesn't negate any bad feelings between you, and you're not responsible for those bad feelings. You loved him. He loved you. You both knew that, and that's all that matters."

She lowered her eyes, shaking her head. "You don't understand. You don't understand what I owed him. Or what it's like to not be able to protect the one you love the most and not even be able to take vengeance for him. I'm weak."

His grip on her turned bruising. "No, you're not."

Her eyes flew to his, surprise there, perhaps at his vehemence.

"Niamh, I do know what it's like. More than you can imagine." Kiyo studied her tormented expression, and he knew he'd never be able to protect her if she couldn't let this guilt over her brother go. Fear welled in him as the words he knew she needed to hear climbed toward his tongue. He was about to confide something he'd never told anyone. But Conall was right. This was about the big picture, and to save everyone, Niamh needed to be saved. And apparently that was his job now.

He let out a breath that was annoyingly shaky. "My mother was the only person in this world I cared about."

Niamh's body stiffened with alertness and her eyes focused. He had her entire attention.

"She was called Kume Fujiwara. The Fujiwara family had money and status. My Japanese grandfather was a powerful rice broker in the mid-nineteenth century. Even though Japan was changing rapidly at the time with industrialization, my mother's family still had great influence in their class of society. Kume was seventeen years old, it was 1872, and my grandfather had hopes of a great match for her because she was very beautiful." His voice trailed off as he remembered her.

"That doesn't surprise me," Niamh replied, their eyes locking. "You must look like her."

The compliment caused him to swallow hard. He had his mother's eyes and coloring, but the rest of him was his father.

"That year an American doctor came to Osaka," he continued, carefully keeping the emotion out of his voice. "William Morris. He was the second son of a wealthy East Coast industrialist who had enough money to doctor wherever he wanted to. He was fascinated by Japan. All things Japan. Including my mother. He fell in love with her. They fell in love with each other and she fell pregnant. My father wanted to marry her. That's what my mother told me." He remembered his time in the States and all he'd learned there. "And I found out enough to know that she wasn't lying. William would have married her if he was a stronger man. But not only did my mother's father refuse the suit, the Morris family threatened to cut William off if he didn't return, alone, to America immediately. My mother wanted to elope, but William was weak and he returned to his family." Bitterness he couldn't contain leaked into his words, and his breath caught as Niamh pressed a comforting hand to his chest.

Right over his heart.

There was no pity in her eyes. Just understanding. And compassion.

His heart already beat too hard, too fast. Sweat beaded on his temple but he forced himself to continue. "I grew up very close to my mother. We were each other's only friend. It was the two of us against a harsh society. Although she wasn't sent away, the Fujiwara blamed her for bringing shame to the entire family. My grandfather was cold and indifferent toward us. I called him *Sofu*. I wouldn't dare call him anything less formal. The same for my grandmother who I referred to as *Sobo*. Sobo was worse than Sofu. She was physically abusive to both me and my mother."

Niamh's fingers curled into his T-shirt.

He lowered his gaze. He wouldn't be able to continue if he kept looking into her eyes. "One afternoon"—his voice grew rough with the memory—"my mother returned home from an errand and she'd been beaten. I thought perhaps Sobo had lost her temper over something and attacked her. She walked with a cane and had no problem swiping my mother with it. Mother wouldn't talk to me about it. For weeks after, she was melancholy. Not even I could comfort her." He stalled, trying to gather the calm to confide the next part. "One morning, I went to her and I found her dead in her room. She'd cut her wrists."

"Oh, Kiyo," Niamh whimpered.

He couldn't look at her.

He could hear the tears in her voice, and if he looked at her and found tears in her eyes, he'd lose his calm.

"Sobo told me the truth then. A group of men who knew of my mother's reputation had beaten her and gang-raped her."

"Oh my God."

Rage still filled him. Rage that would never leave no matter how much time passed. "Sobo said Mother had brought it on herself by acting the whore for the American."

"That old bitch."

The rage receded somewhat and Kiyo finally looked at Niamh. Her anger was exactly what he needed. It calmed him more than her tears could. "Yeah, she was. And with my mother dead, Sofu felt no obligation toward me anymore. He lied and told me he was taking me with him on a business trip to Tokyo. I'd lost my mother. I was desperate to believe that perhaps her death had changed Sofu for the better.

"The truth is, I always felt he blamed me for ruining her potential. I think beneath his coldness, my mother was his pride and joy before her fall. And I was a constant reminder of what he'd lost. As a kid, I was desperate to believe that her death had reminded him of what was important. That he'd want a relationship with me. But it was a trick. He abandoned me in Tokyo. I was twelve years old."

Niamh sucked in a breath. "I was twelve, too, when Ronan and I went on the run. But I had my gifts. What did you have?"

"I had my determination to live." Deciding he'd confided enough, he continued, "Suffice it to say I landed on my feet. And years later, I hunted down the men who raped my mother. I hunted them down one by one and killed them." He looked Niamh deep in the eyes, searching for her horror and finding nothing but understanding. "*I* took my vengeance, Niamh. And it left me with nothing but emptiness. I will never get my mother back. I will never be able to protect her from what happened, and what happened to her happened because of my very existence. But it wasn't my fault. It was those men who took what they wanted like savage animals. And in killing them ... I not only lost my mother, I lost my soul. I won't let that happen to you."

Niamh pressed her hand more firmly against his chest. "You haven't lost your soul, Kiyo. It's just a little bashed up."

"Niamh—"

"No. I won't believe it of you." She released him but only to push up on her elbow, her hair cascading onto the bed between them. "Thank you. For telling me about your mam. Knowing you understand, knowing that vengeance wouldn't have helped anyway ... I needed to hear that."

He nodded. As vulnerable as he felt, he was glad it had been worth it. "I know."

Her expression changed, fear creeping into her eyes. "Kiyo, things have changed. The vision ... someone is alive that should be dead. Someone we really, really need to be afraid of."

15

It was amazing how powerful words were.

How a confidence given could make a person lower their defenses, softened by the trust and kindness of someone confiding in them to make them feel better.

Niamh knew it had been hard for Kiyo to tell her about his mam. She knew because she'd felt the wolf's heart pounding fast and hard beneath her palm; she'd seen the sweat bead on his forehead and detected the slight musky change in his natural scent.

But he'd told her his terrible, tragic story to help her move on.

And in that moment, Niamh felt herself falling.

It was unwise. She knew that.

Kiyo had high defenses and was unlikely to ever return her feelings, even if she sensed he was attracted to her.

Yet Niamh couldn't help herself.

And she so desperately wanted someone by her side, in friendship at least, as they battled what was coming next.

"Who is alive that shouldn't be?"

"Ms. Wainwright, Mr. Kaneshiro." The female voice startled them, drawing their attention upward to the flight attendant who hovered over the suite. She gave them a patient smile. "I'm afraid I'm going to have to ask Mr. Kaneshiro to return to his own suite. It's our policy to have only one person to a suite, for safety reasons."

To Niamh's delight, she felt the frustration emanating from Kiyo. She wanted him to stay with her too. Maybe not for the same reasons, but still ... his reluctance to leave her felt nice.

"My fiancée had a nightmare. Can't you let me stay with her for a bit?" He glanced at the seat-belt sign that wasn't lit up. "If the seat-belt signs come on, I'll go back to my suite, I promise." He smiled at the attendant. It was the first real, big smile she'd ever seen from him. His right cheek creased into an almost dimple, his grin surprisingly boyish. Niamh's belly fluttered and her pulse increased. Kiyo must have heard it because he flicked her a concerned look.

Ignoring his gaze and hoping he didn't notice her flushed cheeks, Niamh looked at the flight attendant who clearly wanted to succumb to Kiyo's gorgeous smile.

No wonder he didn't smile often. It was lethal.

"I'm really sorry, but—" The attendant cut off as her and Niamh's gazes connected.

"Please," Niamh pleaded. Her gift was almost like hypnosis. She didn't know how else to explain her ability to manipulate people into doing her bidding.

"All right. For a little while longer." The flight attendant drifted away, dazed.

Kiyo turned back to Niamh, his elbow to the pillow, his head braced in his palm. He studied her face as if searching for something. Niamh tried to control her heartbeat as she bemoaned his beauty. Not that his gorgeous face mattered. Somehow Niamh knew that even if he didn't look like an Armani model, she'd be attracted to him. It was the contradiction of his brooding standoffishness and the kindnesses he'd shown her, his jumping in front of that bloody dagger to save her, his air of mystery and detachment. All of that was enough to entice her ... but he came wrapped up in a package that involved an unfair quantity of masculine beauty.

He'd turned her into one of those annoying heroines who wanted to save the broken hero.

Damn him.

"What are you thinking so hard?" he asked, his voice rough and rasping across her skin.

Niamh tried to contain a shiver. Maybe she should have let the flight attendant force the wolf back to his suite after all.

"Niamh?" He frowned.

"Astra," she blurted out. Concentrating on the bigger picture was a good distraction from this potent infatuation.

"Astra?"

Niamh nodded. Deciding the next part was way too important to be overheard, she rested her head on the pillow and spoke into Kiyo's mind. *Can I talk to you like this?*

Kiyo showed no sign of discomfort at her use of telepathy. He gave her a subtle lift of his chin in agreement.

Seven of us were born on the same day of the same year to different human mothers. Although we're fae, we do actually have our human parents' DNA too. It's complicated. Most of us were born not knowing what we are. But I was born with knowledge. Of who we are, of how Faerie's interference in the human world led to the birth of supernaturals, of Aine, the Faerie Queen, and her spell. Over the years, a vampire named Eirik sought the fae-borne to kill them so they couldn't open the gate. Eirik and his brother Jerrik were the oldest vampires in the world. So old, they remembered Faerie. They'd visited it often. Jerrik's true mate was a princess of one of the royal fae houses.

Aine had begun to learn that fae and supernaturals were coming together in the true-mate bond. It alarmed her but not so much as when a werewolf bit his fae mate and she turned into a werewolf, losing her fae-ness and her immortality. Those who weren't connected in a true-mate bond found that a werewolf bite was as lethal to a fae as iron. Until that point, there was nothing on Faerie that could kill them.

Kiyo flinched like she'd hit him. He hissed, "My bite can kill you? Why the hell did Fionn not warn me? I could have hurt you without even meaning to. The full moon is in four days."

Niamh wasn't concerned about Kiyo hurting her. The wolf had

more self-control than any werewolf she'd ever come across. *Fionn probably didn't want you to know how dangerous you are to us.*

"I'm going to kill him and now I know how."

Sensing he was only semiserious, Niamh gave him a mock reproving look. *Shall I continue, or do you just want to brood about what a sly bastard Fionn is?*

When he didn't answer, Niamh asked, "Well?"

He flicked her a dark, petulant look. "I'm thinking about it."

She smiled despite herself. *Let me choose for you ... Aine said she was afraid for the human world, that a war was brewing, and she wasn't wrong. But she was afraid for her own people. She hated the idea of them mingling with supernaturals, or worse, becoming like them. The fae are superior beings to her, and while it was okay to have sex with supernaturals, it was most definitely not okay to become one of them. She sent all supernaturals on Faerie back to the human world and closed the gate.*

But Aine is a typical fae. Bored. Complex. Capable of kindness but apt toward wickedness. And she likes her games. She knew there were beings like Jerrik who would do anything to get back to Faerie, so she tormented them with the spell: seven fae children born in the human world with the ability to open the gate. No instructions for when they'd appear or how many were needed to open the gate or how *they'd even open the gate. She just loved the idea of supernaturals chasing their tails trying to find the kids.*

Eventually, we appeared. Niamh gave Kiyo a wry smirk. *But as I said, most of us didn't know what we were. We were vulnerable.* Her smirk died as sadness filled her. *Eirik killed Jerrik, who wanted to protect the children. Killed by his own brother. That's how much he feared the gate being opened again. Over the centuries, Eirik created The Garm. Their sole purpose is to find the fae children and kill them.*

They succeeded with a few. Jael was first. She lived in Jordan. Her powers came to her more quickly than the rest of us. As a baby, in fact. Her parents abandoned her, thinking she was cursed. An international relief organization took her into one of their orphanages. When she was five years old, Eirik tracked her down through rumors of the strange incidents that occurred around her. And he killed her.

"How do you know this?"

Because I saw it. I saw it before it happened. My knowledge of what I was and where we came from was just within me as a child. But Jael's death was my first-ever vision.

Kiyo's eyes narrowed. "You were five years old when you saw a child you were connected to being murdered?"

She nodded slowly, not wanting his pity when she didn't need it. *I've been burdened with knowledge my entire life, Kiyo. I was never allowed to be a child. Not with my visions. But I could handle it.*

He cursed under his breath.

An ache flared in her chest as she realized what he felt wasn't pity. He was angry on her behalf.

I'm okay. I was built for these visions. Built to handle the adult emotions that came with them.

"It would have destroyed an ordinary human kid," he said. "Seeing things like that."

Maybe. Maybe not. Humans are capable of incredible mental and emotional strength.

He frowned. "What happened next?"

Dimitri. He was fourteen when Eirik found him in Kyiv. Dimitri was using his powers, much as I have over the years, but not being quiet about it at all. He crossed paths with a vampire coven who turned him over to The Garm. Ronan and I tried to get to Kyiv to warn Dimitri, but we were too late and then we had to get the hell out of Dodge before The Garm sensed me there.

Then there was Astra. Niamh's stomach flipped anxiously. *When I was sixteen, I started to get visions of Astra. She lived in Bergen, a coastal city in Norway. These visions weren't like the others—these were warnings. About Astra herself. Ronan convinced me not to go to her, not until we understood what the visions meant. But I was pretty sure I knew what they meant. Astra was more dangerous than The Garm and the Blackwood Coven combined.*

Niamh held Kiyo's gaze as she whispered into his mind, *Her soul is ... Kiyo, she doesn't have one.*

"What do you mean?"

The only thing I can compare her to is a psychopath. It's not that she doesn't have wants or passions or that she doesn't feel ambition or loyalty even ... but she has no empathy. It doesn't bother her if she hurts or betrays someone. She doesn't feel it. It's like she has no conscience.

"You saw this?"

Niamh nodded. *She killed her parents when she was twelve. She'd been hiding her gifts from them, but they discovered her over time. They wanted her to be medically examined but Astra knew she'd end up in a lab somewhere and maybe even eventually exploited by a government. So she killed her parents and ... got rid of their bodies ... like I did with the abuser at Moscow Airport. Despite the suspicions of her parents' friends, there was no evidence she'd done anything to harm them, so she was put into the foster care system. She grew close to a girl in her group home, but when the girl became romantically interested in another girl and stopped paying attention to Astra, she used her powers to push the girl down three flights of stairs. The girl ended up in a coma.*

There is a long list of antisocial behavior from Astra. I thought perhaps if I went to her and gave her a family, it might help, but Ronan wouldn't let me. In all honesty, he was right.

When I was seventeen, I got a vision that truly frightened me. The future is never absolute. The smallest decision can affect everything, so the possibilities are infinite. Over the years, I've been shown possible futures. Thea, Conall's mate, endured horrors that none of the rest of us have. I knew if she didn't trust Conall when he was sent to her, Eirik would eventually find and kill her. Her mating with Conall would change that future, so I tried to push them together. The vision I saw before he left ... it showed me multiple possibilities for Thea, Conall, and their pack's future, and in all of them, I'm pleased to say that Thea and Conall are happy.

With Fionn and Rose, it was much bigger than just one person's destiny. Fionn wanted to open the gate so he could take his revenge against the Faerie Queen for destroying his life and turning him fae. He would have succeeded in killing Aine and the fae would rush to the human world to take their vengeance. The human world, as we know it, would have ended.

His mating with Rose, however, changed that. His priority became protecting her and thus protecting the gate.

"So you saved the world?"

Niamh smirked. *Rose saved the world from Fionn.*

"What of Astra?"

If Astra lived, there was a possibility, not an absolute, but a possibility she'd succeed in opening the gate to Faerie. I wasn't the only fae born with knowledge. She has it too. Astra and I are like two sides of the same coin. Same gifts, visions, abilities ... but one of us was born in the light, the other, the dark. She craves power and believes that she can only be truly immortal by returning to Faerie where there is no iron or werewolves ... where nothing can end her.

But she also knows there are several ways to return to Faerie. If one of us willingly *wants to return to Faerie, then we need four of us to open the gate. Four is a sacred number to the fae. They have four countries, four courts, four seasons, four times of day in which the courts are named for— Samhradh, a country of perpetual sunshine. Colloquially known as the Day Lands and location of the Queen's royal seat. Geimhreadh, a country of eternal darkness and called the Night Lands. Earrach, the Dawn Lands, and Fómhar, the Dusk Lands.*

Four. Four of us to open the gate if one *of us is willing.*

If we're all *unwilling, our enemies only need one of us. They don't even need our deaths. They just need to spill our unwilling blood.*

"Why do *you* need four, then?"

Proof that we're deserving to return to Faerie. That one of us at least feels like we're one of them, not one of the supernaturals or humans we were raised among.

"And Astra knew this? She has the sight?"

Yes. But I thought she was no longer a problem. A few months after I had the vision about her plans to find and use three of us to open the gate, Eirik found and killed her. I thought she was dead. He *thought she was dead.*

"What happened?"

He stabbed her in the heart with iron, and she appeared to die a slow, painful death. Niamh couldn't believe Astra had been able to contrive that. *She must have used magic as an illusion. He only thought he was using iron, and she made him see what she wanted him to see. The scary part is that it tricked me too.*

"But now you're getting visions of her again."

Yes. She's alive. And she's on track to take me, Rose, and the last fae-borne, Elijah, to Scotland to open a gate that no one knows about. Everyone thinks the only gate is in Ireland ... but there's another near Edinburgh.

"Is that what the stones were from the vision?"

Niamh nodded. *Standing stones. They mark the gate to Faerie. They were put there thousands of years ago to warn people not to go near. That within the circle, the fabric between worlds was broken and they'd slip into Faerie.*

Kiyo frowned. "Why am I in this vision?"

"I honestly don't know."

He considered this a moment. "Okay. I believe you."

His words caused her to melt into the bed with relief. *Good. Because we need to be on the same team. I said Astra and I were different sides of the same coin, but I feel like her powers have grown exponentially. She may be more powerful than any of us now. She's capable of things ... she can hide from us. My vision told me that's how she'll get Rose and Elijah. We'll sense something but not danger, and not enough to protect ourselves. And if our guard is down with her, she'll be able to manipulate us like we can manipulate humans. I know now, so my guard will be up with her, but I should warn Rose and try to get to Elijah too. It's just ... I feel like Tokyo is the priority and I don't know why.*

Kiyo suddenly sat up, his whole being alert.

"What is it?"

"You can't sense danger from her and she can manipulate you?"

"If my guard was down."

His eyebrows nearly hit his hairline. "Niamh, your guard *is* down. You've been grieving for months for Ronan. Burying yourself in guilt."

"So?"

"Is it possible Astra could make you think you were seeing visions?"

"What are you saying?"

"You haven't been able to make sense of the visions you've been receiving. Visions that are coming too often. Visions that are pushing you toward vengeance ... toward darkness."

You think she's planting these visions in my head to steer me off my path?

"Didn't you say you sensed someone following you when you went after Meghan?"

Niamh nodded, disbelief making her dizzy.

"And that these visions felt different?"

Yes. Aggressive and insistent and like they want me to feel something rather than relay information like the others. Oh my God. Realization caused a wave of nausea. Kiyo was right.

"She's been pushing you for months, and then I arrived and tried to talk you out of it—"

"So she pulled out the big guns: Meghan O'Connor."

"And it didn't work. So she sent you another vision at the airport."

"Where I could feel her following me." Niamh nodded as it all began to make sense, the kind of sense that sat right with her, finally. Despite the awful realization that she'd been manipulated, relief also filled her. Now that she knew, she could take back control. *She was at the airport, trying to push me to kill the child abuser.*

"It's possible, right?"

No, Kiyo. It's not possible. It's what's been happening. These visions never really felt like my true visions. I couldn't put my finger on why, and I was too distracted by my pain to stop and think. She grabbed his arm. *It's Astra. She's been using my grief against me.* Her grip on him tightened. "Thank you. Thank you, Kiyo."

He looked somewhat uncomfortable with her gratitude, but he nodded. "So, what's next?"

"I think she knew," Niamh said. "Perhaps she saw that you would help me. My guard is up now because of you." Concern slammed through her fast and hard. "You're a threat, Kiyo. You're a threat to her plans. That's why you're in my real visions. What the hell is in Tokyo that can hurt you?"

Kiyo pulled away from her, his elbows resting on his knees. "Why can't you see what she's after? Why were you blind to the fact that I might be able to help you? Why didn't you see me coming?"

I don't know. Maybe because you never intended me danger. I don't get visions about things that directly affect me personally, unless I'm in danger and I can't see my own future.

He looked away, seeming to process this.

Kiyo?

A muscle ticked in his jaw. "I'm not aware of anything that can harm me. I was cursed with immortality by someone who knew that eternity would be a form of hell for me."

At this confession, Niamh ached for him. She hated that he found immortality such an awful prospect. It reminded her of Thea and how she'd felt about the possibility of forever, alone as one of the fae.

"No one is invincible in the human world, Kiyo." Niamh tentatively touched his arm this time. *True immortality only exists on Faerie.*

His head bent toward her, his eyes hard as he whispered, "I've had everything imaginable happen to me over the last century and a half. Trust me, nothing can kill me. You saw what happened when the dagger pierced my heart."

Trust me, *Kiyo,* she replied. *You're not invincible, and there's something in Tokyo to prove it. She may not know about it now, but Astra will learn of it. That's what my vision, this real vision, is warning me about. We have to go to Tokyo to protect you.* She curled her hand around his arm and felt longing ripple through her as he glanced down at where she held him. But the longing felt foreign ... it wasn't her longing. It was his. His for her.

It couldn't be.

Only true mates could sense each other's feelings, and Niamh knew that happened between them from the moment they met.

She shook off the bizarre sensation, putting it down to her crush on him.

Ironic, she joked, trying to ease the sudden tension. *Fionn hires you to protect me and yet it seems by merely getting involved in this crazy faerie story, I'll have to protect you instead.*

Kiyo looked decidedly unimpressed with her teasing, pulling back his upper lip to snarl under his breath.

Niamh laughed, if only to cover that his snarl caused a rush of sexy, tingly feelings low and deep in her belly and between her legs.

Damn the wolf for distracting her so badly when they were in the middle of a bloody war.

16

What was around two o'clock in the morning for them was nine in the morning in Tokyo.

Jet lag didn't affect Kiyo, but he wished he'd had more sleep before landing at Narita International.

Almost three decades had passed since the last time he was in Tokyo, and the events of his last visit meant he was on high alert as he led Niamh through the airport.

"Bran booked us into the Natsukashii in Chūō City. I don't know what it's like," he said, "but if it's too conspicuous, I'll move us somewhere else."

"Conspicuous?"

"If it's a luxury hotel." He frowned. "I know you like nice hotels, but we're trying to stay under the radar."

Niamh scowled at him. "I can live without luxury, believe me."

At her clipped tone, Kiyo dragged his eyes away and continued following the signs for the express train at the airport.

It was amazing what a few hours could do.

Suffice it to say, Kiyo had not liked the sudden vulnerability he felt when he realized what he'd divulged to Niamh. He could see how much his words had helped her, and so he was satisfied. He wouldn't regret telling her about his mother.

But there was an air of connection between them that was worse than any attraction he felt.

And Kiyo needed to nip it in the bud.

After returning to his own suite, he'd feigned sleep so he wouldn't have to talk to her. Upon waking, he'd been monosyllabic in reply to her perky chatter. There was an aura around her that hadn't been there before. A lightness. As if the knowledge of this Astra bitch's manipulation had taken a weight off her shoulders.

When the flight attendant offered them a Japanese bento box for their breakfast, Niamh's friendly prattle and delight over the traditional meal should have been annoying. It wasn't.

"I can't make the chopsticks work." She practically pouted. She who could conjure nearly anything on the planet.

Trying to suppress a smirk, Kiyo leaned into her suite and gestured for her to lift her hand with the chopsticks. He took one from her. "Hold the upper chopstick like a pencil," he instructed, "about a third of the way from the top. Got it?"

He proceeded to show her how to use the eating utensils, ignoring her beaming smile all the while. Niamh had gripped noodles from the bento box with her chopsticks and managed to use them with an ease that made her laugh in triumph. "Arigatō."

Kiyo had raised an eyebrow at her use of Japanese and her decent pronunciation. His expression had caused her to laugh again.

"It's the only word I know."

Something about the exchange on top of their earlier cozy, soul-bearing conversation made him clam up.

At first, Niamh, sensing something was wrong, had asked him about it. His cool, clipped responses had caused her to withdraw. Kiyo knew putting distance between them was absolutely the right thing to do when he realized he felt guilty for hurting her feelings.

Kiyo was not a guy who felt guilty for hurting *anyone's* feelings.

Thankfully, Niamh had gone from upset to pissed.

He could handle that better.

"Where are we going?" She hurried to keep up with his long strides.

Kiyo flicked her another look.

Earlier, when she'd returned from the plane's restroom, he'd had to do a double take. Instead of the jeans and T-shirt he was used to seeing her in, she was dressed as she had been in the many surveillance photos Bran had sent him. Her hair fell down her back in braids and loose curls, and she wore a dress the color of fall leaves. It was fitted tightly to her upper body and had long sleeves but the skirt was loose and floated around her ankles. She wore a pair of flat, brown leather boots, dangling feather earrings, and a ring on nearly every finger, each one a different moonstone.

Kiyo was simple when it came to women. He preferred no guessing games; he liked them confident and sexy and only interested in casual encounters. That's why his tastes usually veered toward women who dressed in clothes that left little to the imagination.

Yet, something about Niamh's ethereal femininity sparked a heat in him he didn't understand.

He didn't want to understand.

So instead of asking her about the fashion change or where she got all the shit she was wearing, he ignored her.

"Kiyo," she huffed impatiently. "Where are we going?"

"Express train. It'll take us about an hour to get into the city from here." He slowed to a stop in front of a large route map. Studying it a second, he relayed, "We can get *shinkansen* at Shin-Nihombashi."

"Shinkansen?"

"Bullet train."

Excitement fluttered in her words and she seemed to forget she was annoyed with him. "Ooh, I've always wanted to go on one of those. Is it true they travel at two hundred miles per hour?"

She sounded like a kid at Christmas. His lips twitched as he began to walk again. "At their top speed. We won't hit that. Shinkansen will get us to Chūō City in only two minutes."

"Two minutes? Wow. Something that moves as fast as me. Who knew."

He would not be charmed by her.

He wasn't charmed by anything.

Soulless bastards were immune to charm.

"Oh my goodness, is that a vending machine with noodles in it?" she asked.

He followed her gaze to a bank of vending machines adjacent to food stalls. "You choose what dish you want, pay, it gives you a ticket, and you take it over to the food stall."

Niamh nodded, still wide-eyed. "What does the vending machine with the umbrella mean?"

"Just what it says. You can buy an umbrella from it."

"No way!" She slowed to a stop. "Can I get one?"

It was hard not to smile. In fact, he lost the fight entirely as he turned to her. "You want an umbrella? You, with all the magic?"

Niamh grinned. "I've never had an umbrella from a vending machine before." Her eyes flew back to it and then caught on another. "Oh my God, there's a banana vending machine!"

A chuckle escaped him before he could stop it, and her eyes flew back to his in surprise. He took a step toward her. "We might get to where we're going faster if I tell you that there are vending machines all over Japan and they have pretty much everything in them. Now, can we go?" he asked gently.

Niamh threw the umbrella vending machine one last longing look before she hurried to follow him. "Who needs magic in Japan?"

To his eternal gratitude, Niamh was too busy watching the country pass by to talk to him on the express. She disarmed him, making it difficult to be cool and distant with her. On the train, however, he'd given her the window seat. She took in the soft green countryside, tinged with the paleness of mild winter. This express train took the more scenic route, nature eventually melting away to city as they entered Inzai. Niamh leaned closer to the window as she took in the sight of the city in the distance.

"There are no English signs anywhere." She turned to him at one point.

He frowned in query.

"All the signs are in Japanese."

Kiyo smirked. "Shouldn't they be?"

She blushed. "Of course, it's just ... somehow it's more disorienting in a language that's so unfamiliar."

"Don't worry. The Japanese love to practice their English. You'll get by. Plus, you have me."

She gave him an irritatingly unhappy look and turned back to watch the world fly by.

He didn't want to think about what that look meant. He didn't want to think about much, but between telling Niamh his mother's story and being back in Tokyo, memories and nostalgia threatened to pull him under.

While it had been almost thirty years since he'd returned to Tokyo, it had only been a few years since he'd visited Japan. For a nomad, Kiyo was willing to admit, at least to himself, that he liked to touch base with his homeland often. Perhaps it was because when he moved to the States at the end of the nineteenth century, he did not return to Japan until the 1970s. It was only then he'd realized how much he'd missed it.

Tokyo had become a no-go zone because he'd pissed off some very powerful people there, which was one of the reasons he needed an inconspicuous place to stay. But that didn't stop Kiyo from traveling elsewhere. The one place he'd never returned to was Osaka. Instead, over the decades, he'd developed a fondness for Kyoto. The city on the island of Honshu had kept much of its tradition, even as it developed into a modern city. Moreover, it was surrounded by the bounty of Japan's natural beauty, and on the full moon, there was no better place for Kiyo to roam freely. He owned a home in the mountains just so he could.

He wished like hell Niamh's vision had taken them to Kyoto and not Tokyo. The full moon was in three days. He'd have to travel to the mountains to make the change and avoid his enemies at the same time.

Drifting back to the world from his thoughts and memories, Kiyo was startled to realize they were approaching their station. He'd sat in silence with Niamh the entire hour. Her expression was remote as he relayed it was their stop.

"The station will be packed." He gripped her by the biceps as they descended from the express train. "Stick with me."

Although she felt tense beneath his touch, she didn't resist as he guided her through the crowded station, following the signs for the bullet train to Chūō City. He glanced at Niamh as he led them through the station. Her face was full of wonder and curiosity as she drank in every inch of their surroundings. For someone who knew of the supernatural underworld, of Faerie, who had powers beyond any human's imagination, who had seen visions of the worst atrocities humans and supernaturals could commit, Niamh Farren had "the wonder."

She was a person of immense mental and emotional strength to have the knowledge she had and yet still be able to find beauty and newness in the world.

So busy looking at her, Kiyo bumped into someone, a businessman who snapped at him in Japanese. The impact brought Niamh's eyes to his, and somehow he found himself drowning in her.

"What is it?" she asked softly in that lilting Irish accent.

No human could have heard her over the din of the station.

"Nothing," he lied, and forced his gaze forward again.

At the platform for the bullet train, he released Niamh's arm and stared stonily up at the departure information.

"What does it say?"

"Our train will be here in a few minutes."

Seconds later a bullet train whizzed past them on the opposite platform.

"Wow!" Niamh nudged him, seeming to forget she was irritated. "Is that how fast I am?"

Humor bubbled on his lips but he kept it under control. "You're probably faster."

"Really?" She considered this and then grinned, pleased. "I guess I'm kind of epic."

"I guess you kind of are."

Something must have slipped in his tone because her answering look was much warmer than any of her expressions had been since the plane. The urge to lean in and kiss her lush mouth was suddenly overwhelming. He'd been fighting it for days, and he was tired of resisting.

Kiyo definitely needed to get laid.

But it wouldn't be with Niamh.

The woman was far too dangerous.

Niamh's eyebrows furrowed and her attention flew back toward the platform behind them.

A warning shiver skated down his spine. "What is it?" he echoed her words from before.

Before she could speak, their train appeared, slowing to a stop at the platform. Niamh moved toward it, shooting a troubled glance over her shoulder.

"Niamh?"

"Get on the train." Her voice was cool, authoritative.

Kiyo followed but Niamh didn't move away from the doors. She stared out at the platform as people boarded.

"Niamh?" He searched the crowds, too, as his impatience with her evasiveness grew.

"I sense danger."

Eyes narrowing on the platform, it was just as the doors were closing that he saw three men rush through the commuters toward them. His eyes connected with one of the males who bared his teeth in fury as the train moved away.

Daiki.

Kiyo sighed heavily. "Yeah, we have a problem."

"Other than the ninety-nine problems we already had?"

He looked down at her scowling, pretty face. "I told you I haven't been to Tokyo in a while."

"Yes?"

"The last time I was here ... I pissed off the largest werewolf pack in Japan." He glared out the doors as the world passed by at high speed. Inside the train, however, they didn't even feel it. The train seemed to glide. Kiyo wished it would glide them right off the damn continent.

"You pissed off the largest werewolf pack in Japan, how many years ago?"

"Twenty-five, twenty-six."

"And they're still pissed about it?"

"Apparently. One of those men is an alpha. High ranking in the pack." Kiyo inwardly groaned at the thought of the pack's current alpha. She wasn't alpha back when Kiyo knew her, but her uncle had died and she'd won the right to lead the pack by being the fastest, strongest bitch in Eastern Asia.

Clearly, she was also still pissed.

Women. They had memories like elephants.

"It must have been really bad what you did to them."

"No. They just know how to hold a grudge."

Niamh shook her head in irritation as the train slowed into their station. "I hope you're happy."

"About what?"

"Because of you, my first trip on a bullet train was utterly ruined." The doors opened and she hopped off the train with a haughty sniff of annoyance.

Kiyo might have found it cute if she hadn't just stumbled into a fucking ambush.

17

Too late, all the hair on Niamh's body rose as she stood on the metro station platform. Pulse racing, her eyes flew to the source of the danger. A line of great big hulking men and athletic women guarded the exit. Passengers approached them warily, skittering by when they opened their guard to let them through.

The wolves stared at Niamh and Kiyo.

"I take it this is the pack you pissed off?" she whispered.

So angry at him for being cool toward her ever since he'd woken up on the plane, she'd jumped off the bullet train without listening to her senses.

"Pack Iryoku." Kiyo's hand wrapped around her elbow. "No fighting, Niamh. We go with them."

She glanced up at him, shocked. Worried the wolves might overhear, she spoke into his mind, *Are you nuts? Don't they want to kill you?*

Kiyo shook his head. "No. They more than likely want me to pay a debt they think I owe."

Do you owe it?

"No."

Then let's annihilate the bastards and get out of here.

"Our business is here." He reminded her. "So we'll do the polite thing and go where they want to take us. If we fight, it'll be war, and we'll have to leave Tokyo."

Frustrated beyond belief, Niamh huffed and glared at the brooding werewolves who waited patiently at the exit. *I reserve the right to kill any one of them if they attack first.*

"I have no problem with that plan." His grip on her arm tightened and he bent to whisper in her ear. "And as far as they're concerned, you're a witch."

At the feel of his lips brushing her skin, she tingled, heat flushing down her spine. He lifted his head. His expression was hard, implacable.

Niamh nodded. *I'm a witch.*

Satisfied, he nodded back. Then he murmured, "Haruto is with them. Belying his size, he's a beta. Older than he looks. Coolheaded. Doesn't believe in violence unless utterly necessary. I respected him back when I knew him. If he's here, we should be okay." He led her through the crowd to the wolves who seemed to grow larger at their approach, their scowls forbidding and unnerving. Niamh hoped like hell that Kiyo was right about these people.

The tallest of the wolves, a male with deep-set black eyes and an overhanging forehead, stepped forward and said something to Kiyo in Japanese. His tone was calm, bored even, which gave Niamh hope.

Kiyo's expression remained impressively blank. "My companion doesn't understand Japanese, Haruto-san. May we speak in English?"

Haruto flicked a look at Niamh. Seemingly uninterested in her, he turned back to Kiyo and nodded. "Our *ippikiookami* returns. Arufua-san wishes to know why. She will see you now, if it pleases you."

Despite his respectful words, Niamh knew Haruto wasn't asking.

Kiyo nodded. "We're happy to."

She noted a slight softening of Haruto's expression, as if he was relieved Kiyo wasn't going to give them any trouble.

But then the pack surrounded them, and Niamh stiffened beneath Kiyo's touch, her body readying itself for battle.

Kiyo squeezed her arm. "It's okay. They're just escorting us out of the station."

She tried—and failed—to relax as they followed Haruto, beseiged by the bodyguards that smelled of damp earth and herbs. None of them smelled like Kiyo, with his distinct smoky scent that reminded her of lazy afternoons in a cabin with a log burner.

Niamh didn't know why he reminded her of that, considering she'd never had a lazy afternoon in a cabin with a log-burning fire.

Shaking off her silly wayward thoughts, she asked Kiyo under her breath, "What did he call you?"

"*Ippikiookami*?"

"Yes."

"Lone wolf."

"And what or who is Arufua-san?"

"*Arufua* means Alpha. *San* is a suffix. Like Mr. or Mrs. It's used as a mark of respect. It can be used with first or surnames or in regard to a person's profession. Alpha is a job, a high-ranking job, so their pack will refer to them as Arufua-san. 'Chan' is for those we feel affection toward. 'Kun' is less respectful. I might use it if someone is the same age or younger than me."

Isn't everyone younger than you?

He smirked in acknowledgment, shooting her an amused look that caused little flutters in her belly.

Damn him.

Haruto's hulking form led them out of the station toward black SUVs with blacked-out windows. Niamh's steps faltered.

Sensing her trepidation, Kiyo gave her arm a squeeze, his look one of reassurance.

Then his attention was whipped away by a stream of Japanese from Haruto.

Kiyo scowled and he pulled Niamh more firmly into his side. "Absolutely not."

"What do they want?"

"To separate us."

At the thought, energy crackled across her skin.

Kiyo shook his head at her ever so slightly and spoke to Haruto. "We come quietly together, or we give the people of Tokyo a show right here, right now."

Haruto scowled and then exchanged a look with one of the other wolves. Finally, he nodded at Kiyo. "Together." He opened the back passenger side of one of the SUVs.

Kiyo released Niamh but only to press his hand on her lower back, guiding her forward. It seemed stupid and wrong to get into the vehicle but Niamh had to trust him.

Bristling with agitation, Niamh slid along the leather bench as Kiyo followed her inside. He sat close, his leg pressing against hers.

There was already a werewolf in the driver's seat. He didn't move or speak to them.

Then Haruto got into the front passenger seat and clipped out directions in Japanese.

"They're taking us to the alpha. The pack's headquarters aren't in this ward," Kiyo spoke at a normal level, since even if he whispered, the wolves would hear. "It's in Shinjuku. Roughly a thirty-minute drive."

The darkly tinted windows afforded the passenger a view of outside but it was a muted, gray one. Frustrating for Niamh when she wanted her first look at the city. From what she'd glimpsed so far, it looked like any major city. Tall buildings made of concrete, glass, and brick. Multilane main streets with crosswalks and traffic lights. The only difference was the signs with the Japanese characters. But now and then, she'd see an English word on a sign that made her feel less disoriented.

Silence reigned thick in the car. Niamh tried not to worry about what was ahead of them. If Kiyo thought they could survive this interview with a werewolf pack, then they probably could. After all, Fionn had vowed him to an unbreakable bond. If he got her killed, he essentially got himself killed, so she trusted he wouldn't put her in a too-dangerous position, even if her Spidey senses were telling her otherwise.

Eventually they drove through a greener part of the city. Beautiful trees lined the sidewalks, and she decided she liked this area better for it. When they slowed in traffic, passing what looked like some kind of traditional wall with trees towering behind it, Niamh asked Kiyo if he knew what it was.

"If memory serves, it's Kudankita."

"Hai," Haruto said gruffly from the passenger seat.

Kiyo nodded. "It is. Kudankita is a residential district. Quite prestigious. There's a Shinto-style shrine in there you'd probably like. It commemorates the war. The buildings are traditional, lots of greenery. It's its own little town. Very private. Quiet. You don't really feel like you're in the city when you're in there."

"I like the sound of that."

"For someone who sticks to cities, you seem to like nature, to like green?" he said, his eyes almost smiling.

"I do." She grinned, despite her nervousness. She spoke in his head, *It's part of fae genetics to be at one with nature.* "I like my green."

"I know the feeling."

"I bet you do."

They shared a look that made her heart beat so hard, Niamh knew everyone in the car must have heard it. She glanced quickly away, willing her pale skin not to flush. Instead she concentrated on where they were going.

"It's not how I imagined."

"How did you imagine it?"

She shrugged. "Narrow, crammed streets with lots of market stalls."

Kiyo smirked. "There're plenty of neighborhoods like that. We're taking the main road that cuts through the entire city."

As they drove onward, even though they were still on multilane main streets, the buildings did seem to crowd closer together.

Kiyo leaned over, pointing out the window. "We're in the pack's ward now. Shinjuku. All of these signs"—he gestured—"are neon at night."

Niamh could imagine it in her mind from the images she'd seen of Tokyo over the years. "I can't wait to see it." Her tone was dry as her she spoke into his head, *Assuming I live through this.*

He huffed under his breath but didn't comment again until five or so minutes later when they were suddenly surrounded by extremely tall buildings. "Skyscraper district." He relayed and then clarified. "Business district."

The pack is based out of this district?

Kiyo nodded.

When you said they were powerful, you meant in more ways than one.

Another slight nod.

Shit.

Niamh was concluding that Pack Iryoku were something along the lines of a Mafia.

"This is their hotel."

As Haruto opened the door for her and she hopped out, Niamh nearly broke her neck craning it back. The hotel was tall.

Like really, really bloody tall.

"How many floors does this monstrosity have?"

Haruto shot her a quiet scowl. "Forty-seven. But the hotel is two towers, not just one."

"Oh. Still, it looks about five hundred from here."

Kiyo settled beside her, his hand on her lower back. "Haruto's English is excellent. Try not to call the pack's hotel a monstrosity."

"Oops." Like she actually gave a damn if she insulted the man who was essentially kidnapping them.

He rolled his eyes.

Any irreverence left her, however, as the pack members surrounded them and Haruto led them inside. The lobby was humongous and decked out in all the world's finest materials. It gleamed with expense, from the massive crystal chandeliers to the marble columns, to the antique walnut furnishings.

"This isn't just a hotel," Kiyo informed her as their shoes echoed off polished marble floors. "The last time I was here, there were ten restaurants, a nightclub, a casino, and even tatami suites."

"There is more now," Haruto informed them, looking at Kiyo over his shoulder. "Arufua-san has added much over the years. Thirteen restaurants now, one, a Michelin star. We have exhibitions, tea ceremony, and sushi-making classes, a spa ... The nightclub has been replaced with a whisky degustation bar—we have the finest whiskies in the world and Chef who makes whisky-flavored food." Haruto frowned. "Portions are small but I am told humans cannot handle larger for a six-course menu. Oh, and the casino has been expanded."

"My goodness," Niamh muttered, slightly amused that the somewhat tacit Haruto got chatty like a proud father talking about the hotel. "It's like a city within a city."

"Hai."

"If we weren't currently being politely held hostage, I'd love to explore it."

Haruto grunted as Kiyo chuckled under his breath.

Niamh's gaze flew to his face to see he was almost smiling.

"Diplomacy, Niamh. Diplomacy," he reminded her, though he didn't seem all that upset by her sarcasm.

They were led past a bank of elevators to the one at the end. Haruto stood in front of a panel and swiped his watch across it. The panel opened to reveal a computer screen. He pressed his thumb to it and the elevator doors opened.

He ushered them inside and only one other male wolf got on with Haruto. Niamh almost breathed a sigh of relief. Being surrounded by werewolves was not her favorite thing. Werewolves in numbers had always equaled The Garm for Niamh. The enemy.

The elevator climbed to the forty-seventh floor and when the doors opened, they didn't open onto a corridor.

They opened to a room.

"Wow."

They stepped out onto more polished marble floors. A wide hallway led off to the right while stairs ahead guided down into a sunken living room with hardwood floors. A bank of windows offered a view so amazing, Niamh could see the snowcapped Mount Fuji in the distance.

A glass box sat in the center of the room with flames flickering inside. It was one of the most modern fireplaces she'd ever seen.

If she wasn't mistaken, the music filtering softly into the entire area from hidden speakers belonged to the biggest country-pop princess in the world. Not the kind of music Niamh would have guessed a powerful pack alpha might listen to.

It almost endeared her to the mystery wolf.

They passed interesting sculptures and colorful artwork that did much to break up a plethora of white paint everywhere. Velvet furniture in shades of blues and golds was scattered throughout the room. And as they wandered down into it, Niamh saw there was a stylish modern kitchen fitted at the back.

Standing at an island, chopping vegetables, was an equally stylish and beautiful woman.

Her knife stilled as her dark eyes moved past Niamh to the male at her side.

To Kiyo.

Something about the way the woman looked at her companion made Niamh's stomach flip with uneasiness.

Haruto stopped in front of the island. "Arufua-san." He gave her a sharp bow and then spoke in Japanese.

This ... this was the pack alpha?

She thanked Haruto without taking her eyes off Kiyo. Lowering the knife to the counter, she walked slowly around the island. Niamh's gaze moved to Kiyo who seemed transfixed by the alpha.

Something sharp and painful cut across her chest at his expression.

To her dismay, she realized it was jealousy.

The female sashayed slowly toward them. Her slender but gently curved figure was accentuated by her tight emerald-green pencil dress. It was sleeveless, showing off her toned arms. It had a high collar but a deep cut that split the neckline, showing off more than a hint of cleavage. The sexiness of the neckline was softened by the length of the dress, which hit her toned calves. Her strong, slender legs were elongated by impressive six-inch black stilettos.

Her black hair was sleek and sharp, cut to skim her elegant jawline. Perfect lips were rouged in bright red.

She was classy and stunning and emanated huge amounts of alpha energy. In her stilettos, she was the same height as Niamh.

Her thickly lashed, dark eyes pinned Kiyo to the spot as she stopped a few yards away from them. On closer inspection, Niamh saw telltale lines around her mouth and eyes. She was older than Niamh. Perhaps even older than she looked. She certainly recognized Kiyo and if he hadn't returned to Tokyo in twenty-five years, then it would make sense that the alpha was older than her appearance.

"Kiyo-chan ... Genki?"

Kiyo grunted at that. "English, Sakura."

Sakura's eyes narrowed. "Respect, Kiyo." Her eyes finally flitted to Niamh. She curled her upper lip. "*Mahoutsukai*?"

"Yes, she's a witch. English ... Sakura-*san*. My companion doesn't speak Japanese."

"You bring a western witch to our home, Kiyo?"

Our home?

Niamh's eyes narrowed.

"She's under my protection." He sidled closer to Niamh, which made her feel somewhat better.

That feeling dissipated, however, when Sakura gave him a soft smile and stepped toward him. Right into his personal space.

Something possessive and territorial surged through Niamh as Sakura placed a perfectly manicured hand on Kiyo's chest.

The whole room tensed as lights flickered, and Sakura, still touching Kiyo, shot Niamh a reassessing look. "She is powerful, your little mahoutsukai." She returned her attention to Kiyo as she trailed her fingertips over his pecs.

Niamh wanted to rip her hair out.

"And territorial of my Kiyo-chan," she murmured.

That burn in Niamh's chest, the one she tried so hard to ignore, neared the boiling point at having to listen to this condescending wolf while she stroked Kiyo.

And while he did nothing to stop her.

"She's just concerned you plan to rip out my heart."

"It would only be fair." Sakura's expression hardened. "Since you ripped out mine twenty-six years, three months, and twelve days ago."

Oh crap.

Niamh cut Kiyo a filthy look.

The bloody idiot could have told her this was about revenge of the bloody heart!

You had an affair with the alpha and then skipped town and didn't think that was pertinent to tell me? she yelled in his head.

Kiyo didn't even flinch.

Niamh's anger burned. *Well, clearly you know nothing about women if you thought we could walk in here and walk back out without a fight. Next time you might want to think about keeping it in your pants.*

This time he shot her a dark look that was supposed to quell her anger.

She didn't care.

She wasn't afraid of him.

She *was* afraid of the gorgeous Japanese alpha who was still carrying a grudge twenty-six years after the fact.

"You have not aged. How can that be?" Sakura asked in wonder, stroking her thumb along his cheek.

"You haven't aged either."

"A kind lie." She leaned in to whisper so softly, Niamh was sure only she and Kiyo could hear. "No one knows how kind and gentle you can be, Kiyo-chan. That was always just for me."

Niamh wished she were anywhere else but here witnessing this. She felt like an awkward third wheel, and it was not a nice feeling when you were falling for one of the other wheels.

"I'm not being kind. It's the truth. You've barely aged."

"I have aged. But you ... Oji-chan always thought you were older than your years. So mature for a young man. But he must have been wrong, hai? You had to only have been in your twenties. Which would make you nearly fifty now. Yet you do not look a day over twenty-five."

Oh shit.

Niamh held her breath as Kiyo deftly handled the questioning with a casual shrug. "I have good genes. It'll catch up to me one day."

"Hmm, maybe. After all, everything always does. Speaking of which, we must discuss your debt, Kiyo. It is long overdue."

"We seem to have a difference of opinion on that."

"You were set to fight the biggest fight Tokyo has ever seen. Oji-chan put a lot of money on you ... and you reneged. Kiyo, you owe us that money."

"I don't think I do. But if it'll settle our score, I'll pay you the money. I'm good for it."

Sakura laughed prettily and then pressed her body against his.

Yup, Niamh was going to kill her.

Kiyo's hands came to rest on Sakura's hips and she slid her arms around his neck, settling deeper into him.

Any urge to kill Sakura transferred to him. He might as well have taken his katana to Niamh's chest.

She lowered her eyes, hating that she was jealous over this cold, mercurial bastard.

"You know it does not work that way, Kiyo-chan. You have to pay the debt you owe."

"You want me to fight?"

Niamh looked at them, despite how much it hurt to see their intimate embrace. They looked stunning together.

They looked right.

For a moment it distracted her from what was happening.

"I don't have time."

"You will make time."

Kiyo sighed heavily, his expression softening as he gave her hips an affectionate squeeze. "Sakura, can't we just put this behind us?"

"Do not try to charm me. You will pay your debt or you do not leave Japan without losing a limb. Do not make me do that. You know how I love every inch of you."

Trying to slow her speeding pulse, Niamh dared to speak. "What's going on?"

"Keep the mahoutsukai quiet." Sakura flicked her a dark look. "Or I will do it for her."

Before Niamh could break her fecking neck, Kiyo leaned down and brushed his lips over Sakura's. "Show Niamh some respect … or I walk."

His words should have made her feel better, but they didn't.

That lip brush pushed Niamh further from Kiyo.

She felt like an outsider.

She felt alone.

Always alone.

She couldn't understand why this hurt so much when she barely knew him and she never knew where she stood with him, anyway. Who needed that? If she had a friend and a friend told her about a guy who was nice one second and a cold bastard the next, she'd tell her friend to dump his arse.

Niamh couldn't dump his arse physically, but emotionally …

The alpha seemed to bristle at Kiyo's command, but she didn't respond to it. She slid her hand into his top knot and gripped it, pulling his head toward hers so she could demand against his lips, "You will fight."

"One fight," he relented, to Niamh's surprise. She didn't know what this fight was they spoke of, but she couldn't believe Kiyo was giving in. She hadn't thought anyone mattered to him anymore, not since his mother, but clearly this snooty, stunning wolf had wheedled her way into his affections.

"We will see."

"One fight." He pushed her away gently, his expression hardening. "One fight, Sakura."

She considered this and then sighed. "One fight. But it needs to be a big one. Shinjuku Gyo-en in two weeks' time. We are closing it to the public for a big international fight. Some of the best wolves are coming from all over. Big money, Kiyo. I want you in that fight so I hope you are not going anywhere anytime soon."

"We'll stick around for the fight. We're staying at the Natsukashii. You can send for me when the time comes."

"No. You will stay here."

Niamh's stomach dropped at the thought of being under the pack's guard.

"We have reservations elsewhere. I'm not your prisoner, Sakura. You'll have to trust I'll be there when you need me."

The alpha smirked, her eyes drawing licentiously down his body and back up again. "Oh, you will be there when I have need of you. Hai?"

He stared stonily at her as Niamh felt nauseated.

"Kiyo." Sakura tilted her head and gave him a mock petulant look. "If you want to stay at the Natsukashii, you will be there when I have need of you. Hai?"

"If I'm not busy, then yes."

Niamh couldn't look at him now.

"I call, you *come*."

Niamh really, really wanted to get out of there. *Now*.

Finally Kiyo answered, "You know where to find me ... speaking of which ... how *did* you find me so quickly?"

"We are tapped into all security cameras. Airport, stations ... we have them rigged with facial recognition. You are on our database. As soon as you stepped into Narita, our systems pinged." Sakura grinned. "I never let a debt lie, Kiyo. I am not Oji-chan."

"No. Your uncle knew when to let things go."

Sakura glared at him. "You may leave. But do not think I am not eager to know why you are in my city with a peculiar-smelling mahoutsukai."

Kiyo didn't respond. Instead he turned and nodded his head at Niamh to leave. Feeling as if she were somehow separate from the situation, she seemed to float out of the room, barely aware of Kiyo's hand on her back.

It wasn't until minutes later as Haruto led them across the hotel lobby to the exit that she was aware of Kiyo's touch.

She didn't want him to touch her.

She didn't want anything to touch her.

He'd made it clear when he woke up on that plane that he didn't want any connection with her. He'd regretted telling her about his mother. That was the only conclusion to be drawn after his cold behavior since.

Having thought they'd connected, that she finally had someone who understood her, someone on her side, Niamh had been in a wonderful mood before he woke up.

Ever since, and now more than ever, her mood had swiftly declined.

It was still a relief to know that her visions were manipulations from Astra.

It was not a relief to realize she was still as alone as ever.

Niamh moved away from Kiyo's touch and when Haruto opened the SUV, she slid along the bench until she was pressed right up against the door.

Thankfully Kiyo didn't scooch close to her again.

She felt his gaze on her for a moment.

But it didn't touch her. Not like before.

Nothing could touch her. Her emotions were too dangerous. And she needed to focus on following her true visions and doing what was right. She'd stop Astra.

And then she'd go into hiding again.

Alone.

Far away from Kiyonari Fujiwara.

18

Something was wrong with Niamh.

Kiyo didn't know what it was and so he didn't know how to fix it. More alarmingly, it disturbed him how much he wanted to know what it was so he *could* fix it.

He'd put it down to jealousy, but it was more than that. He could feel it.

And he didn't like it.

He told himself not to question her. To let it be. After all, he was the one who had decided to create distance between them after their conversation on the plane. Niamh was just following suit. Kiyo should be happy.

But even though Niamh was right at his side, she felt millions of miles away. Her remoteness bothered him on multiple levels.

It was easy to keep quiet in the SUV as Haruto escorted them to Chūō City. Kiyo didn't want the pack knowing his business or who Niamh was to him. Sakura's performance at the hotel was born of her own jealousy. She thought Niamh was his female. How she came to that conclusion so swiftly, he didn't know, but her cozying up to him, flirting with him, her less than subtle demand to service her needs when she wanted him, was all to needle Niamh. If Niamh hadn't crackled with energy the moment Sakura touched him, the alpha might not have pushed the topic.

Then again, she might have.

No, she probably would have.

Kiyo sighed inwardly as Haruto dropped them off at the hotel.

"Anything new I should know about the city?" Kiyo asked him as he got out of the vehicle, knowing Haruto would understand his meaning.

"Vamp coven has taken over Akihabara. As long as they leave the rest of the city alone, we stay out. No wolves."

Kiyo nodded. The gaming ward wasn't his cup of tea, anyway. "Anything else?"

"You might have heard Tsukiji Market moved to Toyosu, but the outer market with the food is still there."

He almost laughed. Trust Haruto to think anything regarding food was important. "Good to know."

Haruto nodded, looking satisfied he'd imparted news of great importance. "Arufua-san will call on you when you are required."

Kiyo fought his frustration and nodded in agreement. Turning to Niamh, who waited at the hotel entrance with a coolly distant countenance, Kiyo cursed the damn vision that brought them to Tokyo. He knew Niamh felt they had to be there to protect him (from who knew what) and while he appreciated her motives, it had only landed him in trouble.

And exposed Niamh to Sakura and her pack.

He didn't like that either.

He strode over to her. "Check in."

She nodded and as she turned, he placed his hand on her lower back to lead her into the tower block. Kiyo didn't think anything of it. The gesture was instinctual. Yet he was forced to think about it when she moved away from his touch.

Rejection and anger burned in his gut.

Not anger with her.

But with himself.

He'd fucked up from the moment he woke up on the plane.

Earlier, she'd been pissed at him. He got it. He could handle it.

This ... not so much.

He hurried to catch up to her but didn't touch her again.

Kiyo spoke in Japanese with the woman behind the reception desk, and she relayed that the lobby for checking into the hotel was on the thirty-eighth floor. He told Niamh who again nodded quietly and followed him onto the elevator.

"This place must have some views," he said inanely as the elevator moved quietly upward.

"Mmm," she acknowledged.

He gritted his teeth against a growl.

When the doors opened, Niamh seemed to jump out to get away from him. Her eyes had widened ever so slightly and while the change in her was infinitesimal, Kiyo already knew her well enough to know that the hotel pleased her. It lacked the western opulence of Sakura's hotel. However, Kiyo preferred the Natsukashii's warmth with its hardwood floors, midcentury furnishings, floor lamps designed to look like framed paper lanterns, and walls created entirely from shoji screens. There were open staircases that led down to the floor below. Incredibly impressive floor-to-ceiling windows reached from that floor to the height of the ceilings on the lobby floor. Tokyo could be seen for miles.

"Do you like it?" he asked Niamh as they approached the check-in desk.

She nodded, still not looking at him. "It's beautiful."

"Nicer than the pack's hotel?"

"Much. Theirs is all about showing off how much money they've got. This is about Tokyo and thoughtful design."

He agreed.

"Is Fionn paying for this?"

"Bran called it a bonus."

Silence fell between them again as they waited in a small line at check-in. When Kiyo approached the clerk, he used the name on the passport Bran had provided.

The clerk checked his computer, relaying to Kiyo in Japanese that they had two deluxe suites booked. Kiyo shook his head, replying in their mother tongue, "We need one room. A suite with a sofa bed. And views of Mount Fuji, if you have one available." He didn't know why he added the last part. Maybe because he thought it might cheer Niamh up and pull her out of her strange mood.

"We don't have sofa beds but our suites have sofas."

That would do.

"A suite with a view," he reiterated.

The guy typed and then sighed dramatically. "I'm afraid the only room available with a view of Fuji is our Oriental. It's a one-bedroom suite with a separate living space. Quite an upgrade."

Kiyo didn't know if it was the guy's tone and its insinuation that he couldn't afford it or if it was something even more stupid, like a need to do something nice for Niamh, but he said, "We'll take it."

"It's two hundred thousand yen per night."

Roughly nineteen hundred dollars a night.

Damn it.

Fine.

Fionn was paying him a shit ton of money to protect Niamh. He could afford it. Kiyo would pay Bran back. "We'll take it," he replied more firmly.

It must have been firmer than intended, with a hint more of alpha behind it, because the clerk blanched and hurried to book the room.

A while later, once the clerk had photocopied their passports, he handed over two room cards and seemed relieved when Kiyo turned down the offer to be shown to the room.

"What was that about?" Niamh asked as they got on the elevator.

"Bran had us booked into two rooms. I changed it to one. I'll sleep on the sofa."

"I'd prefer my own room."

Kiyo worked hard to beat down that growl again. "The last time you had your own room, you took off."

"So I'm being held hostage?"

If she'd snapped at him in anger, he could have handled it. But her dull, emotionless tone irritated him. "No. But in case you didn't notice, I have enemies here, and by association, you're in danger. Not to mention the vision you keep having that brought us here in the first place."

"I hardly think Sakura is your enemy," she muttered as the elevator opened.

Following the room signs, Kiyo stopped at their door and swiped a key over the lock.

When they pushed inside, he heard Niamh let out a gasp of wonder, and satisfaction filled him.

They stood in a living room with a huge sectional that looked comfortable enough for him to sleep on. It was stylish, minimal but warm, with the same Japanese midcentury design as the lobby. The most impressive aspect of the room was the wall-to-wall, floor-to-ceiling window at one end where not only did they have amazing views of Tokyo but on a clear day like today, they could see the snow-covered Mount Fuji in the distance.

Niamh moved past him, striding across the room to stand at the window.

He followed, closing in beside her, subconsciously needing to be close to her scent of caramel and spice.

It felt like they were floating above the city.

"What does the hotel name mean?"

"Natsukashii?"

"Yes."

"Technically it means *nostalgia*."

"That's beautiful. The hotel, this room … it's beautiful. You booked this?"

"The room, yeah. Thought you might appreciate the view."

Just like that, the light in her gorgeous eyes dimmed, and she turned and walked away. She picked up her backpack where she'd dropped it upon entrance and strolled through the open sliding doors that led into the bedroom.

His patience snapped.

He followed her in.

The room was long and narrow, with a mammoth bed and dual-aspect windows overlooking the city. Behind him was the door to a polished marble bathroom with a shower big enough for five people and a tub a person could swim in. He studied Niamh as she wandered into the bathroom, fingers trailing across walls and counters, before returning to brush past him. Without a word, she dropped her backpack on the bed and stared out at the city.

"Is this how it's going to be from now on?"

"How what's going to be?"

The growl he'd been holding back rumbled out, drawing her attention. Finally. "What the hell is going on with you? Are you pissed because I didn't tell you about the pack, about Sakura, before we came here?"

"It might have been good to know so we could have avoided an ambush, but I'm not pissed about anything."

"You're something. You've barely said a word to me since we got off the plane."

Her eyes narrowed and the flash of anger in them perversely delighted him. "You made it clear when you woke up on the plane that you didn't want us to be friends. I'm only following your lead."

At the hurt he heard in her voice, the hurt she tried to hide, Kiyo took a step toward her, his voice gentle as he replied, "Niamh, it isn't personal. I just don't have friends."

"Lies. Fionn is your friend. Conall's father and grandfather were obviously your friends. Not to mention Sakura seemed pretty friendly for an enemy ..." She pushed up off the bed and her look of disappointment bothered him. "And it's always personal when someone doesn't think you're worthy of friendship."

"Of course you're worthy of friendship." His anger grew at her disappointment in him. "And do I have to remind you that I've told you things I haven't told anyone?"

"Things you obviously regretted telling me by the very fact you woke up acting like a cold bastard."

He sighed, running a hand through his hair that was coming loose from the top knot. "I don't regret telling you about my mother if it helped you." Kiyo tried to find the words that would soften the impact of what he said next. "But I didn't want you to think my telling you *meant* something."

It was the exact wrong thing to say.

As soon as the words were out of his mouth, he knew it.

Hurt flashed in Niamh's ocean eyes and was quickly chased by anger.

They stared at each other in silence for a moment while he braced for a verbal assault.

Instead, once more she surprised him.

Her expression softened. "I understand."

Discombobulated by the sudden tonal change, he raised an eyebrow. "Understand what?"

"What it's like to be afraid of your own emotions. I don't want to get too attached to you because I know you aren't the kind of man someone gets attached to and comes away intact. And you don't allow yourself to get attached to anyone because you don't trust anyone."

Her bold honesty stole his breath.

She glanced away but not before he saw the dark loneliness in her eyes.

"Niamh ..." He didn't know what to say.

What could he say when she was right?

She stared out at the city. "I don't want to spend the next few weeks or however long we're here trying to decipher what the hell the vision meant with this horrible tension between us." She looked back at him now, meeting his gaze with a sudden fierce but cool determination.

"We're not friends," Niamh stated emotionlessly. "We're here to do a job. Let's be ourselves, not coldly pushing one another away to remind ourselves what we're *not* to each other. We get it. Any conversations or relayed history is given for the benefit of the mission and will not be misconstrued as some kind of connection. Let's just agree to that so we both know where we stand."

A feeling akin to dread filled his gut.

But she was right.

So he nodded. "Agreed."

Niamh looked away again but seemed to deflate somewhat, as if the tension was releasing from her body. "Well," she said, exhaling slowly, "I don't know about you, but I could eat a bloody horse. That bento box on the plane did nothing to fill me up."

Agitation still thrummed through him but Kiyo forced another nod. "Yeah, I could eat."

"Where do you fancy?" She upended the contents of her backpack on the bed. "While you were talking with the guy at reception, I was reading some of their pamphlets. They have a Michelin-starred restaurant in the building. I wonder if they're open for lunch."

Kiyo shook his head, suddenly wanting to show her authentic Tokyo. He thought she'd like that. "Do you like sushi?"

Her brows puckered, her lips twisted in thought. "I don't know," she eventually answered. "I don't think I've ever tried good sushi before."

"I'll take you to Tsukiji Market for brunch."

"Skeeji market?"

"Tsukiji Market is Tokyo's most well-known fish market. There are hundreds of food stalls and restaurants. There's sushi, sashimi, hibachi-grilled fish. There's *okonomiyaki*, *shioyaki*, *imagawayaki*, *tomorokoshi*, *yakisoba*, *nikuman*—"

"Okay, stop naming food." She laughed. "I don't even know what any of it means and you're still making me hungry."

Kiyo chuckled, the sound trailing off as Niamh blinked at him in surprise. "What?"

"You laughed."

"So?" He frowned.

She shrugged, a blush staining her cheeks. "Nothing. I've just never heard you laugh before."

That couldn't be true.

Could it?

Is that how high his defenses were with her?

Fuck.

Kiyo moved toward the living room. "I'll let you clean up first. Let me know when I can use the bathroom." He needed a shower more than he needed food.

"I won't be long," she promised.

NIAMH KEPT HER PROMISE, appearing in the living room fifteen minutes later having showered and changed into a pair of tight jeans and a cropped T-shirt that showed tantalizing flashes of smooth, pale skin.

"Done." She strode past him, moving toward the window. As she did, her scent gusted over him and his body reacted with an intensity that shocked him. Feeling the tightening in his groin and heat on his skin, Kiyo gaped at her.

She'd piled her hair on top of her head in what was supposed to be a messy bun but her hair was so long, strands spilled down over her shoulders. There was something about her carefree style that made a man want to pull her hair tie out to see it all come tumbling down.

And he didn't even want to get started on what the denim jeans did for her ass.

Niamh's body was hard to ignore, as much as he tried. But she was fae, and from what he knew, part of their genetic makeup was their allure to other species.

"You need a jacket."

"I'm never cold."

"People will think it's weird you're not wearing a jacket in Tokyo in February." His eyes lingered on the sliver of skin revealed by the short T-shirt.

Niamh shrugged, leaning against the window without looking at him. "I don't care what people think."

Aggravated, he pushed off the sofa, heading toward the bathroom with swiftness. He didn't want her to notice his very male reaction to her.

But as he stripped and stepped into the shower, his erection raged fierce and strong. The water sluiced down his body, and he felt it course over his skin like fingers. His every nerve ending was on fire with feeling. He couldn't remember the last time he felt like this.

He wanted Niamh.

He'd wanted her from the moment he'd touched her.

It only made sense that days (which felt like months) of repressing his response to her would finally get the better of him when his defenses were lowered by being back in Tokyo.

Still, it was typical that once she'd put herself completely out of his reach with her little speech about them not being friends, he'd start to lose control over his attraction for her. People were fucked up that way. Even werewolves.

Turning the jets up on the shower so Niamh wouldn't hear, he closed his eyes, wrapped his hand around his dick, and went somewhere in his head he promised to forget about later.

Somewhere dark and hot and pulsing.

Somewhere deeply satisfying.

Somewhere with Niamh.

When he came, it was long and hard and he grit his teeth to swallow the loud groan of release that had swelled inside him. Kiyo sagged against the wet tiled wall and let out a huff of disbelief.

As hard as he'd just come ... it wasn't enough.

Damn her.

"Aren't you wondering how I dried my hair so fast?" she asked with a teasing smile as they took the elevator down to the hotel's ground floor.

Still taken aback by his uncontrolled physical response to her, Kiyo grunted in response.

"I used magic. I can use magic to clean myself too. Sometimes I do. But there's nothing like the feeling of a hot shower."

He shot her a suspicious look. Why was she rambling about the shower? Had she heard him in there? Was she teasing him?

Niamh stared back at him with innocent eyes. "That's the thing about magic. I can do practically anything with it, but sometimes doing it the human way is actually more satisfying."

Why did everything she say suddenly sound sexual?

It wasn't her. It was him.

He cleared his throat, trying to think of something that would distract him. "No more visions?"

"You'd know if there were," she replied dryly, following him out of the elevator and to the lobby.

He grunted again before gesturing to the valet to hail them a cab.

"I was reading the pamphlets in the room about places to visit, and I'd really love to go to Akihabara."

She would want to go to the one place they couldn't. "Off limits. Vamp coven territory."

As a taxi pulled up, Niamh grumbled, "Bloody vamps always spoil everything."

Kiyo scooted into the car behind her after tipping the valet and directed the driver to the market.

"We could still go and just be careful," Niamh said.

"What?"

"Akihabara."

"No. It's not about that. There's an agreement between them and the Iryoku." He lowered his voice. "No wolves allowed."

Her brow puckered. "But I'm not a wolf."

"You're not going anywhere in this city without me."

"Kiyo, I was taking care of myself long before you showed up."

"My city, my rules." Part of him said it just because he knew it would piss her off.

Sure enough, she bristled. "I'll go if I want."

"Have you forgotten how you smell?" he said softly, trying to tame the burst of possessive territorialism that he knew was natural to most wolves but had never been to him. Until now.

Niamh sighed but said no more on the subject. Instead she turned her attention to the window, taking in the city with her usual wide-eyed wonder.

It didn't take long to reach the market.

Kiyo placed his hand on Niamh's lower back without thought to guide her, but her cropped shirt meant his palm hit silken skin. His fingers flexed as electricity tingled up his arm. Niamh stiffened and shot him a look, as if she felt it too.

Deciding it was safer not to touch her, he nudged her forward and let his arm fall to his side. The market was comprised of narrow walkways, crowded in on either side with stalls and restaurants with overhanging awnings. The buildings were crammed together, ramshackle and higgledy-piggledy but with their own sense of history and thus order. Smoke and spice and the tangy scent of miso assaulted them, and Kiyo explained what was on offer at each stall. The brunch and early lunch crowds meant the market was packed, its soundtrack one of indistinguishable layers of conversation.

Niamh stopped to watch a young man holding what looked more like a sword than a knife cut through a chunk of sashimi tuna steak like butter. "What is he doing?"

"*Maguro bocho*." Kiyo stepped up behind her, his mouth near her ear, as he pointed to the knife. "It's very sharp. Needs very little pressure and it allows him to cut the tuna sashimi into fine slices. Do you want to try the tuna?"

She glanced up at him. "Is it good?"

"With wasabi, yes." He turned to call out to the young man and ordered two tuna. Taking their containers and chopsticks, he and Niamh stood off to the side to eat standing up.

His lips twitched, watching Niamh stare uncertainly at the tuna. He lifted a piece of tuna with his chopsticks and said, "*Itadakimasu*."

"What does that mean?"

"It's one of our many words that don't have a literal translation. The closest is 'bon appétit,' but it means more than that. It's a way of showing your gratitude to everyone responsible for producing your meal, from the fisherman all the way to the chef."

"Say it again."

He said it slower this time.

"Itadakimasu." She raised her tuna to him in acknowledgment of the expression and then dipped into the bit of wasabi in the corner of the container.

Kiyo stopped eating to watch her.

She nibbled tentatively at it.

Surprise flickered over her face and she ate with more gusto.

Seconds later, two pieces were gone.

"Good?" He grinned.

Her gaze dropped to his mouth before returning to his eyes. "Surprisingly."

Once they'd finished, he guided her to a tea stall. "Green tea?"

"Ooh, yes."

It unnerved Kiyo how much he delighted in watching Niamh discover the market. It took the guy at the shop a little over five minutes to prepare the green tea, and Niamh studied everything he did with fascination.

"So good." She sighed in delight after taking her first sip. She tapped the small white cup. "What's this called?"

"*Yunomi.*"

"Yunomi?"

He nodded. "Hai."

"Hai," she repeated, beaming like a kid on Christmas. It was as if their earlier tension and conversation hadn't happened. "I like that word: *hai*. Will you teach me more Japanese while we're here?"

"If you like."

She beamed at him, eyes bright with joy at the thought.

Kiyo had to look away, searching for somewhere else to take her. It was either that or he would kiss the hell out of her right there in the middle of the market.

As they walked, green tea in hand, he pointed out the narrow back alleyways where the food was produced and told her about pork dumplings, corn with miso, and soba noodles.

The thing that caught her attention, however, was *tamagoyaki*. Pan-fried rolled omelet. At her insistence, he bought her one.

"Mmm," she moaned and nodded happily around a bite she was eating off a cocktail stick. She swallowed and asked, "What's in it?"

"Traditionally, egg, salt, and dashi. It's why it's a little sweeter than the omelets you're used to."

From there they ate grilled fishcake on skewers while Niamh eyed a stall selling *okonomayaki*. Pancakes.

"I was planning to take you for some sushi. Will you be able to eat that too?"

"Hmm. Sushi first. We'll see how I feel afterward."

"You eat more than any woman I've ever known."

"Uh, fae. I can move faster than two hundred miles per hour," she said pretending to be defensiveness. "Can you imagine what that does to my metabolism?"

Smirking, Kiyo nodded and then led her farther through the market. A while later, he took her arm and pulled her gently into a crowded standing sushi bar.

He studied her as she watched the chefs behind their high-top counter create the sushi at tremendous speed and place it on the wooden trays in front of the waiting customers.

"They're so fast," she murmured. His eyes dropped to her mouth. "It does look good. So fresh. But I think I'll still want those pancakes after. And maybe those pork dumpling things you were talking about." She grabbed his arm, drawing his gaze up to her eyes. "Ooh, and the corn with the miso."

Kiyo's shoulders shook with laughter. "You're acting like you haven't eaten in years."

She released him, smiling sheepishly. "I don't know why I'm so hungry. I just ... I want to try everything." She wrinkled her nose; he found it adorable when Kiyo was sure he'd never found anything adorable in his life. "Except squid." She scowled at the wooden tray with said cephalopod on it. "I don't want squid."

"Noted. I'll eat the squid."

Kiyo couldn't believe how much he was enjoying this experience with her. He couldn't remember the last time he'd had such fun. Such *human* fun. Niamh wasn't just hungry for food, she was hungry for life, for experiences, for knowledge, and in that moment with her, he didn't feel jaded and old and trapped by the monotony of forever.

Before, he'd always known what lay ahead. An eternity of wandering, doing and feeling the same things over and over. But now Kiyo felt a freedom he hadn't felt in a long time.

The freedom of not knowing what was ahead after all.

All because of her.

She was so unbearably dangerous to him.

Part of him was beginning to not give a shit if it meant feeling like this even for a while. Her words at the hotel, about them being nothing to each other but the mission, rang false then and even more so now.

Deciding that to think about it was to ruin his mood, he threw the thought away and conversed with the chefs about what they were doing. He then relayed to Niamh what they told him. They stood, drinking warm sake out of cups while they ate at the counter. She went nuts over the yellowtail, so he gave her his portion and took the squid off her tray before she could ask.

She smiled in gratitude and dipped a sushi roll into her soy.

"You got the hang of the chopsticks fast."

"I had a good teacher."

They shared a warm look. Kiyo was so relaxed, so in the moment, her next words pulled him out of it with all the impact of a bucket of cold water.

"So, tell me about Sakura."

He almost choked on his snow crab sushi roll.

Niamh chortled. "What? We've already decided we're not friends and nothing said between us means anything."

Renewed agitation thrummed through him at the reminder. "What do you want to know?"

"You two seem close for someone who doesn't get close to anyone."

He shrugged, finding no reason not to tell Niamh the truth. "I'd started fighting in the underground fights decades before. In the '90s I came to Tokyo for a job. When it ended, I decided to try out one of the underground fights here. Eito, Sakura's uncle and pack alpha, saw me fight. I stupidly agreed to fight in one of his—a more professional setup in the basement of the hotel where people bet on the fights. Eito began to think he owned me. And Sakura pursued me. Since I had no plans to stick around, I didn't see any harm in a casual arrangement. But Sakura got attached. Then she started dropping hints in Eito's ear about what I was to her … and he tried to groom me."

"Groom you?"

"To take over his empire with Sakura as alpha. I'd be her mate."

"What happened?"

"They knew what I was when they got involved with me. I wasn't going to change, and I never gave any signal that I would." He knew he sounded defensive but everything he said was true. It wasn't his fault that Eito and Sakura changed the rules on him. "I couldn't stay even if I'd wanted to. No one could know that I didn't age. But the immediate problem was that they were using me, and I felt trapped.

"On the other side of it was Daiki. Powerful alpha, an orphaned pup who Eito raised. It was assumed he and Sakura would become mates. Daiki loved her, but Sakura thought of him as a brother. Daiki was pissed, to say the least, when he discovered I was screwing his intended," he related dryly. "He and his own little wolf pack were continually trying to fuck with me, and it wasn't worth it."

"*She* wasn't worth it?"

"To him," he answered. "She was worth it to him and I respected that. But she wasn't worth it to me. So I got the hell out of Tokyo."

"Reneging on a fight."

He nodded. "I never promised to fight, but I never said I wouldn't either. Which is why I'll fight for Sakura if it'll get her off my back."

"I don't think she wants off it." Niamh shot him a saucy look. "More to the point, I think she wants you on it."

Her words sparked an answering image but the face of the woman riding him wasn't Sakura.

Kiyo looked away. "She can want what she wants. Doesn't mean she'll get it."

A somewhat tense silence settled between them for a second or two but was abruptly broken by Niamh's panicked words. "Oh no, not here, not now."

Kiyo's gaze jerked to Niamh who'd gone stiff as a post on the bar stool. "What is it?"

She cut him an exasperated look. "I sense danger."

Kiyo let out a snarl of aggravation before gesturing to her to follow him out of the standing bar. He scanned the crowded lane, readying for fight or flight depending on the source.

And then he saw him, marching through the crowds with his men.

"Fuck."

"What? What is it?" Niamh pressed up against his back, and the heat of her sent an overwhelming surge of protectiveness through him.

"It's Daiki."

"The good-looking fella the train doors closed on and who is now coming toward us glaring at you like he wants to kill you?"

Good-looking? He cut her a dark glance over his shoulder. "Yes."

"Why? What does he want with you now?"

"My guess? To warn me off."

"Off what?"

"His mate." Kiyo caught Niamh's eyes. "Sakura."

Understanding dawned. "Oh shit."

Yeah, that about summed it up.

19

"Whatever happens, don't use your powers," Kiyo murmured. If Daiki discovered Niamh, Kiyo would have to kill him. "This is between me and him."

You expect me to just stand by while you fight?

He started at the unexpected sound of her voice in his head. He wasn't quite used to it yet. Kiyo glared at her, bristling with male pride. "I can handle myself."

"Oh, I've seen that," she assured him. "But I'm not sure killing Sakura's mate is a smart idea."

"I'm not going to kill him."

"You could not even if you tried," Daiki growled, overhearing them. He sneered at Kiyo like he wanted to rip his head from his body.

Kiyo straightened his shoulders and tried to conceal as much of Niamh as possible from Daiki and his little pack. The four wolves standing behind Daiki weren't all the same players from the '90s. He only recognized two of them. One was Kobe, Daiki's beta.

"He has barely aged," one of them said to Daiki in Japanese, his tone suspicious.

"It means nothing," Daiki replied. "His bones will have aged, and that is all that matters since I plan to break some."

"What are they saying?" Niamh whispered, stepping up beside Kiyo, drawing the other wolves' attention. He could feel her energy humming at a low level around her, which meant she was readying for battle. Kiyo shot her another warning look, but she was too busy shooting her own warning look at the wolves.

Seeing Daiki's men stare openly at her, their eyes dragging down her body, Kiyo tensed with agitation.

Daiki looked at her but not in the way a male stared at a woman he found attractive. His gaze was more calculating. He turned to Kiyo, something working behind his eyes. "Leave Tokyo. Now."

"English, Daiki."

The wolf shrugged and repeated the demand in English.

"I'm afraid we can't do that. Not just because we don't want to but because your alpha has demanded my presence for a fight."

"I am aware of what Sakura has asked of you."

Kiyo raised an eyebrow. "And you'd try to undermine your alpha?"

Daiki's men shuffled their feet restlessly behind him, clearly uncomfortable with anyone voicing such a thing out loud.

Daiki's face hardened but satisfaction gleamed in his eyes. "I hoped you would see it that way. You and I will settle this now."

Kiyo gestured with his hand. "Lead the way."

"After you." Daiki stepped to the side, and Kiyo grabbed Niamh's hand to keep her with him. Daiki's eyes lowered to where Kiyo held her and a frown puckered his brow.

The wolves surrounded him and Niamh as they marched from the market. Locals darted out of the way, either recognizing Daiki and his men or intuition telling them this was business they didn't want to get involved in. Tourists steered clear because of the sheer amount of energy pouring off them all.

It didn't surprise Kiyo when Daiki led them all the way down to the river and stopped on the loading dock behind a warehouse at the river's edge. They could still be seen, but no one would dare stop them. Not even the police once they realized who Daiki was.

If it looks like he's going to fight dirty, I'm stepping in.

Kiyo turned to face Niamh in answer and gripped her elbow as he tried to communicate silently that she was *not* to make any move toward helping him. At all. Thankfully, Niamh's mulish expression softened, and she gave him a slight nod of acquiescence.

He raised an eyebrow.

I promise, she said softly in his head.

Gratified, Kiyo gestured for her to stand to the side. When Daiki's men sidled up next to her, he quelled the overwhelming urge to warn them off her. He didn't need them to know Niamh was a weakness.

Daiki shrugged out of his jacket and threw it without looking at his men. "Put it on his mahoutsukai. She looks cold."

Kiyo bared his teeth at the men without thinking. "Dare."

Sakura's mate smirked, and Kiyo cursed inwardly. He was testing him.

Irritated, he flicked an annoyed look at Niamh. He'd told her to wear a jacket.

Don't look at me like that, she snapped.

For some reason, her indignation relaxed him.

Which was a good thing. It didn't bode well to enter into a fight when you were tense. Kiyo shrugged out of his own jacket and Niamh stepped forward to take it. To his shock, she slipped it on as if to make a point, and a rush of possessiveness soared through him. His blood pumped hot and fast, and he turned to Daiki with bloodlust in his eyes.

His opponent saw and felt it, baring his teeth to reveal drawn canines.

They raised their arms, fists relaxed, in guard position.

"Let's do this."

Daiki moved first, turning at speed to come at Kiyo with a spinning hook kick. He dodged the maneuver and caught Daiki's leg with a block that threw the wolf off balance. Fast and agile, however, Daiki bounced back up into position and came at Kiyo again with a series of front and side and spinning kicks that forced him back along the riverside.

He kept this up, staying on the defense, rather than offense, to tire Daiki. The alpha *would* tire eventually while it would take much to tire Kiyo.

"*Tatakai*!" Daiki yelled in outrage. Fight!

But the more Kiyo didn't fight, the clumsier Daiki got in his aggression. As Kiyo maneuvered them in a tight circle and back up toward Niamh and Daiki's men, the other alpha lost his footing and had to catch himself from falling. When Kiyo didn't take advantage of the moment, Daiki's face flooded with color and he came at Kiyo with fists of fury.

Kiyo blocked, dodged, and tapped his punches away like they were mere flies.

Then he heard Niamh's voice, her snap of irritation as she warned, "Touch my arse again, dickhead, and I'll tear yours a new one."

Rage flooded him as he whipped around in her direction. Lights exploded across his left eye as he felt his head snap on his neck.

Sucker punched.

"Kiyo!" Niamh cried out in concern.

Daiki took advantage and punched him in the gut. But Kiyo was motivated now. He smashed his fist into Daiki's face, knocking the wolf on his ass, and then he strode toward Niamh, ignoring the swelling in his eye that would heal soon enough, anyway.

"Which one?" he barked at her, his gaze on Daiki's men.

Niamh didn't need to answer. The one closest to her shifted away, guilt and wariness in his eyes.

He was a dead man.

Surging at the wolf, Kiyo swung his dominant arm in an uppercut. The impact juddered down his body and a crack rent the air. Daiki's henchman fell like a sack of potatoes, neck broken.

It was over disappointingly fast.

The other three wolves stood stunned for a moment as Niamh's shocked glance bounced from the downed werewolf to Kiyo.

"What do you think you are doing?" Daiki yelled.

Kiyo glanced over his shoulder as Sakura's mate strode toward him. "He touched her."

Daiki slowed to a stop, staring at his unconscious man. "And that was worth breaking his neck?"

"You think it's okay if a person sexually touches another without their consent?" Kiyo asked, but he already knew the answer. He and Daiki had never gotten along because of Sakura, but that didn't mean Kiyo didn't have some respect for the wolf.

He was a man of honor and all the time Kiyo had known him, he'd never hurt those weaker than him or touched a woman who didn't want to be touched.

"There is more to it than that." Daiki approached, drawing to a halt to look at Niamh. "Who is this mahoutsukai to you?"

Thinking of how easily she distracted him, how protective—and, yes, possessive—he felt over her, Kiyo knew she was more than just a job. More than a mission. He couldn't process how much more. He didn't know if he'd ever be able to. But he had to acknowledge that his and Niamh's conversation in the hotel room that morning had been bullshit.

Turning to her, their eyes met.

"She's my friend," Kiyo replied to Daiki but said with all meaning to Niamh.

Her lips parted on a exhalation she couldn't quite hide. And while something softened in her expression, her eyes seemed to fill with confusion and questions.

"Fine." Daiki broke the silent moment between Kiyo and Niamh. He glowered at his men. "You touch the mahoutsukai and you answer to me."

Kobe, his beta, nodded militantly and gestured for them to back away from Niamh.

Daiki turned to Kiyo. "Let us finish this."

~

AN HOUR LATER, covered in sweat and bruises, Kiyo stood over a sprawled Daiki. "Are we done?"

Daiki squinted up at him through swollen lids and snarled. "Yes. *Kono kuso*."

Kiyo started to remember the reasons he *didn't* like the wolf. Turning from him, he paused when Daiki called out his name. Sakura's mate slowly pushed up onto his knees. He held the ribs that Kiyo had broken in the final fifteen minutes of the fight.

"Stay away from Sakura," Daiki warned quietly.

"I don't want her," Kiyo answered honestly.

Hearing the truth in it, Daiki frowned. His eyes flickered behind Kiyo in suspicion.

Kiyo tensed. He didn't need anyone realizing how important Niamh was to him, but he suspected it was perhaps too late.

Understanding seemed to dawn on Daiki, and hating the idea of the wolf knowing anything that made Kiyo vulnerable, he spoke to distract him. "Sakura made it clear she's not done with me. Instead of warning me to stay away from her, perhaps you should warn your mate to stay away from me. There's nothing more off-putting to me than someone who uses their power to try to coerce me into their bed."

Daiki lunged, faltering as he gasped out in pain.

Enough. Kiyo heard Niamh's disapproving voice in his head.

Without another word, he turned on his heel, eyes to Niamh, and strode toward her as if he didn't feel bruises on his body from the few powerful hits Daiki managed to get past his defenses. It had been a joke of a fight. Other than the sucker punch he'd gotten in, Daiki never got near Kiyo's face again.

Taking hold of Niamh's hand, he marched them past Daiki's wolves who had surrounded the one who was slowly coming back to consciousness. Their furious glares followed him and Niamh, but they didn't dare make a move.

It wasn't until he'd safely ensconced Niamh in the back of a cab that she spoke. "You were toying with him. The fight. Not just the mean dig about Sakura afterward. That fight was nothing to you."

He didn't need to answer. They both knew it was true.

"Then why?" she huffed, her exasperation finally drawing his attention to her face. She stared at him like she didn't understand. "Why fight him at all?"

"Because he wanted it."

"Seriously? So, every time someone wants to fight you, and I'm sure that happens quite a lot, you capitulate?"

"Not every time. Daiki has been waiting for this fight for a long time."

"Why didn't he kill you, then?"

"That wasn't the point."

"Explain the point. Because you just seem like a bunch of Neanderthals to me."

He scowled. "The point was to defend Sakura's honor. He didn't get the chance last time."

"Her honor?"

"He thought I took her virginity. I didn't."

"Why not tell him that, then?"

"It wouldn't be right."

A cloud flickered across Niamh's face. "Because you care about her?"

"No." Kiyo sighed impatiently. He was exhausted. Not from the fight but from the emotional energy he'd expended in the last few days. "Because Daiki needs to believe in Sakura's honor. He needs to believe that her virtue was taken, not given. It's part of the way he views her. Screwed up or not, old-fashioned or not, he needs to believe she's virtuous. Why would I disillusion him?"

Niamh considered this. "While that's very gentlemanly of you, it might have had a bigger impact if you hadn't rubbed his nose in the fact that his mate wants to sleep with you."

Maybe it was Niamh's prudish disapproval or maybe it was just the strangeness of the past days, but amusement bubbled inside him.

Suddenly he was chuckling … and then laughing. He leaned his head back on the cab bench seat, fingers pressed to his closed eyes as his body shook.

Then her voice was in his head, her own laughter dancing through the words as she said, *I don't know why you're laughing but you should do it more. I like the sound.*

A tender ache flared inside him.

He opened his eyes to look at her, his laughter drifting away.

There was something like affection in her expression. "Are we really friends, then, Kiyo? Or did you just say that to make them stop touching me?"

Friends.

What was Niamh to him, really? She was *kyōka suigetsu*. She was a flower in the mirror. She was the moon's reflection on the water. A beautiful but unattainable dream. She was an emotion inside of him that couldn't be described in words.

"Friends," he agreed. It was the truth. But it wasn't the whole truth. The whole truth was something he couldn't admit out loud. And Kiyo felt fear.

For the first time since he'd been bitten, he felt true fear.

20

Niamh was suffering from emotional whiplash.

Just when she thought she and Kiyo had figured out how to treat one another, he turned around and decided the opposite.

It was frustrating to say the least.

At the market she'd been enjoying herself, mostly because Kiyo was finally relaxed around her. She thought he was relieved that she'd decided not to be friends. Perhaps he'd sensed her infatuation with him and now knowing she had no plans to pursue it, he was able to be himself?

And being himself was a wonderful thing. Kiyo was patient and interesting and seemed to enjoy introducing her to Japanese culture. Even if she was slightly confused when his eyes dropped to her mouth now and then or how his dark gaze gleamed with male appreciation.

But getting sucker punched because he'd been distracted by the idiot groping her and then staring deep into her eyes with that intense expression only to pronounce her his friend …

Niamh was bamboozled by the sexy, mercurial bastard.

She didn't want to think about what the sight of him laughing in the cab did to her belly flutters.

So they were friends. It was decided.

Friends.

Did friends cause constant butterflies or hot flushes when you thought about them taking a shower a few meters from you?

Niamh didn't think so.

And now, rather than being stuck in a hotel room with him with a big city outside to escape to if she needed a break, they were on their way to the mountains. Where she'd be trapped with him completely, in a cabin of all places.

Niamh had been blissfully free of any Astra-manipulated visions the last few days in Tokyo. But she'd also been free of *any* visions, period. She could tell Kiyo was growing antsy at the lack of direction, and it was only exacerbated by the moon, which was moving toward its full phase. The morning after their day at the market and Kiyo's impressive fight with Daiki (that did nothing to quell Niamh's belly flutters), Kiyo had announced at breakfast that they were going to the mountains in two days' time. They needed to be there so he could turn in privacy for the full moon.

"I was intending to leave you here at the hotel, but now I'm not letting you out of my sight."

"Because of Daiki?"

"Because of the pack and because of Astra," Kiyo had answered. "She was following you in Paris, which probably means she's in Tokyo or at least knows we're here."

While Niamh slept, Kiyo had been on the phone booking a place for them to stay in the mountains. That's how she found herself three days after their arrival in Tokyo, in the passenger seat of a rented car as Kiyo drove them out of the city. Apparently they'd be staying in an out-of-the-way lodge in the mountains not far from Mount Mito. Niamh obviously didn't know where that was, but Kiyo said it was about a two-hour drive west out of the city.

"Maybe I'll get a vision while we're there," she said in a hopeful tone, knowing he wanted to expedite the mission. He'd spent the last few days playing tourist guide, showing Niamh around the city, taking her to the stunning temple at Senso-ji, and back to the pack's Shinjuku ward but this time to Golden Gai to visit the narrow streets with their post-war bars that were stacked on top of each other via steep staircases. And also to see the Gyo-en National Garden. It was where Sakura's fight would be held.

After strolling through the absolutely stunning Japanese garden, Niamh wondered how on earth Sakura got away with closing it down for a fight. And why would anyone in their right mind want to? What if the gardens were destroyed? There were not only traditional Japanese gardens but landscaped English and French gardens too. Niamh's favorite spot was the Taiwan Pavilion, perched along a pond. Kiyo told her it was a pity it was just a couple of weeks too early for cherry blossom season. Niamh already thought the place was breathtaking. She couldn't imagine what it would be like with the cherry blossoms in full bloom.

The garden did, however, seem vaguely familiar, and she mentioned to Kiyo about the garden she'd seen in her visions. He said there were many Japanese gardens, and if there was nothing specific that stood out for her, they couldn't be sure this was the one from her vision.

"Hopefully not," he replied unexpectedly to her comment about having a vision. "We'll be in the mountains for three days. Full moon phase."

Of course.

Right.

Niamh frowned. "We didn't check out of the hotel. Are you telling me you're paying for that room for three days when we're not even there?"

"It's no big deal."

It *was* a big deal. Kiyo wasn't the type to splash the cash like that. "We should have checked out."

"As long as we're checked in, anyone who wants to know we're in Tokyo will think we're still in the city."

True.

"At least let me pay for my half."

Kiyo snorted. "And have you rob a bank to do it?"

Her cheeks colored. Even though she knew it wasn't a dig, it only reminded her that she hadn't done anything honorable to earn money. When Thea was on the run and on her own, she'd worked every menial job under the sun to pay her own way. She stayed in shitty apartments all over Europe. Niamh had never sacrificed like that.

"Hey ..." Kiyo's voice softened. "I didn't mean anything by it."

"I know. Still, I should probably think about getting a proper job at some point. Putting some money away. Money I've earned."

"You have a job. An important one. Don't forget it."

Soothed somewhat, she shot him a smile he couldn't see because he was focused on the road ahead.

They fell into companionable silence for a while, and Niamh took in the city as they drove through. They slowed in the heavy traffic. Catching sight of a sign that had a wolf painted on it, Niamh thought about the reason for their flight into the woods.

"What's it like?" she blurted out.

"What?"

"The call of the moon?"

He flicked her an amused, questioning look.

She shrugged. "I've never had the chance to converse with a werewolf long enough to ask. I mean, you *have* to turn on a full moon, right?"

"Yeah, there's no stopping it."

"So what does it feel like?"

Kiyo seemed to consider this. "Physically, it's like this tingling sensation down my spine. A burning tingle. It's a pleasure pain. The first time I was forced to turn, it was frightening to not have control over my body. To feel it changing and not be able to stop it. But after a while, the fear went away. I feel connected to the universe during a full moon in a way I don't otherwise. Like the moon and I are bonded. Like it rejoices in my running wild in my wolf form. It's freeing. To soar and leap and be at one with the woods and the earth and the animals. The human part of me might lose control of its body but the wolf is in control of every veer and jump and swerve through the trees."

Something warm and full of anticipation moved through her. "It sounds ... awesome."

Kiyo threw her a quick grin.

"You don't resent being a wolf, then?"

He shook his head. "Strangely not. When I was first bitten, I didn't want it. I was afraid of it. But eventually—and by eventually, I mean quite a few years later—I started to give into it. When I did, I realized that being a werewolf had freed me."

"Freed you?"

"When I was human, I was always treated as if I was different because of my mother's supposed shame. Children who should have been friends used me as target practice. Adults veered between treating me as if I were invisible or as if I were less than an animal to them. It got better as I got older, living in Tokyo away from the past. But I never quite felt myself. Or that I belonged, no matter how people tried to make me feel like I belonged.

"Being awoken to the supernatural world, becoming a werewolf ... I was finally able to let go of the idea that being different was something to be ashamed of. I let go of all the shit that had screwed with my head for years. It was freeing, and I might have been happy as a wolf."

Niamh heard the underlying sadness in his voice and guessed, "If you hadn't been cursed with immortality?"

"Yeah."

"Will you tell about me about it, Kiyo? Will you tell me the rest of your story?"

He slowed the car to stop at a traffic light and looked at her, searching her face for something.

Niamh didn't dare move, afraid any little thing would push him away. He didn't make friendship comfortable, that was for certain. But Niamh couldn't seem to stop wanting to try with him, anyway.

The lights changed and Kiyo turned to focus on the road again.

Disappointment filled her only to melt away as he began to speak.

"After Sofu abandoned me in Tokyo, I tried to survive the only way I could. I begged for food and fell in with some street urchins who taught me how to pick pockets. I hated it, but they kept me alive. It was only some weeks later when I was begging for food in the Kabuto-cho area that things changed. It was the business center of the city, where the bank was. While businessmen were more likely to kick you out of their way than give you yen, those who would give money were often more casually generous than could be found elsewhere. There were a few who handed over yen notes as if they didn't even realize their value.

"That day I was begging, I was approached by a well-dressed woman. When we talked, she seemed surprised by how well-spoken and educated I was. It turned out she was the wife of a construction contractor. She gave me yen and told me to meet her back there the next day for more. So I did. And she kept her promise. This time she'd brought food as well as coin and asked me about my life. Assuming the truth of my illegitimacy would send her running, I lied and said my family had perished in a fire back in Osaka. That I'd come to Tokyo to make my fortune. She was a kindhearted woman and I hated lying to her, but I was trying to survive."

"I understand," Niamh said softly, hearing the self-rebuke in his voice. "You know I understand that. You did what you had to."

Kiyo exhaled slowly and Niamh's breath caught at the tenderness that suffused his face. "Her name was Ichika. Her husband was Yasahiro Watanabe. Theirs was a love match but their marriage had not been blessed with children of their own. When Ichika brought me home with her, I was sure Yasahiro would throw me out instantly. Instead he sat me down and we had a conversation. Whatever he saw in me, it was enough to extract his trust. He decided he would try to help me find work. A good position to suit my obviously good birth.

"But as I accompanied Yasahiro at his work, I took a genuine interest in the construction business. It pleased him. More than I think I ever knew then. Before we knew it, months and then years passed as I lived with them and worked as an apprentice for Yasahiro."

"They sound like amazing people."

"They were. But I couldn't forget my mother or the men who destroyed her. I'd promised myself that I'd return to Osaka one day and wreak revenge on the men who brutalized and violated her."

Niamh held her breath, feeling nervous for him, even though these events had already passed.

"Seven years later, I was nineteen and considered a man. I had a good job and while I wanted revenge for my mother, I was concerned about hurting my new family with my actions. So, I delayed it. And I worked my ass off for Yasahiro and endured Ichika's many attempts to marry me to a respectable bride."

Niamh smirked, imagining how much he'd have chafed at that.

"Yasahiro and I went on a fishing trip to the mountains to schmooze government officials into signing a contract with us. One of the men was a *danna*—the patron of a well-known geisha called Sora. What none of us knew then was that Sora, while taking money and gifts from her danna in exchange for being his exclusive mistress, was carrying on an affair with a young man. And he happened to be a very jealous werewolf called Kurai."

"Holy shit."

"Sora didn't know, of course. That Kurai was a werewolf. I knew that when Kurai changed in front of us. She was as horrified and shocked as we were. I caught up with him a year after he attacked us and asked him why before I killed him. He wanted to kill Sora's danna and when he heard we'd all be in the mountains, he thought it was the perfect chance to get away with it. But when he showed up, he was out of his mind with jealousy. He confronted Sora and her danna and Yasahiro tried to step in to calm the situation down. But Kurai lost all control. We watched him turn into a wolf and I thought I was losing my mind. He ripped through our entire party like we were made of the finest silk. Tore us to pieces. I can still hear the screaming."

Niamh had seen many horrors in her visions, but she didn't know if her heart had ached quite as badly as it did for Kiyo right then. He'd lost so much. And endured incredible violence.

"I was the only one who woke up a day or two later after going through a fever unlike anything I've experienced. I couldn't understand what I was seeing when I woke up. What I was feeling. I raced out of the cabin and eventually it came to me that I was an animal. Out in the woods, somehow I changed back into my human form. I was terrified."

"I can only imagine."

Kiyo flicked her a wry, unhappy look. "For a while, I *really* did think I was losing my mind."

"What happened next?"

"I returned to the cabin and practically threw up my insides at what I found in there. Yasahiro was dead. They were all dead. Worried I'd be blamed, I left. I left Ichika and everything behind to find answers. I eventually tracked down rumors of a wolf pack near the mountains close to Kyoto, and I lived with them for a while. They taught me how to change at will and how to endure a full moon. When I felt emotionally strong enough to return to Tokyo, I hunted down Kurai and killed him for Yasahiro and Sora and every man in that lodge. I killed him for making me into something I loathed. I killed him for Ichika, who'd lost the love of her life and didn't know why. Perhaps she even blamed me. I'll never know.

"I left Japan in search of a cure. Around seven years later, I finally realized there wasn't one, other than death. And I had unfinished business."

"You returned to Osaka to take your revenge," Niamh whispered.

He nodded slowly. "I might have hated myself, but I was powerful now. I hunted those men down like they were animals. Fear ripped through Osaka as worries grew of a wild animal on the loose. I had two men left to take care of when the grandmother of one I'd killed found me. She had magic. What we called a *miko*. A female shaman. They were mostly known for their spirit possession and *takusen*—they served as mediums to communicate with spirits. But they were so much more than people knew."

"They were witches."

"The most gifted of witches. They had psychic gifts. Like the fae."

"What happened with this witch?"

"She was a vengeful old bitch," he sneered. "She didn't care that her grandson had participated in a violent gang rape. All she cared about was her own revenge. She knew what I was, and she had an ability to sense things about people. She sensed my self-loathing and decided to trap me with my werewolf curse for all eternity."

"She made you immortal." Niamh's mind whirled. "But how is that possible?"

"I don't know." He shook his head. "I didn't believe her at first. After I'd killed the last two men, I took off and tried to end myself. Many times." He flicked a look her way. "I even tried to rip out my own heart."

Niamh gasped at the thought.

He smirked. "Obviously it didn't work. And miraculously, even though the thought of forever was a torture of its own, I realized that embracing what made me different was the only way I could live as a free man."

"You're amazing."

Kiyo looked at her fully now. "I just told you I killed a bunch of people, and that's your reaction?"

"You also told me on the plane that revenge didn't give you what you wanted. But maybe it did give you something. It gave you wisdom. It gave you the ability to pass that on to me and to make me feel less alone about all the bad stuff I've done when I'm supposed to be the good guy."

Though he concentrated on the road now, roads Niamh realized belatedly had changed from city to country, Kiyo spoke to her in a way she knew he wanted her to *hear* him.

"The Japanese have a saying: *Wabisabi*. It's a perspective, really. It's the accepting of the fact that life is imperfect and therefore we should appreciate the beauty in the imperfect things. There is light and dark in all of us, Niamh. Sometimes life causes us to let in a little more dark than we're comfortable with. But as long as we remember the light exists to chase away the shadows, we'll be okay." He glanced at her meaningfully. "The dark is our imperfect natures, but without it, we'd never realize how beautiful the light is. How beautiful it is as it dances with the shadows. I know you'll be okay. Astra won't pull you all the way into the darkness, Niamh. I won't let her. More importantly, *you* won't let her."

Emotion consumed her as she stared at his profile while he drove them onward.

His belief in her was something she never knew she'd needed.

And while it was wonderful and exhilarating ... Niamh was afraid to need anything from him.

21

The cabin wasn't exactly what Niamh was expecting. It was definitely more of a lodge on stilts. It only had one floor, accessed by an exterior staircase. The lodge had a triangular roof and a deck overlooking the somewhat misty pond it was perched above. As ever, the cold didn't bother her, but she was aware of how much the temperature had dropped at this elevation.

Nature was dark with brown and rusty bracken, but hints of green peeked through, suggesting the season was about to turn. Icy patches of snow could be seen here and there on the forest floor as if it had only snowed a few days before and was still in the process of melting. The air felt fresher, crisper, and clearer up in the mountains, away from the pollution of the city.

"Will it snow while we're here, do you think?" she'd asked as Kiyo wandered around the lodge, checking things over.

"Possibly." He seemed distracted.

The lodge was minimally furnished and was a mismatch of cultural ideas with tatami mats and shoji screens but a comfortable-looking old leather sofa on either side of a beaten-up coffee table. There was even a log-burning fire in the middle of the room with a flue that went right up and out of the ceiling. One shoji screen opened into the bathroom and the other to the bedroom.

"One bedroom?" she asked.

"I'll be in wolf form throughout the night while you're sleeping." He dumped his bag on the small kitchen's only countertop. "You can take the bed during the night. I'll take it through the day, if that's okay with you?"

Disappointment niggled at Niamh. She hadn't realized they wouldn't be spending any time together, but of course they wouldn't. This wasn't a vacation. Yet, she was still reeling from the outpouring of his story during their drive. As much as she (and he) might fight it, she felt closer to him than ever and didn't want to be far from him.

As if he sensed her feelings of disappointment, Kiyo's lips twitched. "You can conjure a book or two to entertain you, right?"

Instead of childishly sticking her tongue out at him like she wanted to do, Niamh gave him an imploring look. "Or ..."

His expression was wary. "Or?"

"You could let me run with you?"

Kiyo's chin jerked back in surprise. "Run with me? While I'm a wolf?"

She nodded, feeling like an excited child at the prospect. "When you were describing what it was like, it sounded wonderful. I want to experience it."

"You're not a wolf."

"Intelligent observation, Sherlock."

At his answering glower, Niamh switched back to imploring. "Please. You know I'm super fast and will more than keep up with you."

Kiyo seemed lost for words. "I've just never ... I've never met anyone who wasn't a wolf who wanted to run."

"It's safe, isn't it? It's not like you lose a sense of who you are when you're a wolf?"

"No, I'm completely self-aware."

Niamh snorted incredulously but covered it up with a pretend coughing fit, even though his raised eyebrow said she wasn't fooling anyone. She threw him a sheepish smile and persisted. "It shouldn't be a problem, then." But then something occurred to her. "Oh, goodness, unless it's, like, an extremely private moment and my asking is unforgivably rude and against all werewolf etiquette?"

He grinned.

God, she loved his smile.

"It's not private and it's not rude. You can run with me. But I'm out there as long as the moon is out."

"I have a lot of stamina."

Something like sexual avarice flickered across his eyes before he quickly looked away. "I could eat. Could you eat?" He busied himself unpacking the food from the duffle bag.

Niamh nodded forlornly, feeling flustered and frustrated in equal measure.

"Ready to go?"

Niamh turned from her spot on the deck. She was sitting on a wooden lounger that had been left out there, gazing at the sun as it set, light filtering through the trees and dancing across the misty pond below.

It felt like they were at the end of the world.

It was wonderful.

Her eyes widened at a half-naked Kiyo standing in the doorway of the deck and the living room. Her gaze, with a will of its own, drifted down his taut pecs and tightly roped abdominals. The scar on his belly, left there quite clearly by silver, pricked her curiosity. She wanted to ask about it but thought perhaps he'd done enough sharing for one day.

"Well? We need to go. Sun is almost set."

"Sorry." She blushed at his slightly impatient tone. "Just wasn't expecting you to come out wearing only joggers and looking like a Japanese Adonis."

Kiyo shook his head at her nonsense but she caught his slight smile as he walked back into the lodge. She followed him inside as he threw over his shoulder, "The less I wear, the less I have to strip off before the change."

That made sense. Niamh swallowed hard looking at his strong, sleek back and the perfect muscled arse currently hugged by black jogging pants.

She was feeling very warm all of a sudden.

"I see you're dressed for running." He flicked her a wry look as he pushed open the door and gestured for her to go ahead.

Niamh glanced down at the sneakers, yoga pants, and sports bra she'd conjured.

Perhaps she had taken the whole thing too literally.

She noticed his tongue hadn't rolled out of his mouth at the sight of her bare belly like hers had at his. Vanity pricked, she shrugged as she deliberately brushed her chest against his as she squeezed past. "I wanted to run like I was naked without being completely naked." She emphasized the word *naked* both times she said it.

She heard a rumble deep from his chest and smiled to herself as she sashayed across the porch. Niamh could feel his eyes burning into her arse.

Good.

It wasn't fair for her to be the only one smarting from sexual frustration.

The porch light spilled across the outside stairs and as Niamh approached, something caught her eye that she'd missed in the bright daylight. She lowered herself at the top of the staircase, staring at the creature carved on each newel post. It looked somewhat human but had a shell on its back and dish-shaped indentations atop its head. "What on earth is that?"

The smoke and heat of her werewolf companion enveloped her as he crouched down beside her. "That"—his deep voice caused a hot tingling in impolite places—"is a pair of *kappa*. They're believed to live in and around bodies of water, like rivers and ponds."

She turned her head to meet his gaze and found his mouth tantalizingly close.

He really did have the most spectacular lips with that exaggerated cupid's bow.

"It's not a very pleasant-looking thing, is it," she said hoarsely.

Kiyo's gaze followed suit, dipping to her mouth. "No," he responded, voice gruff. "They're said to emerge from the water to do strange things to humans and cattle."

That was somewhat disturbing. "Why would someone carve kappa into a lodge perched on a pond?"

"Because this lodge is owned by a werewolf who rents it out to other werewolves. He doesn't want humans or anyone from outer villages staying near the lodge. If they see the kappa, they'll take it as a warning to stay away."

"Oh."

Their eyes locked, and a saturating heat swelled between them like mist rising across a hot tub.

"Time to go." Kiyo stood abruptly, causing Niamh to rock back on her heels.

Renewed disappointment flooded her as she followed him down the staircase and into the woods.

The sun was still setting, and it shot through the trees in radiant beams of orange and yellows and reds as the pair trekked upward.

"The light through the trees is so pretty," she murmured, a contentment she hadn't felt in a long time sweeping over her.

"*Komorebi*." Kiyo glanced back at her.

"What does that mean?"

"It's the Japanese word for 'beautiful forest with sunlight peeking through the leaves of the trees.'"

Wonder filled Niamh. "There's an actual word for that?"

"*Komorebi*," he repeated. "We have a few words and short phrases that encapsulate a feeling or a moment in time that doesn't have a literal translation in English."

"Japanese is beautiful," Niamh said, feeling that beauty so deeply, her heart ached.

Sensing her sincerity, Kiyo's countenance softened and he slowed so she could catch up to him.

"Do you have a favorite word like that?" she asked, curious about ... well, everything about him.

"I do like *komorebi*," he admitted. "I think of it every sunset in the woods before the full moon." His brow furrowed. "My mother's favorite was *Takane no hana*. Literally it translates to 'flower on a high peak,' but its actual meaning is 'something that is beyond our reach.'"

Niamh's felt a swell of compassion. "Your father?"

Kiyo nodded, eyes to the ground. "She loved him even after he left us. She loved him to her dying breath. He was her *ikigai*." His tone changed as he forced levity into it. "Ikigai is someone's reason for being. What makes them get up in the morning. It's the convergence of four elements—passion, vocation, profession, and mission. In my mother's case, the latter three played no part. It was passion for her. Who she loved." His expression hardened. "No one person should ever be someone's entire reason for being."

It seemed like a warning, another example of him trying to push her away. But Niamh wasn't having it. They'd come too far now. She wouldn't let him spoil the mood. Continuing on in silence, she didn't brood. She didn't give in to the tension that pulsed between them.

She was here to enjoy the run.

Soon the light filtering through the trees was no longer sun but moonbeams. Kiyo let out a seemingly uncontrolled growl that reverberated up from his gut. He slowed to a stop and turned to her, his features strained between pleasure and pain.

Niamh's pulse fluttered as she throbbed deep and hot between the legs.

Kiyo's nostrils flared as if he sensed her arousal. "Change is coming," he warned, hooking his fingers into the waistband of his joggers.

What she really wanted to do was get an eyeful of her wolfy protector, but she owed him more respect than that. Giving him her back, she tried not to let her imagination run wild as she heard the material of his joggers slide down his legs.

Goodness, that magnificent arse of his was on display again and what she wouldn't give for another look at it.

She bit her lip to stem a bubble of girlish laughter.

All amusement died, however, as she heard Kiyo hit the ground behind her and let out a long moan of ... pleasure? Her skin flushed hot and she spun around without thinking to watch his transformation. Last time she'd been too preoccupied with a vision to witness him in wolf form.

Kiyo was on his hands and knees, his head thrown back as he let out a half-human, half-animal howl. All the hair on Niamh's body rose. Her pulse raced.

The surrounding energy amplified, throbbing beyond him to affect her. She could feel his pleasure and the slight burn of pain that didn't do anything to detract from the bliss of the change.

And then his claws sprang free, making her jolt back, startled.

Huge, shining black claws that were utterly lethal.

A crack sounded as his jaw elongated, and he growled unintelligibly as sharp teeth filled his mouth, two big fecking canines slicing into view. His arm snapped the wrong way, making Niamh flinch, and then his legs popped and cracked, too, his ankles shifting and lengthening into hindquarters. Thick, black, shining fur pushed through his skin in patches and clumps, like the magically accelerated growth of grass through the soil.

And then Kiyo was no longer a man.

He was now a great big, bloody black werewolf, twice the size of a regular wolf.

A howl burst forth from his snout.

Niamh gaped, wanting to approach him but not sure what the etiquette was.

Then his head snapped toward her, his nostrils flaring, and Niamh almost smiled. She could still see Kiyo behind those large, dark eyes.

"Well, aren't you unfairly beautiful in any form," she teased with a smile.

Kiyo made a chuffing sound.

"I'm not sure what the polite thing is here ... but ... I don't suppose

I could touch you, could I?" she asked tentatively because he wasn't the cuddliest person when in human form.

To her surprise, Kiyo padded toward her, the muscles in his legs flexing. Jesus Christ, his head was at chest height. A head he lowered for her to touch.

Warmth suffused Niamh as she reached out and ran her hand over his soft fur. "You're a big fella, aren't you," she murmured affectionately.

A giggle escaped her as Kiyo bussed into her touch as soon as she scratched his ears. It delighted and surprised her. Wolf Kiyo was more affectionate than his human counterpart.

After indulging him in some ear scratching, Niamh's hands trailed around his large, strong jaw and his eyes opened, piercing her soul.

"Time to run?" she whispered.

Wolf Kiyo padded slowly away, his tail swishing in the night air. He still smelled like Kiyo. Like earth, smoke, and aged ambergris. He stopped, shot her a somewhat challenging look over his shoulder, and then he leapt through the night ahead of them.

Niamh's pulse skittered and she tore off after him.

He was fast.

Bounding and loping and veering and speeding through the forest, never hitting a tree or the logs or rocks that laid in their path. Niamh wasn't so fortunate. Even though she was faster than him, she wasn't quite as graceful as he was in wolf form, and that was saying something since grace was one of her virtues. But at this speed, in the unfamiliar woodland landscape, Niamh stumbled out of her super pace when her toe hit a large rock or she didn't quite make the leap over a fallen tree that seemed to come out of nowhere.

Yet, as the hours went on and she followed Kiyo, he made a circle in the forest (obviously so they didn't venture too far from the lodge and upon possible human activity) and Niamh's reflexes caught up. Suddenly she was soaring through the woods, keeping up with Kiyo as they shared joyous looks of thrill.

Raccoons, squirrels, snakes, and other small animals hurried and slithered out of their path. The trees were a blur of naked limbs and newly growing buds. The patches of snow barely touched them, they moved so fast. The moon glowed on their skin and it felt like basking in the sun.

It was awesome. They felt connected as they ran. A bond sharp and golden strung between them.

And for once, neither of them fought it.

They gave in.

They were one.

And it was glorious.

Until the massive fecking bear appeared.

Feeling exhilarated but weary, Niamh slowly climbed the stairs to the lodge with every intention of falling asleep on the couch. Kiyo could have the bed.

He, after all, had leapt in front of her to protect her from a bear.

Unfortunately, there had been no time to run in the opposite direction. They were bounding through the trees when Niamh almost collided with the beast.

And it charged.

Wolf Kiyo had lunged in front of her, taking the bear to the forest floor.

To Niamh's horror, however, the bear swiped his claws across Wolf Kiyo's belly and he'd whined and rolled off.

Before the bear could charge again, Niamh used her magic to knock it out.

By the time she got to Wolf Kiyo, he was already healing. Werewolves healed especially fast in wolf form.

Still, she felt guilty and appreciative of him for jumping in front of her like that. He seemed to forget she was just as immortal as he was, but Niamh had to admit that she liked his protectiveness. Even if he did say he only protected her because he was being paid to.

Fecking liar.

Smiling to herself, Niamh stepped into the lodge and let her body fall down onto the couch. "Oof," she grunted, rolling onto her back to kick off her sneakers.

The sun was coming up, and Niamh had left Kiyo to change in private.

Sure enough, she could hear his footsteps coming up the exterior staircase just as her eyes began to flutter closed. The door squeaked open and she felt the heat of Kiyo's gaze.

Her body tensed with hyper awareness as she heard him approach the couch.

"Take the bed," he said softly.

Niamh's eyes flew open.

He stood over her. Half-naked. His hair loose and falling around his chin.

God, he was so beautiful, she thought she might die with the pain of wanting him. "I'm okay," she croaked out. "You take the bed."

In answer, he bent down and scooped her into his arms.

Niamh let out a squeal of surprise and looped her arms around his neck to hold on. "What are you doing?"

He didn't respond. Instead he strode into the bedroom and gently laid her on the futon. Without another word, Kiyo left the room, closing the shoji screen behind him.

Niamh's skin still tingled from his touch.

Disappointment was heavy in her gut.

For a second there, she thought he'd intended for them both to sleep in the bed.

22

To her utter surprise, Niamh didn't wake until not long before the sun was due to set again. She hadn't expected to sleep all day, but the run must have taken more out of her than she'd first thought.

Now she was wide awake and restless as the memories of the night before played over in her mind. More specifically memories tormented her with the closeness and intimacy she'd shared with Kiyo.

She knew it would be reckless to drag her feelings into the open, but Niamh wasn't sure how much longer she could pretend that all she felt was friendship. Was it only a few days ago she'd made that impressively cold speech about them not being friends and being all about the mission?

Stuck in a lodge with him for one night, and all that floated out the window. She wanted him too badly.

And she knew he wanted her.

Stubborn wolf.

Getting quietly out of bed, Niamh pulled on a T-shirt that was barely long enough to cover her arse. She slipped out of the patio doors that connected her bedroom to the deck that ran along that entire side of the lodge.

She peeked into the living room but could only see Kiyo's long legs dangling over the sofa edge. Niamh shook her head. Stubborn wolf. He could've had the bed.

Feeling only a slight tickle of the cold, Niamh sat down on the wooden lounger and drew her legs up to her chest, pulling the T-shirt down over her knees. The cool air caressed her thighs, kissed her calves, and tickled her feet. She flexed her toes, drinking in the late-afternoon sun flooding the pond and the tops of the trees. Imagining how lush and green this place must be in the summer, she almost wished they could stay for a few months so she could witness it.

There was so much peace and privacy. They could never run wild like they had last night while living in a city. It wasn't just the closeness with Kiyo Niamh had enjoyed. She'd loved being able to expend massive amounts of energy. But also to let all her worries go and just enjoy the moment. Almost like a child at play.

Melancholy filled Niamh as she rested her chin on her knees. She'd never be able to live in a place like this. An enemy would find her eventually. That's why she and Ronan were always on the run, always moving.

Niamh wondered what Ronan would think of Kiyo.

He'd hate him, she thought decisively.

Not because of anything he'd know about Kiyo. He'd hate him purely for having Niamh's attention.

Her chest ached at that, but she could think such things about her brother without feeling guilty anymore.

Wabisabi, Kiyo said the Japanese called it. The appreciation of beauty in the imperfect things. Ronan was like everyone, human or otherwise. He hadn't been perfect. He'd been very flawed. And Niamh knew he didn't want her to love anyone other than him. Not just because he didn't want anyone to take her from the lifestyle he strangely enjoyed but because she was the only family he had. And he loved her. He was afraid of losing her like he'd lost their mam. It wasn't a healthy way to love. Niamh knew that. But she could forgive him because he had forgiven her plenty in return.

At the end of all things, Ronan had died trying to protect her.

He'd died for the most beautiful part of his imperfect love.

"Niamh?"

She gasped, swiping a hand over cheeks she didn't even know were wet until Kiyo's voice broke through her musings. Her eyes flew to the doorway to the living room. He stood there, still half-bloody-naked but this time in black pajama bottoms.

His brow was furrowed in concern. "What's wrong?"

The last of her guilt had just floated away into the mountains of Japan. And it was all because of the wisdom of the immortal standing in front of her. She gave him a small smile. "Nothing. Everything's fine. Better than fine."

"You sure?" He strode onto the deck, making hardly any noise in his bare feet. For such a tall man, he could certainly move like a ghost.

Niamh watched him falter as his eyes dropped to her legs. Specifically the top of her outer thigh where she knew her underwear was probably visible.

Heat prickled along her skin as he halted next to the lounger, his legs almost touching hers. His dark gaze glittered in the sunlight and if she wasn't mistaken, his breathing was uneven.

She wanted him to scoop her into his arms again and take her back into the bedroom. This time, however, she wanted him to stay with her. To lift the shirt over her head. To slip out of his pajamas. To cover her body with his.

To bury himself inside her until this damn, gnawing longing within her found some relief.

They stared at each other as if silently communicating all the sexual things they wanted to do to each other. Energy crackled between them as Niamh grew slick with the fantasies rushing through her mind.

Kiyo's nostrils flared, and she knew as his features hardened with restraint, as his hands curled into fists, that he'd smelled her arousal. Movement caught her attention and her gaze flickered downward.

Her breath caught.

She wasn't the only one aroused.

Her eyes flew back to his.

Touch me, then, she wanted to demand, but didn't. Reach out for me. I'll give you what you want.

Instead she watched Kiyo fight against his physical desires, his jaw muscles flexing.

But he didn't move away.

In fact, his expression was challenging.

And realization dawned like a bucket of ice water.

Kiyo was waiting for her to make the first move because it meant he wouldn't have to take responsibility for anything that happened between them. It would be Niamh's fault.

That goddamn, fecking, furry arsehole.

Sexually frustrated and furious, Niamh threw him a dirty look, then lunged out of the lounger but in the direction of the bedroom. She slid the patio door open with enough force to break the thing, but she didn't care, as long as a room separated them.

Blood rushed in her ears with her anger.

A strong hold gripped her biceps and then her body jerked backward in a spin. She let out a sound of surprise as her chest collided against Kiyo's.

He crushed her mouth beneath his.

It was a deep, hungering, punishing, brutal kiss.

And Niamh relished every second of it, kissing him back with as much need and aggression. The taste of him, the heat of him ... he was perfect. He was right.

He fit her.

And it wasn't enough.

It felt like it would never be enough.

She needed him inside her.

His grip was tight around her arms as he abruptly broke the kiss. The lights in the paper lampshades flickered by the bedside.

Was she doing that?

Niamh couldn't think.

Kiyo was glaring at her like a man starving.

She thought he might stop, and if he did, she would more than likely scream from the frustration of it all.

Yet he surprised her once again.

His head bent toward hers, his hair tickling her chin as he brushed his lips over hers. Gently. Just a whisper. The sensation was somehow more erotic than the wet, hungry kiss they'd shared seconds before. Niamh whimpered and leaned into him, feeling his erection dig into her stomach.

He pressed his lips more firmly to hers but the kiss was still soft. Slow. A seduction.

Her palms slid over his hard pecs, her fingers digging lightly into his smooth, warm skin. He groaned against her lips and as their hands restlessly caressed one another, the kiss built in tempo until Niamh was overwhelmed by the taste of him on her tongue.

Her lips were wrenched from his but only because he'd grabbed the hem of her T-shirt to whip it over her head. Kiyo's gaze burned on her breasts as he pushed her toward the bed. Then she was falling, landing across the mattress in a sprawl of hot limbs and desperate need. Strong, agile fingers hooked into her underwear and then they were gone, cool air making her tingle between her legs. Kiyo rid himself of his pajama bottoms faster than she'd seen any man move and suddenly, he was braced over her on the bed.

Kissing her mouth, her neck, her breasts, sucking her nipples.

It was a fever, a hurry, as if he couldn't touch and taste every inch of her fast enough. Every one of Niamh's nerve endings sparked with a sensation that was beyond this world. No one had ever affected her like this. Like they were energy connecting and crackling with impact.

Her hands roamed freely, exploring him, his strong back and the way it dipped in a valley before meeting his muscular arse, the ripples of his hard abs, the flex of his muscles in his arms. Fingers slid through his thick, soft hair, caressed his lush mouth as her own pouted into a moan when he touched that magical spot between her legs.

Her skin flushed so hot, she was sure she was going to burst into flames, her heart hammering hard and fast in her chest as he circled her clit with his thumb, all the while sucking and laving at her nipples until they felt almost painful and swollen with sensation.

"Kiyo," she panted, climbing toward that clifftop she'd only ever reached alone—

His thumb disappeared.

She was about to complain when he kissed her with voracious, sexual intent as he gripped her thighs, spreading her to prod between her legs.

A jolt of realization hit her.

This was about to happen.

And she was pretty certain, even though she was fae, it would hurt like a mother if he just slammed into her. After all, she'd gotten an eyeful of him that night in the park in Moscow and briefly before he climbed over her just then, and he was long and thick. Very girthy.

"Kiyo!" She broke the kiss, taking hold of his face to get his attention.

Niamh shivered at the undiluted lust in his eyes.

She panted for breath, feeling him molten and throbbing at her opening and wanting nothing more than to have him inside her. "I should probably tell you ..."

Kiyo trembled above her, the muscles in his arms popping with restraint. "Tell me ...?"

"It's just, it's probably not a good idea to just ... Maybe you should ease into ... I'm kind of ... well ... you see, the thing is"—her cheeks flushed bright red—"I'm a virgin."

Shock saturated his features. "You're a what?"

23

"You're a what?" he repeated.

Despite the shock of her confession, while his mind yelled at him to abort, his dick grew impossibly harder. It liked the sound of being the only one to thrust inside Niamh Farren.

He squeezed his eyes closed and tried to breathe through the lust. "You're twenty-six years old," he argued.

He felt her stunning, warm, sweetly lush body tense beneath his. "Virgins come in all ages and sizes, Kiyo."

Kiyo watched the fascinating gold that had spread through her eyes as he'd fondled her clit disappear back to aquamarine.

He tried not to look anywhere but there. Not at her swollen mouth or her luscious fucking breasts or the long legs he was dying to have wrapped around him while he fucked her.

There would be no fucking of a virgin version of Niamh.

"I didn't think it would be a deal breaker," she huffed, indignant.

Kiyo gave her an incredulous look, cursed under his breath, and forced himself to roll off her. He sat up, swinging his legs over the side of the bed to stare out the window while he tried to will his erection out of existence.

It was the worst case of blue balls he'd ever had.

Niamh was a virgin.

How the hell did that happen? How had a woman that appealing, powerful, confident, and beautiful not had sex? Ever?

And she wanted Kiyo to be her first?

Equal measures of male pride and emotional terror overwhelmed him. If she'd waited this long, then it was because she was waiting for it to be right. With the right person. With someone who would be gentle and adore her and take care of her.

Why the hell would she give a gift like that to Kiyo?

He didn't deserve it.

He'd only hurt her.

And Niamh was the last person in this universe or any other that he wanted to hurt.

However, Kiyo didn't say any of that.

Instead the first stupid words out of his mouth were said in a mocking, sexually frustrated tone: "I can't believe you're still a virgin."

He heard her sharp intake of breath.

But she didn't answer.

"Niamh?"

Suddenly his senses alerted him that he couldn't smell her as strongly as he had seconds before.

"No." Kiyo glanced over his shoulder.

The bed was empty.

"No." Fury and guilt and resentment and worry collided inside him as he hurried out of the room and into the sitting room. No sign of Niamh. Rushing out onto the deck, he didn't find her there either. And even though he searched the perimeter of the lodge, he knew he wouldn't find her there.

Niamh had *traveled*.

All because he was an insensitive asshole who didn't deserve to touch one hair on her head.

Kiyo was aware of a sharp ache as he turned to look up at the sky.

Niamh couldn't *travel* too far at a time, which meant she'd probably *travel* far enough to find transport and then head back to the city.

Panic and worry set his teeth on edge. What if the pack or Astra or any one of Niamh's enemies got to her before Kiyo could?

Sweat dampened his body at the thought.

What had he been thinking?

He hadn't been!

He'd walked out onto the porch, saw her crying, should have been a decent man who offered her comfort. Instead he'd stared at her like she was a juicy fucking steak. It wasn't just the nonexistent nightshirt that bared those magnificent legs. It was the way she looked at him that broke his self-control.

Niamh looked at him like he made her world better.

No one had ever looked at him like that.

And he'd wanted her so much, he damned the consequences.

When she cottoned on to the fact that he was waiting for her to make the first move, however, he should have let her go. He didn't.

He could blame his lack of control on the coming full moon, but the truth was, Kiyo hadn't been able to think past anything but the desire to be inside her. To look into her eyes as he felt her come around him.

Her confession was a splash of cold reality. A reminder of who she was and who he was and ...

He bowed his head, the sting of self-reproach burning worse than he remembered.

How could he speak to her like that? How he could take his own sexual frustration out on her and—

Kiyo threw back his head and howled.

His self-condemnation pierced the night sky.

He couldn't race after her because he was about to change, but he'd make his way as close to the city as he could so that come morning, no matter if there was still one more night of the full moon ahead of him, Kiyo would be in the city. He was more aware of Niamh's scent than he'd ever been of one single person.

And he'd find her.

If she wanted to kill him when he finally did catch up with her ... well, he couldn't say he would blame her.

24

Niamh hadn't wanted to remain at the hotel.

She felt trapped in the room that smelled of Kiyo.

Perhaps it was her hurt, rejection, her fury, or all three, but Niamh had never *traveled* as far and as often as she had last night. She'd *traveled* with the hotel in mind, popping into the middle of the forest, taking a moment to gather her energy, going again, and popping up in the middle of a small mountain village. Thankfully no one witnessed her suddenly materializing out of thin air.

Niamh continued like this until she landed in a heap in the middle of the hotel room. She was covered in sweat and felt like she'd been weighed down by a hundred leather-covered iron cuffs.

She'd passed out, waking up in the middle of the night to drag her arse into a shower and then to bed.

Come morning, she hadn't wanted to be alone in the room. Not that she thought Kiyo would be on his way back to find her. He had another night of the full moon ahead of him and hurting Niamh's feelings probably wasn't a priority for him.

Not feeling hungry, she forewent breakfast and strolled twenty minutes or so into Chiyoda to see the Imperial Palace. She wandered into the gardens first where she got distracted. Discovering Kokyo

Gaien National Garden was much like any of the other national gardens she'd visited in Tokyo so far: like stepping into another world within the city. Not even the buildings towering over in the distance could take away the sense of peace to be found there. The trees were no longer completely barren but beginning to grow leaves, and the grass was losing that frosted dullness. But more special than any of that, two cherry blossom trees had begun to bloom early.

Niamh neared them, gazing upon the sun sparkling through branches of the pale-pink flowers. They existed in a row of cherry blossoms on either side of a wide path that cut through a section of the garden. She could only imagine how spectacular it would look once all the trees had bloomed.

Finding an empty seat on a bench, Niamh tried to relax, taking in the peek of a view of the Imperial Palace in the distance.

But no matter how beautiful her surroundings were, or how much she watched locals relaxing and tourists taking photos, Niamh couldn't rid herself of the awful knot in her gut.

"I can't believe you're still a virgin."

Niamh winced, hearing Kiyo's scornful voice in her head. She couldn't get it out of her mind. He might as well have called her a pathetic loser. And his distaste for the idea of sleeping with someone of such little experience was obvious.

She was a fool.

Because she'd thought he wanted to make love to her ... to *her*. To Niamh.

She hadn't realized he just wanted to scratch a fecking itch.

Tears burned in her eyes and she pushed them back, her lips twitching into a sardonic smirk. She was one of the most powerful beings on the planet and she'd been reduced to the mentality of a broken-hearted teenager by an emotionally constipated arsehole.

You're Niamh Farren, she heard Ronan's biting tone in her mind. *You can kick his arse until the end of time. You are a fecking goddess, Nee. And don't you forget it. He's lucky you allowed him to touch you.*

Determination thrummed through her and she found herself

throwing her shoulders back. That inner voice was right. Who was Kiyo to treat her like this? And who was she to take it?

Well, she wouldn't.

She had a mission in life, and she wasn't going to be distracted by that wolf any longer.

Pushing off the bench, she ignored the persistent knot in her gut, the sadness deep within the pits of her soul, and focused on a purpose beyond herself. And she couldn't very well do anything to save the world if she didn't fuel up.

Following her heightened senses south, she discovered a casual eatery facing onto the park. She ordered some food and found a bistro table outside to watch the world pass as she ate. They'd been lucky with their weather since arriving in the city. Every day had been crisp and sunny.

"It's a beautiful spot, isn't it?"

Too busy looking at the park to her left, Niamh started, almost choking on her soba noodles.

Seated at her small table, having appeared as if out of nowhere, was a stunning redhead with amber-gold eyes. With her tip-turned nose, full mouth, and the sprinkle of golden freckles across her cheeks, she was hard to forget.

Niamh swallowed, dropping her chopsticks while she tried to remain cool and calm. "Astra."

Astra's smile was beatific but if someone looked closely enough, they'd see that smile didn't reach her eyes. At all. "Sister."

Niamh bristled at the designation, especially as they weren't entirely unalike in physical appearance. "We're not sisters."

Manufactured hurt brimmed in the Norwegian fae's eyes. "We're all family. But you and I are closer than the others. I know you feel it. Two sides of the same coin. We even look the same. More so now that you've dyed your hair." She cocked her head to study Niamh. "I like it, sis."

"What do you want?" Niamh decided it was best to get straight to the point; otherwise she'd end up strangling the psychopath.

"I wanted to talk with you." Astra shrugged. "That filthy wolf was always in the way, but I see you finally rid yourself of him."

It was hard not to react to her snooty, nasty tone. But Niamh kept it together. "You don't like werewolves?"

"They're a dilution. So, no. And I particularly don't like that one." She leaned forward and Niamh tried not to flinch as Astra stroked her fingers over her temple. "He shut the door."

Anger coursed through her at the reminder of what she'd done to her. Niamh grabbed her wrist and threw it away from her. "You'll never get inside my head again."

"You're angry?" Astra seemed surprised.

How the hell could she be surprised that Niamh was furious with her for planting visions in her mind? She said as much.

"I was giving you purpose, Nee." Astra's wide-eyed innocence didn't work on Niamh.

"Don't call me that."

She held up her hands in surrender. "I'm sorry. I won't."

"And you weren't giving me purpose. You were trying to turn me dark like you."

Sadness flickered over Astra's features. "Not dark, Niamh. I was trying to help you right the wrongs of this world while we're stuck here. Does that make me dark? I never thought of it like that. I just wanted to make bad people pay for the evil things they've done. Vampires who kill. Humans who abuse. I thought you and I had that in common."

"It's not our job. We aren't judge, jury, and executioner," Niamh repeated Kiyo's words. "And it's not what you want. You want to open the gate. To destroy humanity."

"No." Astra leaned forward. "I want to return home to where we belong. Aine said the gate will close behind us."

"If you've seen what I've seen, you know it won't."

Astra shrugged. "That's merely a possibility. And a risk I'm willing to take to go home. I want my brother and my sisters with me." Tears filled her eyes. "Thea is already lost now that she's a filthy dog ... Rose is making things difficult consorting with the queen's consort … please tell me I haven't lost you too."

"You never had me."

Fury blazed in Astra's eyes, the gold dancing like flame.

And then abruptly they were amber again.

Wearing a mask of tranquility, Astra settled back in her chair and a coffee cup appeared in her hand. So blatant. So uncaring of the humans around them.

She took a casual sip, studying Niamh over the rim of the cup.

"He's not worth it, you know," Astra said. "Your distraction from the mission. No dog is worth it."

If the cow called Kiyo a dog or any other insulting adjective one more time … Holding on to her restraint, trying not to give herself away, Niamh shrugged. "Why does he bother you? Are you afraid of him?"

"Please," Astra scoffed. "I'm an immortal fae. He's a furry speck in the landscape of time that no one will remember."

She didn't know he was immortal.

Thank goodness.

Niamh relaxed marginally. "Then what's your problem with him? Other than your glaringly obvious prejudice, of course."

Astra scowled. "At first, I really had no problem with him. I didn't mind that someone else was there for you while I couldn't be, to look out for you while you were so vulnerable after Ronan's death. But then the dog began to influence you in ways I didn't like. He guided you off our mission."

"It wasn't my mission. You took advantage of me when I was at my weakest."

"I don't see it that way."

"Of course you don't."

"But I'm sorry if you feel I did something to betray you. That was never my intention. You're my sister."

"We're not sisters," Niamh hissed, energy crackling angrily around her.

Astra smirked. "There she is. Buried beneath that placid persona is my furious, raging, powerful sibling."

Niamh immediately calmed.

Astra laughed. "But there's that self-control of yours I loathe."

"You can't change me," Niamh warned her. "I am who I am, and I know I'm on the right side. You can't make me help you open the gate. I will fight you every step of the way. You'll never get me close to that gate."

Astra gave her a small, smug, knowing smile. "I thought so too. I mean, I don't need you willing, but with you so focused on your pet wolf, it would be very hard to get you where I need you to be. However ... I had a vision. It turns out Kiyo is going to be very useful to me, after all."

Worry burned through Niamh. Despite how hurt she was, her first instinct was still to protect the bastard.

"Haven't you wondered?" Astra leaned forward again, her gaze filled with scorn. "Why you feel such a deep, abiding connection to the dirty lupine? I know you have, Niamh."

Her pulse raced as suspicions she'd kept buried fluttered to the fore.

Astra nodded, expression smug. "Yes, you have. Because you know the signs. And he wouldn't be able to share your visions unless you shared an incredible bond. The only reason you've discarded the idea is because you can't sense his feelings nor he yours."

Her adrenaline kicked into high gear. "How do you know all that?"

"My vision helped me understand quite a bit."

Before Niamh could respond, the familiar scent of earth and smoke caught her attention.

Astra grinned triumphantly. "Perfect timing."

No!

Niamh glanced behind her, fear filling her at the sight of Kiyo hurrying toward them, his angry gaze focused on Astra. Niamh knew when he recognized Astra from the vision they'd shared because he began to run.

No! Kiyo, no! She pushed up from her chair to stop him, but a blur moved past her, kicking her hair around her face.

And suddenly Kiyo was struggling as Astra held him in her vise-like grip. Niamh flew at them, not caring if any humans witnessed their strange interaction.

"Stop!" Astra shouted, raising a syringe over Kiyo's chest. Niamh skidded to a halt.

Kiyo's shoulder jerked, as if he was preparing to fight, but quite abruptly, there was a crack and he went limp in Astra's arms. It was a strange sight—an elegantly built woman, holding a tall, muscled, unconscious male like he weighed nothing.

Niamh's palms were slick with sweat as she stared at Kiyo's broken neck. Rage rushed through her. She moved, ready to rip Astra's head off, when the fae lifted the syringe.

"Ah, ah," she warned.

Niamh's eyes narrowed on the silver liquid inside it.

"Do you know what my vision was about, Niamh?"

She shook her head, baring her teeth at the fae bitch.

"It was about what happens to a fae when the most important bond in her life is snapped and taken from her." Astra smiled sweetly. "It's enough to make even the lightest soul welcome in the shadows."

Understanding dawned too late.

Niamh rushed at the fae, screaming her outrage, but the syringe had already been plunged into Kiyo's heart.

And then Astra was gone.

Kiyo sprawled unconscious in the middle of the park as onlookers watched on in confusion and fear.

Niamh fell hard at Kiyo's side and pulled up his shirt. Silvery veins had already begun to spread from his heart.

She tried not to panic.

Kiyo was immortal.

He already told her he couldn't die.

Sensing humans crowding in, Niamh lifted his unconscious body into her arms, pretending to struggle.

"Do you need help?" a young Japanese woman asked in English.

Niamh shook her head, pushing past people to get Kiyo into the restaurant. She ignored the shouted protests from those around her and dragged him all the way into the restroom.

A wide-eyed woman let out a gasp of shock as Niamh hauled Kiyo into a stall.

His head lolled horribly on his neck as she shut the stall door behind them.

Holding him tight, Niamh thought of the hotel.

After a moment of disorienting darkness, she opened her eyes to find them in their hotel room.

Kiyo swayed in her arms and she lifted him with ease.

Lying him down on the bed, Niamh stepped back on shaking legs to study him.

He looked like he was merely sleeping.

"Kiyo," she whispered. "Why did you come back?"

Creeping forward again, she lifted his shirt to take another look.

The silver veins had lengthened. The spot around his heart was inflamed.

He couldn't die.

He was immortal.

Astra didn't know that.

He couldn't die.

Niamh studied the scar across his belly.

Silver *could* hurt him. It had left a permanent mark.

What the hell would the silver do to his insides?

25

Niamh had never conjured anything as far away as Kiyo's cell phone. Her whole body shook with exertion as she concentrated.

Fifteen minutes later, her hair and clothes damp with sweat, the cell finally popped onto the bathroom counter in front of her. Weary to her bones, Niamh had no time to celebrate. Instead she dialed Bran's number and relayed to him what had happened.

"Isn't the moon still in phase?" Bran asked, his tone far too casual for Niamh's liking.

"Yes," she snapped. "What of it?"

"Werewolves' healing abilities are accelerated when they're in wolf form. As soon as he changes tonight, the transformation will dissolve the silver in his blood. It has to. All my research on Kiyo tells me there is nothing on this planet that can kill him."

In the end, it was Bran's calm certainty that reassured Niamh. She thanked him and hung up after he told her to keep him posted on Kiyo's status.

Niamh strode out of the bathroom and almost swayed into the door frame. She'd overexerted herself. If she'd practiced her powers half as much as Astra had, she'd be able to do all the things she'd done in the last twenty-four hours without it affecting her.

A groan drew her out of her self-recrimination.

"Kiyo." She hurried over to the bed just as he opened his eyes.

After a moment of disorientation, he let out a grunt of pain and clutched his chest. As he pulled at his shirt to have a look, Niamh explained, "It was Astra. She injected you with silver. Right into your heart. I can only assume this was her chosen method to draw out your death for as long as possible."

A sheen of perspiration coated Kiyo's skin. He looked haggard and pale as he turned his head to her.

"I'm sorry." Her hands hovered over his body uncertainly. "I wasn't fast enough to stop her. But Bran reckons when you change tonight, your wolf will heal you."

His face strained with a sudden shock of pain, his eyes squeezing shut as he grimaced.

Powerlessness swamped her. "Kiyo."

Kiyo shook his head. "Don't," he gasped. "Not your fault. Argh!" He clutched at his chest.

"What can I do?" she asked, frantic.

His eyes shot open. "Bran ... right," he hissed. "Fuck ... change will heal ..." He gasped for breath, the misery in his gaze undoing her.

Tears burned in her throat.

"Knock me out," he groaned, flinching either with pain or broken pride. "Until tonight."

Wet escaped her eyes as she pressed her fingertips to his carotid and sent a flare of magic inside to squeeze it.

His body went limp.

Before she could give in to the panic slithering from the pit of her stomach, Kiyo's cell rang. Hurrying into the bathroom, she saw Bran's name on the screen.

"Yes?" she answered.

"Niamh?" It wasn't Bran. It was Fionn.

"Yes, it's me. Can you help?"

"That's why I'm calling. I think Bran is right and the transformation will probably heal Kiyo, but is there anything I can do in the meantime?"

A sob swelled out of her, but she choked it down.

Fionn must have heard it anyway. "I can come to you. Rose will have to stay behind, but I can come to you if you need me."

The offer made her feel less alone, but she doubted Fionn could get there before the full moon. There was nothing to be done but wait.

Yet something occurred to her. "You know things I don't about our magic."

"Yes ..."

"I've had to knock Kiyo out. He asked me to. The pain was too much."

Knowing it had to be an incredible amount of pain for Kiyo to ask that, Fionn cursed in old Irish.

"I'll have to continually hit his carotid to keep him knocked out until the change, unless you know a way for me to keep him in a stasis of some kind?"

Rose's mate was quiet a moment before finally replying, "You can hold him in that moment of unconsciousness by creating a cocoon around him with your magic. Pour your emotions, your want for him to be pain-free, into it. It should hold him within for as long you want."

Feeling more useful, Niamh thanked him.

"Niamh, who is this woman?"

Knowing it was time to warn Fionn and Rose, she told him about Astra and her vision. About how she had the ability to use her mind manipulation against Rose and Elijah if they weren't prepared.

"But we can still stop her?" Fionn asked once she'd finished.

"You know all futures are possible. And she wouldn't be going to these lengths with Kiyo if I wasn't destined for another path."

Fionn considered that and then asked gently, "Does Kiyo know?"

"No," she choked out, knowing what he was asking. Perceptive bastard. "And I doubt he'd want any part of it, even if he did."

"That's not how it works, *a leanbh*." His tone was gentle with a tenderness that surprised her. And although Niamh couldn't remember as much Irish as she should, she was pretty sure he'd just called her "my child."

She frowned. She was the same age as Rose.

"Tell him. Once he knows, you'll only be stronger together against Astra."

She ignored the thought because the hope of it hurt too much. "That castle of yours," Niamh replied. "The one with the spell that hides and protects it from the world."

"You know about that?"

"I know about a lot of things. Take Rose there, Fionn. Until this is over. Astra can't get her hands on all three of us."

"What about this man, the last of the fae-borne?"

"I was hoping a vision would come telling me how to help him." She laughed bitterly. "But look what happened the last time I followed a vision. I came to Tokyo because my instincts told me I needed to be here to protect Kiyo. And look what I've done to him."

"Your visions are never wrong, Niamh. Kiyo will survive this, and you'll figure out why you're there."

She had to believe he was correct.

Otherwise she was completely lost.

"Okay," she agreed. "Okay." She looked up to stare at her wan complexion in the mirror.

"Remember who you are, Niamh."

He was right.

She needed to remember who she was.

"Look after Rose," she demanded.

There was a smile in his voice when he promised he would.

"Remember, the only limitations to your magic are the ones you place upon it. Call if you need me, *a leanbh*." He hung up.

The silence in the bathroom seemed palpable without Fionn's reassuring voice echoing off the tiles.

"Remember who you are, Nee," Ronan whispered in her mind.

Leaning toward her reflection, Niamh placed her hand on the mirror. Energy pulsed from her and she watched as the reddish-brown hair that reminded her too much of Astra dissolved in a shimmer of pale blond.

Strangely, her skin glowed again, and a renewed strength filled her.

It wasn't about returning to her natural blond. She threw back her shoulders.

It was about returning to herself.

Marching out of the bathroom and straight to the bed, Niamh lifted her hands over Kiyo's body, closed her eyes, and imagined her energy surrounding him, cocooning him in warm sleep where no pain could touch him. The air glittered like the sun on her skin until the process felt complete in her mind.

She opened her eyes and stepped back in wonder at the sight of Kiyo looking peaceful beneath a barrier that shimmered gold and pulsed with vitality.

His strained features had smoothed in his sleep, assuring her he no longer felt pain.

Satisfied, Niamh rounded the bed and climbed onto the other side to lie with him.

There was nothing to be done now but wait until sunset.

"Astra, you evil cow," she said hoarsely, "if anything happens to him, I'll drive an iron blade straight through your black heart."

TIME CRAWLED.

Just when Niamh was sure the day would never come to an end, the sun began to set. She knew it was time.

Releasing Kiyo from the magical stasis, she sat up on the bed and watched him struggling into consciousness. He did it with a start, his eyes flying open, stark with pain, as he clutched at his chest.

Niamh reached for him, brushing his hair off his damp forehead. "It's okay, it's okay," she tried to reassure him.

His eyes flew to her, somewhat panicked. "Niamh?"

"The moon is about to rise. The change will heal you."

Kiyo's face flooded with remorse and he gasped out, "I'm sorry."

"For what?"

He tried to grab hold of her other hand but his coordination was totally off. Niamh reached for him instead, still petting his hair. "Try to lie still." There was silver near his throat.

The veins had climbed right up his torso.

Panic prodded her.

She fought it back.

"What I did," he choked out. "What I said. The lodge."

Realizing he was apologizing for his behavior, Niamh shook her head. "You can say sorry later when you're in your right mind."

"I am ..." He winced, hissing. "Oh fuck ... Niamh ... I'm sorry."

"It's okay." She pressed a kiss to his temple. "Shh, it's okay."

Kiyo squeezed her hand so tight it was almost painful, but she endured it as she held him to her while they waited for the moon to rise.

Fear soon swamped Niamh as moonbeams flooded the dark hotel room with light.

And Kiyo didn't change.

"What's happening?" she asked.

Kiyo had settled somewhat, seeming to suffer the pain without shuddering and jerking as much. "The silver ... affecting ... change."

She cursed under her breath.

He needed to bloody transform.

"Argh!" he suddenly roared in agony, bolting upward on the bed, ripping himself from her. His arm snapped the wrong way but then snapped back into place.

"What's happening?" Niamh cried.

Growls ripped from the depths of his belly and he lurched onto all fours. Cracks rent the air as his limbs broke as if to change but then broke back into human form.

"Kiyo." Her hands hovered near him. She was desperate to touch him, to help.

Claws protracted from his fingers, long and sharp and black and deadly, and he bellowed as he tore his shirt from his body.

How Niamh thought to protect their privacy during such a terrifying moment, she'd never know, but she sent out a flare of magic around the hotel room to soundproof it. "Kiyo." She rushed at him, staring in horror at the silver veins pulsing beneath his skin, all over his torso like tree branches. They reached up toward his throat and down his shoulders, stopping just before his biceps. She placed a hand on his sweat-slicked shoulder and he roared in outrage and swiped at her.

Niamh startled, falling off the bed.

His eyes widened in horror. "Niamh."

"I'm okay."

Snarls and grunts fell from his mouth as his jaw elongated, his mouth filling with sharp teeth. Niamh rushed toward him, and he held up a warning hand just as his spine snapped.

"Kiyo!"

"No!" he yelled, eyes wide with terror. "Go! I'm not …" He panted for breath. "I'm not in control." To her shock, tears wet his eyes. "I could kill you. Please. Go."

The thought of leaving him like this broke her. Tears spilled down her cheeks. He couldn't kill her. Not being what he was to her.

But he could bite and change her.

And he'd eventually be lost to her.

Niamh considered it, thinking it might be worth it to stay, to comfort him.

Kiyo saw her indecision and roared as his legs snapped. He clutched the bedcovers, ripping them to shreds with his claws. "LEAVE!"

Niamh sobbed. "I can't!"

Horror filled his eyes. "Please," he begged.

And she saw it. The possibility of hurting her was unbearable to him.

He didn't know he couldn't kill her and being here was making this worse for him.

"Okay," she nodded, swiping at her tears. "Okay."

She *traveled*.

But only into the locked bathroom.

Sliding down to the cold tile floor, Niamh pressed her ear to the door and cried quietly as she was forced to hide and do nothing while Kiyo endured an entire night of torturous torment. She sat hoping, *hoping* to the depths of her soul, that the stunted transformation would eventually heal him.

26

It had been quiet for a while.

Pushing onto her feet, Niamh hesitated a second before she opened the bathroom door.

She feared what she'd find in the bedroom.

Forcing herself to be brave, she stepped out into the room.

Bedside lamps laid broken and damaged. The bedspread and mattress had been torn to shreds and the headboard was cracked in half.

None of that mattered.

What mattered was Kiyo curled up in a ball on his side, on the floor next to the bed. He was now covered head to toe in silvery veins. Even his face.

His breathing was slow and raspy.

He hadn't healed.

"Kiyo."

His eyes flew open. Something warm glittered in them. "I knew you were there. I smelled you."

She'd known he'd probably know. All he'd cared about was that she wasn't close enough for him to snap his teeth at her.

Niamh threw her hand out and the room repaired itself.

Including the bed.

Without a word, she reached for Kiyo and leaned down to help him to his feet. He held on to her, needing her strength. Resolve moved through her as she helped him onto the bed.

"The change didn't work." She pressed her hands to the mattress to lean over him.

He gave a slight shake of his head. He looked so strange with the silver veins spreading up his throat into his cheeks. Niamh wanted to kiss each one away. "The pain is better, though. I know I look bad, but I think my body is healing. I can't die, remember."

Niamh reached for the sheets and pulled them up to cover his nakedness. He didn't look like he was healing at all, and there was a fevered flush to his skin.

"Think it might just take a day or two." He reached for her hand. Trying not to jerk in surprise, Niamh let him thread his fingers through hers. "You changed your hair back."

She gave a startled laugh. Were men supposed to notice these things? Especially when they were ... Her smile died. "I'm me again."

He squeezed her hand. "You were always you. Hair color doesn't change that." Worry darkened his eyes. "You need to eat."

"I'm not hungry. And you should be the one who's eating after ..." She squeezed her eyes closed. "Kiyo, I'm so sorry about Astra. What you experienced last night ..."

"Wasn't your fault." He tugged on her hand. "Order some food. I'll try to eat some too."

She knew he said the last part because it was the only thing that would motivate her to order room service.

Not long later, she placed the delivered meal tray onto the bed between them. Kiyo let her spoon chicken noodle soup into his mouth before shaking his head against any more.

She supposed it was something. Nibbling on a pork dumpling, she studied him. "So we just have to wait this out?"

His breath rattled. "I think so."

"The silver stopped you from changing, didn't it?"

"Yeah." Kiyo didn't hide the torment in his eyes. He let her see what the pain had been like. Her eyes stung as he spoke. “The moon tried to force the change while the silver prevented it.”

For the rest of her long eternity, she’d never forget the sound of his agony.

“I’m okay now.” He slid a hand along the mattress to tap her arm. “Kind of deserved it for treating you like that.”

“Don’t even joke about it.” Niamh glared at him.

“I’m not joking.”

“Kiyo, you might have been an insensitive bastard to me, but I would never want you to go through what you did last night.”

“Hey, hey, okay, don’t get upset,” he replied hoarsely, his brows puckering.

Wiping impatiently at the tears scoring hotly down her cheeks, Niamh couldn’t meet his gaze. He already knew by now that she cared too much about him.

“What I should have said ... what I was actually thinking ... was that I wasn’t worthy to be your first, Niamh. If you’ve waited this long, then you must be waiting for the right guy. You deserve better than me for your first time.” He rolled his head back on his pillow, glaring at the ceiling.

Though the subject made her feel vulnerable, she found herself flicking her fingers at the food tray so it disappeared to outside their hotel room door. Then she laid down beside Kiyo. She felt him looking at her as she stared at the paneled ceiling. “I didn’t mean to wait,” she admitted.

“For sex?”

“Yeah.” She smiled, feeling stupidly shy.

“Tell me about it.”

Niamh turned her head to look at him.

Kiyo smirked. “I’ve got some time on my hands. And I want to know about you.”

Tenderness flooded her and she realized with some discomfort that the wolf could probably talk her into doing anything.

“It was difficult to make connections,” Niamh told him. “Being what I was and always on the run. But it was more than that.” She looked back at the ceiling as she finally admitted, "My brother was a bit suffocating. While he gallivanted all over the place, screwing gorgeous strangers, men and women he picked up in bars and bistros and museums ... I wasn't *allowed* to have that."

"Why the hell not?"

"Ronan used to say it was for my own protection. I let myself believe him. The truth was, he was afraid. Not just of me being found out, but that the life he'd come to love—no matter how much he complained about it—would be taken from him if I met someone. Ultimately, however, I think he was just afraid to lose *me*. He loved me. I was the only family he had. And he didn't want me to love anyone but him."

"That's messed up."

Niamh looked at Kiyo and saw his indignation on her behalf. "I know. But in the end, he did die trying to protect me."

Kiyo's expression softened. "Yeah."

Silence fell between them.

Then he asked, "So there was no one? Ever?"

Blood warmed her cheeks as she remembered Matteo. "There was an Italian." She grinned. "We stayed in Lake Como for a month. And there was this boy from Rome staying at his family's vacation home in the hills. He took a liking to me and wasn't at all put off by Ronan."

"What age were you?"

"Nineteen. He was a few years older, in his last year at uni." Niamh looked at Kiyo and found him patiently waiting for her to continue. "Ronan liked women and men who were already in a relationship. He didn't have to worry about them getting clingy. Well, most of the time. He'd started sleeping around with a man who had a wife and kids. We argued about it a lot. But I was always too afraid to push him because I felt I owed him."

"Messed up," Kiyo repeated.

Niamh exhaled slowly. "So he was off with this married man, and I snuck out to see Matteo. Thinking Ronan wouldn't be back for hours, I took Matteo to the hotel room. I wanted to know," she whispered, feeling her body heat at the memory, not of Matteo's touch but of Kiyo's. "I wanted to know what it was like. I let him undress me and touch—"

"I don't need the details."

Trying not to be delighted by the jealousy Kiyo couldn't hide, Niamh smothered her smile. "No details. Other than to say he was just about to make home base when Ronan burst into the hotel room. They got into a massive fight and Ronan and I had to leave."

Melancholy fell over her at the memory.

She didn't want to remember her brother like that.

"He stopped you from living."

"He kept me on mission," she argued.

Cool fingers curled around her hand and Niamh turned back to Kiyo. His look was one of compassion mingled with frustration. "He kept you from living."

Niamh shrugged, her lips trembling with grief. "But he helped me survive."

Kiyo squeezed his eyes closed as if he felt her pain. His hand gripped hers. "There's more to life than just surviving. *You* reminded me of that."

Emotion swelled hot and thick between them, and hope glimmered in the depths of Niamh's heart.

"Tell me something good about him. A good memory?" Kiyo asked, as if he knew she needed the balance from remembrance.

She searched her memories. "There are so many. How he'd hold me when I had a vision, even though the older and stronger I got, it was really difficult for him to contain me. Sometimes I left bruises," she remembered in remorse. "I told him not to hold me through it, but he said he couldn't see me like that. That he needed to be there to comfort me.

"I think that's one of the things about him I miss most." She struggled against her grief. "Knowing he was there to shield me when I was vulnerable." She chuckled at a thought. "And his sense of humor. Ronan had the most wicked sense of humor. Completely politically incorrect but in a world gone PC mad, he was refreshing. He'd crack me up in the most inappropriate places.

"We visited Vatican City a few years back and he was bored from the get-go, and frankly being annoying. He kept making loud comments about the disproportionate distribution of wealth, the hypocrisy and disgusting display of money when there were people begging for food on the streets of Rome. Whether or not you agree with him, it was pretty bloody embarrassing when you're crammed into the place with thousands of other people, trying to pretend like you don't know the cheeky bastard." She laughed now, remembering his "couldn't give a feck" attitude and how much she'd loved him for it.

"When we got to St. Peter's Basilica, I'd gotten away from him and was standing with a crowd in front of the *Pietà*. Have you seen it in real life?" She turned her head on the pillow to ask him. The *Pietà* was a sculpture by Michelangelo of the Virgin Mary holding the dead body of Jesus.

Kiyo nodded. "I've seen it."

"There's something about it, isn't there? You don't have to believe in God or Jesus Christ to feel it."

"I know what you're talking about."

"I was lost in the moment. Perhaps it was the Catholics around me crying over the sculpture or maybe it was just the sorrow Michelangelo captured in a grieving mother's face. I don't know what it was about it, protected behind its glass wall ... I just knew I felt a deep spiritual sadness." Niamh sighed heavily. "And then my bloody brother appeared and cracked the most blasphemous, terrible, awful joke as loudly as he bloody possibly could." Niamh shook with laughter. "It wasn't even funny, but the moment was so badly ruined that I started to laugh. It was awful. I couldn't stop laughing, and the more I laughed, the more he laughed and the guiltier I felt."

Kiyo grinned as she peeked at him through the hands covering her face. Her cheeks were still hot remembering the moment.

"Oh, it was equal parts horrifying and hilarious. I thought the tourists and guards were going to lynch us. He was such an arsehole," she said affectionately. "He made light of things because everything was always so heavy for me. I didn't really see how much he did that until he was gone."

Niamh turned onto her side, hands to her cheeks. Kiyo's chest rose and fell with shallow breaths as he held her gaze. "I feel like someone stole a piece of me that I'll never get back. Like there's always going to be this emptiness inside me because he's gone. It was different when Mam died. A different kind of aloneness. I loved her, but we weren't close. I know that sounds strange, but we just never bonded the way she and Ronan did. You were close to your mam ... did you feel that way when she died? That emptiness?"

"Yeah," he answered without hesitation, voice hoarse. "It had always been us two against the world. She never blamed me for any of it. She always told me she'd never change what happened because in the end, she had me. My mother was a dreamer." He smiled softly. "She believed in magic and romance even after my father left her. Despite his betrayal, despite her family's betrayal and the way they and everyone else treated us, she still saw the good in people. There was an innocence about her. A light. I see the same thing in you."

Emotion thickened Niamh's throat.

"She used to tell me I was special and that I'd do something special with my life. They weren't just words—she dreamed big for me. Her belief was almost enough to make me feel a part of the world. Almost." He sighed wearily, turning to stare up at the ceiling. "I was angry at her when she killed herself. I didn't understand how she could leave me alone.

"When I got older, I understood that what was done to her broke her. Those men took away her dreams and violated her into darkness. I stopped being angry and started to feel guilty. I kept thinking, what if I had talked with her ... reminded her who she was and tried to pull her back into the light." Kiyo turned toward Niamh, and her eyes filled with tears in answer to the ones she saw in his. "I couldn't do that for her. But I will fight to my last breath to do that for you. Astra can't have you."

Niamh didn't know what part of the high-octane events of the last twenty-four hours had spurred the lowering of Kiyo's defenses. She didn't care.

That hope she felt earlier was rising.

Sliding her hand along the mattress, she took hold of his again. His pulse fluttered weakly beneath her thumb as it rested on his wrist.

Determination filled her as they stared into each other's eyes, lost in the undeniable connection that bound them together.

They laid like that in the quiet for a while.

Just holding on to it. Just holding on to each other.

27

By nightfall, Kiyo was unconscious.

The sheets beneath him were soaked with his sweat and his skin was scorching to the touch.

Niamh stared down at Kiyo, resolution hard in her veins.

He wasn't getting better, and there was a part of her that knew with deep certainty that even if the silver didn't kill him because of his immortality, he wouldn't get better.

He'd exist in this plane of pain and fever for the rest of his life.

And Niamh wouldn't have that.

Her pulse raced but she ignored her own fears and conjured a pair of thick gloves. Pulling them on, Niamh took a deep, deep breath … and then conjured the pure iron blade.

Her hand dropped with its weight and she could feel it trying to burn through her glove. Lethargy threatened, but she curled her hand around the hilt and brought the sharp blade to her bared left wrist.

"Argh!" she cried out, needing to release the misery of what felt like a thousand fire pokers slicing into her.

Kiyo jerked on the bed as if he'd felt her pain, his lids fluttering wildly.

Blood pooled out of the wound. The wound that was slow to close.

Slow enough to let her feed him.

Ridding the blade with her magic, Niamh crawled onto the bed, pushed her opposite arm beneath Kiyo, and forced his lips to her gaping wound.

Blood smeared them.

"Drink, Kiyo!" she begged, panicked the wound would close too quickly.

He grunted but didn't wake.

Hoping he'd forgive her, Niamh sent a jolt of adrenaline into his heart with her magic.

His eyes flew open and his lips parted on a rasping gasp.

Taking advantage, Niamh stuck her wrist right in there. "Drink, damn it."

Kiyo's eyes flared with understanding and he sucked at her wrist, careful with his teeth as he did so.

Within seconds, the veins slithered down his face, disappearing, inch by inch until eventually they were no more.

He released her, her blood smeared across his chin. Then his eyes narrowed on her wound. Her wound that hadn't even begun to close yet. "What the fuck did you do?" he snarled.

Their eyes locked and she shrugged. "Saved you from an eternity of agony. You're welcome."

28

Glaring at the wound slowly healing over on Niamh's wrist, knowing it would leave a permanent scar, Kiyo didn't know whether to yell at her or kiss her.

Moments before he'd been swimming the red-tinged depths of fevered unconsciousness, certain he was lost to it forever.

Now he'd never felt stronger or more powerful with Niamh's healing blood in his body.

She'd taken iron to herself.

For him.

He looked up from her wrist still clutched in his hand and saw the determined defiance in her expression.

And he fell.

Who was he kidding?

He'd been falling for days.

Fighting it every step of the way.

Hurting her.

Pushing her away.

Yet after experiencing the worst pain he'd endured in a long life of violence, worse even than that first change into werewolf form, Kiyo couldn't remember why he was fighting her so hard.

He just knew that when he thought she was in danger from him, he couldn't bear it. He'd born the unbearable in his one hundred and fifty years, but he'd known that if he'd come out of this only to realize he'd bitten and killed Niamh Farren, he would have asked Fionn Mór to find a way to end his miserable existence.

His whole reason for being had become about Niamh. The passion he felt for her, his need to protect her, his ability to do it, and the fact that the world needed her. Her safety was all that mattered. Whether he revealed that to her wouldn't change how he felt. So what was the point in fighting her?

Kiyo might have been stubborn and guarded, but he wasn't stupid.

With stealth of loyalty, affection, of warmth, light, strength, and purity of heart, Niamh had become Kiyo's reason for being.

He stared at her in wonder, not knowing quite how to tell her but knowing how he wanted to show her.

A loud series of raps on their hotel door, however, interrupted the moment.

A familiar scent hit his nostrils and he pulled back his upper lip in a snarl. "It's Sakura."

Niamh's expression flattened at the mention of his ex-mistress. She gently tugged her hand from his. The cut on her wrist had healed but was still red and inflamed. "I put a privacy spell up so no one could hear you last night, so she can't be here because of any reports from the hotel."

There were a few more loud raps and then Sakura spoke in Japanese, at normal volume knowing he'd hear her. "Open the door, Kiyo, or I will break it down."

"What did she say?"

"To open the door." He swung out of bed, amazed at how energized he felt by Niamh's healing. So he wasn't even aware that he was half-naked as he strode into the living room until he felt a crackle of energy around him, followed by the hiss of material on his skin. He faltered.

He now wore a T-shirt to go with his pajama bottoms.

Then Kiyo realized his hair wasn't tickling his chin either. It was in a topknot.

Glancing over his shoulder, he found Niamh standing in the doorway, eyebrow raised. "What?"

He smirked and gestured to the T-shirt.

Niamh shrugged nonchalantly. "I was only thinking of your modesty."

He pointed to his hair.

Niamh flushed and looked away.

"Right." He grinned at her barely concealed jealousy, feeling far better about it than a gentleman should.

She shrugged, still not meeting his gaze. "I also cleaned my blood off your chin."

The reminder of what she'd done to save his life made him want to throw her down on the couch so he could thank her sufficiently. With orgasms. Multiple.

"Kiyo!"

Gritting his teeth at Sakura's impatient snap, he strode to the door and threw it open.

Sakura stood at the head of a small entourage that included Haruto.

"Can I help?"

She pushed past him, sashaying into the room on spiked heels that could be used as a weapon. Kiyo stood back with a sigh as Haruto and four male wolves and one female followed their alpha. They stood to the side of the room in a line, staring straight ahead, as if they had rehearsed this scenario many times.

They probably had.

Kiyo slammed the door shut and crossed the room to stand by Niamh while Sakura skewered Niamh with her dark eyes. Haruto hovered near Sakura's back, always protecting her.

"Where's Daiki?" Kiyo asked, crossing his arms over his chest. "Still recovering?"

Sakura's eyes flashed dangerously. She answered in English. "The full moon took care of what remained of his injuries."

"Are you finally here to reap revenge for it?" Somehow he doubted it.

"If Daiki wants to make a fool of himself, that is up to him. The consequences are his own."

Charming attitude for a mate. "Then why are you here?"

"Word reached me today that you had a strange encounter in Kokyo Gardens yesterday morning. I would have known sooner if not for the final phase last night. So ..." She took a step toward them and without thinking, Kiyo stepped in front of Niamh. He saw hatred saturate Sakura's expression before she quickly hid it with an angry smirk. "Who is the redhead and what the hell did she inject you with?"

He stared coolly at Sakura. There was very little chance she had any real evidence except for gossip. "I don't know what you're talking about."

"You were seen, Kiyo. Do not lie to me."

"I'm not lying. If someone thought they saw me, they were wrong. Niamh and I have just returned from the mountains. Full moon," he reminded her. "Plus do I look like something happened to me?" Thanks to Niamh, he'd probably never looked healthier. "What happened in the gardens?" Kiyo prodded.

Sakura was alpha for a reason. Although she'd let her emotion and jealousy slip over Niamh, she usually had a pretty good poker face. She wore it now. "It is of no consequence if you were not involved."

"I wasn't."

Her eyes flicked to Niamh. "Strange. The description fitted both you and your mahoutsukai. Though she has changed her hair. Not that it does much to increase her appeal."

Kiyo shook his head in mockery. "You're a *wolf*, Sakura. Being a catty bitch doesn't suit you."

The tension in the room grew thick with bristling anger.

Haruto grunted and made a move forward, but Sakura held up a hand to stop him. "He is right. Leave it." She sighed somewhat wearily, amusement glittering in her eyes as she closed the distance between them. Staring up at him, nostalgia warmed her face. "You are the only one who speaks the truth to me. Not even Daiki, unless he is feeling jealous, which is exhaustingly often. I wished you had stayed with me, Kiyo-chan."

"I was honest with you."

Sakura lowered her eyes and placed her hand flat against his chest, over his heart.

He felt Niamh's immediate surge of emotion behind him and wasn't even shocked that he sensed her jealousy and anger and hurt. A knot formed in his gut at the thought. Despite knowing the best way to deal with Sakura was to allow her flirtations, Kiyo took hold of her wrist and pushed her away.

It surprised and angered her as she stumbled on her heels.

"You have a mate," he said softly, "who deserves your respect."

"I'm alpha," she replied with a bite. "I can have sex with whoever I want. If that is the only thing stopping you ... put it from your mind. My pack will not tell Daiki a thing. I ask them to leave, they will take the mahoutsukai from here, and you and I can be alone."

"No."

He felt Niamh's relief at his back. Possessiveness tightened his muscles. He wanted Sakura gone. He wanted them all out of the room so he could be alone with Niamh.

"No?" She raised her eyebrow as if she'd never heard the word in her life.

Kiyo didn't reply. He'd been clear the first time.

"Do you know how many wolves would die to have me in their bed?"

He stared blankly at her.

Her eyes widened at the silent insult. And then her temper got the better of her—she stepped forward to slap him hard across the face.

Niamh was in front of him before he could stop her. She grabbed for Sakura's wrist and let out a wail of distress. Kiyo felt her pain like a slash across the gut. Niamh's knees buckled as she released Sakura and she fell at Kiyo's feet.

He dropped and wrapped his arms around her, confusion buzzing in his ears.

"What the hell?" Sakura cried out in Japanese, stumbling back from them.

Niamh looked into his eyes and shuddered against him. *Iron.*

His gaze flew from her closed hand to Sakura's wrist.

She wore a selection of bracelets and bangles. Some diamond, some gold, some silver ... and one in the middle that stood out from the others for its lack of glitter.

A solid, plain, pure iron bangle.

The alpha glowered at them in confusion. "What is wrong with the mahoutsukai?"

"Flu." Kiyo pulled Niamh closer, trying not to let his panic of her being found out emanate from him. They'd smell the change in his scent. "We thought she was feeling better but she can't overexert herself."

Quick thinking. He heard the pain that still lingered in Niamh's voice. His hold on her tightened.

Sakura's eyes narrowed. Some kind of understanding dawned on her, and Kiyo hoped like hell it was her realizing his feelings for Niamh and not her realizing that Niamh was fae.

"She is lucky I do not kill her for touching me."

"She was defending me." He stared at her, expression hard, filled with warning. "You touch her, Sakura, and I'll take it as a declaration of war."

Niamh tensed in his hold but he didn't care.

Having the pack know that Niamh was a weakness was a risk, but the greater risk was them thinking they could harm her without consequences.

Sakura stepped back as if she couldn't believe what she was hearing.

Haruto placed a comforting hand on her shoulder.

And Kiyo knew ... her feelings for him *were* genuine. He was sorry for it. Sorry he couldn't return them. But she had her place in the world and he had his, and other than the fight he owed her, their paths weren't destined to meet with any permanence.

Sakura shrugged off Haruto's hand and snapped that she was fine in Japanese. Then to Kiyo, she snarled, "You better win this upcoming fight, Kiyo, or I might just give you that war." With that, she turned on her spiked heels and marched out of the hotel room. The others trailed after her, except for Haruto.

He was focused on Niamh's closed fist.

Kiyo stiffened.

Haruto never gave anything away so Kiyo had no idea what the huge beta was thinking as he threw Niamh one last look before following Sakura out. He closed the door softly behind him, and Niamh let out a long exhale. "We can talk. Privacy shield is still up."

"Let me see," Kiyo bit out.

She unfurled her fist and revealed the small but inflamed wound on her palm. It matched the one on her opposite wrist. "Big day," she cracked. "Two iron scars in less than twenty minutes."

"It's not funny." He pulled her to her feet, holding her by the arms. "You okay?"

"Yeah." Her expression turned sheepish. "Just lost my temper when she hit you. I didn't think."

"You didn't know she was wearing iron."

Niamh stepped out of his hold, clutching her fist to her chest. "I didn't even sense it on her. Too distracted by ..." She shook her head. "Why *was* she wearing iron? Does she know about fae?"

"No." Kiyo was certain of that. "I think it was just a coincidence. Not many people believe in the fae legends and even fewer know about pure iron."

Nodding, she seemed to accept that. Then a sadness flickered over her eyes. She wouldn't meet his gaze, which bothered him more than he liked. "I think, despite the femme fatale alpha front she puts up, that she genuinely loves you, Kiyo."

"She cares about me," he admitted. "But you can't love someone if they've never shown you who they really are." He took a step toward her and finally, Niamh looked into his eyes. His heart pounded, hard enough he knew she could hear it. "I've only ever shown one person who I really am. And I'm looking at her right now."

Hope and light and something he was afraid to name turned her eyes almost gold as she whispered his name in wonder.

"I need a shower." His next words caused her to blink in surprise and consternation. Kiyo smiled and held his hand out to her. "Join me."

A flush crested her cheeks and her brilliant eyes sparkled with an alluring mix of sensuality and innocence. Despite what had transpired between them in the last twenty-four hours, there was still a small part of him concerned she'd reject him based on his shitty treatment in the mountains.

Relief flooded him when she took his hand.

Arousal swirled hot and heavy in his loins, but he ignored it for now, leading her slowly into the bathroom and closing the door behind them. Eyes locked with hers, he removed his clothes. After a second or two, Niamh followed suit with her own.

They stood, naked, and explored one another with their eyes.

The delicate, elegant slope of her shoulders, her narrow waist that accentuated the fullness of her lush, perfect breasts. Goose bumps prickled them while her large, rosy nipples were hard and tight and begging for his mouth.

Her gaze lingered on his erection and the blood thickened there the longer she stared. Kiyo could smell her arousal, and his eyes drifted to the neatly trimmed hair between her legs. By the time the night was over, he was determined to have licked and sucked as many orgasms out of her as possible.

It wouldn't be an uncontrolled fuck like how he'd pounced on her in the mountains.

He was going to savor her, give her pleasure, and make it the best first time any woman had ever had.

A gasp escaped her lips as if she'd heard his thoughts, her body bowing with desire.

Forcing himself to go slow, Kiyo reached into the shower and switched it on. Once the jets of water streamed out hot, he gestured for Niamh to step in ahead of him. She did, deliberately brushing her hard nipples against his chest as she squeezed past.

He released a growl of want and practically felt her ass twitch with satisfaction.

His gaze dropped to said ass, catching a glimpse of its heart-shaped perfection before she turned to face him.

Niamh's chest rose and fell with shallow breaths as Kiyo stepped into the shower and crowded her back against the tile. He braced his hands on the shower wall at either side of her head and dipped his nose to touch her throat. Taking in a deep breath of her caramel and spicy scent, his dick grew so hard, he couldn't think past the lust.

Her soft hands settled on his waist and he let out a shuddering exhale.

"Can I wash your hair?" she asked.

He lifted his head to stare into her eyes. He suddenly understood the phrase "to drown in someone's eyes." He nodded and stepped back. Niamh reached past him to the shower shelf and grabbed the complimentary shampoo. He bent toward her so she could reach up to release his hair from its tie. Her fingers sifted through the strands with a sensual leisure that made his skin prickle.

"I love your hair."

"I think I got that." He grinned at her.

"I love your smile more, though."

He cupped her cheek in answer, caressing her shower-dampened skin for as long as she allowed before she continued to wash his hair. She was careful to keep the soap from his eyes. When it was washed out, she grabbed the conditioner.

"Turn around."

He did and felt her crush her breasts to his back as she massaged the conditioner into his scalp. Shivers of mingled relaxation and lust skittered down his nape and spine. As she moved to dig her fingers gently into his scalp, her breasts caressed his back, her nipples catching. Her breathing quickened and he scented how much she needed him.

It took more self-control than he knew he had to stop himself from turning around and thrusting into her.

Instead, once she'd washed the conditioner from his hair and tied it back up for him, he turned her around to face the wall. "My turn."

His gaze dropped down her slender back to where her hips sloped into a generous curve. Her ass really was the perfect heart. Bitable.

The word stopped him.

Although his human teeth couldn't hurt her, he'd never take them to her, even in sex play.

He couldn't chance it.

The thought of accidentally hurting her burned in his gut.

The urge to slip into her, to feel her alive and throbbing around him, grew stronger.

Kiyo reached out and caressed her ass cheeks, squeezing her as he brushed his erection near the valley between.

Niamh fumbled for the wall, gasping. "I thought … you were washing my hair?"

He pressed his dick more firmly between her cheeks, sensation ripping through him making his balls draw up tight. He gritted his teeth as she panted with need.

One day he'd take her there.

But not yet.

He needed to work up to that.

Reluctantly releasing her ass, he took the shampoo bottle in hand. "Tip your head back."

She did and her pale blond hair, turned honey with water, hung past her ass.

He tried not to let his thoughts wander as he washed it, but after rinsing out the shampoo, he massaged the conditioner in and leaned into her so she could feel him hard and wanting. And he whispered, "Did I mention I like the blond?"

She shook her head.

"I do." He kissed her neck behind her ear. "But I'd take you any way I could get you. You could have no hair, Niamh Farren, not a speck of it on that sweet little head of yours ... and I'd still want you."

Something like a sob sounded from between her lips, and he wrapped an arm around her, pressing his hand over her breast where her heart pounded as hard as his.

"When we ran in the woods, I'd never felt anything like it," he admitted. "Like you were my pack."

Her breath caught.

"It fucked with me. And I treated you badly. I don't have words for how sorry I am." He lifted her now-scarred wrist and pressed the most reverent kiss to it.

Niamh turned her head. He lifted his eyes to meet hers. Her lips almost touched his as she whispered, "I forgive you."

Kiyo brushed his mouth over hers. "I want you," he repeated and pressed his hand harder against her heart. "But I want this too. If you can't give me that, you need to say so now because I can't take one without the other. Not with you."

Her whole body seemed to sag into him. "You already have it," she confessed. "I feel like you've had it forever."

Exultation and possessiveness roared through him, and he turned her swiftly in his arms, crushing her against him. "Are you ready?" he growled with need.

She grinned cockily. "I was born ready for you."

Kiyo was surprised by the laughter that rumbled from his chest and in that moment, he fell even harder.

29

If she was dreaming, Niamh didn't want to wake up.

Though Kiyo hadn't said the words, he'd said more than she'd ever thought possible of him, and she knew he loved her.

She wanted to tell him the secret that hung between them, but she was afraid he'd scorn the idea of destiny trying to trap him. That he needed this decision to be his own. After all, he'd made his opinion on the true mating bond very clear.

She throbbed with so much love as Kiyo gently towel dried her body. When he was done, he dropped the towel to the floor and cupped her breasts in his hands.

Niamh's nipples tightened almost painfully as he dragged his thumbs over them. She leaned into him, his own body still a little damp. The urge to touch him was overwhelming, like she wasn't in control of it. Her palm slid down his abs until she reached him, straining as he was. A gasp of need fell from her lips as he squeezed her breasts in response to her fingers wrapping around him.

His chest heaved as she gave him an experimental tug.

Dark eyes gleamed into hers with barely controlled hunger.

"You're so thick," she murmured, squeezing him harder.

He grunted, thrusting into her touch just before he shook his head and pulled away. "Can't." He gave her a friendly snarl. "I'll come."

"Isn't that the point?" she teased.

Kiyo smirked. "Not for your first time. I have plans."

"Oh?" Niamh burned so hot with want, she thought she might expire.

"I plan to make you come first. Many times." His eyes narrowed. "So many, it'll take weeks for the gold to leave your eyes."

The promise made Niamh flush from head to foot.

He held out his hand to her. "This is going to happen like it should have at the lodge."

She took his hand and gripped it tight. "I know I'm a virgin, but I'm going to be good at this. I'm going to blow your mind."

He grinned at her, that wicked boyish smile that he gave her more and more often now. "You already blow my mind." He tugged her close, cuddling her into him like they weren't naked and aroused. He stroked her wet hair off her face. "Your inexperience is not why I stopped back at the lodge. You want the truth?"

She nodded.

He pushed his hips into her so she'd feel him. "Knowing no one else has had this from you makes me hard as hell." He dipped his mouth to hers and growled against them. "The beast in me loves it."

A thrill rushed through her and Niamh couldn't hold it back anymore. She kissed him and Kiyo opened to her immediately, taking control of it. It was an intoxicating mix of gentle exploring and barely leashed rapaciousness.

Niamh needed closer. Wrapped around him. Inside of him. Connected. She climbed him without thought, her inner thigh pressed to his hip as she wrapped a leg around him and pushed against his arousal. Kiyo broke the kiss with a rough curse and swung her into his arms. Expression fierce, he carried her into the bedroom and laid her gently upon the bed.

Then he spread her legs and lowered his head.

Niamh's hands reached for him, her fingers clutching at his hair as his mouth touched her. Sensation rippled up her spine and her legs fell open to invite him deeper. His lips and tongue wrung pleasure from her, building the tension to excruciating tightness until it released in a shower of warm voluptuousness. She throbbed in ripples that craved more.

He did it again.

And again.

Until she was so sensitive and so needful, she begged him in unintelligible moans.

He grinned wickedly as he made his way up her body, scattering warm, wet kisses along her belly before pausing to make love to her breasts. Niamh's thighs climbed his hips as she pushed into his arousal, feeling the wet heat of the tip brush tantalizingly across her swollen center.

He sucked harder on her nipple as they rocked against each other. His hand slipped between her legs, nudging past his hardness to push gently into her. Niamh gasped at the intrusion, their eyes meeting in desire and tenderness as he pushed two fingers inside her.

"Kiyo?" She tilted into the pleasure pain, needing more.

"You're so swollen," he breathed against her lips, sounding like he'd run a marathon. "Can you take me?"

"I need you," she replied, almost on a whine.

"I've never seen your eyes so gold." He crushed his lips to hers, kissing her like he wanted to ravage her. But when she did feel him pushing inside, it was with tentative gentleness. Kiyo released her lips, bracing his hands at either side of her head, his body trembling as he eased into her.

The fullness of him was overwhelming. Niamh cried out at the burning sensation, her fingernails digging into his back as he pressed onward.

His head fell back as he let out a deep, loud, very male sound of pleasure. Not moving, he held still within her, throbbing and thick.

"Are you okay?"

Niamh soothed the nail marks on his back and tilted her hips, causing him to move and growl with need. "Yes ... like that," she gasped, feeling the pleasure from earlier sprinkle goose bumps across her skin.

Staring deep into her eyes with a primal possessiveness, Kiyo began to thrust slowly, measured, controlled glides, creating that alluring tension in her body again.

Niamh rocked her hips in time with his thrusts, reaching for his ass to pull him deeper. When he hit a magical spot inside her, she threw her head back on a cry of pleasure that seemed to break Kiyo's control.

He captured her mouth in a hungry, wet kiss before he pumped into her faster, harder.

It was too much.

She was too hot. Her heart raced too fast. She broke the kiss, gasping for breath.

"Come for me," he demanded, reaching between them.

His thumb hit her clit.

And a release exploded through her with electrical force.

Kiyo made a harsh sound of surprise in her ears, but Niamh saw nothing but sparks of wonder behind her lids as her inner muscles clasped around him in throbbing waves. His hips jerked, he tensed, and then his shout of release filled the room as he shuddered hard against her.

Niamh's eyes flew open, surprised to find the room only lit by the lights of the city and the moon outside.

Kiyo panted, a smirk playing on his lips. "Should I feel proud that you just blew out the hotel's electricity when you came?"

Laughter bubbled from her gut. "I didn't?"

"You did." He chuckled and kissed her, grinding into her like he didn't want to pull out. His mouth left hers but only to trail kisses over her cheeks. "That was ... there are no words for what that was." He squeezed her hips with affection as his lips caressed her throat.

Niamh was languid with satisfaction and bliss.

So it took her a moment to realize he'd frozen above her.

"What?" she whispered, unnerved by his sudden weirdness.

Then he pressed his nose to her throat. And sniffed.

"Kiyo."

He snuffled like an animal, dragging his nose down her chest, along her shoulders.

Some kind of ancient intuition filled her seconds before his head snapped up and he stared at her in abject shock.

"Kiyo?"

"You smell like me," he bit out seconds before he slipped from her body, causing her to wince from the slight smarting pain of it.

He pushed away to sit on his knees. Dragging a hand through his loose hair, he panted. "And not just 'we had sex' so my scent is on you ... you smell like me and I smell like you ... like our scents are *in* each other." His eyes flew to hers. "Our scents are one."

Niamh trembled, not knowing where his reaction was heading.

Then dark territorialism entered his gleaming eyes. "You're my mate. My true mate."

Niamh nodded, still not sure what this meant for him. "I've suspected it for a few days."

Abruptly he reached for her, and Niamh let out a squeal as he pulled her by the legs toward him, only to fall over her again. "Are you sore?" he growled against her lips.

"A little," she gasped.

"Too sore?"

She shook her head.

Without preamble, he thrust into her, baring his teeth as renewed sensation filled her. Her head flew back on the pleasure pain that sparked all the way down to her toes.

Apparently, Kiyo was good with this latest revelation.

Her eyes practically rolled back in her head as his fingers did delicious things to her.

By the time the night was over, he'd claimed her so many times, Niamh fell into a deliriously happy, exhausted sleep curled in his arms. And the last thing she heard as he cuddled her to him was Kiyo murmuring in wonder, "My mate. My pack."

30

"Okay, we have to leave this hotel room today before the fight tomorrow." Niamh strolled into the sitting room, the scent of shampoo fresh in her long hair.

Kiyo stuffed a forkful of eggs into his mouth to stop himself from reaching for her.

This constant need for her was ridiculous.

But he'd been assured it would ease.

Fionn had called a week ago to ask after Kiyo's condition. Apparently, Niamh had contacted him and Bran for help. Kiyo spoke to him while Niamh showered, his mind half on the call, half on the thought of his mate in the shower.

His mate.

True mate.

Fionn had suspected as much. Somehow. The know-it-all bastard. Kiyo saw no point in not confirming. While it was safer to be far away from other fae-borne, he, Fionn, and Conall were bound by the fact that they were true mates to three fae-borne women. War was a distinct possibility in the future, and by default, all of them made a strange team of sorts.

"What was it you called me?" Fionn had mused. "Oh, that was it. Mate-whipped."

Kiyo glowered but stayed silent, chafing at the turnabout.

Fionn chuckled darkly. "I'm surprised you haven't run for the hills by now."

"No, you're not," Kiyo replied.

Fionn surely understood the bond. There was *no* running from it. He didn't want to. The moment Kiyo had scented the change in his and Niamh's alchemy that signified their bond, a savage desire overpowered him to claim her with the knowledge of their bond in his soul.

True-mate sex.

There was nothing like it.

If humans knew about it, they'd never get anything else done.

Only humans, Kiyo scoffed to himself. Human, werewolf, vamp, witch, or fae ... that mating bond was the strongest aphrodisiac in the world.

"No, I'm not. There's no fighting the bond. You don't want to in the end," Fionn replied.

Kiyo eyed the bathroom door, imagining ripping it off its hinges to get to Niamh. "Does it ... get easier?"

He heard the smile in the Irishman's voice. "In some ways. If you're talking physically, the first few weeks are the worst. You'll want to do nothing but fuck." He chuckled. "But it eases. You start using your big brain instead of the wee one. For the most part. Emotionally ... that's a different game, Kiyo. She's all that's going to matter to you from now on."

It was the most heartfelt conversation the two males had ever had, and Kiyo wanted to be done with it. He'd hit his quota on talking about his feelings and the only one he cared enough to share them with was Niamh.

A week had passed and the connection between them was so acute, they could sense each other's emotions. Sex was phenomenal. Knowing exactly what the other wanted was incredible.

And the two of them were acting like sex-craved addicts.

However, apparently, Niamh thought it was time they tried to shake past this part of the bond. Kiyo tried not to pout over his breakfast. He could have gone another few days in bed. Maybe even a week. Or two.

Or a month.

Fuck.

"Yeah, we probably should," he agreed reluctantly.

She grinned as she took the seat beside him and lifted the cloche covering her breakfast. "Ooh, you went English on me."

They'd been living off room service the whole time and while the food was good, he thought his Irish girl might be growing tired of rice and grilled fish for breakfast. He'd ordered the more substantial traditional English breakfast of eggs, bacon, sausages, blood pudding, mushrooms, tomatoes, and baked beans. "Thought you might like a change."

Niamh fell on the plate like a woman starved, so he guessed he'd been right.

He smirked as he took a sip of coffee.

She raised an eyebrow. Swallowing a bite, Niamh waved her fork at him. "What's that smug look on your face?"

"Nothing. You just seem to have worked up quite an appetite."

"Don't." She pleaded, surprising. "Every time you look at me like that, I want to jump you. And I cannot spend the rest of my eternity in a sex bubble."

"A sex bubble?" Laughter trembled on his lips.

"Don't laugh! You laughing makes me want to jump you even more. And I have a mission. Correction: *we* have a mission. I'm blaming the orgasms for my lack of visions."

Kiyo chuckled harder.

She threw a piece of toast at him and it landed in his coffee.

Niamh stared at it sheepishly but he could tell she was dying to laugh.

"I was enjoying that coffee."

"It was unintentional."

"That may be." He pushed his chair back from the table. "But a punishment is still in order."

"No." She shook her head. "I'm enjoying my breakfast."

"It'll wait." He covered her plate with the cloche before he rounded the table to haul her into his arms.

She wrapped herself around him like a monkey as he carried her into the bedroom. "I've just had a shower."

"You can magically clean yourself afterward." He threw her on the bed and reached to unbutton her jeans.

"Kiyo." Dark desire flooded her expression. "Promise we will leave the hotel room after we have sex. *Today*."

"Okay," he grunted as he whipped off her jeans and underwear.

"You need to pr-promise," she stuttered as he unzipped his own jeans and pushed them down just far enough to free him.

Dragging her down the bed to meet him, he gripped her hips in his hands, lust and love making his heart thunder in his chest. "I promise." Then he thrust into her tight, wet heat, exulting in her cries of pleasure.

"I CAN'T BELIEVE we're outside our room."

Kiyo strolled at Niamh's side as they moved with the crowds across Tokyo's famous Shibuya crossing. They'd been to this part of the city before, but Niamh still took everything in like she was seeing it for the first time. Did she know what a gift her sense of wonder was? "You keep saying it like that, you might bruise my ego."

"Oh, please." Niamh threw him a wry look. "You know if it weren't for the mission, I'd have tied you to the bed myself." Worry darkened her eyes. She spoke in his mind now. *It's been days and days without a vision. And Astra is out there and probably now knows you're immortal.*

Niamh had since told him what Astra said in the garden. She'd known he and Niamh were true mates before they did. Had a vision about it. And she believed the only way to turn Niamh dark was to break the bond between her and Kiyo, i.e., kill him.

Grabbing hold of Niamh's wrist, his thumb caressed her scar as he pulled her out of the crowd and guided her up against the wall of a shop. He braced his hands on the building, cocooning her. "Nothing is going to happen to me. It can't."

"I've told you before. No one on earth is impervious to death."

Not wanting to argue when she was so certain, Kiyo shrugged. "Fine. Okay. Say something happened to me … I know you. You won't turn dark."

He felt a wave of shame emanate from her and his jaw tightened with anger.

Not at Niamh. At Astra, for planting thoughts in her head.

"She had a vision that I do," Niamh reminded him.

"She *said* she had a vision. There's no evidence she actually had a vision of you going to her side and opening the gate. You know what there is evidence of? Her trying to manipulate you. Or do you not remember she planted visions in your head?"

That feeling of shame he sensed disintegrated and an intense flood of tenderness hit him. "You're so bloody wise," she said and leaned up to brush her lips across his. "You always make me feel better, Kiyo-chan."

He grinned at her endearment and pressed a quick kiss to her lips before pulling back. If he lingered any longer, they'd end up back at the hotel. They walked again, heading north toward Meiji Jingu. Niamh wanted to see the Shinto shrine and gardens, and without any current direction, Kiyo saw no reason they shouldn't enjoy the city and each other's company while they could.

Niamh had put up a barrier spell around their room that stopped anyone from entering. Something like that might have drained her years ago, but every day she seemed to grow stronger in her abilities.

Now that they were outside, Kiyo was in guard mode, alert to the fact that their enemies could show at any moment.

When Niamh reached for his hand while they strolled, his first instinct was to drop it. He'd never been the hand-holding type. Yet, when Niamh sensed this and relaxed her hand to release him, Kiyo found himself gripping it tight.

She gave him an understanding smile. "It's okay. I get it." She tugged on his hand.

He didn't let go. If his mate wanted to hold his hand, he'd get over himself and hold her hand. His expression seemed to translate his feelings because Niamh grinned happily.

Her happiness made it worth it.

Fionn was right.

He was mate-whipped.

Fifteen minutes later, they were only around five minutes from Yoyogi Park when Niamh suddenly jerked his hand as she halted. Her features looked strained. And he knew without her having to say the words.

"Vision?" He grabbed and pulled her against the stone wall that ran along the sidewalk. Foot traffic was quiet, but the roads weren't. He covered her with his body, trying to hide her—

Niamh convulsed hard in his arms and he gritted his teeth as he clasped her nape to stop her head from smacking against the stone. Her eyelids fluttered rapidly and powerlessness overwhelmed him.

He hated seeing her like this.

Pain, like being smacked in the forehead with a rock, sent bright lights flashing across his eyes. Images flooded his head. Niamh. Him. Rose. Astra. Elijah. Standing stones. Four. Gardens. Tokyo. Gardens. Jade pendant. They hit him one after the other on repeat.

Then just as abruptly as they'd come, they disappeared.

Kiyo's eyes flew open.

He and Niamh were huddled on the ground. She was tucked into his chest like a child.

"Niamh?"

She lifted her head, her eyes flying up behind him.

He followed her gaze and saw two young men staring curiously at them as they walked by.

Kiyo glared until they hurried away.

Once they were on their feet, he pulled Niamh into his arms, cuddling her tight against him as he rested his chin on her head. "You okay?"

She nodded, squeezing him. “It was the same as before. Nothing new.”

“Not quite.”

Niamh pulled away just enough to look at him. “What do you mean?”

“I know where those gardens are. And the jade pendant was new.”

Niamh frowned. “No, it wasn’t. It’s always been in them.”

Kiyo shook his head. “Not the one I saw last time.”

She considered this. “Actually, I think you’re right. But it was in the first one I ever got. What does it mean?”

“The gardens belong to the house I was renting in Osaka back in the 1800s when I was taking my revenge against my mother’s rapists. I was cursed in those gardens.” His grip on Niamh tightened unwittingly as he remembered. “The jade pendant belonged to Mizuki Nakamura. The miko who cursed me.”

Niamh pushed away from him. “Then we have to go to Osaka. Kiyo … that pendant.”

Something like panic clawed at his gut as realization struck. “It’s a talisman.”

And I’d bet my eternity that it holds your curse within. Destroy it and … She clung to him now, fear pouring from her.

“Best-case scenario, I become mortal. Worst-case scenario … I die.”

Which was exactly what Astra wanted.

A fierceness overcame Niamh with such strength, her eyes bled gold and strands of her hair lifted of its own accord. Electricity crackled around her. “That’s not going to happen,” she vowed, her voice sounding different.

“*Komorebi* …” He reached for her, his tone calming. “The show, while arousing, is unnecessary. We’ll find the pendant.”

Just like that, the surrounding energy flamed out and her eyes were aquamarine again. She looked at him in wonder. “What did you just call me?”

“We need to get back to the hotel. Can you do your thing when no one’s looking?”

"Answer my question first."

"I called you *Komorebi*," he answered impatiently. "Now can we go?"

Niamh stepped into his waiting arms, smiling up at him like he'd just given her the whole world. "You told me *Komorebi* means a beautiful forest with sunlight peeking through the leaves of the trees. And you think of it every time you ready for a run through the woods."

"Yeah," he muttered, feeling too much. Way too fucking much for it to be comfortable.

She slipped her arms around his neck. "Trust you, my darling, my brooding wolf, to give a woman the most romantic endearment on the planet."

His grip on her tightened but he just grunted in acknowledgment.

Niamh leaned up to whisper across his lips. "Don't worry, your secret is safe with me." She pressed her mouth to his, and he felt a strange disorientation.

When he opened his eyes, they were standing in the middle of their hotel room.

31

"Finally!" Niamh cried. She lifted her head from the tablet they'd borrowed from the hotel staff. "I've got a hit that sounds promising."

Half an hour ago, she'd started googling Osaka and Mizuki Nakamura. Considering Mizuki was an old woman when she'd cursed Kiyo in 1898, he wasn't hopeful they'd find much on the internet. While Niamh searched, he'd stewed in restless anger over the fact that he'd just assumed Mizuki had used a human sacrifice to curse him. She'd brought a young girl with her to the gardens that night. Mizuki told him she was the most impressive miko she'd encountered in years. Both he and the girl thought she was there to help Mizuki deal with him.

Instead she'd killed the girl, siphoning her energy to curse Kiyo.

In the morning, when he awoke after being knocked unconscious by the curse, the gardens he laid in had begun to die.

All of that pointed to the fact that Mizuki had channeled her power through nature.

He'd never suspected that she'd used a powerful talisman to contain her spells and curses for longevity.

Feeling impatient with self-directed anger, he strode across the room and Niamh handed him the tablet.

"It's a blog entry from a travel blogger in the US."

Wondering at the relevancy, Kiyo read the paragraph Niamh pointed to.

Of course, I can't write a post on Osaka without mentioning the atmospheric and creepy tavern my sister and I stumbled upon on our last night there. Buried within the Sakai ward near the port of Osaka Bay is the home of the WEIRDEST experience Lucy and I have had since arriving in Japan. We'd been talking with a local girl about how fascinating the miko culture was. For those who missed my post on that, mikos are shrine maidens. Or female shamans to you and me. They're pretty respected in Japan, and Lucy and I love anything with a hint of supernatural or occult to it. Anyway, our new friend told us that a famous family of miko lived in Sakai and the latest generation owned a tavern.

Well, we had to go, right?! So we found the entrance to the tavern down a very narrow alley between a bunch of buildings crammed together. We'd never have known it was there if our newbie friend hadn't told us.

Kiyo sighed with impatience. "Does she get to the point anytime soon?"

"Yeah, keep reading."

As soon as we stepped inside, it was like the dark little place was charged with electricity. It's hard to describe. All I can say is that the bartenders were the least friendly people we've met while being in Japan. It was like they didn't want us there or something!!! And the clientele ... off the charts CREEPY. The whole vibe was very mystical and goosebumpy.

"Goosebumpy? Really?"

Niamh laughed. "So she's no Shakespeare. Just keep reading."

. . .

When we asked the lady bartender about the so-called family legacy, she said if we didn't get out, she'd CURSE us! Lucy and I almost stayed just to see if it would happen but, seriously, guys, we freaking believed her. Call us crazy all you want, but you'll understand what we mean when you visit. And for an authentic mystical Japanese experience, you HAVE to visit Nakamura Izakaya in Sakai to hang out with the descendants of the über-famous Mizuki Nakamura, the most powerful miko in the history of Japan!

"Shit," Kiyo breathed, not believing what he was reading.

"It has to be her, right? Sakai is the area she lived in?"

Kiyo nodded. "The Nakamuras lived in the Sakai ward. Their men were involved in trade."

"Then I guess we're going to their tavern to ask a few questions. If we're lucky, they might have a jade pendant hanging on the wall as a souvenir."

He threw her a wry look. "Yeah, it'll be that easy."

"It's our only lead."

He exhaled heavily, dropping the tablet on the sofa. "Then I guess we're going to Osaka."

"What about Sakura's fight tomorrow?"

"We'll return in time for the fight ... and hopefully we'll have the pendant and we can get the hell out of Japan and go somewhere Astra can't find you."

Tokyo Station was busy but nowhere near as crowded as it would be in a few hours when it was rush hour. Upon checking which type of shinkansen would get them to Osaka the fastest, they bought tickets on the Nozomi. That bullet train would get them into Osaka in two and a half hours. Despite the gravity of the reason for the trip, Niamh was openly excited about getting to ride on a bullet train for more than a few minutes.

"And first-class tickets that cost an absolute fortune," she said gleefully. "You didn't have to do that."

Kiyo slid his arm around her waist, pulling her into his side as he guided her through the station toward their platform. "Did it make you like me more?"

She grinned. "I like you enough as it is. If I like you any more, I'm likely to succumb to the affliction."

He shook with laughter, understanding completely.

But his amusement died instantly when he saw five wolves pushing through the crowds toward them.

"What the hell?" Niamh tensed. "What now?"

Kiyo tightened his hold on her as they found themselves encircled by the werewolves. Passengers gave them a wide berth and the station guards turned their backs, recognizing the high-ranking members of Pack Iryoku. Kiyo glared into the familiar light brown gaze of Kobe.

He sneered at Kiyo and asked in Japanese, "Going somewhere?"

"What's it to you?" Kiyo answered in English.

"Arufua-san commanded your presence in the city," Kobe returned in English, his eyes bouncing between Kiyo and Niamh. "Neither you nor the mahoutsukai can leave without permission. We thought this was made clear to you."

"No. I have a deal with Sakura that I'll fight for her tomorrow night. That's where our deal starts and ends. You can't tell me where I can and cannot go."

"You come with us. Sort this out with Arufua-san."

"We have somewhere to be."

"Yes, you do." The wolves moved in closer.

Kiyo, let's just go with them, Niamh spoke in his mind. *Let them think we're doing what we're told. I can get us on that train afterward.*

He squeezed her waist in acknowledgment but kept his eyes on Kobe. "Fine. We'll go back to our hotel."

"No. You come with us."

He tensed, ready to fight.

No, my darling. Let's just go with them. If we can get out of this peacefully, we must try.

Realizing she was right, Kiyo reluctantly allowed Kobe and his men to escort them out of the train station.

Bloody déjà vu, Niamh muttered in irritation in his head.

THIS TIME when they strode into the pack's hotel, Kobe led them to an office on the thirtieth floor. To Kiyo's surprise, Daiki awaited them. He pushed out of a leather chair situated behind an impressive walnut desk. His bruises and injuries from their fight were long gone.

After he gestured to the two seats in front of his desk, Kiyo stared impassively at him. "I think we'll stand."

The door to the office closed, the other wolves outside. Kobe stood guard at the door.

"Where's Sakura?" Kiyo sighed. "I was so sure she was behind this power play."

"She is." Daiki sat on the edge of the desk, looking far more relaxed than when they last saw him. "Apparently, she does not like your mahoutsukai."

"So you're doing her dirty work for her."

Daiki shrugged. "It is part of the job of being her mate."

"You seem awfully chipper for a bloke who got his arse kicked," Niamh observed, her eyes narrowed suspiciously.

"What does this *chipper* mean?" Daiki sneered at her.

Kiyo tried not to chuckle. "Niamh merely means that you seem in a surprisingly good mood."

"Oh. Well, I was not at first when Sakura said you had turned up at Tokyo Station and we needed to stop you from leaving. Then she reminded me of all the money we will make when you win that fight tomorrow, and I felt my mood change." He crossed his arms over his chest and sighed dramatically again. "But still I was not happy that I would have to see you and be the one to offer a warning that if you try to leave the city before the big fight, we will find you and cut you into little pieces and make your mahoutsukai watch us. Then we will allow the boys to have her for as long as they want. When they are done with her, they will kill her too."

Kiyo lunged at him.

But Niamh was fast and strong, holding him back, murmuring reassuring words in his ear. Slowly, he calmed. But he wanted to claw that smug look off Daiki's face.

"And that"—he gestured to the two of them—"is why I am in such a good mood. As soon as you walked in the room, do you know what I scented?"

He and Niamh tensed.

Daiki grinned. "Your scents are one. Kiyo. Of all the poor bastards in the world it could happen to, it would be you. How many supes actually discover the true-mate bond? One or two percent? And it happened to you." He chuckled madly.

"Why is he laughing?" Niamh stared at the alpha like he'd lost his mind.

Kiyo wasn't sure he hadn't.

Daiki eventually stopped, wiping tears of amusement from his eyes as he straightened up on the desk.

"What's so funny about it?" Kiyo asked.

"Oh, you can give me that cool tone like nothing affects you, but it is too late. I know what she"—he indicated Niamh—"means to you now. And so will Sakura. And that is why I laugh. Finally, she can let you go knowing you are forever out of her reach. It is a good day, Kiyo."

"Can we go, then?" Niamh asked.

Daiki considered her. "I admit I have never seen the fascination with mahoutsukai. I prefer the sensuality of a wolf. But I can see the appeal in yours, Kiyo. There is something about her that makes a wolf want to howl. And her scent ... that must draw the vampires, hai? I do not envy you the bond with one such as her. You will never have peace."

If you understood what I had with her, the jealousy would eat you alive. "We're done here." Kiyo took Niamh's hand and turned toward the door. Alpha energy pulsed from him and Kobe immediately slipped into a fighting stance.

"No need for that," Daiki said behind them. "Let them go on the previous warning of mutilation, violation, and death if they try to leave the city before the fight. And as you have seen, we have cameras everywhere."

Thirty minutes later on a bullet train to Osaka ...

Niamh turned her head as she settled into her seat and grinned mischievously at Kiyo. "Not everywhere."

32

It was the water garden from her dreams.

A green pond. Arched stone bridge that led to the small but beautifully crafted pagoda. Cherry blossoms were in full bloom. Lush greenery surrounded the beautiful pink flowers. Exquisite Japanese maples with spaghetti-like branches and orange leaves. Plants she had no name for that dripped and hung and hugged the garden in a variety of shades of green. The sweet, intoxicating scent of jasmine surrounded Niamh.

Why was she here?

"There she is."

Niamh whipped around at the familiar voice, but no one stood on the large stepping stones that led across the pond to the traditional Minka house in the distance. Niamh squinted. It seemed blurred at the edges.

The whole garden was blurred at the edges.

Where was she?

Why was she here?

Hadn't she just been with Kiyo?

"This is where he was staying." Astra's voice echoed around the garden.

Niamh's pulse raced. "Where are you?"

"I am everywhere, sister. You'll never escape me. Not even your immortal mate can stop me."

Niamh's let out a shuddering breath, searching through the quickly growing darkness for the fae. "You don't want to come at me again, Astra. After what you did to Kiyo, you'll be lucky to walk away."

"Don't taunt me with your anger, Niamh. It gets my hopes up."

"Where are we?"

"In your head," Astra's omniscient voice answered. "In your dreams. I came to ask you where you are, thinking I might catch you unaware, but your defenses really are back up again. He's healed you." Her tone was mocking. "How quaint."

"So you don't know where I am?"

"I'll find you. Eventually. But your scent seems to have changed since the mating bond, so I can't get a read on you until I see you again."

"You can follow me by scent?"

"Only if we're close enough. I got busy and distracted while you were getting busy and distracted by your dog. Next thing I knew, you were gone and your scent trail was gone."

"What a shame." Niamh smirked. Mating bond for the win.

"I wouldn't be smug, sister. Now that the bond has snapped into place, you're one step closer to being what I need you to be."

Remembering Kiyo's words from earlier, she threw back her shoulders and called out into the now-dark garden, "Even without him, I will never walk away from who I really am."

"You say that now, but once he's dead—and when I'm done, make no mistake, he will be dead—you won't be able to contain your grief. It will swallow you in its darkness and you'll need me to pull you out. I'm the only family you'll have left."

Thinking of Rose and Thea, Niamh shook her head. "You're wrong."

Astra sighed wearily. "Only time will convince you otherwise."

"Astra."

"Yes, sister?"

"You underestimate my mate. He's ready for you now. You come at him and he'll tear you to shreds with his bare hands."

"Mmm, how savage."

Niamh narrowed her eyes. "But he'll leave you for me in the end. I'll be the one to put the iron in your heart."

"And add another patch of darkness to your soul in doing so."

"Oh no." Niamh shook her head. "Killing you will be saving the human world. That, my dear psychopath, keeps me on the right side of good. Your end won't blacken my soul."

An animalistic snarl flew at her from the pagoda. Niamh raised her arms to defend herself and—

She flew upward out of her seat, letting out a gasp of fright.

"Niamh." Kiyo pulled her toward him.

Her skin was damp with sweat, the blood rushing in her ears as she tried to orient herself. She was on the bullet train with Kiyo, heading to Osaka.

Panting, she took in her mate's concerned countenance and slowly calmed down. The woman across the aisle peered at her curiously.

Niamh slumped back in her comfortable chair.

"Was it another nightmare?" Kiyo asked, smoothing her hair off her forehead as he leaned into her.

She reached for his hand, slipping her fingers through his. "No. It was ... Astra invaded my dream."

"What?" he bit out quietly. "How the hell can she do that?"

"She said she was trying to manipulate me into telling her where I was. But good news"—she smiled wearily—"she might be able to get into my dreams, but she can't manipulate me in there. And she was tracking me through my scent, but the mating bond changed it. Apparently, she was off doing villainous things while you and I were giving each other happy times. When she got back, we were gone, and my scent trail with us."

"Because our scents have mixed."

"Exactly."

"Did she say anything else?"

"Oh, just her usual threats. She's getting a bit boring, actually."

Kiyo didn't look so amused as he leaned in to steal a kiss. He settled back into his seat but didn't let go of her hand. "It's good to know she has no clue about Osaka."

"None whatsoever. Which means we have a head start on finding that pendant."

Following Google Maps' directions to Nakamura Izakaya, they found themselves wandering the streets near the port of Osaka Bay. Niamh hoped they found the jade pendant fast because from what they'd seen of the city as they drove through it, she was beyond excited to explore. Maybe it was because this was where Kiyo was born. If it wasn't too painful for him, she would like to return to the area of his birth. To imagine Osaka as it had been when he was a boy. She did sense uneasiness from him about being in the city, but his strongest emotion was urgency. He wanted to find that pendant. So did Niamh. Tourist shit could wait. Leaving the car behind, they began to walk in search of their destination.

Kiyo explained that an *izakaya* was a kind of bar that sold drinks and snacks. Nakamura Tavern was apparently hidden in amongst a bunch of commercial establishments a few yards ahead.

Feeling a hum of energy the closer they got to their destination, Niamh asked Kiyo if he could feel it.

"Yeah," he answered, his face hard with thought as they neared the alley that led down to the bar. That hum became a cloying warmth on their skin as they walked down the alley toward the entrance.

It stood before them, a black-fronted building with a brown, ragged awning over the door. One small window covered in peeling black paper allowed some light from inside to peek through.

It looked as welcoming as a morgue.

"That's a spell," Niamh whispered, referring to the hum of energy.

"To keep nonsupernaturals out." Kiyo raised an eyebrow. "The travel blogger and her sister walked right through it ... they can harness magic and they don't even know it."

"Latent witches. That's how they got past the spell."

"Looks like it. I think we should be grateful they don't know. If someone can mutilate the English language with words like 'goose-bumpy,' imagine the horrors she'd commit with magic at her fingertips."

Niamh let out a bark of laughter as Kiyo's eyes gleamed with amusement. "You're funny."

"You don't need to sound so surprised." He gestured to the door. "Ladies first. I've got your back."

"Let's do this." Niamh strode in front of him, pushing open the door to the tavern and blinking her eyes to adjust to the darkness. All she got was an impression of the interior—dark wood everywhere, low-lit lanterns, framed photographs cluttering every inch of the walls. A bar ran along the back of the room.

What really had her attention were the vamps and werewolves that made up the clientele.

Holy crap.

She heard the not-so-subtle sniffing noises from the patrons as Kiyo followed close at her back.

Niamh ignored the flashing silver eyes of the vampires who stared like they wanted to suck her dry.

Damn her fae blood and a vamp's weakness for it.

Hurrying toward the bar where a small, middle-aged human woman with long salt-and-pepper hair glared from behind it, Niamh was halted when a tall vampire popped up in front of her.

"Oh." She stumbled back into Kiyo.

The vampire licked his lips as he zoned in on her throat. He asked something in Japanese.

Whatever it was, Kiyo took a distinct dislike to it. He demonstrated this not by words but by thumping his palm against the vampire's chest.

The knock sent the vamp flying across the tavern into a table of werewolves who immediately pounced on the vampire as if it had been his fault he was now their table decoration.

Niamh raised an eyebrow at Kiyo.

He was too busy issuing a silent warning at every supe in the tavern to notice.

She shivered, feeling hot and tingly in her southern region. Niamh shook her head at herself, not quite used to the idea that as much as there was a primal side to Kiyo's territorialism, there was an equally primal side of her that reacted to it physically.

A stream of Japanese hit their ears from behind the bar.

Kiyo turned to the woman and replied in English, "We're not here to cause trouble."

Glancing at Niamh, the woman sneered. "The mahoutsukai has a troublesome blood scent."

"And a human would know that how?" Kiyo stepped up to the bar. "You're a miko."

The woman glared. "No more."

"We're here about an ancestor of yours." Niamh sidled into Kiyo's side. "Your—"

"Mizuki." The bartender rolled her eyes. "Tourists. They all want to know about Mizuki. Do I look like tourist guide to you?" she snapped. "You want to know things, you go to museum. They took everything from my family. It all there."

"Who took everything?" Kiyo asked.

"The state. Of great cultural importance, they said. And we have no money," she relayed, the bitterness clear in her eyes. "So we sell to state and now they charge tourists to view my family's things."

"I'm sorry," Niamh offered sincerely.

The woman frowned, studying her carefully. "You mean that." Heaving a sigh, she grabbed a napkin and a pen and wrote characters on it. She slid the napkin to Kiyo. "The address. It in what used to be Mizuki's home. There is whole room of her things."

"Arigatō, miko-san." Kiyo gave her a grateful nod as he took the napkin.

"Why do you want to know?" She leaned over the bar. "You are not just tourist, are you? Strange mahoutsukai and her werewolf."

"I'm fascinated by women like me," Niamh replied with a smooth lie. "Mizuki is one of the most famous miko in Japan. I talked my boyfriend into taking me to Osaka just to learn about her."

Kiyo plastered on a comical expression of said beleaguered boyfriend and shrugged as if to say, "What can you do?"

Mizuki's descendant bought it. "Fine. Now go before the vamps decide your boyfriend is worth the fight to get to your blood."

She didn't need to tell them twice.

Kiyo placed a claiming hand on Niamh's lower back and led her out of the tavern. She exhaled in relief as soon as they strode out of the alley and back onto the main street.

"Where to next?"

Kiyo raised the napkin with the Japanese characters on it.

"You really need to teach me how to read Japanese."

"Which language?" he answered sardonically.

Remembering there was Hiragana, Katakana, and Kanji, Niamh shrugged. "All of them."

"Is this before or after we're saving my ass?"

"After. But first we need to save the world. Then you can teach me Japanese."

"If we save my ass and then the world's, I'm not celebrating by teaching you Japanese." He gave her a pointed look that made her hot and needy.

"You can't give me that smoldering-sex look when we're smack bang in the middle of a mission."

Kiyo looked far too happy about her description.

"I feel like you're not taking this seriously at all." She snatched the napkin from his hand. She stared at the alien characters. Fionn's voice filled her head: *The only limitations to your magic are the ones you place upon it.*

Holding tight to the napkin, Niamh stepped closer to Kiyo's body. He instinctively put his arms around her and she smiled up at him as she concentrated on the symbols on the napkin. Her magic pulsed and the characters began to leave the napkin, slithering into her hand and melting into her skin.

Kiyo's expression was blank but she felt his shock.

The knowledge on the napkin became a part of her.

"Hold on to me."

A momentary darkness, a slightly off-kilter but familiar feeling surrounded them, and then they were there.

She'd *traveled* to the address on the napkin.

Kiyo looked up at the house he told her was of the Minka style, much like the one from her dream. Minka was a blanket term now for traditional Japanese architecture. It was large and stuck out on the residential street crammed with modern homes.

Thankfully, no one was on the street when Kiyo and Niamh popped out of nowhere.

Her mate took hold of her hand, turning it over and finding only the scar left by Sakura's bracelet. "How?" His eyes flew to hers. "Have you done that before?"

Niamh shook her head. "It was something Fionn said. The only limitations to my magic are the ones *I* place upon it. I think he meant I'm capable of almost anything. Cool, huh?"

Kiyo shook his head, his expression veering between awe and exasperation. "Try to leave me some things to do that make me useful."

Niamh gave him a saucy smile before turning to climb the steps to the museum. "Oh, there are parts of you that are incredibly useful to me."

"You're going to pay for that." He hurried to catch up with her.

"How?"

"Where's the fun in telling you?" He winked before guiding her inside.

Despite their current reason for being in the museum, Niamh couldn't help the happiness that filled her. Every day, Kiyo grew less and less brooding. And she knew it was because of their bond. Even here in Osaka, somewhere he hadn't returned since being cursed, he was lighter than before.

She made him happy.

She made an immortal werewolf who hadn't known true contentment in over a hundred years happy.

That was cooler than any magic she could ever hope to do.

While Niamh was woolgathering over their bond, Kiyo paid their admission into the quiet museum. Renewed urgency seemed to have taken over him now that they were in the large home with its tatami mat flooring, wall scrolls, and shoji screens. Small plaques written in Japanese and English were placed on the walls next to scrolls and photographs. Other objects were encased in glass.

Kiyo read signs above doorways and led them with quick efficiency into the largest room at the back of the house. "This is it."

They separated, taking one side of the room each. Niamh scoured old newspaper clippings and eyed beautiful kimonos, vases, and stones that were considered objects of power for Mizuki.

Then she stumbled to a stop upon an empty glass stand.

The plaque beneath it read:

The Nakamura Jade Pendant

Mizuki wore the Nakamura jade until the day she died. Despite requesting the jade be buried with her ashes, the request could not be fulfilled by the Nakamura family as the stone belonged to the next generation of miko. Rumors that the jade could not be borne, however, by anyone else but Mizuki spread through Osaka when Sayuri Nakamura, her successor, was killed trying to use its power. It was locked away in the family Tamaya (memorial altar dedicated to deceased ancestors) and never seen again, until now.

"Uh, Kiyo."

"Yeah." He hurried across the room. "Did you find it?"

"Sort of." Niamh pointed at the empty glass, trying to quell the tears of frustration burning in her eyes. "It's gone."

She was confused as Kiyo abruptly strode away, though not so confused when he returned with a concerned-looking staff member who went a ghostly white when they showed him the empty glass case.

A rapid-fire conversation in Japanese ensued, the man growing more distressed as Kiyo's anger swelled.

"What's happening?" Niamh interrupted impatiently.

"He doesn't know how it got out of there," Kiyo snapped just as the man fled the room. "He's checking the security cameras."

"Kiyo ..." She placed a hand on his arm. "Who would know?"

"Astra?" he growled in question.

"She made it clear she didn't."

"Or she's trying to throw you off the trail."

The thought of the pendant in Astra's hands scared the shit out of Niamh. Kiyo pulled her into his embrace. "It'll be okay."

She nodded, pressing a kiss to his throat.

They waited like that until the museum guy returned ten minutes later looking flabbergasted and freaked out. He and Kiyo had another conversation in Japanese.

"He says the pendant was in the case last night. At 2:04 a.m., it disappeared. No one in the room. Just gone. He says you can clearly see it popping out of thin air on camera."

"It just disappeared?"

"Yeah."

Magic, she said telepathically.

He nodded, expression grim.

Astra.

33

Kiyo sat on the edge of the bed, elbows on his knees, head bent as he stared at the floor in serious contemplation.

Never in Niamh's life had she felt this kind of all-consuming fear and worry. All because of how much she bloody loved this man.

Loved.

What a pitiful word to describe how she felt.

"*Kyōka suigetsu*," she whispered unthinkingly from her spot near the bathroom door. Kiyo brought his head up to stare at her with that heartrending intensity of his. He'd taught her that phrase this past week. *Something that is visible but can't be touched, like the moon's reflection on the water. Or an emotion that can't be described with mere words.*

That was her love for him.

And she was terrified of losing him.

"*Komorebi*," he murmured and held out his hand. "Come here."

Niamh shook her head. If she went to him, she'd again beg and plead with him not to go to this fight. But Kiyo had already shut her down.

"It's too dangerous," Niamh had complained that morning.

After catching the bullet train back to Tokyo and *traveling* to the hotel so as not to alert the pack, Niamh had exhausted herself trying to connect to Astra. If it was possible for Astra to invade her mind with visions and dream-walking, then surely Niamh could do it to her.

She'd tried so hard, she was pretty sure she'd burst a blood vessel or two on her forehead until Kiyo had demanded she stop before she hurt herself.

Despite all the worries consuming her, she'd fallen asleep in his arms and awoken to his glorious lovemaking.

It was after as he got up to get ready for the day that she remembered the fight.

"I made a promise," he'd thrown over his shoulder as he walked his remarkable naked arse into the bathroom.

Niamh marched in after him. "The pendant is missing. Astra could be anywhere with it. A chaotic, crowded fight in the middle of the city leaves you vulnerable. It's stupid and we should get the hell out of here now."

Kiyo's expression darkened as he stepped into the shower. "I can look after myself."

"I'm not saying you can't," Niamh huffed in exasperation. "But I don't understand why you can't just walk away when things are this uncertain."

"Last time, I made no promise to fight. This time I did. I honor my promises. Without my honor, Niamh, I really am just a soulless bastard."

She flinched. "How can you say that? We wouldn't be mated if you didn't have a soul. You couldn't feel anything for me."

"Right now, I'm feeling impatience. I fight, I win, and then I'm entirely free from the pack."

"And if Astra attacks during the fight?"

"Then we fight back."

"This is idiotic!" Niamh had hissed in outrage. "What about the promise you made to Fionn to protect me? Is that less important than your promise to Sakura?" She'd known it was jealous and childish as soon as she said it, but Niamh was too frightened to care. She'd hurried out, slamming the door behind her. She fought back tears as she glared out the window at the city beyond.

The bathroom door opened seconds later.

He didn't say anything.

Just pulled her back to his chest, wrapped his arms around her waist, and pressed a tender kiss to her temple.

"I didn't mean that." Her tears leaked as she covered his arms with hers. "I'm angry at myself. I'm supposed to be one of the most powerful beings on this bloody planet, and I can't even protect my own mate."

He squeezed her. "That's not your job."

"She's stronger than me, Kiyo. I can't find her, I can't get into her head—"

"Shh." He turned her in his arms and she sank into his embrace, uncaring that his skin was damp from the shower. "We'll find the pendant and then we'll get out of here and go where she can't find us."

Hours later, it was time to leave for the fight and Niamh felt no more reassured than she had this morning.

"Come here," Kiyo repeated, his hand still held out to her.

"No," Niamh said. "I'll fall apart."

Anger flashed across his face as he stood. "So, your plan is to punish me for going through with this."

"If you think that, then you don't know me at all."

He cut her an exasperated look before striding into the sitting room. "Then the problem is your faith in my skills as a fighter."

Ugh, men.

"I know you can kick the arse of every supernatural who'll be at that fight tonight. Except for one."

"Astra." Kiyo shrugged into a leather jacket, looking way too handsome and distracting in it. "We're on our guard. We go there expecting her to turn up. It's better this way than her catching us completely unaware."

Niamh felt irritated that there was a kernel of common sense in his words.

"Fine," she huffed, striding past him to their breakfast table. Lifting her hands over the surface, she gathered her magic to the fore.

"What are you doing?"

"Shh. I'm concentrating."

Seconds later, three pure iron blades gleamed atop the table. Lethargy crawled through her.

Kiyo crossed the room to peer down at them. "What's wrapped around the hilt?"

"A protective covering. I can handle it without burning myself. I'll still feel weakened by it, but it won't leave me with any scars if I wield it."

"Where did you get them?"

"Somewhere. Who knows? Same with the protective covering on the hilt. I just think of what I want and my magic retrieves it for me."

"And where are you planning on concealing them? We'll be checked for weapons before we enter the gardens."

"I'm not taking them with me. I'll leave them here. If Astra does come to the fight, I can conjure them to me." Niamh stepped back, her legs weak. "But I think we better leave the room now. Forgot how much of a toll that bloody iron takes."

A forbidding scowl marred Kiyo's brow, and a wave of feeling flooded from him. Startled by it, she followed him quietly out of the hotel room. The weakness faded almost as soon as they shut the door. Kiyo, however, strode down the corridor, pulsing with self-directed recrimination.

And guilt.

Hurrying to catch up with him, Niamh slipped her hand into his.

He quirked a brow at her. "*Now* you want to hold my hand."

"Don't be spiky just because you feel guilty for breaking my neck twice and trapping me in a room filled with iron."

His emotions flooded her, including annoyance, but Niamh didn't care. She'd forgiven him for that ages ago and he should know it. He tried to pull away, but she held on tight. "Kiyo-chan, it's in the past. Let's leave it there. I know you'd never intentionally hurt me."

He whirled on her, grabbing her face in his hands to pull her to him. He crushed her mouth to his, his wild abandon way too sexual and hungry to be happening in a public hallway.

Niamh moaned, her back bowing as she melted into his voracious kiss.

Finally he released her lips but didn't let her go. His gaze was fierce. "Next time I ask you to come to me, you come to me."

Goodness, he was still chafing about that? "I'm yours to command, my darling, but only when we're making love. Outside of that, my feelings and actions are my own."

Kiyo released a groan of exasperation as he leaned his forehead against hers and squeezed his eyes closed.

"We'll get used to it," she promised, understanding. "All the feelings for one another ... one day they won't overwhelm us."

"I feel like I'm wearing my insides on the outside."

Niamh grinned at his unromantic but accurate description. "Like I said ... we'll get used to it."

Her mate kissed her again, soft and sweet this time. When he released her, he brushed his thumb over her mouth and said with grim seriousness, "Tonight you'll do what I say at the fight. I know these wolves. I know how these fights work. I need you to follow my lead."

Niamh had no problem with that. It made sense for him to take charge in a situation completely unfamiliar to her. "I'll follow your lead."

That seemed to reassure him and he led her to the elevator. When the doors opened, he shuffled her inside. Silence fell between them.

Then ...

"When you say you're mine to command in bed ... what are we talking about exactly?"

Niamh shot him a mock annoyed look and didn't reply. Not until the elevator stopped a few floors down for an older American couple who greeted them as they stepped inside.

Then Niamh belatedly replied, "I was thinking light bondage. At least to start with."

She felt his arousal hit her with full force. The Americans

exchanged confused and somewhat disturbed looks while Niamh grinned wickedly.

Amusement danced in Kiyo's eyes even as he promised silent retribution for turning him on when he couldn't do anything about it.

ANY AMUSEMENT NIAMH had been feeling died as their cab dropped them off outside one of the entrances to Shinjuku Gyo-en National Garden. Epic levels of energy leaked from the park.

"There's a spell here. A powerful one."

Kiyo nodded. "Sakura pays a local coven to put a barrier spell up to stop the public from getting in."

"A coven?"

"Yeah."

"You never mentioned Sakura had connections to a coven."

"Does it matter?"

Niamh shook her head, but something niggled at her. Trying to shake off the feeling, she asked, "How does she get away with a fight in a public garden?"

Kiyo eyed the five hulking werewolves guarding the entrance. "Pack Iryoku has werewolves in positions of power within the government. No one will take action against Sakura for closing the park."

A note had arrived at the hotel a few days ago with detailed instructions of which entrance Kiyo was to use and where the fight was taking place. As soon as they reached the security werewolves, Niamh felt the pulsating energy from within reaching beyond the barrier spell.

The place was filled with supernaturals.

Kiyo gave his name to the werewolf who stepped forward. He wore an earpiece and spoke in Japanese to someone elsewhere. He nodded and turned to Kiyo. "Haruto-san is on his way. We check you for weapons."

The security guard moved in for pat downs. When it was Niamh's turn, Kiyo bristled with so much tension waiting for the wolf to make the wrong move that everyone in the vicinity felt it.

The wolf patting her down shot her a wry look as he gave her a clinical once-over.

Niamh's nervous butterflies made her feel antsy as they waited. She was unaware her physical jitters were so obvious until Kiyo grabbed her hand and pulled her into him to whisper in her ear, "It'll be okay."

She nodded just as Haruto arrived to escort them.

He stared at them with the same blank expression he always seemed to wear. "This way."

They followed Haruto into the gardens. He led them past people Kiyo relayed were pack members.

"How big is the pack?"

"Biggest pack in East Asia. Sakura has her work cut out leading this many wolves. That's why she is the way she is."

"Don't make excuses for her, Kiyo."

He frowned. "I'm not. Just stating facts."

Niamh hated that she was jealous of his past with Sakura, or any woman, for that matter. She wanted to be above such emotion. Maybe one day, hopefully, when they'd settled into the bond, Niamh would be.

The pack watched them as they passed, wolves in casual and formal wear drinking and eating and socializing around the landscaped French garden area.

Niamh's looked beyond Haruto to the massive open park ahead of them. The large green area surrounded by trees had been transformed from the peaceful park she'd visited almost two weeks before.

Folding chairs were spread in a circle around what looked like a professional boxing ring. The chairs were already filling fast with spectators, and standing near the back row of seats in a bloodred, skin-tight dress that left little to the imagination was Sakura. Daiki stood at her side, and they were conversing with a huge werewolf Niamh didn't recognize.

Scenting them, Sakura turned her nose toward them. When

Niamh's stare connected with hers, she could have sworn she saw bolts of absolute hatred spark from Sakura's eyes. But it was as if Niamh had almost imagined the look because Sakura appeared nothing but smugly pleased by their arrival.

Haruto stepped to the side as they drew to a halt in front of the alpha and her mate.

Sakura ignored Niamh, giving her entire attention to Kiyo. "You *can* keep a promise."

Kiyo didn't give her the satisfaction of an answer.

"Well." The alpha gestured to the werewolf who was built similarly to the mammoth Fionn Mór. The male was at least six foot six and bursting at the seams of his T-shirt with muscle. "This is Emil König. He has come all the way from Berlin for our fight. Emil, meet Kiyo. He is your opponent for the evening."

Emil gave Kiyo a nod of respect, which he returned.

"Your fight is the most anticipated and the most exclusive," Sakura explained. "Only the wealthiest of our patrons have been allowed to place bets. Your arena is across the bridge"—she gestured to Niamh's left—"in the smaller park. It will take place in thirty minutes. I hope that meets with both of your approval."

While Emil and Kiyo agreed, Niamh couldn't ignore the niggle in her gut. Since her pulse had been racing since leaving the hotel and butterflies had raged all day, it was hard to differentiate those feelings from what might be her sixth sense warning her of danger.

Feeling her anxiety, Kiyo shot her a questioning look.

I'm okay, she promised.

But she was highly alert.

"The mahoutsukai ..." Sakura's reference to her brought her attention back to the alpha. Sakura didn't look at Niamh as she said, "Will remain here."

"Not a chance," Kiyo replied. "Niamh stays with me."

"My fight, my rules."

Daiki stepped up beside Sakura. "I see no harm in letting Kiyo's *mate* stay with him."

Sakura looked like she'd tasted something sour but gave an abrupt nod. "Fine."

Daiki winked at Niamh.

Oh, he was enjoying holding this true-mate thing over Sakura way too much.

How awful, Niamh thought. To be stuck in a mating where there was nothing but unrequited feelings and resentment. Awful for Daiki. She couldn't care less how Sakura felt. Especially as she wouldn't stop staring at Kiyo like he was something she wanted very badly to own.

Possessiveness welled inside her, and Niamh took a deep breath to contain it.

At the feel of Kiyo's hand on her lower back, she relaxed marginally and allowed him to guide her as they followed Sakura, Daiki, Haruto, and Emil through the park. Niamh couldn't even enjoy the beauty of the arched wooden bridge that took them over a tranquil greenish-blue pond. The pathway beyond led through a cluster of trees and then out into another open park.

It was much smaller than the other. There was no boxing ring. Just a circle in the middle of the swanky, gold-plated dining chairs. Men in suits and women in glamorous gowns filled the smaller seating area. Waiters and waitresses carrying trays of canapés and champagne and whisky floated around Sakura's wealthy patrons as they waited patiently for the main event.

Niamh's searched for any sign of Astra.

"Take a moment," Daiki said to them as Sakura wandered off to introduce her guests to Emil. "Drink, eat, and enjoy both while you can. Emil has not lost a fight in ten years. We are hoping he loses this one, but I am also hoping he breaks a bone or two before he does." Daiki smacked Kiyo hard on the shoulder. With a dark laugh, he sauntered off after his mate.

Haruto hovered nearby, as if he'd been instructed not to let them out of his sight.

A wave of panic rose through Niamh and she turned into Kiyo, resting her hands on his chest. As she stared up into his beautiful eyes, an ominous sensation was quick on the heels of panic. For a moment, it felt like this might be the last time she ever saw him.

He gripped her elbows. "What is it?"

Not wanting to voice something out loud that might upset him before the fight, she shook her head at her own nonsense. Her anxiety was getting the better of her. "I know you can handle yourself ... I just don't like the thought of anyone hurting you."

"I'll be fine."

"I'll be watching." She then spoke telepathically. *You'll only hear my voice in your head if Astra or anyone else is approaching.*

Kiyo nodded and gave her arms a gentle squeeze.

What Niamh really wanted to say ... what she wanted to tell him was something he already knew, even though she'd never said the words.

She wanted to tell him she loved him.

Yet his head needed to be in the fight. Not on her.

And she didn't want him to feel pressured to return the sentiment. He didn't need to. For her, actions spoke so much louder than words. Anyone could tell you they loved you. But it was the showing of it that demonstrated its truth. And Kiyo had shown her that he loved her before he even knew it himself.

"Kick his arse, yeah?" She laughed shakily.

His answer was to kiss her. A sweet, languorous, luscious kiss that was given as if they had all the time in the world.

They didn't.

Which was proven not long later when Haruto approached to tell them it was time.

Kiyo nodded and shrugged out of his jacket, handing it to Niamh. His black T-shirt was whipped off and he handed that to her, too, his scent and heat on it proving a comfort as she watched him stride fluidly through the small crowd to meet Emil in the center of the park.

Niamh watched Sakura whose eyes were trained on Kiyo.

Uncertainty moved through Niamh.

What if what Sakura felt for Kiyo wasn't merely infatuation?

What if she was dangerously obsessed with Niamh's mate?

But if that were true, wouldn't she have spent the last twenty-five years searching for him?

Something was off about it. Niamh just couldn't quite put her finger on what it was.

The sound of steel hitting steel startled her attention back to Kiyo. Niamh took a step toward the spectators. Her mate and his opponent were brandishing katana that had appeared from who knew where. Kiyo hadn't told her this was a sword fight!

While the seemingly civilized men and women watching jeered and snarled like wild animals as they rallied behind their chosen fighter (with the majority apparently behind Emil), Niamh's entire focus was on her mate.

It was the opposite of what she'd promised herself when she walked into that park.

But watching Kiyo was hypnotizing. The crowds grew more agitated as his skill became more obvious. The way he moved was a like a dance. So graceful and powerful. Heat and love and pride suffused her watching him push Emil into a corner over and over again.

Finally, his blade met flesh, scoring a cut across Emil's pecs.

The spectators went wild as Emil's face darkened with anger.

He came at Kiyo with harder blows, but her mate's feet moved swiftly, agilely changing direction this way and that before powering back against Emil's katana.

"He's bloody magnificent," she murmured in awe.

"Hai." Sakura's voice caught her off guard.

Niamh startled, gazing down at the alpha who'd crept up on her.

"I hear you are pretty magnificent too." Her gaze flicked behind Niamh's head. "Do it."

Before she could compute what was happening, something slammed into her lower back like a blade of the hottest fire. A hand clamped over her mouth as a wail of agony wrenched from her throat. Black dots peppered her vision as the misery of a pain she'd never experienced the like of overwhelmed her senses.

34

He'd been focused.

Learning Emil's tells, weaknesses, and strengths as quickly as possible.

It was a balancing act. Giving the crowds a show but ending the fight as expeditiously as possible. Kiyo would allow this to draw out for another twenty minutes and then he'd end it so he and Niamh could get the hell out of there.

Blocking Emil's increasingly aggressive swing, sensation blasted into Kiyo, sending him stumbling backward.

The feeling was pain.

Agony.

He felt it as if through a barrier.

Like he felt Niamh's emotions.

Fear lurched in his chest as spun to stare out through the rows of spectators to where he'd left his mate.

He couldn't see her.

Moving forward, he scanned the park, not seeing a familiar head of pale-blond hair.

Or Sakura.

Or Daiki or Haruto.

Fire slammed into his temple, taking him to a knee, and he couldn't see in his right eye.

Blood.

There was blood in his eye.

Turning just in time to stop another blow from the hilt of Emil's katana, Kiyo channeled all his fear and rage into the German.

He forced the hulking giant back and moved at supernatural speed, a blur, spinning until he was behind the wolf. With two quick slashes, he cut the wolf's Achilles tendons and watched him sprawl to the grass in a roar of pain.

Dropping his katana, he straddled Emil, took his head in hand, and snapped his neck.

Then he was moving.

Niamh.

What had happened?

Was it Astra?

Why was Sakura, Daiki, and Haruto missing too?

"Hey, where do you think you're going?" A werewolf dressed in a tuxedo stood in his path. "Get back in there and give us a real fight."

Kiyo broke his neck in less than two seconds and watched in satisfaction as the rest of the complaining crowd melted away. He ran. He ran at full speed, cutting through the crowds as he followed his mate's scent out of the park and into the city.

The skies opened above him as if in answer to his anguish and rage. Kiyo cared nothing for the humans witnessing his super speed, for the way he lunged over moving cars like an animal in the jungle or the way he handled the rain-slicked streets the way an ice dancer's skates became one with the ice.

Humans in his way were shoved aside by his speed and strength, but he didn't care. It wasn't in him to care about anything but Niamh in that moment. It took him only five minutes to reach the hotel where Niamh's scent was the strongest.

Kiyo skidded to a stop across the street from the familiar building, his chest rising and falling, not with tiredness but fury. Sakura, the arrogant bitch, had kidnapped Niamh and taken her back to her own hotel.

Did she really think she was powerful enough to withstand a war with Kiyo?

Drawing in a deep breath, Kiyo zoned in on Niamh's scent.

The basement. Where the fights used to be held.

He couldn't feel her, though.

He couldn't think about what that meant.

If he entered the hotel, their security cameras would alert them to his arrival.

But what Sakura didn't know was that her uncle had entrusted much knowledge to him.

There was another way into that basement. Through the public subway.

A woman hurrying down the street in a light green dress lifted her umbrella to see where she was going. She halted at the sight of Kiyo standing in the rain half-naked.

In the time she took to blink, Kiyo was already gone.

It was worse than the time in that horrible apartment with Kiyo. The weariness was so much worse.

And there was also the pain.

Niamh laid on her stomach panting against the damp concrete floor, unable to move, as though paralyzed. Torturous flames of sensation shot up her spine and down both legs.

"You are awake," Sakura's voice drifted somewhere above her.

Niamh let out a grunt, trying to ask her what she wanted, but the words came out a mere whisper.

What was wrong with her?

"You have a very large iron dagger stuck in your spine," Sakura answered, as if Niamh had voiced the question out loud. "You are not going anywhere anytime soon, faerie." Her face came into view as she bent low to the ground to stare into Niamh's pained eyes. Horror suffused Niamh as Sakura swung a familiar jade pendant in front of her face. "And our Kiyo-chan will not be able to save you."

35

The silence in the abandoned tunnels that led to the basement of the Iryoku Towers was palpable. Kiyo could hear the overly loud, much too fast beating of his own heart as he tried to move swiftly without making a sound.

Rats fled his alpha energy as he rushed through the earthy, metallic darkness. If he wasn't careful, Sakura would sense him before he even got there.

He had to calm.

He didn't know how to be calm.

They'd taken Niamh, and whatever they'd done to abduct her had caused her pain.

Rage burned in his gut.

Sakura and her mate would be lucky to survive the night.

Slowing to a halt, Kiyo's night vision revealed the blacked-out door off to the side of the tunnel. When Eito was so sure Kiyo wouldn't be able to say no to being Sakura's mate, he'd shown Kiyo this secret entrance. It led into the basement where they hosted their supernatural underground fights.

The key was hidden in a pipe across the tunnel.

Kiyo shooed a rat out of the way and felt cool metal touch his fingers. Wrapping his hand around it, he pulled out the old-fashioned key and returned to the door.

The door opened on hinges kept oiled to perfection so it made no sound as it swung into darkness.

Beyond was a narrow corridor blanketed in more shadows.

Kiyo snapped his hands out at his sides, his long, black claws slicing into the air. Opening his mouth, he forced his canines out.

Then strode onward to meet the shadows face-to-face.

He was silent as the night, pulsing in the blackest depths of the low-lit basement.

It had taken much not to rush into the gargantuan room once he'd reached it.

Years ago, the room had been decorated in cool greens and gold wall coverings, three fight rings in matching colors set along the center of the room.

Tatami mats had been placed over nearly every inch of the concrete floors.

Now there was nothing but empty echoes in a space that resembled an underground parking lot.

Except for the sconces attached to concrete pillars. Real flames lit them.

It reminded Kiyo of hell.

Except it couldn't be because Niamh could never belong anywhere but in the light, and his mate was in the room.

Lying sprawled on her stomach, seemingly unable to move.

A long iron blade protruded from her lower back.

Kiyo grew cold and silent.

This was a new level of rage he'd never felt before.

"I can feel you," Sakura said from her spot near his mate.

Kiyo stared at her. He didn't see a woman he'd once known intimately. A wolf he'd once admired and respected.

He saw nothing but an enemy.

Daiki and Haruto stood off to the side like two watch dogs.

Were they fools? Did they think they were enough to protect Sakura from him?

Kiyo strode into the light, his eyes glancing over the three of them as he tried to calculate the fastest way to end them all so he could get to Niamh and remove the dagger.

His mate emitted a soft moan and he felt it, much as Emil had felt his katana slice at his Achilles tendons, taking him to his knees. It took much to keep moving as though it hadn't affected him.

"Take him down but try not to kill him," Sakura commanded.

Kiyo assumed she was talking to Daiki and Haruto, but the air shimmered across the room in front of him and the feeling of magic prickled his skin.

Fifteen werewolves, male and female, appeared out of thin air, standing in a row between him and Sakura. Some carried silver blades.

They lunged at him.

Kiyo was faster than any of them. He moved as a blur and was able to take five down by breaking their necks before he felt the first blow across the back of his head. He used the momentum from the hit and fell forward in a shoulder roll, grabbing up the silver katana one of the downed wolves had been carrying. Springing to his feet, he turned to face ten members of Sakura's pack.

The first was easy. The male came at him without a weapon, and Kiyo slashed the katana across his gut, low near his groin, and the wolf fell to the ground howling in pain. The next had a sword, and Kiyo had to defend with his katana while kicking out behind him as other wolves tried to approach.

A moan of anguish from Niamh made its way to him through the grunts and clangs of the fight, and his impatience became a well of strength. He kicked out with a roar at the male in front of him, sending him and the three wolves behind him soaring across the basement. He lunged at the nearest female, dodged the air around her as she slashed out at him with a silver knife, and spun around to punch a hole through her back. Tearing her heart out, Kiyo held it as he scowled in warning at the rest of the wolves.

They'd momentarily frozen, shocked by the death because until now, he'd just been incapacitating them.

"You still will not kill him," Sakura's voice echoed around the room. "But take him down. I grow impatient."

Kiyo was a cyclone, a tornado of vengeance. Within seconds, four more wolves lay on the ground without their hearts.

Snarls of outrage filled the basement and the remaining wolves launched themselves at him in unadulterated fury. They closed in on him, giving him little room to move as fists and feet hammered into his body. One snapped his wrist and the katana slipped from his grasp.

A burn scored up his back and then down his hip as two of them slashed him with silver. Ignoring the pain, Kiyo unleashed his claws and spun, feeling their clothes and skin tear, the impact juddering up his arms.

As they fell back, wounded, Kiyo found a way out of their circle.

It was more expedient to snap their necks. He took out three in seconds but as he approached the last, she turned, blood dripping from her chest where his claws had raked her. Fire blazed up Kiyo's neck as she swung a katana at his throat, connecting. Despite Sakura's orders, her intention had been to decapitate him. The curse binding him in immortality rebounded on the blade, and it shattered.

Terror flooded her expression as she realized the extent of his invincibility. Something flickered inside him, a soft feeling he'd blame his mate for, and it stopped him from killing the wolf. Instead he snapped her neck. As her body crumpled atop one of her downed comrades, Kiyo touched the cut on his neck and hissed.

Blood was leaking from several areas of his body.

Silver poisoning the wounds.

He was bruised and battered.

Covered in sweat and dust from the disused basement.

But there was still enough fight in him to take down a fucking army.

And he was going to kill Sakura for this.

"Impressive," she said, walking toward him. "It was a test, and you passed. What would it take to stop you? Twenty, thirty, fifty werewolves? Oh wait ... I know." Sakura lifted her arm and something gold winked in the light as it unraveled from her hand.

It was a necklace.

Kiyo halted in utter shock.

Dangling from the end of the chain was Mizuki's jade pendant, the stone shaped like a water droplet.

"Hai." Sakura smirked, slipping the necklace over her head. "Before you think about killing us to get to her, think again. Or I will smash this jade to pieces and we will watch you crumble to dust."

How the hell did she know?

Sakura took a few steps toward him. His wounds seemed to hurt more the longer Niamh had to lie there with the iron inside her. He wished she'd speak to him in his mind. Assure him she was okay.

Sakura snapped her fingers. "Look at me. Not her."

Revulsion rolled through him. "All of this because you and I fucked three decades ago."

Daiki snarled behind her. Kiyo cut the puppet of a wolf a murderous look.

"How arrogant to think this is about that." Sakura shook her head, sighing dramatically. "Oh, I admit that I was obsessed with you for a while. Kept track of you on your adventures out in the world, hoping you would come back to me."

Daiki cursed under his breath and turned his back on her.

Kiyo didn't blame him.

"I know about your little house in the mountains of Kyoto." She nodded smugly. "And every year that you returned, you never seemed to age. Word in the supernatural world got out about a mysterious Japanese American werewolf who rarely lost a fight in the underground. Rumors spread that he was not what he seemed. So I did some digging. It is amazing how money and connections can speed up the research process. And what did I find"—Sakura fingered the pendant—"but a puzzle. Small puzzle pieces that all fit together, leading back to 1898 and Mizuki Nakamura, Japan's greatest miko."

"How?" he asked flatly.

"You taught me all about poker face, Kiyo, but I have never surpassed my teacher. You look so unaffected, but I know better." Sakura stepped dangerously close to him. "You made a mistake all those years ago. You slipped up and confessed your real name to Oji-chan, as well as your place of birth. And *he* told *me*. Kiyonari Fujiwara from Osaka. My researchers scoured letters, documents, contracts—every piece of literature connected to the supernatural community in Osaka. What did we find? A diary stolen from Mizuki. It was in the private collection of a coven. The Yamamoto Coven."

"The Pack Coven," Kiyo replied, feeling the pieces come together. The Yamamotos had been on retainer to Pack Iryoku for nearly a hundred years. "They spelled the wolves just now?"

"Yes." Sakura glanced to her left and he followed her gaze. He saw nothing but darkness. "Three coven members. They left when they saw the blade of the katana break when it should have cut off your head. Cowards." She turned back to him. "Still, they have their use. They were happy to let me have a look. And there you were. An entry about a werewolf—made, not born—who took vengeance on Mizuki's grandson for the rape of your mother. I commend you, Kiyo. I would have done the same. But Mizuki took offense to your killing her grandson, and she sacrificed another miko to curse you with immortality. She said in her entry that you loathed being a werewolf. That tormenting you with an eternity of being trapped as a wolf was a greater revenge than death. I think she was wrong. I know no wolf as connected to his animal as you are. Watching you take out my wolves like a beast was highly arousing." She snapped near his lips with her teeth, and it took everything within him not to rip her fucking heart out.

But her hand was still wrapped around the jade.

Sakura narrowed her eyes. "So here you are. The world's only immortal werewolf."

"How long have you known?"

"About eighteen years."

"And you kept my secret all this time?"

Her face softened. "Even from Daiki. You see ... in her diary, Mizuki spoke of this jade talisman and how it held all of her spells within. No other miko had the power to contain it. She tried to warn them to bury it with her, but they did not. Unfortunately for you. Destroy the talisman, and her spells would be undone. Never mind what chaos that might unleash upon Japan ... what if it meant you did not just become mortal but that you would die?"

Sakura's eyes brightened. "I did not want you to die, Kiyo."

He was untouched by her emotion. "It looks like you've changed your mind about that."

She shrugged and retreated a few steps. "I have a difficult life, Kiyo-chan. It is a constant struggle as a woman to remain alpha of one of the world's most powerful packs. You have no idea what I have to deal with day to day."

"Get to the point, Sakura."

Her eyes flashed in warning. "It happened the day the fae grabbed at my wrist. Haruto saw it burn her. My iron bracelet. I knew nothing of the fae other than the myths. The bracelet was a gift from Haruto's family, who have a deep belief in the legends. And he knew about the pure iron and how it hurt the fae. At first it seemed ridiculous to imagine the fae as real, let alone walking among us ... but she smelled and felt so different from any other creature, and she did react strangely to the bracelet.

"Haruto told me more about the gifts of the fae. How their magic is limitless. How they are not bound by the laws of nature. How they do not have to pull the energy from the world to power their magic. They *are* energy. They *are* pure magic. To have such a being within my control ... I will never again have to worry about losing my position as alpha."

He was going to kill her.

There was no question of it now.

"There was still part of me that did not want to hurt you ... that did not want to be your enemy." She curled her lip in bitter disappointment. "You were my one weakness, Kiyo. And I wanted to be your weakness. But that will never be now that you are true mates with the fae. So, in lieu of being your weakness, I now *own* your weakness. Both of them. The fae bitch and the jade. I had the coven steal the pendant from the museum in Osaka last night.

"I do not want your death. Even now. But the fae will remain here with me," she announced proudly. Arrogantly. "And you will leave Japan. No arguments, no fighting ... or I will stick iron through the fae's heart before I smash the jade to pieces."

A loud grunt stopped Kiyo from lunging forward to rip out Sakura's heart. Their eyes shot toward the sound to see Haruto and Daiki both dropping to their knees, their bodies loosening like their strings had been cut.

They sprawled forward lifelessly, and a figure behind them stepped into the torchlight.

A stunning redhead stared placidly at them, Daiki's and Haruto's hearts clenched in her hands.

Astra.

Sakura's scream of grief wrenched Kiyo out of his stunned stupor.

"While I appreciate your expeditiousness in removing the other wolves from the picture," Astra said to Kiyo, "I'm beginning to grow impatient with this conversation while my sister is in torment."

Realizing what Sakura did not, that they were in the presence of a far more powerful enemy, Kiyo blurred toward Niamh, falling at her side. His fist wrapped around the dagger in her lower back. He tugged it out, his stomach lurching at how deeply embedded it had been.

"*Komorebi*," he murmured, throwing the dagger away. Kiyo leaned down, brushing her hair off her face. "*Komorebi*, wake up."

"A-a-wake," she replied hoarsely, barely audible. "C-can't move."

Fuck!

He glanced over his shoulder at the piercing howl that echoed around the basement.

A black wolf, much smaller than Kiyo, bared its teeth as it prowled toward Astra.

Sakura.

His eyes searched the floor near Sakura's clothes, but he couldn't see the gleam of gold and green from the pendant.

They'd have to leave it.

"Come on." He slid his arms under his mate. Ignoring the ache from his own wounds, he swung Niamh up into his arms and eyed the exit—

A shimmer of gold flew up in front of them.

He turned and another wall appeared.

And another.

And another, until he and Niamh were trapped in a magical cage.

"What's happening?" she mumbled wearily against his throat.

He kicked at the barrier and it hit back with such impact, it took him to the ground and Niamh with him. She cried out in pain and his heart splintered.

"You're not going anywhere!" Astra yelled as she blurred out of Sakura's way.

She was toying with the wolf.

Tell her to bite Astra, Niamh's voice sounded stronger in his mind. He looked down at her to find her staring out at the fae and wolf.

"No. It's not safe for Sakura to know about that."

Niamh turned her head slowly, like it weighed a ton. *Astra will kill her.*

"I know," he responded grimly.

Shaking her head, Niamh pushed against his hold. He grunted as she hit the wound on his hip. She tensed. "Kiyo?"

"I'm okay."

She fumbled for his shirt, revealing his silver-inflicted wound. Then her eyes flew to his throat where the cut ached the worst. "What happened here?"

"One of Sakura's wolves tried to decapitate me with a silver katana. Now let's go."

Just like that, the color returned to her cheeks. Dark circles remained under her eyes, but the indignant rage flooding out of her fueled a renewed strength.

Niamh pushed to her feet as Astra laughed gaily.

They looked out of the cage to see her *traveling* from one spot to another to avoid Sakura who grew more aggressive with frustration. Niamh raised her hands against the barrier. Energy pulsed from her like a light bulb at the end of its life.

"Niamh—"

She shook her head, fierce determination filling her expression. "How many times did they wound you?"

"Niamh?"

"How many?" She glared at him.

"There's a cut on my back as well."

At that, she shocked the shit out of him by throwing her head back on a scream of pure anger. That release was like the doors of a dam breaking open. Golden light streamed out of her in warm, pulsating waves.

When it faded, the cage was gone.

Sakura and Astra had stopped their fighting to stare in wonder.

Astra grinned, pride in her eyes. "There she is."

A growl ripped through the air and Sakura raced for Niamh, canines out.

Kiyo's heart lurched into his throat and he rushed forward, pushing Niamh out of the way.

But there was no need.

Astra appeared on Sakura's back, her arms wrapped around the alpha's neck. With a hard twist of bones, muscle, and tendons, she tore Sakura's head from her body. They collapsed in a heap of wolf remains.

"That was unpleasant." Astra threw Sakura's head from her hands. She looked down at the carcass she was still sprawled atop and beamed. "But worth it. This is just what I've been looking for."

Gold and green gleamed from beneath fur and gore.

Neither he nor Niamh were fast enough.

Astra picked up the jade pendant and stepped away from what was left of Sakura. She shot Niamh a satisfied smile. "I told you we'd be together finally."

Kiyo blinked.

A mere blink.

And Niamh was gone from his side and standing behind Astra, one hand gripping her by the hair, the other hovering above her chest. She wielded one of the iron daggers she'd conjured back at the hotel room.

"Give me the pendant or I'll kill you," his mate promised.

Astra laughed. "Oh, Niamh ... you wouldn't hurt your sister."

"What makes you so sure?"

"I've seen it."

"Yeah?" Niamh leaned closer, the iron dagger now touching Astra. "That's the thing about visions ... they're only guides to what can be. They're not absolute. Do you know why?"

Astra winced as Niamh pressed the dagger deeper.

"Because none of us are Fate's bitch. Even true mates make the choice to be with each other. And I choose Kiyo. It's the kind of choice that leads to other choices ... and if you don't hand over that pendant, I *will* choose to end your pathetic existence."

Of all the many emotions Kiyo was feeling right then, pride was at the forefront.

His mate was the most majestic female on this world, or any.

Astra, sensing Niamh's sincerity, lifted the pendant. Niamh let go of her hair to grab it, and the pendant immediately disappeared.

Now it's somewhere no one can find it, she told Kiyo telepathically.

He wanted to feel relief, but they still had a pyschotic fae to deal with.

"You're coming with us," Niamh ordered.

Something glittered in Astra's eyes, something that had Kiyo lurching forward, alert. Her lips curled as she glanced down at the iron still hovering above her chest. "One last thing before we go ... a confession, really."

The hair on the back of Kiyo's neck rose in warning.

"Why do you think a seemingly good coven would kill an innocent human, like Ronan, knowing that one human couldn't create enough power to take out a fae?"

Niamh's eyes hollowed. "What?"

It wasn't us. She made us do it.

Realization dawned on Kiyo as he remembered Meghan's babbling. "Niamh." He took a step toward her.

"I got inside their heads," Astra grinned. "Just like I got inside yours, sister. I needed Ronan out of the way. I don't like to share."

Niamh's eyes flared bright gold as a wave of fury blasted out of her. She lifted the dagger as if to plunge it into Astra's chest and suddenly, Astra was gone. She reappeared behind Niamh with the dagger in hand, and his mate whirled in outrage to face her.

"You would have done it." Astra seemed pleased. "You would have taken that final step into the shadows for vengeance." She looked at Kiyo now, smug. "One day … she will choose me."

Then she was gone, Niamh's cry of frustration ringing across the basement as she stumbled back from clasping at air.

Before she could do or say anything else, Kiyo breached the distance between them and gathered her into his arms. His nose hit her throat, right at her pulse, and he trembled against her to feel her alive and warm.

Niamh held on to him, her voice soothing in his ears, even as he heard the tears in them.

A shift in the surrounding space caused him to lift his head just as everything went dark. Then color blurred, and they were in an unfamiliar room. His arms tightened on Niamh as his questioning gaze found hers.

"We're in a hotel as close to the station as possible," she explained. "It was as far as I could get us. We need somewhere safe where I can recharge and we can heal from our wounds before we get the hell out of here."

Kiyo was lost for words. Where did he begin to apologize for Sakura? He was supposed to protect Niamh from the people who wanted to use her, and he'd led one of them right to her.

"None of that." She seemed to sense his thoughts, nestling against his chest in weariness. "No guilt, no blame. Just healing and sleep. Please."

"What about Astra finding us ... What about Ronan?"

Niamh's face crumpled. "I don't ... I can't think about that right now. As for her finding us ... something happened to me tonight. Like some part of my power unleashed that's been sleeping. I can *feel* her, Kiyo."

His arms tensed around her. "What do you mean?"

"I think that's how she's been able to keep tabs on me. Anytime we're in the same city, she's been able to feel me. It wasn't about my scent at all. You changed the alchemy of my very being when our souls bonded. That's what threw her off. Now she knows how this new me feels, she can sense me here. It's how she found me in the basement."

"But you can feel her now too?"

"Yes. It's hard to explain. I just know that she's here in the city, but she's not near us."

A sense of relief moved through Kiyo. "So you'll know when she approaches."

"Exactly. She'll be watching the station, the airport, so I think it's best we *travel* onto a bullet train going to Osaka Airport." Niamh yawned. "Let's sleep, Kiyo-chan. You need to heal." She kissed his chest and slumped against him, abruptly passing out.

Kiyo pressed his fingers to her pulse, even though he knew nothing but iron through the heart could kill her. He needed the reassurance. With a sigh, he swung her into his arms and carried her to the bed.

Drawing her close, he tried to sleep but couldn't.

Kiyo didn't think he'd be able to sleep until he knew for certain they were as far away from Astra as they could get. But perhaps what they should be concerned about was Pack Iryoku. Once they realized their alpha, her mate, and her most loyal beta were dead, as well as the pack members Sakura had used to test the extent of his powers ... they'd do whatever they could to stop Kiyo and Niamh from leaving Tokyo.

36

Niamh's scream wrenched Kiyo out of sleep.

Heart in his throat, he reached for her and found the bed empty where she should be. "Niamh!"

"In here." Her head appeared around the doorjamb of the hotel bathroom. "Are you okay?"

His relief was so intense, he could have wept like a goddamn babe. "Bad dream." He exhaled shakily.

Niamh's expression was one of understanding. "Come shower with me." Her head disappeared.

Needing to feel her beneath his hands, Kiyo swung his legs out of bed, his eyes dropping to the new scar near his hip. The wound was completely healed. Touching his neck, he felt the raised skin of the scar there too. It wasn't the first time someone had tried to take his head off. It was the first time they'd tried it with silver.

Stepping into the dimly lit bathroom, he drew to a halt at the sight of his naked mate.

She had her back to him, angled toward the mirror above the sink as she stared at herself.

Or more precisely at the scar on her spine. Her eyes flew to his in the mirror and then moved to the scar on his neck. "What a pair we make, covered in battle scars."

Kiyo divested himself of his jeans to join her in her nakedness. Then he moved to her, every part of him aching with a strange emotion that almost felt like grief. What happened to her last night had yet to leave him. He didn't know how long it would take, if ever, for him to recover from it. Lowering to his knees, he clasped her warm hips in his hands and kissed the scar. It was nestled on her spine just above the sexy dimples on her lower back.

Goose bumps pebbled her skin as he brushed his mouth over the raised area.

"Does it hurt?" he whispered.

"All healed," she replied, hoarsely.

Kiyo pressed another kiss to it, wishing he had the power to erase the memory for her. With that feeling of powerlessness came an urgency to make her forget. If only for a while. He caressed her hips, trailing his fingers downward until they reached her gorgeous ass. He squeezed her cheeks as he rose slowly upward, peppering wet kisses all the way up Niamh's spine.

Her gasps of excitement were the equivalent of her soft hand wrapped around his dick.

His hands followed his rise, chasing around her silken stomach. As his lips reached her shoulders, he palmed her breasts, catching her taut nipples on his thumbs.

"Kiyo," she panted, arching into his touch as she rested her head against his collarbone.

Catching the erotic sight of them in the mirror, Kiyo turned her gently toward it. Her eyes were closed as she mewled at his fondling. "Open your eyes."

They flew open, bright gold with arousal.

His reaction was immediate. All blood shot south.

They looked phenomenal together. Her golden paleness against his dark fawn. Their eyes locked in the mirror. Kiyo released one of her breasts to skim his hand down her belly, and he felt her tremble with anticipation. Her gaze dropped to follow his hand and her mouth parted on a quiver of want as his fingers found her clit.

"Kiyo." She bit her lip, pushing into the touch, as he rolled hard circles over the peak of her while massaging her breast with his other hand. The act of watching her watch him bring her to climax had him so ready, he could feel the wet leak from his tip against her ass.

Niamh's hands came to his outer thighs to steady herself as she rocked against his fingers, her moans and cries of pleasure echoing around the bathroom. Then she tensed. "Kiyo!"

She shuddered as the orgasm rolled over her.

Barely giving her a moment to process it, he grabbed her hair in his hands and twisted her head to kiss her, his tongue licking at hers, needing her taste and scent and sweat on every part of him. Breaking the kiss, he growled against her lips, "Bend over the sink."

The gold that was bleeding back to aquamarine drenched her irises in liquid sunlight. She nodded, a little unsteadily, before she pulled away from him to bend over, hands to the sink.

Kiyo took her perfect rump in his hands as their eyes locked in the mirror again. "Spread."

Niamh's breathing grew shallow as she did what she was told.

His body was hot with anticipation. His mate hadn't been joking when she said he was welcome to order her around in the bedroom. It was something he was definitely going to explore to its limits. Later. Right now, he just needed inside her.

Without another word, he tightened his hold on her hips and thrust hard into her, groaning with sheer bliss at the feel of her wet warmth clasping him so tight.

"Ahh!" Niamh's back bowed at the intrusion but she kept her eyes on his.

He stayed still, giving her a moment to adjust until he felt her desire for more seep through the bond. Sliding a hand up her spine and beneath the strands of her long, pale hair, Kiyo found and gently gripped the nape of her neck. Holding her at the hip and the nape, he kept her locked there, unable to move, only able to take.

And he fucked his mate, holding her gaze in the mirror so she could see the savage possessiveness darkening his face as he pumped into her in powerful, hard strokes.

Niamh's eyes fluttered closed as she lost herself to pleasure.

He smacked her ass and gritted out, "Open your eyes. Watch me fuck you. Watch how you belong to me." He bent over her as her eyes opened, the change in angle causing her to moan in desperate want. He held still inside her, feeling her throbbing need, as he murmured in her ear, "Watch how *I* belong to *you*."

Her inner muscles tugged around him as Niamh cried out his name in orgasm.

He grunted in surprise at her sudden climax and straightened to pump his hips against her ass, riding her through it until he couldn't hold back any longer. Kiyo's flooded into his mate with a yell of her name, his hips jerking and shuddering against her as she wrung every last drop out of him.

Every last drop of his essence, of his soul.

Of his fucking heart.

Wrapping his arms around her, he pulled out of her but only to bring her down to the floor with him. Niamh turned in his embrace, straddling him so she could kiss him. Soft, lazy, sexy kisses that worked like an aphrodisiac until he was hot and hard and wanting against her soft belly again.

Niamh moaned, feeling his arousal, and pressed kisses down his chin until she reached the scar on his throat. She kissed it sweetly then met his gaze.

Her fingers sifted through his hair. "That was the sexiest thing you've ever done to me," she admitted.

"I got that." He grinned, his arms squeezing around her. "There's more where that came from."

"Unfortunately, I think we better get a move on." She pouted and then kissed him again. She grinned, pulling back. "You need to shave. I've never felt you all prickly before."

"Been kinda busy."

She rubbed her cheek to his like an animal bussing into its mate.

"I like it," she whispered in his ear, deliberately pushing her hips into him.

Kiyo smoothed his hands down her spine until his palm rested over her scar. "As much as I want you again, you're right. We need to move. The pack are probably already maneuvering against us."

Niamh exhaled and reluctantly stood. "Then you better call Bran and ask him to book us flights out of Osaka. Do you have a destination in mind?"

Kiyo shook his head as he got to his feet. "Up until now, we've been following your visions."

"There's nothing new on that front."

"Why don't I just ask Bran to book wherever he thinks best," he suggested.

She chuckled. "It might be fun to see where he sends us. I'm not sure he likes you very much."

"It's better than no plan at all."

"True." Her amusement died. "And for now, we need to get the hell out of Japan. As much as I'll be sad to say goodbye."

While he was pleased his mate felt such an affinity for his homeland, she was also absolutely right. They couldn't return to Japan for a while. Maybe years. A feeling akin to homesickness touched him. Sensing it, Niamh cuddled into him in comfort.

"We'll find a way to come back," she promised. "I won't let the bastards take your home from you."

Overwhelming emotion for this woman sought to rob him of words. But he needed her to know exactly what she meant to him. "They won't ever take my home," he replied, pressing a kiss to her hair. "They can't when my home is right here in my arms."

"I love you, Kiyo," she said in answer.

He tilted her chin to look into her eyes. "If you need those words, I will give them. I love you, *Komorebi*. But know this ... what I feel for you is so much bigger than three words."

She smiled, understanding him completely.

37

Piling her now-dry hair up into a loose knot, Niamh listened from the bathroom as Kiyo finally called Bran. She'd conjured their things from the other hotel. This was after they'd taken a shower that had quickly turned into the kind of love-making that made her tingle from the tip of her toes to the ends of her hair.

Niamh shivered in renewed want.

Her mate definitely knew how to go beyond satisfying her.

And distracting her.

Finally, they'd tumbled out of the shower with more urgency to get out of the city than they'd displayed heretofore. Niamh could forgive them for losing themselves to the bond, though. After what happened the night before, they both needed to feel the other alive in their arms in the most primal way.

Upon pulling his cell phone out of his bag, Kiyo had called out to Niamh that he had five missed calls from Bran that morning.

Kiyo rang the vampire; the line picked up after only two rings. "Where the bloody hell have you been?" she heard Bran ask over the speaker.

Frowning at Bran's urgent tone, Niamh hurried out of the bathroom and leaned against the doorjamb to listen in.

Kiyo wore a concerned scowl. "Hiding. Why?"

"Hiding where?"

"In the city."

"You're in Tokyo still?"

"Yeah, why?"

"You're in Tokyo and you have no bloody idea what's going on? Where the hell in the city are you?"

"I don't know. Niamh took us to a hotel we could hide out in." Kiyo marched over to the window and opened the blind. As soon as he did, he let out a curse of shock.

Rushing to his side, Niamh looked out at the city and saw the plumes of smoke buffeting into the sky from several points in the distance. "What is that?"

"Maybe you should turn on the TV," Bran suggested. "News channel."

Without searching for a remote, Niamh used her magic to power the TV on the wall, flicking to the news. A female reporter was standing in the middle of the city while all the emergency services could be seen moving through the streets behind her. There was smoke and rubble everywhere. "Kiyo, what's she saying?"

Kiyo stared flatly at the TV but she could sense his inner distress. "A suspected terrorist attack in Shinjuku. Several buildings were bombed this morning, including the Iryoku Towers."

Horror and understanding flooded her. "The Pack."

He turned to her. "All the buildings she mentioned ... pack. Their businesses, their apartments ... all of it gone. Along with thousands of innocent tourists and bystanders."

Tears burned in Niamh's throat. "Astra did this."

"Astra?" Bran's voice cut through the air, reminding them he was on the line. "Why would Astra take out one of the largest packs in the world?"

"Because she couldn't risk the idea that any one of them might have known what Sakura knew." Niamh's tears escaped as she thought of all the people who had just died because of her. "That I'm fae."

A muscle flexed in Kiyo's jaw and he shook his head. "No. You are not going to blame yourself for this."

"I am to blame."

"Niamh—"

"Someone want to catch me up?" Bran interrupted.

Kiyo let out a growl of frustration but answered Bran. He gave him a quick run-through of the events of the night before, never taking his eyes off Niamh.

She needed him to anchor her to his heart, a place that held no condemnation toward her.

Technically, she knew she wasn't to blame for what Astra had done. But with the knowledge hanging over her head that Ronan's death had been intentional just to get to Niamh ... it was hard not to succumb to overwhelming guilt. Especially now. There was no getting around the fact that Astra had destroyed nearly an entire ward to keep Niamh's identity a secret, just as she'd destroyed Ronan to make Niamh more vulnerable to her.

"Jesus Christ," Bran bit out when Kiyo was done. "Well, that explains much. Before Shinjuku was blown to bits, I was alerted to high magical energy use in Tokyo. And so was every other fucker paying attention. Including the Blackwoods. I guess that was you, Niamh, when you were fighting Astra."

Niamh sighed wearily, slumping onto the bed. "I guess so."

"The Blackwoods have ties to the Yamamoto Coven and they've called in a favor. They're watching the airports and stations in and out of Tokyo. On top of that, while the humans think this is a terrorist attack, the supes can feel the epic fucking magical signature coming off the explosions. The coven knows this is supernatural. As does the East Asian Council. They're on their way to investigate." Bran referred to the council of witches and warlocks who acted as a governing and policing body against dark magic users.

"It was definitely Astra, then." Kiyo cursed under his breath.

"Yeah, but Niamh might get confused for the evil shrew, so I'm thinking you need to get your arse out of there—now."

"Niamh is going to get us on the next bullet train to Osaka. We'll bypass the station. We need you to book us flights out of Kankū Airport."

"Going where?"

"Surprise us." Kiyo hung up and strode over to Niamh. Lowering to his haunches, he rested his hands on her knees. "We need to leave. By the looks of it, we're in Musashino. I'll get us to the nearest station, you get us on the train."

She nodded.

It felt like her heart was breaking.

"*Komorebi.*" He gripped her knees now. "You are not to blame for what Astra did."

"I know. But in a way I am."

"You're not going to do this to yourself." Kiyo stood and took her hands in his, pulling her with him. "No mourning. No self-recrimination. Astra is to blame for Ronan and for this and one day, you'll mete out justice for it. But not today. Today I need to get you to safety. There are too many powerful people on the way to this city who could try to take you from me."

Hearing the plea in his voice, Niamh threw off her guilt to focus on getting out of Tokyo.

For her mate's peace of mind, but also to protect him too.

Plans to bring Astra to justice for the atrocities she'd committed would need to wait.

Determination hardened through Niamh as she followed Kiyo out of the room. If Niamh had to wait decades or a century or a millennium, she would. She had all the patience in the world.

But Astra *would* one day answer for what she'd done to Ronan, to this city, and to the people in it.

38

Four weeks later (late March)
Kamala rainforest, Phuket, Thailand

Niamh's scream of agony wrenched him out of sleep.

Kiyo flew up in bed, damp sheets clinging to his body. His eyes flew to his side and panic suffused him at the empty spot where his mate should be.

"I'm here."

Her soft voice soothed him as he followed it and found her outside the bedroom, climbing out of the small pool attached to the tree house. Niamh loved the precariously positioned pool that dangled over the rainforest from their deck.

The sun blazed against her back through the thick trees as she crossed the balcony, water trickling down her long, bikini-clad body.

Still gripped by the terror of his dream, he wanted to haul her into the bed and prove to himself that she was alive and well and safe.

"Another nightmare?" Niamh asked, stopping to lean against the sliding door that closed the bedroom off from the deck.

Kiyo ran a hand through his hair, letting out a slow exhale. He didn't need to answer. She already knew that it was. He'd been having the same nightmare since they left Tokyo. Memories of the night Sakura stuck iron in Niamh's spine. Except the dream changed the memory at the end. After taking the iron out of her back and grappling with Astra for the pendant, Niamh didn't win.

Astra twisted in her arms and drove an iron blade through Niamh's heart.

And he launched out of sleep, adrenaline coursing through his body, until the reality of his mate sleeping at his side soothed him.

"They'll go away eventually." Niamh crossed the room to sit down on the bed. Magic tingled in the air along with a cloud of heat as she dried herself before pushing him back onto his pillow to snuggle into him.

Kiyo wrapped an arm around her, his fingers finding the scar on her spine and massaging it.

"It'll just take time. It's only been four weeks."

Four weeks. It felt longer and shorter in equal measure.

By the time they arrived in Osaka, Bran had sent information that there would be a private plane waiting for them. The plane would log false passenger information and itinerary. Kiyo didn't ask questions. A private plane with a false itinerary was the safest way for them to get out of Japan.

He'd been feeling grateful to the vampire—until they'd landed in Thailand.

In Phuket, to be exact.

Where a young Thai man awaited their arrival to drive them in his four-seater jungle buggy and left them in the middle of the rainforest next to their own jungle buggy. When he tried to contact the vampire for answers, he got a single text from him.

Look up. Tree house and buggy belong to Fionn. Consider this a honeymoon present. Enjoy. You lucky fucking dog.

In a sense, Bran and Fionn had forced Kiyo to take his first-ever vacation.

Whatever aggravation he felt about that had melted away because of Niamh. She had the wonder in her eyes again as their driver shot through the forest, and her excitement hit new levels when they looked up and glimpsed the building far above their heads. There was no way to get to it unless you were fae and could *travel*. Taking hold of his hand, Niamh *traveled* and then oohed and ahhed over what Kiyo had to admit was a pretty impressive tree house.

It took three weeks for Kiyo to believe Niamh when she said Astra had no idea where they were. Bran had contacted them to confirm that they were safe. The East Asian Council was investigating the Yamamoto Coven for the attack against Pack Iryoku and seemed pretty happy to lay the blame at their door since there was a long history between the magic users and the wolves. There was evidence of strained relations over the past twenty years since Sakura took over as alpha, including the murder of a high-ranking coven member. The attacks had been ruled to be the consequences of a secret cold war. The coven would pay for the crimes despite their protestation of innocence.

Tokyo was slowly recovering from the devastation. Human governments publicly investigated terrorist organizations while those in the know about the supernatural world grew more ruthless in recruiting supes to their secret armies. If the supernatural world was beginning to cause devastation in the human world, they wanted to be prepared if war was coming.

It felt like the world was changing beneath most humans' very noses.

Kiyo hurt for Tokyo, but he didn't like to talk about it with Niamh. She already blamed herself for it. Instead, he'd distracted her with explorations of Phuket with its stunning beaches, aqua waters, and amazing food. And there was the sex. They'd indulged in a lot of sex this past month.

However, the restlessness he felt within himself, he also sensed in Niamh.

They were waiting for Niamh to have a vision. Something that would tell them what their next move should be.

So far she'd been visionless. Not that Kiyo minded. He hated witnessing her experience a vision. But it was driving his mate insane with frustration.

She sighed beside him. "As beautiful as it is here, I think we should leave."

"And go where?"

"Maybe the US."

"Why there?"

"It's where Elijah is."

"The last of the fae-borne?"

Niamh nodded.

As restless as he was, Kiyo replied, "You're safe here. No one but the people we trust know we're here. And it's not exactly a crappy view." He gestured the stunning blue sky beyond the tops of the trees.

"I know." But she sighed heavily again.

"Those are big sighs, *Komorebi*."

Niamh pushed up off him, her palm pressed to his chest. "I can sense your restlessness, too, Kiyo. This place isn't exactly full-moon friendly."

She referred to the fact that he'd been relegated to a small section of the jungle to run in during the full moon. There were too many tourists in nearby resorts for it to be safe for him to venture any farther. It wasn't ideal, but it wasn't anything he couldn't bear.

"This isn't the life you're used to. You're not used to hiding from anybody and ... I don't want you to come to resent me."

Her worries baffled him. Hauling her across his body so she straddled him, he plucked at the ties on her bikini top as he growled, "I can't listen when you talk nonsense at me."

Grabbing her bikini to stop it from falling away from her breasts, Niamh's expression turned mulish. "I'm not talking nonsense."

Kiyo pulled at the ties at her hips holding the bikini bottoms on.

"Oh, for goodness' sake," she huffed, but he could feel her mood changing to meet his. "We're in the middle of a conversation."

"Well, I feel bad after my shitty dream and I need my mate to make me feel better."

Her eyes narrowed but she dropped her hands, letting the bikini fall away. Her nipples pebbled even in the thick, warm air of the bedroom. "You're a manipulative bastard, Kiyo-chan."

He launched upward to drag a delicious nipple into his mouth and sucked it hard until she rocked into him. Releasing her, he kissed his way up to her mouth and whispered against her lips, "I will never resent you. All that matters is keeping you safe. If you want to leave, we'll leave. But I want a few orgasms out of you first."

Kiyo pulled away the sheet that acted as a barrier between them and then flipped her onto her back. He crawled down her body, spread her thighs, and nuzzled into her sex to make good on his promise.

Later, after she'd returned the favor and made his eyes roll back into his fucking head, they laid sprawled across the bed, staring at the mosquito netting they never needed to use because mosquitos apparently hated supes.

"What do you want to do today?" Kiyo asked lazily.

Niamh pushed off him and gave a sexy, sweet smile. "I'm going to go for another swim and then maybe we can eat at that place I like on the beach."

He nodded, feeling replete from their fooling around but unsettled by the uncertainty he still sensed in her. Leaning up on an elbow, he watched her strut outside, her bikini magically back in place, and he wished he knew what the next right move was.

Just as she walked toward the steps that led down to the overhanging pool, she faltered, swaying.

"Kiyo," she moaned in distress. And then her head slammed back on her neck with the force of an incoming vision.

"NIAMH!" Kiyo was a blur across the room to the deck, catching her in his arms seconds before she would have fallen over the security railing around the balcony. It was a hundred-foot drop.

Pulse pounding, he restrained her hard judders as he hauled her backward, fearing if he connected to the vision, they'd both go over.

This time, however, he saw no flooding of images; he felt no overwhelming swarm of emotions from Niamh that usually triggered his connection to what she was seeing.

Instead he fell on his ass on the floor, cradling her tight to his body as the vision seized hold of her. When she grew still, Kiyo's pulse slowed.

Niamh's eyes fluttered slowly open, and her eyes focused. Kiyo brushed her hair off her face, patiently waiting for her to return to herself.

"You caught me," she breathed out in relief. "Would have survived but I didn't fancy a broken neck this morning."

His tone was bland, belying the terror he'd felt at the thought of her going over the edge of the tree. "Turns out this place isn't so safe."

She saw right through him. "Did I give you a fright?"

He glowered at her.

"I gave you a fright," she answered her own question before pressing a reassuring kiss to his throat. "Sorry."

"Not your fault. I got to you in time. Vision?" he asked somewhat reluctantly. The vision had brought home the reality that Niamh's destiny waited outside the borders of the rainforest and one day, they would have to face Astra again.

It came at Kiyo suddenly that for once, he didn't want to face something head-on. He wanted some peace and quiet with his mate, and he wanted it to last more than a few goddamn weeks. He wanted to cling to the idea of Phuket. To a hidden nirvana where there was nothing but a safe, happy Niamh, and the pleasures they could wring from one another's bodies.

But he knew that wasn't their fate.

He knew that even before Niamh took a deep breath and announced, "It's time to get a flight to London."

39

Three weeks later (mid-April)
Munich, Germany

It was difficult to get anywhere near Margaret Lancaster. During the day, there was always at least one werewolf stalking her. At night, two vampires. The supes were well trained, and it seemed that Margaret had no idea she was under constant surveillance.

As soon as they'd spotted her twenty-four-hour guard from The Garm, Kiyo wanted to bail.

But as Niamh patiently explained to him, this was their current mission.

Margaret was a chess piece. She might not be the king or queen. Really, she was a lowly pawn ... but a central one, and she needed to be moved to further the game.

So they'd gone to London where they found her and discovered she was under surveillance, which only signified Niamh's vision was on point. Niamh had to *travel* into the financial building Margaret worked in on Canary Wharf to get a surveillance shot without drawing The Garm's attention.

At forty-eight years old, Margaret Lancaster was still a very beautiful woman. And she was the spitting image of her daughter.

From there, Niamh had broken into the personnel department of Margaret's company and stolen copies of her personal information. She and Kiyo had used it to track down photographs of her dead boyfriend, his medical files, and the death certificate for the daughter who had been stolen from them. During their own surveillance of the woman, Kiyo had discovered she visited a therapist every week. Niamh decided to break into the therapist's office and steal copies of that file too. It wasn't right for Niamh to look through it, but her daughter might be interested in what was in the file.

Information in hand, they'd finally arrived in Munich.

Much to Kiyo's disgruntlement.

Munich was the new headquarters for The Garm. Probably Niamh's most dangerous enemy since the Blackwoods didn't want to kill her, but The Garm most certainly did.

However, Echo Payne, the adopted daughter of William "the Bloody" Payne, new leader of The Garm, was about to become an important player for the fae-borne. She was raised as William's adopted human daughter until she was twenty years old, and then he'd turned her into a vampire. In human years, she was twenty-six—a newbie vampire in the grand scheme of things—but rumor had it she was powerful and intelligent. She'd also been raised by William to fear the fae-borne and to treat them as the enemy.

Now that just won't do, Niamh thought to herself as she and Kiyo stalked through the streets of Munich at dawn.

Kiyo bristled at her side with heavy tension, his ears pricked, his gaze swinging from side to side.

"This way." Niamh gestured to an apartment building two streets over from Echo's. Kiyo followed at her back, watching it for her, as she used her magic to break into the building. Following the stairwell up to the very top, she unlocked the door to the roof and they strode out into a rooftop garden. "Ooh, I like this. What a grand idea."

"Niamh," Kiyo bit out impatiently. "Focus."

"I am. I'm just saying, those tomatoes look amazing. Ooh, and look at all these potted herbs."

"Keep walking."

"I'm walking," she threw over her shoulder. "Bossy bastard." Then she turned back around.

"I heard that."

"You were meant to."

"Did it ever occur to you that as I am an actual illegitimate child, I might take offense to the word?"

Niamh rolled her eyes, even though he couldn't see her. She suddenly ran, leaping across the small gap between buildings. She landed silently on the next building and heard Kiyo land behind her, almost as quietly. "No," she answered as they continued across its lackluster, bare rooftop. "The only thing you take offense to is me wearing clothes."

At his lack of response, she glanced over her shoulder.

"I can't argue with that." His nostrils flared and he grabbed for her, pulling her down beside him in a crouch.

What is it?

Kiyo murmured close to her ear. "I smell wolves."

"Guards?"

He nodded.

Niamh searched the roofline ahead of them and across the street. "I don't see anyone."

"Look down. White van with a satellite dish."

Glimpsing it down on the way, Niamh sighed. Echo's apartment was at the other end of the street, so the van wasn't in sight of her place. Were they guarding Echo or surveilling her?

Clutching the satchel filled with the info she needed to deliver to the vampire, Niamh turned to her mate. "I want you to stay here. I'm going to *travel* into Echo's apartment."

Kiyo shook his head and hissed, "No. You have no idea from this vantage point what room she's in or how many supes are in that apartment with her. Never mind the fact that they're clearly listening in."

"Well, I could mess with their equipment but that might bring them to her apartment to check on things," she mused. "I guess I'll just have to be really quiet."

"Niamh."

"Kiyo." She held his eyes, her expression deadly serious. "This is too important. This affects Elijah."

"Or we could just warn Elijah about her and be done with it."

Niamh grimaced. "You know that's not the point. They need to meet, and she has to learn to trust him. Without this"—she patted the satchel—"she's just another one of William's puppets."

Letting out an exasperated sigh, Kiyo gave her a sharp nod. "You better be back here in five minutes. Five minutes. I'm counting. Or I'm coming for you."

After pressing a swift kiss of reassurance to his lips, Niamh concentrated on the thought of Echo's apartment and everything went black for a moment before the world blurred back into focus.

The blackness barely lifted, however, as she found herself standing in the middle of a large sitting room with tall windows fitted with state-of-the-art blackout blinds. Niamh's eyes adjusted to the dark and she spun around, looking for a doorway. It was behind her. The best thing to do, since it would force Echo to look, was to empty the contents of the satchel across the vamp's bed. Niamh took a step toward the door but was halted by the shadowy appearance of a female.

Eyes flashed silver in the dark.

Artificial light filled the room as the ceiling spotlights flooded on.

A beautiful blond with pale skin stood in the doorway wearing nothing but oyster-pink silk shorts with scalloped lace edging and a matching cropped camisole. Her arms were relaxed at her sides but in her right hand, she clutched a handgun and in her left, a dagger.

Niamh knew vamps had good hearing, but how the hell had she been alerted to her presence so quickly?

As if reading her mind, Echo Payne replied in an accent borne from living in Canada most of her life, "Silent motion-detector alarm."

With a discreet flick of her wrist, Niamh created a soundproof bubble around the room so the feckers listening out in their van wouldn't hear their conversation. "I'm not here to hurt you."

"I hate to tell you this, *witch*, but I'm a vampire. I'm not the one who should be worried right now. What did you just do? I felt magic."

Niamh raised her arms in a surrender gesture. "I just made it impossible for the members of The Garm sitting in their surveillance van down the street to hear what we're saying."

Echo smirked, her green eyes like icy chips. "You think I don't know my apartment is bugged?"

"I don't think *they* know you know."

"Who are you?" The vampire raised her gun to point it at Niamh.

"I'm a friend."

"I don't need a friend."

"Then think of me as a friendly messenger." Niamh counted the minutes in her head, and worry made her tense. If she didn't get out of there very soon, Kiyo would come crashing in. "The message is in my satchel. May I open it?"

"You may not." Echo pulled back the safety on her gun.

Done with taking the slow route, Niamh thought of the documents, the air around her tingled with magic, and then they scattered at Echo's feet.

She cursed, jumping back, her attention fixed on the pile that included the photographs of her supposedly dead mother, the therapy session notes, and the medical records that described her dead father's fatal injuries. The most important aspect of which was the puncture wounds in his neck and the fact that his body had been drained of blood.

Satisfied she had Echo's attention where it should be, Niamh *traveled* back to the rooftop.

Only to find Kiyo fighting three werewolves.

Anger burned through Niamh as the wolves crowded Kiyo into a tight circle that didn't allow him space to fight off their hits with much success. Just as she moved to approach, her mate let out a grunt of fury. He jabbed his fist upward, a flash of silver held within it, through the chest of one of the wolves.

Niamh sent magic across the rooftop, the energy hitting the other two wolves' carotids. They slumped and collapsed on top of each other as Kiyo stumbled back. He had a cut on his lip but otherwise seemed fine. The silver dagger with its protective leather hilt was clasped in his hand, the tip smeared in blood. He'd started carrying the blade since they'd arrived in Munich.

His expression was grim. "We have to go. More will be coming."

"Okay." She held out her hand. "We'll *travel*."

He gave her a hard look. "They've seen my face—and yours. If they were anyone else but The Garm ..."

Understanding what he meant, Niamh's stomach knotted with indecision. Had it just been about her and Kiyo, she would've let the wolves live. But no one could know what she'd delivered to Echo. Her visions led her to believe that Echo would keep her brief visit a secret from The Garm. If these guards told William, there would be too many questions.

"Where did they come from?"

"The white van. They must be surveilling the rooftops. But they probably sent communication for backup."

Indecision and guilt pricked her as she said, torn, "No one can know about Echo."

Kiyo was a blur of movement, sticking the silver through the other wolves' hearts while they laid unconscious. Once that was done, he hurried to Niamh's side. "Decision taken out of your hands. Let's go." He wrapped his arms around her and then they were *traveling*.

They popped into the grubby motel room as far away from Echo's apartment as her gift would allow. Avoiding the station and airport, which was under heavy guard from The Garm, they'd driven into Munich—and they'd have to drive out. Niamh had naively hoped they'd finish their mission without any casualties.

Now she felt guilty that Kiyo had had to make that decision. "I—"

Kiyo took her face in his hands and pressed a comforting kiss to her lips. “Don’t say you’re sorry. We’re in a war, *Komorebi*,” he reminded her. “You have your job and I have mine. If I can save you from those hard decisions, I will. I don’t regret it. I keep you safe while you do what you do. I’m good with that. Okay?”

She nodded, leaning her temple against his, her love for him overwhelming.

“Did you get the files to Echo?”

Niamh stiffened. “She caught me.”

He pushed her away, a flare of fear passing across his eyes. “She saw your face?”

“Don’t worry,” Niamh assured him. “She won’t tell anyone about meeting me. Not after she’s looked through those files and put two and two together.”

Her mate didn’t argue. With a faith in her that Niamh had come to crave as much as his love, Kiyo accepted her word. “Where to next? The States?”

Niamh shook her head. “Elijah doesn’t need me. Not yet, at least. No. I have somewhere I want to take you. But it’s a surprise.”

EPILOGUE

One week later (late April)
Kyoto, Japan

Trekking through the mountains of Kyoto was not where Kiyo expected to be. Without Pack Iryoku, his homeland was no longer off limits. But their return, so soon, had taken him aback.

Even more intriguing was that this surprise of Niamh's was leading toward his home in the mountains. Even though he'd been a nomad for sixty years, he'd kept an apartment in New York and his cabin in Kyoto.

He'd mentioned the spot in passing to Niamh weeks ago. Any questions about why they were here had gone unanswered, so Kiyo kept his mouth shut as they climbed through the forest.

The trees disappeared and to his utter shock, they stepped out of the woods and onto a sharp cliff. This shouldn't be here. His cabin wasn't anywhere near the Sea of Japan. "What the hell?"

Niamh reached for him, grinning mischievously. "Trust me?"

He clasped her hand in answer.

Then Niamh walked forward as if walking off the cliff and onto thin air. Instead of falling, however, a golden shimmer haloed her body and then she was disappearing through a seam between magic and reality. Kiyo followed and felt a shiver of heat—like Niamh's magic—trickle over him as the bracken crunched beneath his feet again.

Astonished, Kiyo gazed at the familiar forest that led to his cabin about three miles away. He glanced behind them and saw only forest. "What?"

"It's a spell," Niamh explained. "Anyone approaching our land will think they've reached the sea edge. It'll confuse the feck out of them, but there's nothing they can do about it." Her light laughter caused a pleasurable ache within him. "Fionn did it."

"Fionn?" He knew that Niamh and Fionn had been in touch over the last few weeks. Not just because of Astra but because Kiyo had finally confided to Niamh what Fionn suspected: that Niamh was Fionn's descendant, and that's why he'd been so determined to protect her. The thought of having a blood relative, however distant, had been a welcome surprise for Niamh, and a closeness had formed between her and the warrior king fae.

More than Kiyo had known, apparently.

"It's how he spelled his place in Galway," Niamh explained. "I can't *travel* in or out until I'm beyond the boundary spell, but neither can anyone else. Including Astra. It's a totally safe place where we can stop for a while if we want."

It was a home.

Something neither of them had had for a very long time.

"Thank you," he said, somewhat hoarsely.

Niamh gave him that loving smile of hers, squeezed his hand, and trekked onward with him in silence. The house appeared, and Niamh drew in a surprised breath. Though she'd organized the spell for him, Kiyo realized she'd never seen his place.

Pride flickered through him.

The cabin sat on the edge of a clearing in the forest near a fresh-water pond. Kiyo had landscaped it and turned it into a mini Japanese garden with stepping stones to a pagoda and an arched bridge that led to the cabin.

"It's heaven." Niamh gaped.

"I'm glad you like it." Since it was their home now.

A FEW HOURS LATER, after christening their bed, Kiyo had enjoyed the quiet of watching Niamh as she stood outside the sliding doors between their bedroom and the wraparound deck. She wore only his shirt. It barely covered her ass as she leaned against the railing and stared out at the forest.

Rolling out of bed, Kiyo stooped to pull on his jeans and then strolled out to join her. He leaned his elbows on the railing and stared down at her face. Niamh turned to look up at him.

"Shall we stay here for a while, then?"

He nodded. "I think we could do with a little peace and quiet."

"And if I have a vision?"

"Then we follow it." He reached out to caress her cheek. "I'll follow you."

She bussed into his touch, but the serious, slightly worried darkness in the back of her eyes didn't leave.

"What is it, *Komorebi*? Not this nonsense about me needing to be on the move again? I'm content to stay put for a while."

"It's not that." She turned into him, resting her chin on his shoulder. "I've been thinking about something."

He kissed the tip of her nose and nodded for her to continue.

"The true-mate bond is significant. It has to be. In the coming battle against Astra, I mean."

"How so?"

"Think about it. Very few supes find their true mate ... but Thea did, Rose did, I did ... and we've hopefully just set things in motion so Elijah does too."

"What about Astra?"

“I don’t know if it’s possible for someone without a soul to have a soul mate,” she answered in grim wryness.

“But the other fae-borne have all met theirs, or will.” It was a hell of a coincidence.

“Something about the bond ... I think it’s the reason the chances of the gate opening have gotten lower and lower over the last two years. I don’t know if that was Aine’s intention or if Fate is some omniscient being bigger than all of us, deciding to play a hand against the Faerie Queen. I don’t know. I just know I’ll protect the bonds for as long as they need my protection. Not just ours ... but all of them. All the bonds my fae siblings share with their mates.”

“And I’ll help you.”

Niamh’s eyes brightened. “If one day, in the distant future, when nobody needs us but each other, if we ever start to grow weary of never aging ... you *could* bite me. Your bite would turn me into a wolf like Conall’s turned Thea.”

The very thought made his blood run cold. Kiyo pulled away from her. “You would eventually die,” he reminded her. “And I wouldn’t.” The *thought* of existing without her was sheer torment, never mind what the reality would be like.

But he knew if Niamh asked it of him, he would give it to her.

He wouldn’t let her drown in the misery of eternity if he could save her from it. “Okay.” He tried not to glower out at the forest but probably failed. “If that’s what you want. I promise to do that for you when the time comes.”

“No, you silly male.” Niamh cuddled into him.

Despite his grim mood, he instinctively welcomed her burrowing into him.

“I don’t mean I would leave you here. I meant I could become mortal, and then when my time came to die, you could smash the pendant and meet me in the afterlife. If there is one.”

Kiyo frowned. His mate had not thought this through. “And unleash whatever spells or curses are held within it on Japan? Who knows what chaos that could cause.”

“Oh.” Niamh’s face fell. “I never thought of that.”

"Never mind that I would have to watch you grow old while you watched me stay the same age."

"I just wanted there to be an option for you." Niamh shrugged, everything she felt for him brimming over in her beautiful eyes.

Kiyo had never known what it was like to be someone's entire universe. He almost thought it would chafe. Too much responsibility. But when you felt the same way as that person, it was a peace he never expected to find or thought he deserved.

"I know eternity is not something you ever wanted," Niamh continued. "And I just want to give you everything that makes you happy."

Slipping his hand beneath her shirt, Kiyo glided his palm up Niamh's belly until it rested over her heart, beneath the warm weight of her breast. She sucked in a breath and he sensed her immediate desire for his touch, but this moment wasn't about that. Feeling her heartbeat against his palm, he realized it beat in time with his own.

"There's a saying people use here, especially to describe the short cherry blossom season. *Mono no aware*. It's an appreciation for things that quickly pass or are soon lost. I hated that damn saying because nothing has passed quickly for me in almost a hundred and fifty years. Until now."

He bent his head to her mouth, their eyes locked as he confessed with rough emotion, "I used to resent forever. And now, because of you, Niamh Farren, forever will never be enough."

He felt her tremble slightly as she clung to him, eyes wide with the wonder that he could love her so much. "We're bound by forever," she whispered, her bliss and awe wrapping him in love, loyalty, and desire. Her emotions tasted like caramel and spice on his tongue; they felt like power and heat and electricity.

They were Niamh.

They were everything that made up who she was.

Not just fae-borne.

Not just one of the most powerful beings on earth.

Those were how others would see her.

To Kiyo, she was simply Niamh: the other half of his soul.

His to love and his to protect.

And his to follow where she led.

That might chafe other alphas. In fact, he would have scoffed at the very idea only months ago.

Now he felt only pride that Fate had chosen him to be what she needed.

"Bound by forever, *Komorebi*," he purred, nudging her into the bedroom. He might follow her in life, but he was still a male, still an alpha, and he needed somewhere to channel his bossiness. Kiyo grinned wickedly. "Conjure some restraints, Niamh-chan. I'm feeling literal this afternoon."

ACKNOWLEDGMENTS

Diving back into the world of adult paranormal romance with Niamh and Kiyo by my side has been an absolute adventure and true escapism during this strange year we call 2020.

I have a fascination with Japanese culture and it was so much fun to research Japan for this book. Unfortunately, as you can imagine, a research trip was out of the question, so I relied on non-fiction novels and internet research to provide me insight into Tokyo. I also reached out to readers who have lived in, or spent time in, Japan for their insights into the country. Thank you to Jacy Tayler Leavitt and her friend Tobin, Madoka Kamimura Mason, Françoise Giang, Catherine Trieu, Dawn Kelly, Janet Lofthouse, Katie Phillips, Annie Krall Buehner, Fame Valentine, Suzanne Andora Barron, María WieBitte Navalón-Castillo, Stéphanie Lambert, Lena Boe, Tanja Kunej and Maria Leronimides Metsikas. I love my reader group, Sam's Clan McBookish, and I appreciate your time and support more than you know. How lucky am I, to have readers such as you?

I've endeavored to be as thorough as possible, cross-checking references, especially with regards to translations. The Japanese language and culture are immensely beautiful and my sincerest hope is that I've done Japan's beauty justice. Any research errors are my own.

For the most part writing is a solitary endeavor, but publishing is not. A massive thank you to my editor Jennifer Sommersby Young for taking a process than can sometimes be excruciating for a writer and making it pretty painless. I love working with you!

Thank you to my bestie and PA extraordinaire, Ashleen Walker, for handling all the little things and supporting me through everything. I love you lots.

The life of a writer doesn't stop with the book. Our job expands beyond the written word to marketing, advertising, graphic design, social media management and more. Help from those in the know goes a long way. Thank you to Nina Grinstead, Kelley Beckham and all the team at Valentine PR for making sure Niamh and Kiyo's story finds its audience. You have no idea how grateful I am to you. You ladies are tremendous!

Thank you to every single blogger, Instagrammer and book lover who has helped spread the word about my books. You all are appreciated so much. A special shout out to Natasha Tomic of Natasha is a Book Junkie. Natasha, your enthusiasm and support for this series means more than you'll ever know. Thank you, friend. You are a positive, glowing example of how wonderful this book community can be.

To my family and friends, for listening to me ramble as I tried to untangle the many ideas and thoughts I had about Kiyo and Niamh's story.

Moreover, to Regina Wamba for beautiful cover image photography that the exceptional Hang Le used to create yet another stunning cover that I cannot stop staring at. Your talent knows no bounds and I'm so grateful to you. Thank you, Hang.

As always, thank you to my agent Lauren Abramo for making it possible for readers all over the world to find my words, and for always having my back. I can't imagine doing this without you.

And finally, the biggest thank you of all, to you my reader. Writing in this genre feels like coming home. I couldn't come home without your support.

ABOUT THE AUTHOR

S. Young is the pen name for Samantha Young, a *New York Times*, *USA Today* and *Wall Street Journal* bestselling author from Stirlingshire, Scotland. She's been nominated for the Goodreads Choice Award for Best Author and Best Romance for her international bestseller *On Dublin Street*. *On Dublin Street* was Samantha's first adult contemporary romance series and has sold in thirty countries. *True Immortality* is Samantha's first adult paranormal series written under the name S. Young.

Visit Samantha Young online at
www.authorsamanthayoung.com
BookBub
Instagram @AuthorSamanthaYoung
Facebook @AuthorSamanthaYoung
Facebook Reader Group
Goodreads

CPSIA information can be obtained
at www.ICGtesting.com
Printed in the USA
FSHW010502181120
76068FS

9 781916 1740